Someone was coming.

Ketti scrambled to her feet and glanced around for a place to hide. She didn't want to be seen, as it was obvious she'd been crying. Then she remembered the ladder to the loft. She edged away to quickly climb the rungs to the upper floor, where the sweet fragrance of hay seemed to welcome her.

Then she heard the barn door open. An eerie stillness settled over the barn, and now all she heard were the distant sounds of laughter and music, the pagan drumbeats echoing in the silence of the loft. Unnerved, she whirled around to flee, but she was brought up short by the man who'd just ascended the ladder.

"John," she whispered.

As he watched her, a shaft of moonlight shimmering on her long hair, her dark eyes round with fright, he could think of nothing but taking her in his arms. For a moment he simply stood there; then he hesitated no longer.

Dear Reader,

Welcome to the world of Harlequin Historicals. This month, we bring you another tale from the faraway islands of Hawaii with Donna Anders's *Ketti,* the story of the daughter of Mari and Adam from the author's April release, *Mari.*

For those of you who have long enjoyed her contemporaries, we are pleased to have *Odessa Gold,* Linda Shaw's first Harlequin Historical. Don't miss this delightful tale of honor and betrayal set against the backdrop of turn-of-the-century high society in Saratoga Springs and New York City.

Private Paradise by popular author Lucy Elliot and Jennifer West's first historical romance, *Passion's Legacy,* complete the roster. To start your summer reading off right, look for all four Harlequin Historicals at your local bookstore.

From all of us at Harlequin Historicals, our best wishes for a relaxing and enjoyable summer.

Yours,

Tracy Farrell
Senior Editor

Ketti

Donna Anders

Harlequin Books

TORONTO • NEW YORK • LONDON
AMSTERDAM • PARIS • SYDNEY • HAMBURG
STOCKHOLM • ATHENS • TOKYO • MILAN

Harlequin Historicals first edition June 1991

ISBN 0-373-28681-3

KETTI

DONNA ANDERS

delights in every aspect of writing, particularly the research. Her explorations have led her into some pretty strange situations, such as being stranded in a remote area of Mexico and spending the night at the only lodging available—the local brothel. She is an enthusiastic reader of just about everything, but her first love has always been historical romance. In addition to her historicals, she is the author of short stories and children's books. When she isn't conducting writing workshops, working as an office administrator, or, of course, writing, she loves to spend her treasured free time reading, painting and taking long walks.

For my dear friend, Margaret Chittenden

Chapter One

The image of herself in the mirror was hardly recognizable to Ketti Foster. The diaphanous fabric of her white, sleeveless, low-cut gown fit her slim body to perfection, and complemented her long dark hair and eyes. It was difficult to believe the vision of beauty reflected in the glass was really she. She was used to seeing herself in a long-sleeved waist with a high collar, tucked into an ankle-length black skirt—her daily attire as a teacher in the private Catholic school from which she'd graduated one year ago.

She whirled around and hurried to the door. It was time to return to the ballroom on the top floor of the three-story Victorian mansion. As she moved up the marble steps, the wide sweep of her petticoats and skirts whispered around her legs. But as she reached the landing, she hesitated at the large windows to look out over the lights of San Francisco. It was such a beautiful city of steep hills and broad vistas, and this particular view was from one of the highest hills. She sighed, tearing her eyes away from the city that sparkled at her feet like a carpet of diamonds, and continued up the wide staircase. Her escort, James Rawlston, would be wondering why she took so long in the powder room.

She marveled at the opulence of the house. It was owned by the very rich Simpson family, who were friends of the Rawlstons, the family she'd been living with during the years she'd attended school in California. The Rawlstons, highly

respected and rich in their own right, were related to one of
the old missionary families in Hawaii, and knew Ketti's
parents, who owned one of the largest cattle ranches on the
Big Island.

She paused when she reached the upper hall. Beyond it
the ballroom was crowded with elegantly gowned and be-
jeweled women dancing with formally attired men. The
string band was playing a waltz, the music as light and
frothy as the garlands of spring flowers that decorated the
huge room. Crystal chandeliers cast a glittering brilliance
over everything, including the dancers who dipped and
whirled over the highly polished floor.

Excitement bubbled up within Ketti. It was a wonderful
party, given by the Simpsons to celebrate their daughter's
twenty-first birthday. Although she'd hardly danced with
James—her program being filled with the names of other
young men who wanted to partner her—the next dance was
his. Still she hesitated; her heart was suddenly beating too
fast, and she knew she had to calm her nerves.

Although James had been away studying law at Harvard
during the years she'd lived with his family, his return a year
ago had prompted her decision to stay on in California after graduation. He was so handsome with his curly brown
hair and teasing hazel eyes, so charming and so hard to resist. And he had soon let it be known that he was interested
in Ketti. That other women also found him attractive had
sometimes bothered Ketti, for he enjoyed their attention.
She'd often had to remind herself not to distrust him; he
simply had an open, friendly personality.

And now she believed he was about to propose to her. The
thought was exciting...and disturbing. Marrying James
would mean living the rest of her life in San Francisco. Not
that she didn't love the city, she did. But it would also mean
she would never live in her beloved Hawaii, the place of her
birth.

Ketti's thoughts whirled faster than the dancers, and instead of entering the ballroom, she went to the far end of the

hall and sat down on a window seat built into a bay window. Obscured by a decorative trellis of greenery and pastel flowers, Ketti tried to calm her anxious state. Again, she looked out over the twinkling lights of the city below her, lights that were reflected in the water of the bay in the distance. But her thoughts were in Hawaii, in the high country of the Big Island where her family lived. It seemed so far away, so mystical with its legends of ancient Polynesians who believed in old gods like Madam Pele, the fire goddess of the Hawaiian volcanoes.

Deep in her own thoughts, she didn't hear the approach of a man and woman, but gradually she became aware of their low voices on the other side of the trellis. They obviously didn't know she was there. About to make her presence known, she suddenly realized that the couple were speaking in intimate tones—and she was in the embarrassing position of being an eavesdropper.

The woman giggled. "You mustn't. Someone will see us." Her words protested, but her tone was inviting.

Ketti squirmed, and wished there were a way to go past them before they saw her. But there wasn't, and she had no alternative but to stay put and hope she wasn't discovered.

"No one can see," the man whispered. There was something familiar about his voice.

After another short silence during which Ketti suspected they were kissing—she couldn't see through the greenery even if she wanted to—the woman giggled again. "James!" she protested, her voice flirtatious. "If we're seen, then you'll have compromised me. My father would insist you do the right thing in that case." She teased and coaxed him on, but there was a ring of truth in her manner as well. "Like marry me instead of that prissy, foreign schoolmarm, Katherine Foster!"

Hearing the man's name had brought a frown to Ketti's brow. But the woman's final statement jolted her, and sent a flash of fire into her face. *They were talking about her!* It was James—making love to another woman!

"Who says I'm marrying Ketti?" he retorted, his voice husky with desire for the girl. "Maybe I want you instead."

"Everyone," the woman went on, as Ketti stiffened, horrified and humiliated. But when the sensual banter continued on the other side of the trellis, anger erupted within her to cancel out any other feeling. How dared they discuss her as if she were an aging spinster, and not a young woman of nineteen who'd been pursued by most of the eligible men in San Francisco.

Lifting her skirts, she flounced around the trellis and faced them. They jumped apart, the woman's fair complexion as pink as her gown. Shock registered on James's face, much to Ketti's satisfaction.

"Everyone may say so," Ketti cried, her words dripping ice, and her dark eyes flashing. She tilted her chin haughtily. "But *I* haven't said so." Her gaze raked James, from his widened eyes, over his stocky figure, to his feet. His square jaw now sagged with guilt. She looked him straight in the eyes. "I'm not so desirous of marriage that I would ever consider a—a *philanderer!*"

"Now, see here, Ketti," James began, sudden color suffusing his face as he blustered. "I don't appreciate you making a scene over nothing."

"Nothing?" She almost choked on the word. "Surely you're joking?"

He took her arm, but she shook him off. Ketti had recognized the other girl as Andrea Simpson, the blonde whose birthday they'd been celebrating, and was even more infuriated to see amusement on her smug face. Ketti only managed to keep her temper in check because she saw it was useless to argue. She turned on her heel to leave them.

James tried to grab her again and steer her toward the ballroom, but she jerked away as though he had the plague. She didn't want him touching her. How could he dare after what she'd just witnessed!

For long seconds she glared into his eyes, suddenly seeing the spoiled, only son of rich parents who'd doted on his every whim. Because he was so attractive and attentive, Ketti had turned a blind eye to his faults. Now she wouldn't have him if he offered her the whole earth served up on a diamond-studded golden platter. At that moment she hated him.

"Come on, Ketti," James said, his manner condescending. "This is 1892, not the Dark Ages. Can't you be a sport?"

"Sport—*sport?*" It was the last straw. Before she could control herself, she slapped his face, the crack sounding above the music that wafted into the hall from the ballroom.

With a rustle of skirts, she turned to flee and almost crashed into a tall man behind her, bringing her hasty exit to an abrupt stop. He clicked his tongue, his blue eyes glinting like molten silver under hooded lids, as he took in the scene. Lazily, he stepped aside. Ketti only gave him a passing glance, but she saw amusement quirking the corners of his well-defined lips, and then a flash of white teeth.

"Bravo," the stranger drawled. "That was quite a performance." His glance shifted to the other girl. "And I must say, you had it coming, Andrea." His tone was bored, as though they were all children having a spat, and he were the only adult.

Ketti shot him a withering glance, resenting his interference. "I'll thank you to mind your own business. This is none of your affair, *sir!*"

Then she left them all staring after her, the stranger's faint chuckle following her, ran down the stairs and headed for the front door. She was glad she lived within walking distance. She certainly wouldn't allow James to escort her home.

Once she was outside the tears came unbidden. She was humiliated, devastated—and homesick for Hawaii. I don't belong here, she told herself. It's time to go home.

* * *

The Chinese girl bolted into the street in front of Ketti's horse. The action was so sudden that Ketti almost lost her seat in the saddle when the stallion reared. Fighting to control her startled mount in the narrow, crowded street of Chinatown, Ketti had no time to see that the girl was being chased by two Chinese men dressed in black. Or that her ebony-dark hair had come loose from its chignon, that her eyes, wild with fear, were filled with tears that ran down her cheeks to soak into her sea-green, satin jacket.

As the stallion came to a skittish stop, Ketti slipped from the saddle and quickly tied the reins to a hitching post, knowing the animal must settle down before she continued to her destination on the next block. Her horse had a wild streak, and although she took pride in being the only one who dared ride him, she should have known better than to bring him into the busy streets of San Francisco, even if she had been pressed for time. She hadn't wanted to miss saying goodbye to Char, her old friend and son of the Chinese cook on her Grandfather Webster's ranch in Hawaii. And she'd wanted to see if it were possible to book passage for herself; though the Rawlstons didn't know it, her trunk was already packed. And she'd managed to avoid James since she left the party the night before.

Like her, Char had been sent to school in San Francisco—she at fifteen, he at eighteen. Four years ago when she arrived to attend the Mission School it had been a comfort to know that Char had already lived in the city for three years with his uncle's family. Although she and Char didn't visit often, their social circles being so different, they both enjoyed the reminder of someone from their beloved Big Island of Hawaii. And now Char, who had just graduated with a law degree, would sail on the evening tide for Honolulu, to rejoin his proud peasant family as the first member with a college education.

A sudden cry jolted her thoughts back to the present, and Ketti's gaze darted to the two men, who'd started to drag the Chinese girl down the sidewalk, the resistance of her small frame no match for their superior strength. She pleaded with them in Chinese, and although Ketti couldn't understand a word they said, it was obvious that the men were taking the girl against her will. To Ketti's surprise, other people in the street avoided looking at the girl and her two captors, and didn't offer help.

Impulsively, Ketti stepped in front of the men, blocking their way. "Let go of the girl," she told them crisply. "She doesn't want to go with you, so let her alone."

They stopped abruptly, their expressions incredulous. The girl's gaze darted to Ketti's, and her black eyes pleaded mutely for help, while her whole body shook with fear.

"Do not give trouble!" the taller Chinese man snarled at Ketti in a menacing tone. "Or you pay price." His hold tightened on the girl's arm and she cried out in pain.

Oblivious to possible consequences, Ketti bristled. Although both men glared threateningly, she was determined to find out what was going on. Since completing her studies at the Catholic Mission School a year ago, she'd been teaching, helping the Sisters with their work among the poor and homeless—another reason, aside from James, for her delaying her return to Hawaii. During those months she'd spent time in Chinatown as a volunteer to teach English. She'd heard all about the girls being brought from China to the brothels of San Francisco, girls sold into slavery by their own fathers and forced into prostitution by their new masters. Ketti wanted to make sure that this was not one of those girls.

"Is this girl your daughter?" she demanded, and took a step closer. She wasn't about to be intimidated by their manner.

They glowered back in silence, their expressions darkening even further when Ketti didn't step aside.

She gestured to indicate her meaning, but suspected they had understood her. "If this girl is not your daughter, then you have no right to detain her," she continued fearlessly, virtually certain now that the men were up to no good. "This is America, not China."

"Let pass!" the other man growled finally. "Not your affair."

They started to push her out of the way, and as Ketti stood firm, the Chinese girl renewed her attempts to free herself. Beyond where they stood, a crowd had gathered. Pigtailed men, garbed in the traditional dark trousers and high-necked quilted jackets, were chattering and pointing, as though something of immense importance were going on before their eyes. Ketti disregarded them; it was becoming more obvious that the girl was probably a recaptured runaway slave. If so, she needed help.

With a sudden movement, the girl stumbled free of the hands holding her. Instantly, Ketti stepped between her and the men, and bracing herself, she confronted them.

"I'm taking this girl to the Mission School," she informed them tersely. "The nuns will get to the bottom of this since you can't seem to explain," she added. She tried to hide the shiver of fear that their inscrutable faces evoked, as they now turned the full force of their wrath on her. Ketti knew that most white people wouldn't have interfered, that she probably shouldn't have, either; but she somehow sensed the girl was doomed to a terrible fate—and that she was the girl's last chance.

The men's expressions hadn't altered, but Ketti felt them tense, as though they were about to pounce on her. Fear trickled down Ketti's spine. Somehow she managed to keep her apprehension hidden and resisted the urge to take flight herself. The absolute terror of the girl was contagious. She clung to Ketti's riding skirt with a desperation that shouted louder than any words: the men were indeed dangerous!

"Female white devils!" one of the men whispered with contempt, and Ketti knew he was referring to the Sisters, as she'd heard the term before. Her angry retort died on her lips as a gleaming knife suddenly appeared in the man's hand. Shutters lifted from his black eyes, and Ketti saw hatred reflected in their depths a moment before he lunged forward.

In the split second before she had time to react, a tall, sandy-haired man bounded out of a doorway near Ketti, a small revolver in his hand. His shot in the air stopped the attacking man in midstride.

"What in hell's going on here?" the newcomer demanded, his voice deep and commanding—and familiar. His glance flickered between the women and men, dismissing Ketti before she could reply, as he focused icy-blue eyes on the men, his pistol leveled and ready.

Despite her relief, Ketti was pricked by annoyance. The stranger's brief glance hadn't been approving. She tried to place where she'd seen him before—an extremely handsome man whose dark skin was a startling contrast to his light brown hair and blue eyes. Even though he had saved her from a brutal attack, her momentary gratitude vanished. Damn his arrogance! she stormed instead.

Then she remembered him. He was the man at the ball, the one who had observed her humiliation by James and Andrea Simpson!

At once both attackers, the knife still in the one man's hand, spoke in Chinese, and her rescuer seemed to understand their language. It was clear the confrontation was not over, and only the newcomer's pistol prevented a renewed attack.

Instinctively, Ketti dropped a protective arm around the trembling girl while she contemplated the tall stranger. She realized she hadn't even heard his name the night of the party. She wondered if he could really hold off the Chinese men with his words, for his gun would never be able to stop the gathering crowd, should they side with the abductors. She studied him now, as she had only glanced at him in passing as she fled the Simpson mansion. He was well over six feet tall, and the lean hardness of his limbs under his well-cut suit spoke of strength and hard work. As her gaze traveled up the length of him, from his booted feet to his wide-brimmed hat, she wondered what a man of his obvious means was doing in Chinatown. Then a glance at the building he'd been visiting told the story: he'd exited a gambling den and brothel.

Suddenly realizing they could make an escape while everyone else's attention was focused on the men, Ketti gestured to the girl, who understood her plan at once. Quickly they backed away toward Ketti's horse, which now waited peacefully at the hitching post.

"Not so fast!" the stranger cried, stopping both girls in their tracks. Ketti whirled around to face him, and again placed herself between the girl and the men. The stranger's eyes were narrowed and his features had a hard cast, as though he'd suffered in his life, Ketti thought in passing. Then her gaze was caught by the compelling quality of his intense, blue eyes, which glinted like spun silver—reminding her of how the sun was reflected on the surface of the Pacific Ocean when viewed from the high country on the Big Island.

"You have a knack for finding trouble, Miss Katherine Foster," he drawled, surprising her.

A flush stole up Ketti's neck into her face. So he did remember her. But before she could respond, he went on forcefully.

"And what in damnation are you doing in Chinatown?" He waved the pistol, which was still aimed at the men who waited, their eyes watchful. "Do you have the vaguest idea of what you've involved yourself in? That you've poked your pretty little nose into something that's none of your affair? A crime you once pointed out to me," he added dryly. "In fact, Miss Foster, it's dangerous, to the extreme."

His words stung, but Ketti tilted her chin, defying him. "How dare you talk to me in that tone!" she retorted with a burst of anger. "And I only realize one thing—Mr. Whoever-you-are. I saved this girl from an abduction by these men, who—"

"Are highbinders, Miss Foster." He spoke harshly, looking her up and down.

She stared, and swallowed back sudden fear. *Highbinders!* She willed herself to maintain her composure, knowing she couldn't allow the men to see how frightened she felt.

"Do you happen to know what that means?" His voice was deceptively low as he continued, but it barely concealed his leashed fury with her. His eyes again raked her from her trim booted feet, up her divided green riding skirt, over her matching jacket that molded her breasts, which were suddenly trembling from her accelerated heartbeats and on to her face that burned from more emotions that Ketti could identify.

The pins in her hair had become loose, and her sombrero hung by its cord against her back; she knew she didn't present a proper picture of feminine decorum. The pink in her cheeks deepened as she noted that the stranger was taking in all aspects of her dress, and the fact that she wore a divided skirt. Even Sister Mary Agnes, her favorite nun at the school, had been shocked when Ketti first wore the riding habit she'd commissioned a Chinese tailor to sew—until Ketti had explained that such garb was more seemly than the pants she'd always worn when riding the rangeland at the family ranch in Hawaii.

"I asked you a question, Miss Foster," he said, holding her regard by the sheer male force of him. "And it would behoove you to answer at once—before this little drama really gets out of hand."

She didn't like his tone one bit. Hiding her growing fears, Ketti spoke tartly, playing for time while she tried to come up with an escape plan. "I'm sorry, but I don't believe I heard your name. I don't have to answer questions from a stranger." She knew she sounded ungratefully inane, even childish, but she was in a desperate situation.

He drew in his breath sharply. "Damnation, woman! Do you think this is a game? I suggest you get on your horse and leave matters, and the girl, to me."

All attention was now focused on Ketti, and she licked her suddenly dry lips. Highbinders—*paid assassins!* She'd been right; the girl must be a runaway slave, and the highbinders had caught her. *Help us, Lord,* she prayed in desperation, and flicked a glance to the terrified girl behind her.

"Give girl so we take back to her master," the taller highbinder demanded. "Then you go free."

Turning back to the men, Ketti straightened in resolve. She just couldn't leave the girl to her fate—it was unthinkable. And slavery was against the law, she reminded herself. But she also knew that the law wouldn't help her now; she must appeal to the highbinders in another way.

"I'll buy the girl from the—uh—master!" she announced, and as her words sank into the minds of the onlookers, there was a ripple of surprise. But before anyone could speak, the crowd parted to allow two men to approach Ketti and the others.

"Char!" Ketti cried in relief, recognizing the slight frame and serious face of her friend, and his elderly, plump uncle beside him. "I've never been happier to see anyone in my life!"

"Ketti! For God's sake, what have you done?" Char asked, his round Chinese face registering shock as he took in the situation.

Quickly she explained, while the Chinese girl cringed behind her, and Char's expression went from concern to absolute disbelief. Then he raised a flat silencing hand and interrupted her. He directed his next words at her rescuer, who still held the highbinders in abeyance with his gun, an odd expression on his face—as if he knew something Ketti didn't.

"John Stillman, I want to thank you for your intervention," Char told him with typical Oriental politeness. "If not for you, Ketti might have been hurt."

Ketti glanced between the men, and tried not to allow a new concern to grow within her. She was surprised that Char knew the rescuer, and appeared to respect him. She also detected a strangeness in Char's tone; if she hadn't known him, she would almost have wondered whose side he was on.

When Char's uncle, a man Ketti knew only as Mr. Kee, the head of a large clan, stepped forward and motioned to the girl, everything suddenly became clear. The girl cringed and cried out in a torrent of Chinese, tears streaming from eyes that still pleaded for help.

Mr. Kee was the girl's master!

Rumors she'd heard surfaced in Ketti's mind; she recalled the whispered claims that Char's uncle was a tong lord, though at the time she'd disregarded the stories as idle gossip.

Although the stranger, John Stillman, now spoke rapidly to Mr. Kee in Chinese, and it was obvious that the conversation was heated, Ketti couldn't wait to voice her own demands: the girl was going with her no matter what the price!

"Mr. Kee," she began, knowing from the times she'd visited his house that Char's uncle spoke English, "I'll buy the girl from you."

When Char started to protest, his fears for her suddenly apparent on his usually inscrutable face, Ketti waved him away and again addressed his uncle. "This girl is too fragile for your—needs," she said, and went on quickly when she saw his expression darken. "I'll pay you whatever price you wish."

For long seconds Mr. Kee considered her words, peering at her from behind thick spectacles; he looked more like a benign peasant than a man who controlled the lives of others less fortunate. Ketti was glad she'd never have to see him again after Char left his household, and wondered how she could have been so fooled. Then Mr. Kee nodded to the highbinders, indicating they could go.

But as they turned away, John Stillman stopped them. "Not so fast!" His words were a command that brooked no refusal.

"It's all right, Mr. Stillman," Mr. Kee informed him, as calmly as he would have asked for a cup of tea. In that sec-

ond Ketti glimpsed the power behind the peasant face. "The
matter is finished," Mr. Kee went on in the same mono-
tone. "These men won't bother Miss Foster again."

"Do we have your word on that?" John Stillman looked
doubtful—and dangerous—and Ketti wondered if he was
involved in the same things as Mr. Kee. One thing was certain: she didn't trust him any more than she did Char's
uncle.

Anger glinted briefly in Mr. Kee's narrowed eyes, but he
gave a slight nod, and held his tongue.

John Stillman studied the elderly Chinese tong lord for
long seconds, then, satisfied that the man spoke the truth,
he lowered his pistol. A moment later the highbinders disappeared into the crowd without a backward look.

Char stepped next to Ketti, as though he were allying
himself with her, and making it known that he expected his
uncle to honor his words. The slave girl cringed between
them, her long lashes lowered, her whole posture one of
submission to her fate.

"I agree to sell her," Mr. Kee said, in a singsong voice.
"But only if you agree to my terms." He hesitated, and the
sunlight suddenly caught on his spectacles, the reflection
obscuring his eyes. A foreboding chill touched Ketti's neck
and was gone, but not before she realized that the man,
family or not, could be deadly. "You will pay three thousand dollars, that is first term," he told her in a low voice
that couldn't be heard beyond their small group. "Then you
and girl leave city at once ... forever."

She nodded, hoping she could arrange passage for two on
Char's ship.

"It set," he went on, still toneless. "Those are terms—or
I might not be able to keep you safe."

Before she could speak, Char broke in. "He's right, Ketti.
Those men don't like the kind of attention you just brought
down on them and they could retaliate if they see you in
Chinatown again."

"When you interfere in matters you don't understand, you pay the consequences, Miss Foster," John Stillman added dryly.

Her gaze flew to the sardonic face of the man who towered above all of them. Their eyes locked, and Ketti felt the jolt of some strange sensation all the way down to her booted feet. "I don't need your philosophy on my actions, Mr. Stillman," she managed tartly.

Apparently her response amused him and he grinned, taking her completely by surprise. Years dropped from his face and Ketti realized he was probably only in his midtwenties. But it was a passing thought, for his disarming smile banished all rational thought from her mind and momentarily robbed her of breath. He read her face and his grin widened to show teeth that were a startling white against his brown skin, which was darker than she'd have expected for one with such blue eyes and light hair. It took all her willpower to control her traitorous reaction to him.

"I accept your thanks for my coming to your aid," he quipped, a reminder that she hadn't thanked him, had in fact not seemed grateful at all. He kept his eyes fixed on her and wasn't unaware of the effect. But even as he recognized that, he realized his own breathing had become a bit irregular. The girl before him was a beautiful creature. Slender and with delicate features, she was also a study in contrasts. Her hair shimmered like black silk and her eyes, almost as dark, were a stunning foil to her flawless light skin. He wondered about her background, and then with regret set such thoughts aside. He had no time to speculate on Ketti Foster. He had affairs to tie up before his ship sailed within a week's time.

He tipped his hat to her, reminded Mr. Kee that he must stick to his agreement and then strode off before she could even open her mouth.

Ketti let out her breath in one long sigh, strangely relieved that he'd gone, yet embarrassed that she hadn't thanked him for probably saving her life. As she took the reins of her horse and followed Char and Mr. Kee to their house to finalize the transaction, she told herself that she was glad she'd never see John Stillman again.

"But damn his arrogance!" she muttered under her breath. *Why did he have to smile and become human before he went?* She knew it would be a while before she'd forget his handsome face.

Char's ship sailed on time, and Ketti watched as it sliced through the bay toward the Golden Gate. An immense longing to be home took hold of her, and she knew she was lucky to have booked passage on the next ship for Hawaii, set to sail in five days. There had been space for only one more passenger on Char's ship, and she'd booked it for the Chinese girl.

She sighed as she remembered the meeting in the Kee house, when she'd agreed to leave the city—as though it hadn't been her goal since the night before at the party—as one of the terms of agreement in her buying the slave girl. She smiled wryly, and wondered what her parents would say when Char brought the girl to them, along with Ketti's letter; in the letter she briefly described the girl's plight, and said that she herself would arrive on the next boat from California and explain everything then.

She watched until the ship disappeared, then mounted and rode up the street away from the teeming waterfront, toward the Rawlston mansion on Nob Hill. She didn't feel regret that she'd soon be leaving. Although they'd always been kind to her, the Rawlstons hadn't always approved of what they called "her headlong ways" during the time she'd lived with them. She knew they'd be shocked when she told them she needed three thousand dollars, money she'd repay when she contacted her family in Hawaii. Her parents would understand her action, of that she was sure, as they believed as she did—that everyone deserved a chance.

At the top of the hill she reined up and turned in the saddle for a final glimpse of the ship before it disappeared into the evening darkness. The final light from the sun, as it slipped below the western horizon, was a brief golden opalescence on the water. Then the spectacle vanished with the ship into the night.

For another few minutes she lingered, watching as the lights twinkled on over the city below her, and were reflected on the water of the bay like constellations of diamonds. Oh, how she loved San Francisco. How she'd miss it after she was gone. She'd made a place for herself in California, working with the Sisters to help the poor, work she'd intended to stay involved in after she married James. She swallowed hard, and forced her thoughts away from the painful memories.

Ketti kneed the stallion, amused that the animal was so docile all of a sudden, as though it sensed that their wild rides on the beach were coming to an end. As she rode home her mind whirled with the images of the past four years, and of the people she'd miss after she was gone.

When Ketti dismounted at the stable next to the Rawlston mansion, she was startled when Mrs. Rawlston, elaborately gowned for dinner, ran out the side door to greet her.

"Ketti! Where on earth have you been? We've been to the school—everywhere—and couldn't find you."

"Just riding," Ketti replied, surprised. "I apologize for being late. The time got away from me." The Rawlstons had never approved of her trips to Chinatown, so she had decided some time ago not to share information that would only upset them. But now she would have to explain, as there was the matter of honoring her agreement to pay Mr. Kee. Preoccupied with how to broach the subject, Ketti wasn't paying attention to Mrs. Rawlston's rambling until she heard James's name mentioned.

"What did you say?" she asked sharply, coming to an abrupt halt at the top of the porch steps.

"Ketti! I've been telling you!" the plump woman cried, wringing her hands. "James was called away on business, to Sacramento to see the governor. It's a great opportunity for his future law practice.'' The older woman hesitated. ''But he wanted to see you before he went, said he had to get things settled with you. When you didn't get home, he had to leave.''

''I'm happy for him.'' Ketti tried to put enthusiasm into her words.

''Well, you can tell him yourself when he returns in a week,'' Mrs. Rawlston said, and followed Ketti into the house.

Ketti braced herself. The next five days wouldn't be easy. Maybe John Stillman was right after all. She had a knack of finding trouble.

Chapter Two

The buggy rolled over the steep hills in record time, and Ketti hardly had time for a final glance at the streets and buildings that had become so familiar to her during her time in San Francisco. She'd said her goodbyes to the Sisters, and to the Rawlstons, who'd tried to talk her into staying until James returned and could reason with her. But she'd been adamant; she was returning to Hawaii.

As the driver reined in the horse near the wharf where Ketti was to board the ship, she sighed, hardly able to believe that she'd tied up all her loose ends in only a few days. Even Mr. Kee had been paid by a loan from the Rawlstons. At first they'd refused, disapproving of Ketti's involvement with Chinese slaves and tong lords. But when Ketti had explained her own peril if she didn't fulfill her promise, they'd agreed to the transaction. She smiled just thinking about it. In the light of her Chinatown escapade, she suspected they were glad to see her go after all.

Her trunk was unloaded by two stevedores so they could take it aboard. She climbed down from the buggy onto the planked wharf, smoothed the skirt of her light blue traveling suit over her hips, repositioned her straw hat over her pinned-up curls and glanced around. The final rays of the setting sun had dramatically struck the bank of clouds rimming the horizon. The beauty of San Francisco Bay, she thought sadly. She wondered if she'd ever see it again.

The chain of her chatelaine bag over her arm, she picked up her skirts and started for the ramp. Although the ship didn't leave until dawn, she'd been advised by the captain to board the night before. Sailing time didn't wait for anyone.

"Ketti!" she heard a man call. "Wait, Ketti!"

About to step onto the ramp, she turned, her heart sinking as she recognized James dismounting. *Oh God!* she thought. She'd hoped to be gone before he returned from Sacramento.

She braced herself and waited as he tied his horse to the hitching post near the street; then he hurried toward her. She didn't like the angry, set look to his handsome features. As though he was the one who'd been wronged! she fumed suddenly. Like a spoiled little boy who'd been told no.

"What's the meaning of this?" he demanded as he approached.

Her annoyance turned to anger. "Just what it looks like," she retorted coldly. "I'm boarding this ship to go home."

"Like hell you are!" he cried, indignation sparking from his narrowed brown eyes. His pants and shirt looked as though he'd slept in them, his dark hair was tousled and he needed a shave. She suspected that Mr. Rawlston had wired him to come home at once.

She glared back, her cheeks hot with outrage. How dared he think he could stop her from leaving! He hadn't even apologized for his behavior at the party, or for the fact that he'd humiliated her. And now he thought he could tell her what to do? Ketti turned her back on him and started up the ramp. There was nothing more to say.

He grabbed her arm, yanking her to a stop. "See here, Ketti. I won't have you embarrassing me like this. You aren't going. You're staying in California and marrying me."

"Too bad you didn't think of that before your dalliance with that Simpson woman," she told him coldly. "I'll never marry a man who cheats!"

His expression darkened further. He wasn't used to being turned down. "You're just hysterical—reacting like a jealous woman. Running off to Hawaii won't change your feelings. You know you're in love with me. Besides, if you go, people will think you turned down my proposal," he added, his words a whine.

She suddenly saw that his social image was his main concern, not her feelings. "And that's the important thing, isn't it, James? What people will think? You don't give a damn about the fact that they'd snicker behind my back if I was a ninny and stayed."

She shook off his arm and would have marched off but he grabbed her and pulled her roughly against him. Her straw hat flew off her head and she dropped her purse as she struggled for freedom. Suddenly James was yanked backward, freeing her so abruptly that she stumbled and would have fallen but for the railing behind her.

"Didn't you hear what the lady said?" a familiar male voice drawled.

Ketti's gaze flew to the man who'd rescued her, meeting the cool blue eyes of John Stillman. Her heart jolted in her chest and new heat flooded her cheeks. She couldn't believe it. The man always seemed to materialize out of nowhere when she was being accosted. Suddenly speechless, she could only stare.

"Stay out of this, John!" James cried, but his tone had lost its note of authority. "I'm just trying to keep Ketti from making a terrible mistake."

"Which is?" John's words were deceptively casual.

"She's to be my wife, and she's letting a little misunderstanding get out of hand."

"That so?" John looked at Ketti, taking in her flustered state and the rise and fall of her breasts under her formfitting jacket. "Are you betrothed to this man?" he asked her.

"I thank you for stopping this—this silliness," she managed with a semblance of restored dignity. "And I'm certainly not engaged to James. He never even asked me to marry him." She hesitated, not liking the sudden humor she saw in John Stillman's eyes. "Not that it's any business of yours!"

She picked up her purse and hat and, with her head high, she mounted the ramp to the ship. When James called her name she turned once more and looked down at the two men, one ruffled and obviously upset, the other watching lazily, impeccably dressed in a dark frock coat and trousers, his wide-brimmed hat tipped back so that he could view her better.

"I'm asking you to marry me now," James called up to her. There was a pleading quality to his voice, a desperation because he realized she was really going; she knew he would have followed but for the taller man who stood next to him.

"Now is much too late," she retorted. "And I'm sure you'll get over my refusal very soon, as soon as you realize your precious reputation is still intact." Her tone was as flat as she felt and without another glance, she started forward again.

The captain, a tall man whose weathered face showed no reaction to her hasty departure from the men on the dock, came forward to greet her. "Welcome aboard, Miss Foster," he said. Only the twinkle in his blue eyes gave away the fact that he was amused by the exchange. "We'll see to it that you have a pleasant voyage home."

"Thank you, Captain Wade," she replied, liking him even though he looked rough around the edges. When she'd secured her passage, it had heartened her to know that he knew her father.

"You'll have your meals in the galley with me," he told her, his manner reassuring, as though he were telling her to pay no mind to James, who still glared from the wharf.

Again she thanked Captain Wade, and went below deck to her cabin. Only then did her rapid breathing begin to slow. And it wasn't James who'd caused the condition; he'd never affected her so. It was that damnable John Stillman, and his knowing eyes, that caused her such discomfiture.

She was just glad she was putting the Pacific Ocean between herself and both men.

She settled into her tiny cabin, undressed to her petticoats and then rested on her bunk. I'll get ready for bed a little later, she told herself, feeling too emotionally drained at the moment to bother with ablutions. She dozed, and the gentle rocking of the ship lulled the disturbing thoughts that whirled in her head. She concentrated on the high country of the Big Island, and the timeless peace that permeated the land. Before she knew it, she was asleep.

Ketti sat bolt upright on the bunk. For a moment she didn't know where she was. The motion and the gentle rush of water against the hull reminded her that she was aboard ship—a ship that was now at sea. Ketti slid her legs from under the blankets—sometime in the night she must have covered herself—and stood up on the mattress to look out the only porthole. It was already daylight; the sun was peeking over the eastern horizon. She'd slept right through the night and missed the sailing time. She could see that the ship had already left the Golden Gate behind and was headed out into the Pacific Ocean.

A great sense of loss suddenly enveloped her. Although she wanted to go home, to see her parents and grandparents and brother again, doubts almost overwhelmed her. Had she made a mistake in not giving James another chance? In giving up her work with the Sisters? And a position in San Francisco society?

With a great sigh, she turned back to the cabin and began her morning toilette, using the water from a pitcher that rested on a small washstand. No, she reminded herself. She'd done the right thing. She could never marry a man she didn't trust, and in any case, the incident in Chinatown had made staying impossible. Feeling a need for fresh air to clear her head, she hurriedly opened her trunk and chose a high-necked afternoon dress with puffed sleeves that narrowed to fit tightly on her lower arms. The light green garment was accented with ribbons of forest green that matched the jacket Ketti also donned before leaving the cabin.

Once on deck Ketti leaned against the rail, watching as the captain saw to the deckhands, who were securing the ship for the voyage across the ocean. He waved in passing and told her breakfast would be served shortly in the galley. She nodded back, and enjoyed the feeling of the salt breeze that caressed her face and ruffled her long hair that she'd left unpinned. The day was glorious, the brilliant sky flawed only by a bank of clouds on the distant horizon.

The ship, being a freighter, would take two weeks to reach Honolulu. But Ketti didn't mind; she felt fortunate just to have secured passage, as there was space for only a few passengers. Already she felt better, more prepared to meet the future. She decided not to worry about what she'd do once she was back on the ranch. She knew she'd never be content unless she were involved in some type of work. After all, she didn't have expectations about marriage; she didn't even have a beau.

Although the morning was already bright with sunshine, the water was choppy from the wind, which had become brisker as they'd left the land behind. Ketti found she had to hold on to the rail in order to keep her balance.

"So, how are you finding the ship—not too deprived of conveniences, I trust?"

Startled by the man's voice, Ketti turned so quickly that she was caught off balance when the ship hit an exceptionally large swell. Strong arms grabbed her. She was held secure against the man's hard chest, the support saving her from a fall. Then her eyes met his, brown colliding with silvery blue. Her mouth dropped open in surprise.

"What are you doing here?" she managed.

John Stillman grinned down at her, then slowly released her from the protection of his arms. His sandy-colored hair blew rakishly against his forehead and his strong features were relaxed by a smile that widened into a broad grin. The white of his teeth caused her again to take notice that his skin was darker than she would have expected from one with such fair features. He cocked a brow in a question, and she realized, to her further embarrassment, that he'd caught her staring, assessing him.

"Not fleeing a rejected suitor like you," he replied finally.

She bristled and would have retorted, but he raised his hands in a gesture of truce. He looked so contrite, so attractive; his long muscled legs were braced against the roll of the ship, his white lawn shirt was open at the neck to reveal a brown column of neck, and his well-defined lips curved into an expectant smile that was very different from the sardonic one he'd worn only seconds before.

He watched her mental gears shift from surprise to annoyance to contemplation of him. By heaven, she was a beautiful creature, he thought. He'd never seen such flawless ivory skin on any woman, especially a woman with such dark lustrous hair—hair that shimmered like rich silk in the sun—or such expressive dark eyes, fringed with black lashes so long that they lay against her upper cheeks when lowered. Even her slender body was perfect: small waist and full breasts that were molded by the cotton of her dress, their nipples not completely obscured under the garment. Something stirred within him, and he recognized it for what it was—a desire to possess her. But he knew she would not be an easy conquest; she was courageous and headstrong, as he'd learned from their previous meetings.

"Well? What do you think?" he said, and his words sounded sincere to Ketti. "Should we start over, forget— uh—earlier impressions, and be friends?"

She licked her lips, not realizing how seductive she looked to John, and considered his suggestion. It was a long trip, she reasoned and there were few passengers, who would be thrown together frequently, at meals if nowhere else. She nodded finally. "I agree, so long as you don't mention my— uh—former connection to James."

"Agreed," he replied at once, and turned the full force of his grin on her.

She was glad she was holding on to the railing, for her legs were suddenly shaky and her heart felt as if it were ready to sail right out of her chest and take flight with the seabirds riding the air currents overhead. Somehow she managed to keep her reaction to him from being reflected on her face. She'd never before felt so weakened by the mere presence of a man, and wondered what it was about him that affected her so intensely. She'd even liked the feel of his arms around her, when he held her against his chest. The thought was provocative and she lowered her lashes at once, so that he couldn't read her thoughts in her eyes.

"I'd be delighted to escort you to breakfast," he offered. "I believe it's being served in the galley."

Her gaze flew back to his, but he appeared perfectly serious. For a moment she'd thought she detected a return of amusement in his voice.

"Thank you. I am hungry." She hated the prim note she heard in her voice. But somehow her reactions were all off with this man; she was too *aware* of him.

He took her elbow to steady her as they walked to the companionway and down the steps to the galley. Ketti didn't glance at him, but felt his eyes on her, and she wondered what he was thinking. That she was a shrew who'd jilted her suitor? Or a loose woman who frequented places like Chinatown, a foolish woman who took on highbinders?

But his thoughts followed a completely different course. He'd noticed the rosy stain on her cheeks that revealed more than she knew, that she might in fact feel the same attraction to him as he felt to her. He smiled to himself. The voyage might not be as tedious as he'd expected. Not with Miss Ketti Foster aboard.

Over the next week Ketti often found herself in John's company. They played chess in the galley after dining with Captain Wade, and walked the deck in both the morning and the afternoon. During their conversations, she learned that John had been in Chinatown that day on business, finalizing a property sale so he could relocate on the sugar plantation he'd inherited from his parents. He explained that his parents hadn't lived in Hawaii for many years, and now that they were both dead, he'd sold the family holdings he'd been managing in America and was moving permanently to the islands. She didn't mention that she'd noticed him coming out of a brothel or gambling den, and wondered if that establishment had been part of his "holdings." The details sounded a bit vague to Ketti, but since it was none of her affair, she didn't press for more information.

Now, as they sat in deck chairs after supper, watching angry clouds gather on the evening horizon in front of the ship, John spoke more about the plantation he meant to run. "It's on the Big Island of Hawaii," he told her. "On the Hilo side, which is tropical."

She'd been watching the waves, and his words swung her attention back to where he lounged, his lids half-lowered over his eyes.

"I thought your plantation was near Honolulu." She felt almost breathless, a reaction to him that had gotten worse over the days. His revelation was unexpected. "I live on the Big Island, too," she began. "My family has a ranch near Waimea in the high country." She broke off as it was his turn to look surprised.

For some reason neither had mentioned their exact destination, and both had assumed Honolulu. Their eyes met, and locked. Ketti wanted to look away, but the silvery-blue intensity held her gaze like a magnet, until she felt she was drowning in the fathomless depths. It was strange how their paths kept crossing, and now they were to be neighbors. It was almost scary. Ketti's Hawaiian grandmother would surely say it was preordained—the will of the old gods. Ketti gave herself a mental shake. She was being silly. It was all coincidence, anyone could see that.

"So, we'll be neighbors, Miss Ketti Foster," he said, but his voice sounded stilted. All of a sudden his expression was unreadable. "I didn't make the connection, I'm afraid. You must be Adam Foster's daughter."

She nodded, and wondered why his smile had faded. Then she had an awful thought. Surely he wasn't one of those people who was offended because she had Hawaiian blood in her veins? Several times in San Francisco she'd run into such prejudice.

But when he excused himself a few minutes later, leaving her to return to the galley alone for a chess game with Captain Wade, she wondered. And when he didn't return by the time she went to bed, she found puzzlement had turned to anger.

If that's how you feel, John Stillman, then I don't care a rap, she thought. But that was the problem. As she stared into the night, hearing a storm gather force around the ship, she knew that she did care.

By morning the storm battered the ship, and Ketti was not permitted on deck. By late afternoon it had abated enough to allow her to go topside for a few minutes of fresh air. But when Ketti took advantage of the opportunity, she found herself alone at the rail, gripping it tightly to balance herself against the roll of the ship. The oilskin coat that she'd flung over her dress whipped frantically around her skirts, as if it had a life of its own. The heavy rain had stopped, but Ketti could see that it was only a lull, for another squall was churning toward them over the ocean, angry black clouds that flashed with zigzags of lightning.

Captain Wade was on the upper deck shouting orders to the crew, his tone urgent. Then he spotted Ketti on the lower deck. "Miss Foster!" he shouted. "Get below—at once!"

For a moment she only stared back, wondering why he was so upset. Didn't he know that one of the hands had given her permission to be there? As she was about to explain that she hadn't gone against his orders, the squall hit the ship broadside, and she was flung away from the rail. The rain was so sudden and heavy that it was as if a curtain had dropped around her, obscuring her vision and soaking her in seconds; the oilskin had blown open and hardly protected her clothing. Above the din she heard shouts from the men. But all that was secondary to her need to reach the companionway. The ship was bucking and balking so hard that she was thrown first one way, then the other, so quickly that she wasn't able to grab anything that could anchor her. She suddenly feared she was about to be washed overboard.

Tossed backward again, she was slammed into something solid, hitting so hard that little lights exploded in her head. The day dimmed, and helplessly, she felt herself falling into a dark abyss. She struggled against it, knowing unconsciousness would mean certain death—her limp body would be swept overboard.

She slipped deeper into the blackness rimming her mind, but was still aware of sliding over the wet deck like a rag doll, dangerously close to the edge. Then strong hands grabbed her and jerked her to safety before she was swooped up in equally strong arms. The man seemed tall, and sure of his strength, for he carefully measured his steps to the roll of the ship. In seconds they'd reached the safety of the companionway, the hatch closed to the fury behind them. A minute later another door opened and was kicked shut and she was lowered to her bunk. Her oilskin was removed and tossed aside. Her eyes fluttered open to meet the concerned gaze of her rescuer.

"John," she managed faintly.

"Are you all right?" The lines around his mouth were white with strain, and his eyes were narrowed, as though he'd just suffered a severe shock himself. All at once Ketti felt silly. Why was it always John who saved her from some awful fate? Suddenly embarrassed, she glanced away, her eyes fastening on the drops of rain that still clung to his hair and dripped onto the shoulders of his dark frock coat.

"I'm fine now," she reassured him, but was horrified to hear her whispered words crack. She was shaky, too, and wondered if it was a reaction to the blow on her head. She dismissed the thought; she was feeling better with each passing second. It was John's presence that was disconcerting her now. Being alone with him in her closet-sized cabin was bad enough, but he'd sat down on the edge of her bunk—*and his face was only inches from hers.*

Her reassurance had a strange effect on him; the tenseness went out of his face, but his eyes were suddenly blazing with anger.

"Then what in hell were you doing on deck, Ketti? Didn't you hear the captain forbid it? This is a serious storm!"

She licked her lips, surprised by the abrupt change in him. She felt like a child being chastised for bad behavior, and that thought brought the warmth back into her chilled flesh. "One of the deckhands said I could. He said—"

"I don't give a goddamn what he said!" he interrupted savagely. "You should have known better. Someone could have drowned trying to keep you from going overboard!"

She squirmed into an upright position, too upset to care that they faced each other, so close that she could feel his breath on her hot cheeks.

"You?" she taunted, throwing caution to the wind. "Were you afraid of being washed overboard?"

He drew in his breath sharply. Even as she spoke Ketti knew she'd gone too far. No man would stand for being accused of cowardice. But she couldn't stop herself, because somewhere in the back of her mind she knew anger was safer than the other feelings she had for him—feelings she feared to identify. His effect on her was too drastic, too emotionally draining when she already felt so shaky.

His hands were suddenly on her arms, in a grip that pressed painfully into her flesh. "You little spitfire! I should show you what fear is, as you seem intent on one dangerous situation after another."

"No, thank you!" she snapped back, but her lashes fluttered nervously, and the heat in her cheeks was spreading downward into her body, quickening her breathing and sending a quivery sensation deep inside of her. "And I know when I'm in danger." She brought her chin up defensively. "I can take care of myself!"

"Can you, now?" His words were silky, but something flickered in his eyes, something that held her gaze even though she wanted to look away. Slowly he shook his head. "Did you know that you would have gone overboard if I hadn't grabbed you just in the nick of time?" He lowered his eyelids to shutter the silvery glint that so mesmerized her, and his tone became a hoarse whisper. "Do you know that you're in danger, right now, from me?"

Her anger drained away like water through a sieve. She was suddenly aware that she was at his mercy. Although she'd come to know him better, was in fact attracted to him, she really knew very little about him. As she stared, a knowing smile touched his lips and was gone. She licked her own, and the silence that lay between them, silence heavy with her awareness of his masculine power, only seemed to accentuate the violence of the storm raging beyond her porthole. The captain and his men were busy fighting the weather; there was no one to come to her rescue now.

The thought disturbed her even more. Was she in danger from John? What had he meant? As realization struck her, she tried to edge away from him, but there was nowhere to go.

"I asked you a question, Ketti?" he drawled. "Don't you know that I'm more of a threat to you than the whole damnable ocean out there?" His words slowed even more, seductive, coaxing her glance back to his.

"Of course I don't know that," she lied. Her hands fumbled with her sleeve, pretending an indifference she was far from feeling. Gathering her ragged emotions around her, she went on. "I do thank you for rescuing me, though. I'd struck my head and—"

She broke off as his hands moved to circle her back, gently drawing her closer to him. She dared not look up, and tried to ignore his gesture. "But I'd like to rest—so—so you can go now." She knew she was stuttering and babbling, and she hated the breathless quality to her voice.

Before she knew it, he'd pulled her closer still, her breasts crushed against his chest. One hand tilted her chin so that she had no option but to look into his face. Her breath caught. He was so close that she could see herself reflected in his eyes.

"No, John, no!"

His lips on hers was his answer, softly brushing her mouth at first with a gentleness that moved her beyond any protest. Despite her earlier determination to resist, her lashes fluttered as she shut her eyes. Vaguely she wondered why she was allowing him such liberties, why her arms had crept up to touch him, then hold him, and why it felt so right to be with him like this.

And then something happened. The tiny cabin was suddenly too small to contain the passion that exploded between them. Her newly awakened senses threatened to overwhelm her, like molten lava coursing over the land. She didn't want his kiss to end; she no longer wanted anything on earth but to stay in his arms, and be taught the language of love.

His kiss deepened, demanding and overpowering in its passionate possession of her lips, and the two fell back onto the bunk. She opened her mouth under his probing tongue, almost swooning as tentacles of fire surged through her veins into the most private part of her. She heard him groan, as though the sound had been wrung out of him—as though their passion surprised even him.

His hands moved over her, his touch soothing as velvet, to stroke her face, his fingers tickling and tantalizing as they traveled over the smooth column of her throat, and then lower over the cotton fabric that covered her breasts. And now it was her turn to moan, the sound lost against his mouth, as her nipples tingled and her flesh turned to fire. Between her thighs, deep within the very core of her, a hot, throbbing ache of desire was born.

Ketti felt him fumble with the buttons of her blouse, and she managed another feeble protest. His fingers didn't seem to hear her, for they didn't even hesitate. A moment later she felt a rush of cool air when her breasts were freed from their confines. John sucked in his breath sharply a second before his lips moved lower to capture one of the nipples, traitorous buds that strained toward him. She lay under him, her eyes closed as waves of desire clouded her reasoning. At that moment nothing else in the world existed but the fiery sensations spreading through her from his touch.

Briefly he lifted his head and Ketti's long lashes fluttered open to find John looking down at her, a strange expression of soft longing in his eyes.

"God but you're beautiful," he whispered, his words hardly more than a groan. He took in the flush that stained her skin, from her heaving breasts all the way up her delicate throat to her cheeks. She was even more exquisite than he'd dreamed, more perfect than any woman he'd ever known. Her flesh was smooth as satin, and her long hair that fanned out in a black cloud around her was scented with a fragrance that went straight to his head. As he drank in her loveliness, denying for the moment his need to possess her, to tame the wild spirit he'd sensed from their first meeting, her lips, sensual and swollen from his kisses, parted in wonderment. For long seconds both John and Ketti were caught by a powerful emotion neither understood.

At first they didn't hear the knock until a voice hollered above even louder knocking on the door. "Miss Foster! It's Captain Wade. Are you all right?"

"Jesus!" John muttered, and shot a glance at the door only a couple of feet away.

The spell was shattered. Desperately, Ketti pulled away as John stood. With frantic fingers she rebuttoned her blouse and then smoothed her disheveled hair.

"Yes—yes. I'm fine now!" she called back.

After a final glance to make sure Ketti's appearance was restored, John opened the door to the captain, who stood holding a cup of steaming coffee. He glanced at one, then the other, and Ketti wondered what he thought. But John appeared completely at ease, cool and suddenly remote—as though he hadn't been about to make passionate love to her. She shivered from the draft that wafted in through the open door.

"I'm still a little chilled," she managed as Captain Wade stepped into the cabin. She gave a nervous laugh. "It seems that John saved my life."

"Aye," the captain agreed, and kept his face carefully noncommittal. He could sense that there was something between them, and that he'd interrupted it. "I thought you a goner for sure." He handed her the cup. "I added a little whiskey," he said, "for medicinal purposes to calm your nerves."

The captain clucked over Ketti, making sure she hadn't been injured in the mishap. Then he turned back to John, who'd stood in silence, watching them with unreadable eyes. The captain indicated they should go, and John inclined his head in agreement.

"We'll continue our talk later," he told Ketti.

"Thanks for keeping me out of the ocean. You saved my life, John—at the risk of your own."

A slow smile touched his lips, and his eyelids drooped suddenly. "The risk was worth taking."

A moment later they took leave of her. As the door closed behind them, John gave her a final glance, one that sent her blood surging once more.

Ketti gulped her drink, then suddenly too uncertain about her feelings to do anything more, she threw off her clothes and climbed under the blankets. The whiskey took hold of her, dulling her senses, and she drifted into a strange daydream where a tall man with eyes that glinted silver told her she belonged to him—that he loved her. And she forgot everything else, and allowed herself to sink deeper into the ecstasy she'd only just discovered. She knew she wanted more, far more.

Chapter Three

The mystic pull of the islands grew stronger as the ship neared Hawaii. The voyage offered Ketti time for introspection, and as she thought about the mountains and valleys of her home in the high country, her anticipation grew. By the time they docked in Honolulu, she was anxious to catch the steamer for the Big Island, and felt fortunate that she'd made the connection with only a several-hour delay. She wondered who would meet her at the port of Kawaihae.

Impatiently Ketti watched the deckhands secure the vessel, and then lower the gangplank. She glanced around. She hadn't seen John all morning, and he'd seemed preoccupied the night before during supper with Captain Wade. She didn't even know if he intended to catch the steamer or lay over in Honolulu. Again she mused about how little she really knew of him, aside from the fact that he'd inherited a sugar plantation on the Hamakua coast.

But she did know about her reaction to him. Since the night of the storm John had been carefully casual, although she'd often caught him watching her. They'd still played chess and talked and taken walks on the deck, but they never had occasion to be alone again. Each time he took her arm or sat next to her, she remembered the powerful passion that had taken hold of them that night; it still hovered in the air between them. One good thing had come out of all her confused feelings—she no longer thought of

James, and indeed realized that what she'd felt for him was only a girlish infatuation. Her feelings for John were far deeper, and she couldn't help but wonder where they would lead. Although her traitorous body longed for his touch each night, her mind cautioned her about falling in love with a man she hardly knew.

"Ready to go, eh?"

Startled, Ketti turned from the rail to meet John's amused smile, and hesitated. He'd appeared as though conjured from her thoughts and had caught her unawares. She wondered how long he'd been watching her. The slow heat stirred within her, then its tantalizing fire surged through her veins. He looked devastatingly handsome in casual, thigh-molding trousers tucked into boots, and a white cotton shirt that accented the darkness of his skin. The morning sun was already hot, and he'd rolled up his sleeves to expose brown muscled forearms. A Stetson was tipped back on his head. She was hit with the full force of his penetrating gaze, which swept over her, just as she was, in fact, assessing him.

Instantly embarrassed, she lowered her long lashes to screen her eyes, which were already shaded by the straw picture hat she wore atop her pinned-up hair. She was suddenly aware that he'd noticed her low-cut, short-sleeved pale rose dress, and that his eyes had lingered on her upper arms and the curve of her breasts. Her cheeks warmed to match the cotton she wore.

"The captain said you're taking today's steamer to Kawaihae," he told her as he leaned against the railing, his arm brushing hers.

Ketti inclined her head and waited. She willed herself to forget that his face was so near, that his arm rested against hers, skin against skin, and that he stood closer than necessary when the whole rail was available.

"So you're to come along with me, as I'll be on the same ship," he went on suavely, as though she were just another passenger—*not a woman he'd made love to.* "It wouldn't be wise to walk on the waterfront unescorted," he added when she didn't reply at once, a trace of humor in his tone. "And the captain can't spare men who have cargo to unload."

"That'll be just fine," she managed primly, pleased she sounded equally casual. *Damn him!* she fumed. Was he deliberately trying to disconcert her? Why he'd do such a thing, she couldn't guess.

"Ready to go then?" He half turned so that he could peer into her face, his eyes squinting against the sun.

"Any time you are," she told him. "I just have to collect my things from the cabin." She would have gone at once but for his hand, which took her arm, detaining her.

"Did I tell you how pretty you look today?" His brows lowered as his eyes swept over her once more, jolting her with an electric current that almost stopped her heart. "Being back in Hawaii agrees with you."

Despite her breathlessness, she smiled. "Thank you, John. You're quite right. I'm very happy to be home, happier than I expected." Then, lifting her skirt, she strode to the companionway, suddenly anxious to feel the ground under her feet, even if it still wasn't the Big Island. And she was glad she'd managed a gracious retreat from the man who wielded such extraordinary power over her senses, glad that she'd been able to hide that reaction from him.

Ketti said goodbye to the captain and went with John to the other ship. Although he was friendly, she sensed a withdrawal in him and wondered what was disturbing his thoughts now. Once on board, she went with the mate, who carried her trunk to her cabin. When she returned to the upper deck, John and the captain had gone to see to his own crates and luggage being brought aboard.

Now as she stood alone in the stern of the steamer and watched Honolulu diminish behind the wake that marked their passage from the bay, Ketti forced her thoughts from John and her attraction to him. Instead she took a good look at the city, which had grown in the four years she'd been away. She wondered about the changes on the Big

Island. How could I have stayed away so long? she asked herself, her gaze on the lush green mountains, which rose above the coconut palms and other exotic flowering shrubs that flourished on the lowlands near the beaches. She'd almost forgotten how beautiful and fragrant everything was— how heady to the senses. Even the gentle trade wind was a soothing rhythm, a continuous breeze that tempered the heat of the brilliant sun in the pure sapphire sky above her.

Shifting position, she glanced seaward toward where the Big Island was just beyond the distant horizon. The home of the goddess Pele, she thought with a tinge of uneasiness. But then she grinned as she thought of the ancient superstitions, the old taboos that her Hawaiian grandmother claimed had long been a plague on the family, because the old woman had once married a *haole,* foreigner.

Turning back, Ketti saw that Honolulu, and the island of Oahu upon which it rested, had all but disappeared into the afternoon haze. She stared at the sun-silvered water, and the images of her parents rose in her mind; Mari, her blond, dark-eyed mother, who'd come as a girl from New Bedford to join her father, Russell Webster, a former whaler who'd remarried and settled down on a ranch on the Big Island; Adam, her tall, dark father, the only son of a Norwegian father and a Hawaiian mother of high birth. Mari and Adam's union had produced two children, Ketti and Charles; Charles was now married to a Hawaiian girl, much to the delight of Ketti's grandmother, who lived with the family on the Foster ranch.

Remembering her Hawaiian grandmother brought Ketti another smile. They'd always been close, the old woman taking delight that her only granddaughter had the dark eyes and hair of her Hawaiian ancestors, even though her features were delicate like her mother's and her fair skin too light for a native. Her grandmother Foster was the only one who'd sided with Ketti in opposing school in California.

Amazing, she thought as she walked back to her cabin. At first she'd resisted liking San Francisco and the Mission

School. It had been chosen for her by her mother, so that
she would be educated in the religion of Mari's own Irish
mother, who'd died long ago in New Bedford. Ketti had
grown to love California, had believed the roots she'd put
down would be permanent; and now here she was, returning to Hawaii.

One thing was still true, she reminded herself. It was her
brother who'd eventually inherit the huge Foster ranch, not
she. And although her mother owned a half interest in the
adjoining Webster ranch, left to her by her father's partner
when he died, she suspected that, too, would go to her
brother, Charles. Although she loved him, she felt it was
wrong that daughters inherited nothing but a dowry.
Daughters were expected to marry well, and unless things
had changed on the island, the number of eligible men was
limited. Ketti had never liked the thought of being dependent on marriage in order to have a productive future.

Her cabin was hot and stuffy after the door was closed,
so she opened the porthole for the sea breeze. Then unbidden, John's face appeared in her mind, his silvery eyes
mocking, as though he were reminding her that he was eligible, and would be living on the island.

Unsettled, Ketti tried to erase his image. It was ridiculous that the man should so occupy her thoughts. She admitted to herself that she more than liked him, that she often
found herself reliving the night when their lovemaking had
been interrupted. She wondered what would have happened if the captain hadn't knocked on the door. If John
had taken her maidenhood, would he still seem so aloof?
That thought was even more disturbing.

Faced with nothing to do, she decided to take off her
gown and have a nap until supper was served in the galley.
Once on the hard bunk, she dozed. The fragrance of the sea
flowed in through the porthole to lull her senses, and she
drifted into a deep sleep.

Ketti sat up with a start and glanced around, for a moment disoriented. Then she realized that she was in her

cabin, and that the first rays of dawn were shimmering the water with light all the way from the eastern horizon.

"Oh my goodness!" she cried aloud. "I've slept right through the night!"

Completely awake now, Ketti hurriedly began her morning ablutions, washing the sleep from her eyes and then taking clean undergarments from her trunk. She decided against wearing a corset; her waist was small enough without it, and dress on the islands was never too formal. She took a pale blue cotton gown from a trunk hanger and placed it on the bunk, contemplating whether she should wear it. Although it was the latest fashion with its bell-shaped skirt, tiny waist and wide hem, the neckline was almost too low for daytime wear. Ketti shrugged and put on the dress anyway. Its matching jacket with mutton sleeves would do for the buggy ride to the ranch in the uplands, and cover her bodice if necessary. Then she dressed her hair in a casual long style, as she knew the trade winds would only blow the pins from any upswept confection she could manage. Besides, she reminded herself again, happily, this was Hawaii, not San Francisco.

Finally ready, she closed her trunk again and left it for one of the deckhands to lift ashore after they arrived. Then, after adjusting her wide-brimmed straw hat on her head, she pulled on white lace gloves, picked up her chatelaine bag and went to the galley for something to eat before continuing on to the deck to watch the growing shoreline of the Big Island.

The ship anchored off Kawaihae, and when Ketti and her trunk were finally on the dock, she realized there was no one there to meet her. She wasn't surprised; there had been no way of sending word that would have arrived before she did, other than the message she'd sent with Char. But if worse came to worst, she knew she could take shelter in the Foster cabin located in the village, a shelter the family or their *paniolos,* cowboys, used when in the tiny port to ship cattle. Even John was nowhere to be seen.

The morning was already hot, and she stood in the bright sunlight and drank in the beauty of her cherished island. She'd almost forgotten how much she loved the dark cinder plains of volcanic rock, the coconut palm-lined beaches, and the high peaks of Mauna Kea in the north and Mauna Loa to the south, high mountains that sloped upward out of the sea to almost 14,000 feet. The mountains divided the island, and she marveled that the west side, where she stood, was as arid as a desert, while the east side was humid and tropical, and the high country to the north, the cattle country, was similar to the American west. An island of diverse terrain, she thought. Oh how she loved it all—and had missed it!

She left her trunk to be fetched later and strode off the dock to shore. As her feet touched ground she hesitated as a slight tremor shook beneath her. Her gaze automatically turned toward the distant peak of Mauna Loa. Her smile began deep inside her. She'd just experienced one of the many tiny earthquakes that jolted the island on a regular basis. The old ones would say it was only Madam Pele, fire goddess of the volcano, welcoming her home.

"And thanks to you, too, Madam," she cried, her sudden joy too much to be contained. She couldn't believe she was really home. She had a sudden impulse to dance, but contained herself.

"And thanks to you," a familiar male voice drawled behind her. "Although I dare say I'm not a madam."

More startled by the voice than the quake, Ketti whirled around to face John. He was standing in the shade of stacked crates that had been unloaded from an earlier ship, a pencil and pad in his hands, and it appeared that he was taking an inventory of the boxes.

He tipped back the brim of his Stetson and cocked his brow rakishly. But it was the full force of his startling eyes that had made her heart go so fluttery that she doubted she had the breath to utter a word.

Silence fell between them, and he just stood there, as though he, too, were trapped by the invisible force that held her. A smile touched his lips—and Ketti remembered how those lips had felt against hers, his tongue probing with liquid fire that even now was singing through her body. The sound of winches and men working and sea birds all drifted on the soft, fragrant air currents, swirling around them but outside of their suspended state. She knew he was remembering, too.

Tall and lean in riding pants that molded his thighs, his off-white cotton shirt opened down his chest to expose his bronze skin, one booted foot still resting on a small box, he was so devastatingly handsome that she suddenly felt overpowered by his very presence. But when she saw the small knowing grin that tugged at his mouth she forced herself to glance away.

"Are these yours?" she asked with a wave of her hand to indicate the crates.

He nodded. "Came on an earlier ship. The one that brought your friend Char—and your Chinese slave girl."

His tone had a cutting edge when he mentioned the girl. It was the first time he'd alluded to the incident in Chinatown, and his disapproval was evident.

"She's not my slave girl!" Ketti retorted hotly, and didn't care that her tone was defensive. A strand of hair blew into her face, and she nervously pushed it back. He may have made love to her, but that didn't give him the right to probe into her affairs, she fumed, and was glad that her sudden surge of anger was diluting her awareness of his male power over her.

He watched her, his bearing not giving away his own attraction. He'd never seen anyone more beautiful, and even the anger that touched her face briefly didn't detract from her charm. If anything, she was even more beautiful when her wild rebellious nature surfaced. She's truly a child of Hawaii, he thought suddenly. The blood of her pagan ancestors ran through her veins, and all the trappings of the civilized world couldn't change that.

When he'd first glimpsed her in Chinatown defying the highbinders, he'd assumed she was Chinese with her long silky hair almost black, and her eyes almost as dark—but there the similarity stopped. Her skin was like flawless ivory and her eyes, fringed with long thick lashes, were large and round and passionately expressive. Ketti Foster had depths that even she didn't yet understand, he thought, and had a sudden urge to be the man who awakened her. But as his gaze flicked down her slim figure to linger on her full breasts, their upper swells exposed by the daring cut of her gown, her cheeks flushed angrily. She tilted her chin, as if to defy the touch of his knowing glance. It was then he knew that he *would* be that man.

But Ketti had no way of knowing the thoughts behind his oh-so-male regard. Anger, awareness and attraction were suddenly all tangled in her mind. Again her breath was trapped in her lungs, as a tingling sensation surged into the warm, moist place between her thighs, the strangely tantalizing feeling she'd experienced before with John.

"Come on, Ketti, don't be angry." He was beside her so fast that she didn't have time to react. He took hold of her and gently pulled her closer, although not against him, aware of the men within view. "We're going to be neighbors." His tone was low, seductive, as though he'd not been disapproving only seconds earlier. "So let's stay friends."

As she was about to remind him that he was the cause of her anger, their attention was suddenly diverted by the approach of a fast-moving, two-seated buggy drawn by a pair of high-stepping bay horses. She recognized the blond hair of her brother, Charles, and the woman beside him as Panana, his wife. With a quick nod of agreement to John, she raced to greet her brother. She was unaware that she again demonstrated her impulsive nature by holding up skirts that revealed far more of her legs than was proper, and equally unaware that the amused John stared after her, even more intrigued. All thoughts of strange and alluring sensations were gone from her mind. At that moment she only wanted to be held by her big brother.

The horses were reined in and the buggy stopped with a jolt and a swirl of volcanic dust. Even before it stopped creaking and rocking, Charles leaped to the ground, yanked his sombrero from his head, grabbed Ketti in an enfolding hug and whirled her around, her feet barely skimming the ground.

"Ketti, Ketti!" he crooned. "I'm so glad you're home. I've met every ship from Honolulu since Char told us you were coming."

She leaned against him, so glad to see him that she could do little more than hug him back. Finally she pulled free and looked up into his sun-browned face, which was so like their father's. He was a big man, his dark features a legacy of his Hawaiian ancestors—except for his blond hair, which he'd inherited from their mother. He was an extraordinarily handsome man, one who'd had all the island girls at his feet, Ketti remembered fondly.

"Marriage agrees with you, Charles," she told him, grinning. "Never thought I'd see the day when my big handsome brother would really tie the knot."

"Yes, it does." He glanced lovingly at his wife. "I'm a lucky man."

"And so am I." Panana had climbed from the buggy and joined them, a petite, graceful girl whose dark exotic beauty was a perfect match for Charles. It was obvious that the couple was very much in love. "Welcome home, Ketti," she said, smiling, and embraced her with a fondness that had begun in childhood.

"I'm sorry I couldn't be at the wedding—" Ketti broke off as Charles interrupted.

"We missed you." About to say more, he hesitated as he noticed John. They exchanged greetings and Ketti was surprised to realize that they seemed to know each other, and, in fact, appeared to be on friendly terms.

"We went on with our marriage plans," Charles said with a shrug as his attention returned to Ketti. "After you wrote that you were staying on in San Francisco for another year."

A lump formed in Ketti's throat. San Francisco seemed far less important now, and she suddenly knew she should have come back to Hawaii after completing school.

"That's understandable," she managed, suddenly near tears at having missed her only brother's wedding. Because he was four years older, he'd always been protective, the one who'd been her confidant during her growing-up years.

"And Mother and Father, how are they?"

"Same as ever." Charles grinned suddenly and hugged her again. "I'm so damn glad you're back. For a while there we feared you'd stay in California. Mother was blaming herself for sending you when you hadn't wanted to go in the first place." He gave a laugh, and Ketti was reminded of him as a child. "And Grandmother—you know how she is," he said fondly. "She was beginning to believe it was the old taboos at work, taking you away forever."

"That's Grandmother," Ketti agreed. She tried not to notice John, who was talking with Panana. The brim of his Stetson was adjusted so that his eyes were shaded, and she couldn't see where he was looking. She had an odd prickling feeling that he was watching her.

"Well, let's get started for the ranch!" she cried, unable to wait any longer to see the rest of the family.

In a few minutes Charles, with the help of John, was loading Ketti's trunk and other boxes onto the back of the buggy. While they worked, Ketti chatted with Panana, catching up on the events of the island. Then another buggy pulled up near them.

"Oh! It's the Reverend Mead and his sister, Sarah," Panana told her, indicating the man and woman in the buggy. She flashed Ketti a grin. "I bet I know why they're here."

Ketti somehow knew that what was coming next would be upsetting, and she wasn't mistaken. As Panana and Ketti watched, the two newcomers descended from their vehicle. The reverend, a thin, severe-appearing man garbed all in black, nodded in the direction of Ketti and Panana. His sister barely spared them a glance, and Ketti sensed that she didn't meet the woman's prim and proper approval. In a gray dress, her poke bonnet shading her sallow complexion, the woman was drab and uninteresting.

"He's the new minister in the church near John Stillman's plantation," Panana whispered as the reverend and his sister greeted John warmly.

"This isn't John Stillman's first visit to the island, I gather," Ketti commented, and tensed even more.

"Oh no," Panana replied. "He's been making trips for the past two years, getting his affairs settled before moving here permanently." She turned to Ketti with a conspiratorial grin. "Now that John is here to stay, island gossip says that the reverend will be announcing Sarah's betrothal to him."

Stunned, Ketti did all she could do to appear normal. For a moment the sounds of the surf and port receded, and her mind was filled with the memory of John making love to her. And all the time he was committed to someone else. He was no better than James!

Then the buggy was loaded, and John saw them off. He told them he'd see them soon, but his eyes were on Ketti. It was as if he were saying that they still had personal business to finish.

How dare he! she fumed. She flounced onto the back seat. As the horses started forward for the climb into the high country, Ketti held her head high, and ignored whatever message John was trying to convey. She would not be trifled with again.

It was as though Ketti had never left; the beauty of the ranch seemed untouched by the passage of time. After a burst of conversation, they'd traveled the miles up the long sloping road to the high country in companionable silence, and the eternal peace of the land had finally helped Ketti to relax. By the time Charles slowed the bays for the turn into the driveway, all thoughts of John had been replaced by her anticipation of seeing her family again.

Charles brought the buggy to a stop by the stairs to the veranda. The same hibiscus and bougainvillea bloomed on either side of the steps in a riot of scarlet and orange. Impatient to see everyone, Ketti nevertheless hesitated after jumping to the ground. Slowly she turned, taking in the familiar setting. Mauna Kea loomed above the ranch several miles to the south, and beyond the two-story, well-maintained house, down the long sloping land, the distant Pacific Ocean sparkled under the late-afternoon sun. Then, for the first time, she saw the new house, resting in the curve of the hill beyond the paddock. It was some distance away, commanded a spectacular view and belonged to Charles and his new bride.

"When you've settled in, we want you to visit," her brother said, following her gaze.

As she grinned back her agreement, her parents and grandmother burst out of the house and down the steps to greet her.

"Ketti! Oh, Ketti! You're finally home with your family!" Her mother's dark eyes brimmed with tears as she held her daughter in a tight embrace.

Then it was her father's turn. "My little girl, all grown up," he crooned as he folded her against his broad chest. A surge of love filled her; she felt protected and safe.

"And now me," her grandmother said, her round face alight with love for her granddaughter. She was a small, elegant woman, her hair a little grayer and her face more lined than Ketti remembered.

Charles and Panana stood to one side, smiling and nodding, and then followed the others up the steps to the veranda. As the family entered the house, everyone talking at once, Ketti thought she'd never been happier. Her mother was still slim and vital, her blond hair undimmed by years, and her father was still the strong, handsome man she'd always imagined as the embodiment of the mythical Hawaiian gods. Only her grandmother appeared older, a thought that saddened Ketti. Her grandmother had come to this very house as the bride of a Norwegian sailor, a man she married despite ancient taboos that forbade her to marry a *haole*. Her grandfather had been killed in a freak accident long before Ketti's birth, and her grandmother had never stopped grieving, had never really accepted that his death wasn't the revenge of the old gods. But whatever had happened in the past, Ketti was just so glad to be home.

Once inside the cool entry hall they went into the salon. There had been changes to the interior of the house, if not to the exterior. Although the koa paneling remained in the hall, shining like polished mahogany, the furniture in the salon was different; it was in the Edwardian style, and had been imported from Europe. So had the damask that covered the walls, and the exquisite lamps and paintings that gave the room an elegance to match any of the mansions Ketti had visited in San Francisco.

"Panana and I have the old furniture," Charles remarked, seeing she was pleased with the beautiful room. "Our mother has a knack of making things nice."

Pleased, Mari stood with her arm around her husband, who looked down at her with love and pride in his eyes. "I couldn't have accomplished any of it without Tutu," she said, meaning Ketti's grandmother.

Again everyone talked at once, but in the back of her mind, Ketti felt at peace. Her life in San Francisco was over. Her new life in Hawaii was beginning. Tomorrow she'd start thinking about her future, and how she could contribute to her family. She'd consider her work options, for she couldn't bear to be idle, just waiting for a husband to fill her life. She glanced beyond the velvet-draped windows, and could see the distant Pacific Ocean, reflecting a sky that was awash with the brilliant crimsons and purples of the setting sun.

Suddenly travel weary, Ketti longed for a bath, and after another round of hugs, she went upstairs to her room. Instantly she felt as though she'd stepped back in time. A glance told her everything was as she'd left it. The polished koa walls seemed to enfold her with all the love she'd always known from her home and family. The bedroom was still decorated in the pale rose chintz of her childhood: bedspread, dressing-table skirt, drapes and ornamental cushions and pillows. Even the Oriental carpet on the floor and the French wallpaper on one wall were of a rose and pink floral print. She moved to the window seat and sat down, for the moment too drained to do anything else.

For a long time all she could do was gaze out the window at the mountainous land and the lush valleys, beyond which the ocean was a constant background, darkening now as the day ebbed away. Land that once belonged to the ancient kings, she mused, caught in sudden melancholy. Land haunted by the Night Marchers, the ghosts of ancient warriors, according to the old Hawaiian beliefs. But I don't believe in ghosts, she reminded herself. I don't believe that the mythical Polynesian gods take revenge on *haoles* if they settle on sacred ground.

Standing, Ketti shook off such thoughts, and turned away from the window. For the first time she noticed that her trunk had been placed by the closet, together with her bag and straw hat. Another urge to bathe reminded her that she was hot and grimy from the buggy ride, and that her dress was soiled. She began to undress, anticipating a long soak in the tub, which the Hawaiian housekeeper had filled with lavender-scented water.

As she bathed she allowed her mind to drift. But when the faintly sardonic man with silvery blue eyes suddenly popped into her thoughts, she reined them in. She wouldn't allow her unsettled feelings about John Stillman to upset her reunion with her family. Abruptly she stood up and began to dry off.

But one thing she did know. She wasn't going to let him play with her emotions. She'd show him she was a woman to reckon with...not a hoyden who was forever getting into a scrape.

Chapter Four

The night felt warm to Ketti as she stood in her petticoats trying to decide what to wear to dinner. She'd finished her bath and put on her undergarments, then brushed her hair until it shone, and now she was unsure of how to dress for her first meal with her family in more than four years.

Impulsively, she went to her window and looked out over the black landscape. A light breeze flowed into the room, touching her with the cool fragrance of night in the high country. She sighed, allowing the peace to enfold her. *I'm really home,* she thought, and a sudden joy almost overwhelmed her. Her fatigue had been banished by the long soak in the tub, and by her growing sense of knowing she belonged to this beautiful island in the Pacific Ocean.

The thought struck her that it was getting late, that maybe the family was awaiting her presence in the dining room. She went back to her open trunk, and after another quick glance over the gowns, she decided on a black skirt, flat in front and full in back, and a high-necked, scarlet ruffled blouse with huge leg-of-mutton sleeves. Once she'd finished with the buttons and adjusted the skirt over her hips, she went to the mirror for a final assessment.

Even though her dark eyes had caught the light from the lamp, and her attire was prim and proper, the young woman looking back at Ketti didn't appear sedate. Instead, the high color in her cheeks and her long shimmering hair the exact shade of her long dark lashes, seemed to offset the sophisticated effect of her dress. *Good Lord!* she thought. At the moment she looked more like a schoolgirl than a young woman who'd furthered her education in America.

But after a final grin at her image in the glass, she whirled away to the door. Girlish or not, there was no time to pin up her hair now. Besides, it was her family downstairs, not some beau she was trying to impress. She went along the hall to the stairs, and hesitated, her gaze on the banister.

She ran a hand over the smooth koa wood, and remembered all the times she and Charles had slid down the banister's slippery length. She'd done it from the time she was old enough to get around the house alone, and was still doing it when she left for San Francisco. Why not? she asked herself mischievously. There was no one in the lower hall; she could hear everyone talking in the salon.

Pushing up her skirts, she flung a leg over the highly polished handrail, then carefully balanced herself. As she let go, sliding downward faster and faster, and rounding the curve into the front hallway with lightning speed, she let out a giggle. If only Mr. John Stillman could see her now, she thought gleefully.

As she prepared to stop herself at the bottom, she was startled by hands that suddenly brought her to an abrupt halt, and yanked her against a hard male chest.

"If it isn't Katherine Foster. I should have known," John said as she rested against his arms, for a long, horrifying moment unable to gain her balance and extricate herself. A chuckle sounded just behind her ear, and she felt warm breath against her cheek.

Ketti twisted her head around and her gaze was instantly caught by the amused eyes of John. Embarrassment engulfed her in a great wave of fiery heat, even as her flesh quivered under his touch. Her pulse began to beat unsteadily in her throat. Her skirts were caught up around her knees, exposing her lower legs, and she wondered how she could climb off the banister without making matters worse. Then anger came to her rescue.

"Please be a gentleman and turn around!" she told him tartly. "I'm perfectly able to help myself, thank you!"

But he didn't move. Instead his brows shot up and the corners of his mouth quirked as he suppressed a grin. Then, with one quick motion, he lifted her from the polished rail and set her down on the hall floor.

"That takes care of an awkward situation," he drawled, standing back to let his eyes travel over her pink cheeks, and her breasts that rose and fell with each rapid breath. Outwardly cool and amused, John didn't let her see how aware he was of her, of her wide-eyed stare that had gone from childish glee to embarrassment and then anger. She was quite a woman, and even as he held her gaze, his manhood stirred with longing for her.

The moment he dropped his hands she stepped back, indignant that he hadn't respected her wishes. "You're no gentleman!" she spit at him. "A lady expects consideration."

He laughed out loud. "Since when do *ladies* slide down banisters?"

"Ladies can do as they please in the privacy of their homes!" she returned hotly.

"Is that right?" His tone was lower, as though he read a different meaning into her words—*as though he were remembering the last time they had privacy*.

Something glinted in his silvery eyes a moment before his lids lowered to hood whatever he was thinking. But Ketti got the message, and she knew the red banners of color in her cheeks flagged her knowing to him as surely as the quick rhythm of her breathing strained her breasts against the scarlet silk.

She licked her lips nervously and glanced around the wide hall, hoping no one else had witnessed her entrance. With relief, she saw it was empty. She wondered how she'd missed seeing John. And when had he arrived at the ranch? Were the minister and his sister with him?

Thinking of the minister's sister, Sarah, was even more disconcerting. How dared John bring another woman into her house, after he'd— She broke off the thought as her anger grew. "I can't thank you because I didn't ask for your help," she said primly. Then she picked up her skirts and swept past him, her chin tilting upward as she glimpsed a flash of white teeth.

She hesitated in the doorway to the salon, and felt John come up behind her. The narrow-faced Reverend Mead sat in an overstuffed chair, intent on the conversation he was having with Ketti's father and brother; his sister, Sarah, a handsome but severe woman, sat with the other three Foster women. No one seemed to notice the couple in the doorway.

As Ketti was about to enter the room, John leaned forward and whispered in her ear. "I forgot to mention how lovely you're looking tonight, Ketti."

He still sounded amused and she'd didn't dare glance at him. Instead she retorted, "I expect you say that to all the women, including your friend Sarah."

But she spoke louder than she thought, and the three women glanced up. "Oh, there you are dear," her mother said, and came to take her arm and lead her into the room. "We've been waiting for you. Cook says dinner is ready."

Everyone stood, and Sarah immediately took her place next to John as they walked to the dining room. Ketti's mother explained that their visitors had stopped on their way across the island when their buggy broke down, and that Adam had insisted they spend the night and continue the journey in the morning after repairs had been made to the wheel.

All through dinner Ketti felt puzzled. Each time she looked up she caught John watching her, and she knew Sarah noticed as well. One thing was for sure. He certainly didn't act as if he were betrothed to anyone, let alone the minister's sister.

The conversation was stimulating to Ketti, for she heard the news about the island. The one sour note was hearing that there was political unrest in Hawaii, related to tariffs on sugar and the depressed economy. There was even talk of a secret organization that plotted to overthrow the queen. Talk of more personal family matters was avoided because of the guests, and Ketti looked forward to long conversations with the members of her family. She caught a glimpse of Siu, the Chinese girl from San Francisco, who'd since taken a job with the Fosters, as she brought some of the hot dishes from the kitchen. The two girls exchanged smiles and glances. Ketti was anxious to know the ex-slave girl better, and was happy to see her so obviously settled into the Foster ranch life. She intended to seek out Siu tomorrow so they could talk.

By the time the diners finished the roast and fresh vegetables and had been served dessert, Ketti began to feel fatigued, and was unable to stop her eyelids from drooping. After everyone went back to the salon for coffee, she asked to be excused, pleading her tiredness.

"Of course, Ketti dear," her mother said, and immediately hugged her. "I can see you're exhausted."

Her father kissed her. "Go to bed, little Ketti. We'll see you in the morning."

Her grandmother stood, too, and joined Ketti, explaining that she was also ready for bed. After a final smile that included everyone, Ketti turned to go. But not before her eyes had been captured in a brief but heart-stopping moment, by John's, in a look that told her they would meet again.

Once upstairs, the two women paused before separating. Her grandmother's face crinkled kindly as she pulled Ketti close. As she stepped back, her expression sobered. "You have become a beautiful young woman," the old woman told her thoughtfully, the words drawn out. "So lovely that even the goddess Pele is no more beautiful."

Ketti pulled the little woman close in a long hug. "Oh, Grandmother, I love you so. And I'm so happy to be back with you."

She knew the reference to Pele was the ultimate in compliments from her grandmother. Ketti suspected she put more credence in the old gods than the family realized.

"You go to bed now, child," the old woman said, her expression filled with love for her granddaughter, who so reminded her of herself when she was young. "We'll talk tomorrow."

Then they both went to their rooms. As Ketti closed the door and felt the enfolding warmth of her childhood, she knew she'd sleep the clock around. In minutes she was under the covers, the cool breeze caressing her face with fragrant breath. But as she closed her eyes, she saw John's. And then she remembered no more.

The night wind of the high country was the only sound Ketti heard when she opened her eyes, wondering what had awakened her. Moonlight poured into her room, illuminating her bed with its magical spell. Ketti strained her ears but the house was silent. Everyone was asleep, including their guests.

She pushed back the covers and slipped out of bed to pad barefoot to the window seat. She tucked her feet under her as she sat down on the soft cushion. Beyond the house Mauna Kea stood like a massive black shape against the lighter sky, while far below, the moonlight lay like a shimmering ribbon across the ocean. Ketti suddenly wondered if the mountains were haunted by Night Marchers, and found herself scanning the remote reaches of peaks and valleys for a flicker of light. It was said that the old warriors always carried lighted torches. She smiled to herself; it was amazing how quickly she'd been pulled back into the mood of the land.

Wide-awake now, Ketti knew she wouldn't fall right back to sleep, so she picked up her sheer robe, which matched her white gown, and put it on. Then she moved quietly to the door, and after a peek to determine the hall was empty, she left her room and went down the back stairs to the kitchen and then outside to the garden. The light, melodious rhythm of the little waterfall her father had made long ago for her mother still tinkled from the corner of the garden under the cluster of flowering trees. Ketti headed for it, knowing there was a bench next to the pond where she could sit and allow the night to wrap her in velvet arms.

As she sat, a flood of memories raced through her mind, memories of warm childhood days when she'd played games beside the fountain. After the going-away party her parents gave her when she was about to leave for California, she'd sat on the bench crying her eyes out that she had to go. She smiled now, thinking how quickly the time had passed. So deep was she in her thoughts, she didn't hear the footsteps, didn't know she wasn't alone, until the shadow of a man blocked out the moonlight. Startled, she jumped up.

Immediately, hands steadied her, and the touch seemed familiar. Then he stepped from in front of her so that the moonlight shone on his face, and even though there were still shadows, she recognized John.

"Take it easy," he said soothingly. "I thought you heard me coming. I didn't mean to frighten you."

"I'm not frightened," she managed, but she sounded faint. "You just startled me, that's all."

"I'm sorry," he replied, but he didn't remove his hands from her upper arms. Ketti suddenly felt the coolness of the night, and began to tremble. Instinctively, he pulled her closer, so that she was folded against his chest. "You're cold," he whispered somewhere above her head. "You need to be warmed, before you catch a chill."

For a long moment Ketti allowed herself the pleasure of being in his arms. Then, as though aroused from a drugged sleep, she tried to pull away. Her sudden realization that she was next to naked was alarming, especially when she was so near John whose very presence somehow shattered all her resistance to him.

But he still held her and she couldn't free herself. "Don't resist me," he whispered, and with two fingers, tilted her face to his. Bending his head, he kissed her. At first his lips were gentle against her mouth, soothing, his tongue exploring her softness, tasting the sweetness of her breath. Again she tried to wrench away, before she no longer had the willpower to do so. She reminded herself that Panana had said he might be committed to another woman, Sarah, who even now slept in one of the guest rooms.

Ketti choked on a ragged, indrawn breath, as his hand slid down the silk of her robe, lingering on her ribs beneath the swell of her breast. Every muscle in her body tensed, as a wild longing bloomed within her, sending her blood surging through her heart so that it beat erratically. She managed to press her hands against his chest in an attempt to free herself. But her strength was ebbing away in exact proportion to his mounting urgency, and the language of their bodies, which strained against each other.

Feeling her hands fluttering against his chest, John tightened his grasp. Somewhere in the back of his mind was the belief that he couldn't let her go, couldn't allow all the reasons why he should stop to cloud the moment. He wanted her, and when he saw her sitting in the moonlight like a pagan goddess of the night, her long dark hair accentuating the pale perfection of her skin, flesh he could glimpse under the sheer fabric of her gown and robe, all rational thought had fled from him. The feel of the warm and vibrant woman in his arms, molding her limbs to his even though he knew she wanted to resist, was an aphrodisiac he couldn't deny. He moved his lips to feather her face, felt her lashes flutter helplessly, and then moved on to her ears, nipping at them, before lowering his mouth to the soft column of her neck.

"Ohh." Her word was a long, whispered moan.

Her heartbeat quickened, and her blood was racing through her veins, until she felt a dizzying light-headedness. Her hands stilled against his chest, then moved upward to encircle him, one arm moving lightly over the fine linen that covered his back, the other around his neck, her fingers gently combing his crisp hair. Her lips parted for his tongue when he again took her in a kiss that demanded more. As she melted into him, he plunged with deeper thrusts into the softness of her mouth, a tantalizing rhythm that sent flashes of hot throbbing need into the moist, soft folds between her thighs. When he pulled her back onto the bench she didn't protest. When he held her so close that her breasts pressed against the hardness of his chest, she only wanted to be closer. She could feel the ridged muscles of his thighs next to her own smooth ones, and she thought longingly of her bunk on the ship when he'd made love to her before. As though he, too, remembered, his heart thudded even faster than hers.

"God, but you feel soft," he whispered hoarsely against her lips.

She couldn't reply, for his mouth had immediately closed over hers again. She tasted brandy and tobacco, and she reveled in the thought of tasting him, and exploring his deliciously abrasive tongue. Her awakening responses were soaring and expanding even more than on that night on the ship. She was aware of everything about him, the way his arms felt holding her, the strength of his long lean form, and the male smell of his body.

Vaguely she was aware of him loosening the tie of her wrap so that it fell from her in a whisper of silk, and then his hand sliding down the front of her gown. But when he took hold of her breast, a protest rose from within her. It died into a low moan as he brushed a finger over the taut peak of her nipple, sending a rich flow of sensation deep into the lower part of her body, so that it throbbed for his touch.

Sensing her response, John tilted her back onto the bench so that she lay under him, one of his arms cushioning her back from the wooden seat. For a heart-stopping moment he looked into her face, and even in the moonlight he could see the flush of passion staining her smooth cheeks, and the need of him in her eyes. Something caught in his throat as an intangible connection seemed to hold them in a timeless grip. She filled him with a wonder and desire he couldn't resist. With a groan born of his own hardening need, he lowered his face to trace a path of fiery moist kisses from her eyelids to the fine curve of her jaw, where he paused to outline the bottom of her face with his tongue, then downward over her neck to the hollow of her throat, and then lower still to the swell of her trembling breasts.

Ketti could feel his breath warm on her flesh. Every cell in her body seemed on fire for him, her veins sang as her blood coursed frantically through them, and her ardor grew to overwhelm her with wanton disregard for consequences. John pushed the top of her gown aside so that his tongue captured first one nipple, then the other, but when his hand slid under her gown and tickled over her stomach to touch the soft hairs between her thighs, the muscles of her abdomen convulsed with the exquisite pain of pure rapture.

"Ketti, Ketti." She felt his words vibrate gently against the globes of her breasts. "I must have you—now, while you want me."

His urgency swelled in his words even though his voice was hardly more than a whisper. And as he spoke he lowered the top of her gown so that her breasts were completely exposed to the blue fire of his eyes, as he bent over her. The moon had moved farther down the sky, casting the bench into the shadows of the surrounding trees. The night was heavy with the fragrance of tropical blossoms and the water from the fountain rushed with a musical tribute to the lovers' increasing frenzy for each other.

Ketti felt his hardness against her thighs, and for a moment reason asserted itself. What was she doing? He was about to make love to her as she lay pressed against the hard bench. "No John, no." She tried to move away but she

couldn't. He wouldn't let her. And somewhere in the back
of her mind she was glad—glad he took the decision from
her, for she wanted him with all of her heart, all of her
being.

The sudden glow of a lamp from one of the upstairs bed-
rooms cast a swath of light across the garden. Although they
were some distance beyond it, Ketti was startled. Her gaze
flew to the window to see a woman gazing into the night.
Although she knew they couldn't be seen, Ketti was abruptly
conscious of her surroundings, that anyone could wander
into the garden and find them. The thought was sobering,
and it drained her passion.

"It's all right, darling," John reassured her softly, aware
of what had caused her to pull away from him. "We're safe
here. No one will come."

But his words had the opposite effect. They both knew the
woman in the window was Sarah, peering out as though she
sensed something was amiss, something that would have a
direct bearing on her own future. Ketti knew she couldn't
stay a moment longer with John, couldn't allow his lovemaking to continue to the point of no return. Tomorrow
morning when he left with Sarah she'd hate herself, and
wish she had never ventured into the garden.

With a cry like a wounded animal, Ketti twisted out from
under him and jumped to her feet. With a quick motion she
adjusted her gown and swooped up her wrap where it had
fallen on the stone floor that surrounded the fountain.
Then, unable to meet his eyes, aware that he made no move
to stop her once she'd rejected his words and touch, she fled
back along the garden path, keeping to the shadows until
she reached the safety of the back entrance.

John watched her go, a ghostly form in her blowing white.
He knew it was no use to force her. He wanted her, but he
wanted her to want him as well.

A glance at the window that had just grown dark told him
the woman still stood there, and it was as though she were
trying to see into the garden without the encumbrance of

lamplight behind her. John adjusted his clothing, his thoughts curbing his previous passion, his gaze still on the shadowy form above him. During John's previous visit to the island, Sarah's brother, Reverend Mead, had approached him concerning a possible alliance between John and Sarah. John had listened, and had seen the sense in the man's proposal. It was true there weren't many eligible men as possibilities for Sarah's hand, nor had there been many women in John's life who would have considered living on his plantation—certainly not the women he'd known in San Francisco. John intended to stay on the Big Island, and to raise a family one day, and that meant having a wife. He'd indicated to the reverend that he'd give consideration to the minister's frank talk.

John smiled wryly into the soft night. Even before he'd met the unpredictable Ketti Foster, who had set his emotions on end from his first glimpse of her, he'd finally dismissed the reverend's suggestion, knowing such a cold-blooded arrangement wouldn't suit his needs. Now he sat down on the bench, sobered by another thought. The Fosters were unaware of his background, that his heritage was as deeply rooted in the islands as their own...and that once his family had been intertwined with theirs. If they found out, John knew they might never approve of him.

The night had gone flat and he felt suddenly depressed. Abruptly he got up to stride back to the barn. Checking on the *paniolo* who was staying up to fix his buggy would be more productive than brooding over events he couldn't change. He quickened his step, unaware that his progress was noted by the woman who still stood at the window.

Sarah bit her lip, letting the lace curtain fall back in place. She just knew the man she'd been watching was John, but she hadn't been able to make out what the movement of white had been in the shadows. For an instant she thought of the legendary Pele, but immediately discounted that idea as rubbish. She didn't put any credence in the heathenish beliefs of the Hawaiians.

Her eyes narrowed as she turned back to the bed. It was true that the drawings and paintings of the pagan goddess resembled Ketti Foster, right down to the slim build and long flowing hair. She hesitated, adjusting her high-necked, long-sleeved muslin gown, the very garment that had made her too warm to sleep. Was Ketti the person who'd been with John in the garden? she asked herself. Resolve tightened in her. No one would come between her and John.

With that thought she closed her eyes and willed herself to sleep, while sleep eluded Ketti, in another part of the house, and John, who intended to be gone by first light.

Chapter Five

It was midmorning when Ketti went downstairs, having overslept. At first she thought the kitchen was empty, until Siu came out of the pantry. Ketti was delighted to see the former slave girl, who looked typically Chinese in her high-necked black jacket and willow-green pantaloons. She wore a colorful pair of *tabis* on her feet, which fortunately—because Siu was born a peasant—had not been bound.

The girl gestured and smiled. "So glad to see you," she greeted Ketti in very broken English.

Ketti smiled back. "And I'm happy to see you here, happy that you seem so—"

"Happy!" She waved her hands in a feminine manner. "Char says I do fine...with English."

"Where is Char?"

"Honolulu," Siu replied, dragging out the word. "But he come soon, to visit." Her delicate face glowed and her silky hair bobbed back and forth as she nodded emphasis.

Ketti was thoughtful. Siu couldn't hide how she felt about Char, and Ketti wondered about their sea voyage. Had it been like hers with John? Had Siu fallen in love with Char, as she'd—Ketti broke off her thoughts abruptly. She didn't want to face her feelings—yet. Since awakening, she'd purposefully kept thoughts of John in abeyance. As though she read Ketti's mind, Siu continued with her faltering words and quick hand gestures.

"Mr. John—others—left long time ago," she offered. "Wheel all fixed."

Ketti only nodded, and was relieved when her mother, wearing a pale blue day dress that accentuated her still-slim figure, her blond hair pinned sedately on top of her head, entered the kitchen and immediately hugged her. Siu went back to her work, but Ketti told her they'd talk later. Then, with a coffee cup in hand, she followed her mother into the dining room where a place was set for her breakfast.

Siu brought out eggs and fried pork and freshly sliced bread. Even though Ketti wasn't hungry and would have been satisfied with only coffee, she began to eat, not wanting her mother to think something was wrong.

"Oh, Ketti," Mari began in a rush of words as the Chinese girl went back to the kitchen. "It's so good to have you back. You don't know how many times I wondered if I'd done the right thing in insisting you go to school in San Francisco. Then, when you stayed on, I just knew I'd been wrong."

"I don't regret my education, Mother," Ketti replied, and was suddenly worried that her mother might hear the flatness in her tone.

A short silence settled between them, but when Mari finally broke it, her words were direct. "You were interested in James, weren't you?" she suggested softly, having picked up a sadness in her daughter's words. "Are you all right now, dear?"

Ketti's gaze traveled over her mother's lovely face, reading her concern, and it suddenly felt good to have a mother who cared. She smiled sweetly, conveying her love to the older woman. "Oh, Mother, it's not what you think. I thought I cared for James, even believed we might marry." She hesitated. "And then I found him sneaking around with another woman, and that was the end of any deep feelings I might have felt for him."

"The damn fool!" her mother cried, her large eyes flashing anger. "You're better off without him. Once a cheat, always a cheat!"

Ketti laughed. "Oh, Mother! I didn't get hurt by it, really I didn't. And on the voyage home I even realized that what I'd felt for him was only a childish infatuation."

Mari looked thoughtful for a second, but whatever she was going to say was prevented by Siu's bringing more coffee. Ketti was relieved. She didn't care to discuss anything else about her trip home.

And her mother, watching her face, hoped Ketti had not rebounded into feelings for someone else, someone who might not deserve those feelings. But for now she would content herself with her daughter being home, and trust that the preoccupation she'd glimpsed on Ketti's face was only fatigue after a long sea voyage.

They discussed how Siu was settling into ranch life, and how much everyone liked her. Ketti explained fully what had happened in Chinatown, and why she'd bought Siu from the tong lord.

"You did the right thing," her mother agreed, "although it was dangerous." Mari watched her daughter's changing expression, and realized Ketti might be even more strong-willed than she herself had been as a girl.

Ketti smiled fondly at her mother. She'd known her parents would take Siu in, understand why she had to buy her. They'd already sent money to repay the Rawlstons in California.

"So it was John Stillman who rescued you?" Mari was thoughtful, realizing that John had also been on the same ship from San Francisco as Ketti. Ketti only nodded. Mari wondered what might be between them, but decided not to pry further at the moment.

Ketti finished eating, and the conversation turned to her grandmother. Mari explained that she was napping.

"Tutu is well, isn't she, Mother?"

Mari nodded. "Just slowing down, as we all do in time."

Then she went on to talk about Charles's wedding, and to say that Panana would like them to stop by so Ketti could see her new house.

Ketti inclined her head, and realized how much had changed in only four short years. But she looked forward to seeing her brother's new home. Charles was fortunate to have married his longtime love, Panana. One day she hoped she'd be as lucky. But in the meantime she needed to be thinking about some sort of job for her own future. She meant to discuss the possibilities with her parents as soon as she'd settled in.

The next week was filled with activities around the ranch. When she'd unpacked, Ketti was taken on a tour of the outbuildings and rangeland by her father and brother, who proudly pointed out all the changes in the past several years. The herds had increased in both size and quality, a feat accomplished by segregation and new breeding practices. Even the crew of *paniolos* was larger. It was fun for Ketti to watch the cowboys roping and branding, practices that hadn't changed. Panana gave her a tour of her new house, and Ketti couldn't help but envy her and Charles's happiness, as she saw how cozy their home was, how obviously filled with love.

As she observed the changes on the ranch, one thing became apparent to Ketti; her brother was being groomed to take over its management when their father retired. And there was no position for her other than that of a beloved only daughter in a family that placed all future hopes in the son.

As Ketti sat in the salon one night after dinner, enjoying a cup of coffee, she realized she couldn't idle her days away forever, that she must find her own goals for the future. With that thought in mind, she waited until her grandmother had gone off to bed and she was alone with her parents. Her mother always sat next to her father on the sofa near the fireplace, and Ketti was reminded of how deeply they cared for each other, that they were one of those rare couples who'd married for love and had stayed in love. The pattern had continued with Charles and Panana. *But what about me?* Ketti watched the flames lick at the wood, the fire taking the high-country chill out of the June night. *Will I ever find that kind of love?*

The face of John Stillman abruptly surfaced in her mind, and she shifted uncomfortably on the cushion of the over-stuffed chair. Forcibly she pushed the image away, as she'd done all week. She hadn't seen him since the night in the garden, which had left her confused. Did all men try to take advantage of women, when they had no serious intentions beyond the moment? she wondered. Then she became aware that her mother was speaking to her, and that both parents were watching her.

"I'm afraid I was daydreaming," Ketti explained, and smoothed her hand over her cotton print skirt.

"I just asked how you were settling back into life on the ranch," Mari said with a smile, and glanced at Ketti's father. He flashed a grin.

Ketti, looking at him from an adult perspective, realized how devastatingly attractive he must have been when her mother met him, and she marveled at how handsome he still was, looking so Hawaiian even though he was half-Norwegian. In fact, both of her parents hardly looked old enough to have grown-up children.

"Just fine," she replied. "I so love the ranch." She glanced down at her hands clasped in her lap. Then she took a deep breath and began to explain further about her need for her own work, that there wasn't enough to keep her occupied in the house, and that she couldn't be content to sit idly by and accomplish nothing.

"And as I'm not in line to be married in the near future, I want to work," she finished with a little laugh.

They digested her words, and her father was the first to reply. "Sounds like our daughter takes after her mother," he said, and although his eyes were warm on Mari, his words were a little clipped. "Don't tell me you want to ride with the *paniolos*—because I can't agree to that."

"Your father is just remembering all the trouble I got into when I rode with my father's *paniolos*," Mari added quickly. "And now, as I look back, I can understand why no one approved." She paused, her expression gentle. "But I still remember how I felt, and I sympathize with you needing your own goals, because I certainly did."

"Headstrong, that's what you were," Adam said with a grin. "But always courageous, and I admired that."

Ketti bit her lip. She'd heard the stories many times. How her mother had come from New Bedford as a girl, and hadn't been welcomed at first by her father, Ketti's Grandfather Webster, who still lived on the adjoining ranch with his second wife, Agnes. But Mari had won the approval of her father's partner, Ev, and he'd ultimately made Mari heir to his half of that ranch. Ketti sighed. One day the two ranches would be combined in one, with her brother Charles in charge of it all.

She drained her cup and set it down on the small table next to her chair. Then she addressed her mother and father.

"I don't plan to ride with the *paniolos*," she said. "Although I like to ride on the range, as I've always done in the past, I want a different kind of job, one that will pay me wages." Before her parents could respond she went on quickly. "Times are changing. Women do work at certain jobs in California, like the one I was doing for the school."

"But this isn't California," Adam remarked. "Women going out to work would never be accepted on this island."

"Your father's right, dear," Mari said softly, as though she were trying to keep the peace in what could become an explosive topic. She knew Adam would never consent to his daughter having a job. "But you could help me with my school for the Hawaiian children. Of course it doesn't pay, but it has been very successful in educating boys and girls who might otherwise stay illiterate."

Feeling suddenly tired, Ketti stood up, still facing the two people she loved more than any others in the world. "Thank you, Mother, but no. I'm not asking for your permission," she went on, "although I'd like to have your approval. I'm simply being practical about my own future."

"Rubbish!" Adam retorted. "You'll always have a future here—until you marry, whenever that is."

"Your father's right," Mari agreed. "And besides, you've been home only one week. It's too soon to discuss such heavy subjects."

"Perhaps," Ketti said, her voice carefully calm. "But I just wanted you to know how I'm feeling. I enjoyed my work in San Francisco, and would like to be involved here. So I'm considering my options, and I wanted you to know that."

Adam stood and went to her. "Your mother and I love you, little Ketti, and we only want happiness for you. That means we have to remind you that working women are frowned on in polite society—if not in California, then surely here."

Ketti reached up and gave him a kiss on the cheek, then as her mother stood, she kissed her, too. "Thanks," she told them with another smile. "But I would appreciate it if you at least considered my feelings in this. Being a woman in a man's world isn't always easy."

Ketti took the tray to the kitchen, leaving her parents to consider the fact that their daughter *had* grown up in the four years she was away.

Several days later Adam asked Ketti if she could ride into Waimea to order supplies that would be brought to the ranch later. Ketti suspected her father was trying to make her feel helpful so she would stop thinking about a job. Whatever the reason, she was glad to be in the saddle on the familiar road into town. It was the same road that led beyond Waimea, over the Kohala Mountains of the north, to the

Hamakua Coast on the Hilo side of the island—the road
John had taken to his sugar plantation.

A familiar ripple of heat swelled within her at the thought
of him. But she also felt anger. He hadn't said goodbye and
he hadn't contacted her since. When she thought of what
had happened on the ship and in the garden, her anger grew.
She'd never be alone with him again, she vowed.

The day was filled with sunshine, and often as she rode
she glimpsed its brilliance on the Pacific Ocean many miles
down the long slope of the land. There was a stillness in the
high country, broken only by the whisper of wind, a faint
rustling sound that reminded her this was an ancient land
once peopled by Polynesians from Bora Bora, fearless men
and women who'd crossed hundreds of miles of ocean in
primitive open boats. As she glanced around the grassy
mountainous terrain, Mauna Kea looming at the south end
of the northern range, she could almost see those people in
their bright feathers and flowers, happy even though they
were governed by strict rules of conduct, with punishment
that often meant death.

Her mount went through a stand of ironwood trees and
taller evergreens whose wispy, long-needled branches swayed
gently in a fickle breeze. Upon reaching the outskirts of
town, she kneed her stallion, and with a creaking of stir-
rups and leather, he took her right to the door of the store.
As she tied the reins to the hitching post, she noticed few
people on the street.

Ketti was able to place her order at once, then ambled
down the boardwalk, while she waited for the clerk to sack
flour that the Fosters' cook needed for tomorrow's baking.

The street was dusty and there wasn't much to see in the
small town, so Ketti decided to go back to the store and wait
in the shade. As she turned abruptly, she collided with a
man coming out of another building. Her sombrero flew off
her head to hang by its cord on her back, and her hair tumbled out of its pins. As two hands shot out to steady her, she
met the amused gaze of a man with startling blue eyes. His

skin had darkened since she'd last seen him, and his hair had
streaks of blond, as though he'd spent those days in the sun.
But when he flashed a sudden grin of recognition, Ketti's
heart accelerated with a jolt, and for a second she feared she
might faint. Her blood raced so fast through her veins that
it was a wonder she didn't.

"John," she managed faintly, hating the tremor in her
voice, hating that he'd taken her so unawares—*again!*

He stepped back, tall and lean, the play of his leg muscles apparent under his fitted riding pants as he stood, oh so
sure of himself, watching her with appreciative, but mocking eyes. His shirtsleeves were rolled, and she noticed that
even the hair on his arms was sun-bleached, a startling contrast to his brown skin.

His grin broadened and he cocked his brows as he made
his own survey, from spurred and booted feet up her slashed
leggings that clung to her legs and thighs, to her blouse that
was open at the throat where she'd tied a bright red bandanna.

"So," he drawled, and adjusted his Stetson so that it
again shaded his upper face. "You're now a *paniolo?*" His
gaze lowered to where her breasts strained the buttons of her
blouse, and he disconcerted her even further as he added,
"But not quite, eh?"

His tone hinted at disapproval, and irritation at his criticism came to her rescue. "And you?" she queried hotly.
"What are you? A gentleman planter who lets his help dirty
their hands rather than his own?" She gestured to an older
man who was loading supplies into John's wagon. She knew
she was being unfair, but she didn't care. How dared he
disapprove of her. *She disapproved of him!*

Before she could gather herself together and storm past
him, he grabbed her arm and led her toward the end of the
street to a cluster of ironwood trees. They were suddenly cut
off from the curious eyes of anyone on the street.

Ketti shook off his hand and quickly stepped back. Her
eyes flashed and her breasts heaved under her blouse. She

could feel the heat in her face. He had his nerve! Always trying to get her alone so he could . . . Instantly, the quivery sensations began within her and, try as she might, she couldn't quell them.

He watched her, noting how her hand plucked nervously at her leggings. She was so damn desirable that, despite his own resolve of indifference, his manhood made known its need for her.

"Why did you drag me over here?" she demanded, abruptly aware of the growing silence between them—and of his hooded, knowing eyes.

"Only to explain why I haven't come to visit," he replied nonchalantly.

"You don't have to explain anything to me!" she retorted.

"Don't I, Ketti?" He stepped closer and she had a sudden urge to run. "Have you already forgotten how it feels for me to kiss you?"

"You—you—" she sputtered. "How dare you mention that!"

"I dare much more, my sweet." His eyelids lowered suggestively. "And so will you."

Instantly her body was overwhelmed in heat—it seared through her veins to rush into her heart where it almost stopped her breath. For long seconds she couldn't respond.

"You insult me!" she cried finally, and would have fled but his hands prevented her, as she was brought up against the lean length of him. With two fingers he tilted her chin so she had no option but to meet his eyes.

"No," he replied in a low tone. "I excite you. Isn't that the truth?"

Her mouth dropped open. The arrogance, the impudence! she fumed, frustrated that he read her feelings so easily. Then as the portly older man who'd been loading the wagon appeared around a building, she was saved from having to respond to John's taunt.

"John," the man called, and Ketti could see his hesitation. "Sorry to interrupt. I didn't know you were—uh—occupied." The man shuffled his feet, embarrassed. "I've got the wagon loaded and—"

"Good, Joe." John inclined his head, dismissing the man. "I'll be right with you."

Ketti took advantage of the opportunity to extricate herself, and quickly stepped backward. Before Joe could move away, she did, giving John a curt nod, more for the benefit of the observer than for John. Then she hurried off, nodded to the older man as she passed him and strode on toward the store. She was relieved to see that the clerk had already tied the sack of flour behind her saddle.

"I'll see you within the week!" John called after her, and she was further unsettled by the humor in his voice.

Ketti mounted without a backward glance and headed the powerful animal onto the road back to the ranch. She felt John's eyes until she rounded a bend that left the town behind, unaware of the picture she presented to the man watching her hasty departure: hair flowing and slim body molded by her *paniolo* garb.

"Pele incarnate," John reflected under his breath. And just as willful and unpredictable. As he sauntered toward his overseer, he was thoughtful. Goddess or mere girl, whoever Ketti was, he knew she would be his.

Ketti, her confused feelings under control, reined in next to an unfamiliar bay horse tied to the hitching post in front of the ranch house. As she wondered whose it was, Char emerged through the side door, Siu beside him. They stopped their flow of Chinese when they saw her dismounting.

"Char!" Ketti ran to him and grabbed his hand. She'd have hugged him but for the fact that his cultural beliefs precluded such a public display of affection. "It's so good to see you. What are you doing here? I thought you were in

Honolulu, setting up your law practice?'' Even as she asked
she knew the answer. Siu.

He grinned, looking every inch the successful son of an
uneducated Chinese immigrant, in his black frock coat and
trousers. "To see that you made the voyage safely," he replied, avoiding the real reason. "And to check on Siu here."
He glanced sideways at the small-boned girl beside him.

Siu bobbed her head, keeping her eyes lowered in the
proper manner. But it was obvious to Ketti that she hung on
Char's every word.

"Can you stay for tea?" Ketti hoped he could; they had
so much to talk about.

He glanced at the late-afternoon sun, which was already
descending over the Pacific. Char shook his head. "I'm
expected back. I promised my honorable parents." His
laugh dispelled his Oriental proprieties. "This was an unexpected trip, and I'm returning to Honolulu on the steamer
tomorrow."

Ketti nodded, understanding. His father had been the
cook on her grandfather's ranch since before she and Char
were born. After goodbyes were said, Char mounted his
horse, but as he took up the reins, he hesitated, smiling first
at Siu, then shifting his gaze to Ketti.

"I'd hoped we could talk, as I have a proposition for you,
but it'll have to wait until my next visit, which will be in two
weeks."

Ketti cocked her head, and waited for him to go on.

"You enjoyed your work in San Francisco, teaching the
Chinese to speak English, did you not?"

"I did," she agreed. "Very much." Again she waited for
him to continue, intrigued by what he was leading up to.

"I'd just like you to consider the possibility of teaching
again. There are many of my countrymen who need to learn
the language of their adopted country." He raised a silencing hand as she was about to speak. "Not now," he said,
smiling. "I don't want your answer yet. It would mean
you'd live part of the time in Honolulu. Just think about it."

He glanced at Siu. "There are many like Siu who are fast learners. The job would have many rewards, as well as a good salary." He sobered, his expression serious. "And there would be no tong lords or highbinders to interfere—I guarantee that!"

Before she could reply, he placed his black derby on his head, and with another grin, clicked his tongue and jerked the reins, sending the horse down the driveway to the road Ketti had just left.

As the two girls walked into the house together, Ketti couldn't help but notice the high color in Siu's cheeks, giving her an exotic look.

"Char is a good man," Ketti offered.

Siu nodded. "Yes—good man."

"And he'd make a fine husband for some fortunate girl," Ketti went on.

The color in Siu's cheeks deepened, and her lashes fluttered like a delicate fan. "Yes—would make good husband for nice Chinese girl."

"Maybe for you?" Ketti suggested softly, wanting to let the girl know she was free to marry should she desire. Ketti had not brought her to own her, but to set her free.

"My thanks," she said in her faltering English, understanding what Ketti had implied. "But first I make place in new land. First I be own person."

Once in the hall, Siu bowed gracefully, her eyes filled with gratitude and offered friendship. Ketti knew her own gaze reflected that she would like to be friends, too.

Then Ketti went upstairs to bathe, feeling better about everything. She shared a common goal with the former slave. She wanted to be her own person as well. And Char had just offered her what might be a step in that direction. She was certainly going to consider it.

Chapter Six

John tied his traveling bag behind his saddle, then turned to give final instructions to Joe, his overseer.

"I'll only be gone five days, Joe," he told the older man, who lived with his wife in a cottage behind the main house. Joe's wife did John's cooking and cleaning, and often the three of them ate together. As he lived alone, John didn't worry about proprieties, although he knew that would change when he married one day.

He glanced out over his sugar fields. The first planting, done four months ago, already had cane six feet high, and he knew by the time the harvest was ready at the end of two years, the growth could be thirty feet. He intended to stagger his fields, so that he would always have a crop... and money, he added wryly.

Pulling on his riding gloves, he mounted his horse, while continuing the assessment of his property. His fields were looking better all the time, and his stable was in good repair, but the house—that was a different story. Although it didn't look too bad from the outside, the inside needed redecorating, and new furniture. He'd poured his money into the land, knowing there was a great future for sugar, so long as the Hawaiian economy was straightened out. And that meant new tariff agreements with the United States, the islands' major sugar market.

He knew it was a gamble, but he was determined to put down his roots here where his mother's people had lived for centuries. But paying off his father's debts, thousands of dollars' worth, had depleted his capital, and he wouldn't have enough money to keep him going if his first crop could not be shipped because of current tariffs. But he still had time, he reminded himself. Almost two years. Not like other planters whose crops were ready now, and rotting in the fields.

"Take care of things, Joe," he said, and headed the horse toward the road to the Foster ranch, where he'd break his journey to Kawaihae. "Make sure the irrigation ditch keeps flowing."

As he rode, John was thoughtful. His trip to Honolulu concerned a meeting of the planters, and the current tense political situation in Honolulu. The queen needed to do something about the sugar crisis, before it was too late and the monarchy was lost forever.

He sighed. The only hope was in annexation, which he knew would come sooner or later—and he also hoped that the monarchy could be a part of that change. At the meeting he intended to voice his position on the issue.

As he rode across the mountains, his thoughts turned to Ketti. He looked forward to seeing her. She was another of his hopes for the future—if his plantation became solvent, and if his background didn't turn her against him. But neither of those obstacles would keep him from her. Their feelings precluded it. Of that he was certain.

The creaking of leather, the striking of hooves on the rocky trail, and the occasional jangle of the *paniolos'* long, jagged spurs were the only sounds that came to Ketti's ears as she rode beside her father. They'd ridden out before dawn, on their way to the high slope of Mauna Kea, where they would separate cattle that had wandered from the lower grasslands. The morning sun had risen in a blaze of golden light over the dewy rangeland of the high country, and for a short time, before its rays gained the powerful heat of the day, everything sparkled like a fairyland. Ketti could almost imagine the little people, the *mehehune,* who the Hawaiians claimed were supernatural creatures that only came out of their hiding places at night—peeking at her and the *paniolos.*

Her imagination brought a grin to her face. It was so easy to believe the old myths while riding in the lonely places that spoke of timelessness. She glanced at her father beside her, and saw that he, too, was influenced by the mood of the early morning. The stillness was broken only by the everlasting whisper of wind that drove upward from the sea, bringing with it a whiff of the infinite ocean below them. Having left the quiet forest behind, they were now traversing the area between the Kohala Mountains of the north and Mauna Kea, and would soon begin the ascent to their destination. Only the occasional cloud scuttled across the sky, like a great white clipper ship on a voyage to the horizon. It was a perfect day, and as Ketti breathed in the pure air, she felt a sense of well-being. She was reminded that it was the isolation of the high country that she loved best, the feeling of oneness with the ancient Polynesians from which she was descended.

Her father glanced at Ketti, nodded and then motioned toward the lowlands between them and the ocean. "That's part of your Grandfather Webster's property," he told her. "It extends almost to the old lava flows—where your mother was almost caught in the big eruption back in '68."

Ketti nodded and looked where he pointed. She knew the story well: the time Mauna Loa and Kilauea Crater had erupted together, causing such a holocaust that it was feared the very island would be destroyed. Tidal waves, mud slides and molten lava had taken property and lives. Ketti shuddered and shifted her gaze past the dormant Mauna Kea, to the peaks of Mauna Loa and Hualalai to the south. The much smaller cone of Kilauea couldn't be seen from the northern part of the island. She just hoped that nothing like that would ever happen again, although everyone knew it could. The fire goddess of the volcanoes, Pele, was unpredictable.

Another long silence fell over Ketti and her father, but Ketti could hear several of the *paniolos* talking over the day's work in low tones. She couldn't help but wonder at how differently her life would have been had she married James and stayed in San Francisco. But that was another life, one not meant for her.

But what is for me? she asked herself. Although she'd been riding with both her father and brother in the past week, she knew that she was not really helping in any way. She appreciated their efforts on her behalf, but realized they didn't understand her need for her own work. Her mother understood, having once experienced similar feelings. But Mari's needs had been rooted in a search for family, while Ketti's grew from a desire to maintain herself, should she not marry. And she would never marry for anything other than love.

The image of John came so quickly that she didn't have time to block it. She didn't know how to read him, what he wanted from her aside from the passion that existed between them. It was confusing and disconcerting, and she didn't need another man in her life to deceive her. James had been enough.

"Your Uncle Seth is returning to the island. Did you know that, Ketti?" her father asked, interrupting her thoughts.

Glad for the diversion, she inclined her head. "For a visit?"

"To stay. Your grandparents are almost jumping with joy. They thought he'd always stay in New England."

"I'm happy for Agnes and Grandfather," she replied. "I know how disappointed they were after he completed school several years ago and stayed in New England. Why is he coming home now, after all these years?"

Adam shrugged. "The pull of the islands? Who knows. We'll find out when he gets here."

"And when is that?"

"Sometime in the winter, maybe early spring. There's no set date yet. He'll travel across America on a train, then take the ship from California."

Again Ketti was thoughtful. She understood the strange pull of Hawaii, with all its ancient taboos, myths and gods. Hadn't she herself felt it and ultimately returned?

She glanced back to her grandfather's land in the distance. It wasn't prized land like her father's, but it was good rangeland. Her grandfather Russell Webster, once a whaler out of New Bedford, had gone to sea after the death of his wife, a girl he'd married despite family disapproval. He'd left his small daughter, Mari, with his strict parents, and Mari had eventually run away to join her father in Hawaii. Russell had left the sea to form a ranching partnership with another man, who had bequeathed his half to Mari. Mari had found her father married to Agnes, a missionary's daughter, and the father of a son . . . Ketti's Uncle Seth.

The men reined in, having come to a fork in the trail. As Ketti's mount grazed, her father gave instruction to the cowboys, and within minutes the *paniolos* had separated to go off in twos to round up the stray cattle. Soon only her father and the foreman were left, and as they were about to continue up the trail, she hesitated.

"I'd like to ride down on Grandfather's land," she told them. "To the high point with the view of the ocean. I haven't been there in years."

Adam grinned as he adjusted his sombrero, understanding his daughter's need for solitude. "Meet us back here at noon?"

"No, no, I'll just go on back to the ranch later," she told him, suddenly changing her mind about the day. Somehow the mood of the land had reached out to her, had altered her enthusiasm to watch the dusty process of cattle separation. Her thoughts had reminded her that she needed to make

plans for her own future. For all that her whole family loved
her, would take care of her if she chose that way, none of the
land or houses would ever be hers. They would go to the
sons, Seth and her brother Charles.

Thoughtfully, Adam watched her ride off, looking every
inch a *paniolo,* her slim body garbed in leggings and boots,
sombrero and bright cotton shirt. Although it wasn't woman's attire, it was the only sensible clothing for riding the
range. As he watched her descent among the rock out-
crops, some of her hair loosened to fly behind her, like a
wing of a great black bird. Adam sighed. He loved her. She
was so much like both his mother and his wife, and he
wanted only the best for her. But something was troubling
his daughter, he could see it in her eyes. Maybe just settling
back into ranch life after San Francisco, he told himself.
And getting over that damnable James. If he'd had his way,
Ketti wouldn't have gone any farther than Honolulu for her
education. America was becoming too liberal as far as he
was concerned.

As Ketti disappeared, Adam turned his horse to follow his
foreman. There was work to be done. He'd have a talk with
Ketti when the time was right, try to get to the bottom of her
troubled expression.

The yelping sound was so sudden that Ketti's stallion
reared up on his hind legs, almost unseating her. Her sombrero blew back on its strings to lie with her unpinned hair
against her back. It took all of her strength to calm the animal; as it settled down, Ketti jumped off, more fearful of
hurtling over the nearby edge of the cliff than of the sounds
that came from behind a wind-twisted tangle of cactus,
typical terrain below the tree line of the high country.

Quickly, before the skittish horse could bolt, she tied the
reins to a scrub tree that had long since lost its branches to
the harsh Pacific storms. Then she grabbed her lasso to use
as a whip should the wild critter—whatever it was—attack,
although it sounded more as if it was hurt.

Cautiously, she stepped forward so she could see behind the cluster of brush and cactus, and met the large dark eyes of a dog—a wild dog!

An instant jolt of fear flashed through her. Wild dogs were vicious. A moment later, she realized the dog, although almost grown, was still a puppy, and it was hurt. A little voice in the back of her mind urged her to remount and get out of there before the mother returned. Still, Ketti hesitated. Something wasn't right; a mother dog, even a wild one, wouldn't leave her young. And where were the other pups? There were always six or eight to a litter. The animal whimpered and hung its head, as though resigned to its fate.

"Come here, boy," Ketti crooned softly, and it stopped whimpering, its dark eyes watchful.

"I won't hurt you," she went on, noticing that despite its dusty coat, it was a fine-looking dog, totally white from its feet to the tip of its ears. Only its nose and eyes were dark, an unusual combination for one of the wild marauders that would attack cattle for food, and even people when cornered.

It was backed up against a rock outcrop that extended to the cliff, and there was no way for it to run except past Ketti. The brown eyes didn't waver, keeping a wary watch. But gradually it seemed to realize Ketti meant it no harm. Slowly the dog stepped forward, sniffing at Ketti's outstretched hand. Once it cleared the brush, the pup stood still, trembling.

It was painfully thin, and Ketti realized that something must have happened to the mother, as the male pup looked starved, and was probably thirsty. Without any sudden movement, Ketti backed away to her horse and untied her canteen and packet of dried meat, her own lunch, and went back to the dog. She poured a tiny portion of the water into her cupped palm and offered it to the dog. She knew that any *paniolo* would cringe at her action, for the animal was wild and might bite her. But she had to do it, or the pup would die. She couldn't resist the dark eyes that seemed to beg for help.

Hesitant at first, it crept forward, licked at the water, then hung back, its eyes constantly on Ketti, who kept up a soothing litany of words. It finished the water and Ketti poured more, which he licked from her hand. Then she gave him the piece of meat and it was gone in seconds. She spread her hands to show him the food was gone, and he seemed to understand.

Taking great care to move slowly, she touched the white head, and when he let her stroke his back, Ketti knew she couldn't leave him to die. But she didn't know how to get him back to the ranch. She doubted the horse would allow her to hold the dog while she rode.

I could tie my lasso around him and lead him back, she thought suddenly, but wondered if he could endure the uphill trip; she could see that his belly and one hind leg had deep scratches that were covered with dried blood. But the meat and water had strengthened him; and he was steadier now on his feet. She decided to try it.

Again she took her time, tying her lasso around his neck and then mounting before looping the rope to the pommel of the saddle. The stallion whinnied and rolled his eyes, but he allowed the pup to trail him as they started up the path in a slow walk.

Each time Ketti glanced to make sure the dog kept pace, his dark eyes met hers. Occasionally, she talked to him, and once she saw his tail wag a response, and felt satisfaction settle over her. He would be her dog, she decided. Somehow she knew she couldn't give him up now. Besides, once tamed, he could never survive in the wilds again.

Her gaze moved outward, beyond the cliff where she'd intended to contemplate her future to the broad infinite Pacific, its brilliant blue water shimmering with a glaze of silver sunlight.

It's a day for changing plans, she told herself with another glance at the dog. But she didn't mind. She'd come
back to the cliff another day.

Ketti's grandmother stood on the veranda with Mari,
talking to the tall man who'd just ridden in. Several *paniolos*
were nearby mending a fence, and they glanced up as Ketti
crested the hill and turned onto the driveway to the house.
The stallion still walked sedately, but his saddle was empty.
Ketti and the white dog walked side by side, the reins in her
hand as she led the horse.

The Hawaiian cowboys stood as though frozen, their eyes
on the girl, whose long flowing hair had freed itself to frame
her face and flutter under the touch of the gentle trade wind,
and on the white dog that trod at her side, docile and accepting of his new mistress.

"Pele!" one of the men said, his voice ringing so that the
people on the veranda heard. "*Auwe!* It's the goddess Pele,
with her white dog!"

The old woman's gaze lifted at once, first darting to the
paniolos, then following the direction of their eyes. She
drew in her breath sharply. The men were right. Aside from
her riding clothes, Ketti instantly brought the Hawaiian
goddess to mind. She looked like the old drawings of Pele
walking with the mythical white dog.

"Where in the world did Ketti find a white dog?" Mari
asked no one in particular.

Her mother-in-law didn't answer, her own beliefs reas-
serting themselves in her mind with a suddenness that momentarily robbed her of words. Was it an omen? she
wondered. A portent for the future that could bring bad
luck to the family—as had happened in the past? Her own
husband died young, and for many years she hadn't been
able to shed the belief that his death was retribution from
the gods, because she'd married a *haole,* and not one of her
own people. And Mari's family had also suffered adversi-
ties; after Mari's stepbrother, Seth, was born, his mother,

Agnes, never managed to carry another pregnancy to term. The old ones claimed it was the curse of bad fortune for all *haoles* who lived on sacred land that had once belonged to Polynesian kings.

John, who had ridden in only minutes before Ketti, watched with the women, as curious as the others. Ketti and the dog seemed oblivious to the stir they were causing, and she appeared to be talking to the dog as she kept it on a tight rein.

God almighty! he thought. She was the most beautiful woman he'd even known. Even now, dressed in her riding clothes, her hair flying and her cheeks flushed from the outing, so at one with the wild, mountainous land, she couldn't have looked more desirable to him, more mysteriously feminine. Although he slouched against the veranda railing, an amused expression on his face, looking completely in control of his emotions, he'd never been more aware of his need for a woman. *This woman,* he corrected himself.

"Where did you get the *'ilio?*" one of the *paniolos* asked, indicating the dog as Ketti approached them. Both men whipped off their sombreros, holding them to their chests in a posture of deference.

"I found him," Ketti replied, loud enough for the people on the veranda to overhear. "He's only a puppy and he's all scratched and cut. His mother must have been a wild dog, and for some reason, she abandoned her pup."

"You didn't see the mother?" the older *paniolo* asked.

Ketti shook her head, and realized they were troubled about her bringing a wild dog to the ranch. "I couldn't let him die," she began. "And he would have if I'd left him. He's weak from hunger, and probably loss of blood. It's a wonder he could even walk the whole way."

The dog was still at her side, watchful and alert. When the men stepped closer, a low growl sounded deep in his throat. Ketti soothed him, and at once he was silent. The men exchanged glances, but moved away.

"I'll take him down to the barn," Ketti said over her shoulder as she led the dog away. "Don't worry, I'll make sure he doesn't cause trouble. I'll keep him tied until he's used to his new surroundings."

"Ketti," Mari called from the veranda. "Did we hear you say the dog is a wild one?"

Ketti's gaze darted toward the house, for the first time noticing her mother and grandmother... and John. For a brief second, as their glances collided, she was rocked by her sudden reaction to him. The jolt to her body felt as if the very ground shook under her feet. She and the dog both stopped in their tracks.

"Yes," she managed, returning her gaze to her mother. "But he's only a puppy—even though he's a big puppy."

"Does your father know you brought the dog home?"

Suddenly Ketti felt like a child who'd misbehaved. Although she understood her mother's concern, she was too old for a reprimand. "No, he doesn't," she replied at once, and stepped closer so they could see for themselves. "But I'm sure he'd agree with my action. The dog isn't vicious. He came with me without a fuss."

Her grandmother moved to the dog and held out her hand, as though she were testing Ketti's words. The dog looked at her for a moment, then briefly sniffed her hand before backing off.

"Ketti's right, the dog isn't vicious," the old woman said slowly. "It's unbelievable, but seems to be true." Behind them she could hear the two *paniolos* discussing the odd behavior of the wild dog, and she knew what they were thinking—that the dog belonged to Pele, that there was a deeper reason behind the dog coming to the Foster Ranch.

Then John approached the dog, leaving the women several steps behind him. Ketti stiffened, unsure of the dog's reaction. "Here, boy," John said, and let the dog sniff him. To everyone's surprise, the tail suddenly wagged. John raised his amused gaze to Ketti. "Your new pet seems to accept me." He lowered his voice so only she could hear his next words. "Maybe he's trying to tell you something, my sweet." John's lids lowered, so that she wondered if she'd only imagined the wickedly teasing glint in their blue depths. "Maybe he's telling you I'm the man who's been chosen for you—by Pele herself."

Ketti's cheeks darkened with more color, making her even more attractive to the man who watched her every nuance. "So, you know the myths, too," was all she could manage, suddenly breathless.

"I should," he said, his tone abruptly ambiguous. Then, as though he'd said too much, he straightened to include the two other women in the conversation.

"I have to be going," he told them. "My ship won't wait if I'm late."

"You're leaving the island?" Ketti blurted.

He glanced back to her, humor filling his eyes. "Only on a turnaround trip to Honolulu," he replied. "Don't worry. I'm on the island to stay."

"I wasn't worried, I was only—"

"Curious?" His brows quirked as he interrupted.

"Of course not!" she retorted, aware that her mother and grandmother were watching with interest. Before she could protest further, John was already in the saddle, saluting them, ready to go.

"I'll be back in time for the barbecue," he told the older women. "Thanks for inviting me. I wouldn't miss it."

His eyes had lingered on Ketti while he spoke, as though she were the reason he wouldn't miss it. Then he was gone, headed down the driveway to the road that would take him to Kawaihae.

Contriving an indifferent shrug, Ketti went on to the barn, her new dog at her side. "We'll get you all settled, and then give you a big bowl of food," she told him. But her thoughts lingered on John, and the upcoming barbecue, and the hulas and *meles* that were a part of that day.

The dog wagged his tail, as though he understood every word.

And Ketti's grandmother, watching them go, couldn't help but wonder what it all meant. Because she was sure it meant something—something that would change Ketti's life forever.

Chapter Seven

The barbecue was an annual event each July at the Foster ranch, going back to the first year Ketti's grandfather started his cattle business. It was a day for *paniolos* on the island to compete in roping, tying and horse breaking. Long tables were laden with food for a feast, which was followed by dancing and singing the old *meles*. For the past week no one on the ranch had thought of anything but the planning of the big celebration. Now, as Ketti finished her toilette and stood before her mirror in her undergarments, she was thoughtful, her mind on seeing John. She assumed he'd be there, as he'd said before riding off to the ship the week before.

It was still midmorning, but she could already hear the horse-drawn buggies arriving, and the chatter of neighbors being greeted by her parents. The day was clear, with the heat of summer tempered by the cool trade winds off the Pacific. Even the mountains were clearly visible in all their glory, as though bestowing their blessing on the celebration.

Sitting at her dressing table, she shadowed her eyes with charcoal, touched her lips with a dab of rouge, then brushed her long hair until it shone like polished ebony; her eyes sparkled under their thick silky lashes. As she put down the brush, a knock sounded on her door, reminding her that she

needed to hurry. Ketti quickly grabbed her wrap before she
called, "Come in."

The door opened and Siu stepped into the bedroom. She
smiled, and Ketti thought there was a glow to the Chinese
girl's face, a brighter shine to her eyes. Then she remembered. Char would be at the celebration, too. She grinned
back. She and Siu had become friends; she'd been helping
the girl each day with English lessons, and they'd shared
bouts of helpless giggles when Siu mispronounced some of
the words. But more than that, they'd shared feelings of
being independent, of making their own way.

Siu had offered to help Ketti dress her hair, but Ketti de-
clined as she'd decided to leave it long in the Hawaiian way,
as this was a day for the old traditions.

"Very good," Siu said in her broken English. "Looks
best."

"Thanks, Siu," Ketti replied. The Chinese girl was wearing a pale yellow cotton dress in place of her usual pantaloons and high-necked top, and Ketti thought she looked
exceptionally pretty, her hair swept up in an elaborate chignon. "You look so lovely," she told her. "Char will find
you very hard to resist."

Instantly, Siu's cheeks colored and her long lashes swept
downward. "Char too busy to notice Chinese slave girl,"
she said softly.

"Nonsense!" Ketti retorted. "There'll be no one at the
barbecue prettier than you. And don't forget, you're no
longer a slave girl and you have the day off. You're a guest
today, not an employee."

"I thank you, Ketti," Siu said, looking up. "You are very
good to me . . . change my life—"

"And you are a good friend," Ketti interrupted her,
touched by the girl's gratitude.

"And Mr. John will come, too?" Siu tilted her head,
smiling. "He in love? Maybe?"

Now it was Ketti's turn to blush. "He'll be here," she began slowly. "But I don't know if he's in love. Panana said there is island talk that he might be interested in Sarah."

Siu wrinkled her nose. "No, no! John love other girl." Her expression was suddenly impish. "The girl who love him."

Quickly, Ketti turned to her pale blue dress hanging on the wardrobe, and took it from the hanger. Siu helped her step into it, and then buttoned it up the back as Ketti watched their reflections in the mirror. The gauzy cotton was trimmed with white point lace and deeper blue satin ribbons, the material of the full sleeves even more sheer for coolness, and the bell sweep of the skirt accentuated Ketti's small waist. But it was the neckline she wondered about. Was it too low for afternoon?

"Not too low," Siu said, anticipating her fear. "Very— how say? Attractive," she ended, pleased with herself.

Impulsively, Ketti hugged her, then turned back to the mirror to place her wide-brimmed straw hat over her hair. "Come on," she said and, taking Siu's hand, drew the girl toward the door. "It's time we made our entrance."

But Siu was suddenly apprehensive and shy. "I—I—"

"Don't worry, Siu. Once Char sees you, you'll be fine." And with those words, the two girls went to join the celebration.

Ketti was surprised by how many people had already gathered when she and Siu walked outside. It was obvious that John wasn't there, and she wondered if he'd returned from Honolulu. Char was there, however, looking every inch the successful lawyer from Honolulu, in spite of his casual dress. After a warm greeting to Ketti, and a promise to talk later, he immediately took charge of Siu, leading the hesitant girl off to watch the rodeo events that were about to begin down in the corral.

The competitions between *paniolos* from different ranches lasted all afternoon, amid cheers and shouts of their friends. Ketti enjoyed the events and was proud when the Foster cowboys took their share of awards. One of her Grandfather Webster's *paniolos* took the top prize in roping, while a Foster *paniolo* won first prize in bronco riding. Agnes, her step-grandmother, not much older than Ketti's mother, Mari, spent most of her time with the Foster women, who were attentive to their guests. But there was a pall on the day for Ketti—because John wasn't there. Even though she didn't understand the man's motives, she hadn't realized how much she was looking forward to seeing him until he didn't turn up.

A whole steer and several pigs had been roasting all day in open pits, and the aroma drifted on soft air currents, combining with the fragrance of the lush tropical flowers that bloomed in the gardens surrounding the house. Long tables were being set up by the kitchen help, and Mari was making sure that there were enough chairs so that all the guests would be seated when the food was served later.

In midafternoon a buggy approached on the driveway, and as it drew closer, Ketti saw that it was driven by John. Her heart jolted an instant response, suddenly beating so fast that it was almost a continuous flutter. Then she saw who was with him: the Reverend Mead, unmistakable in his black suit, and Sarah, dressed in gray with a matching poke bonnet.

At once her anticipation turned to anger. How dared he bring that woman to her house! A second time! She watched as John, garbed in a tan shirt with rolled-up sleeves and formfitting trousers tucked into riding boots, nonchalantly jumped to the ground and then helped the other two from the buggy. One of the Foster hands took the vehicle to be parked behind the barn, while the new arrivals were greeted by Mari, and Ketti's grandmother.

"Damn him!" Ketti muttered under her breath, as he removed his Stetson so that a lei of greeting could be placed around his neck. Whirling around, she flounced down the trail to the corral, and for the next hour, until the competitions were almost over, pretended an enthusiasm she was far from feeling. *Damn him!* she thought, again and again. When she saw John coming toward her, she avoided him, unsure of her feelings, and how to react to him escorting Sarah once more.

Moving within the crowd, she maintained her distance, but when someone came up behind her, she jumped. "Oh, Char!" she cried. "You startled me!"

His dark eyes were amused. "So I see. Were you expecting someone else—or avoiding him?"

Intelligence shone in the whole set of his features, and Ketti suspected that he knew why she was so jumpy. But she wasn't about to admit to anything, so she shook her head and changed the subject.

"Are you enjoying the day?" She'd already noticed that Siu was not beside him.

"Very much." His gaze was suddenly direct, his posture erect, and Ketti remembered that he'd always taken that approach to a serious matter, since he was a small boy tagging after his mother on the Webster ranch. He had something to say to Ketti, and she waited for him to begin.

"I thank you, Ketti, for treating Siu like a friend—"

"She is my friend," she interrupted. "That is, we've become friends. I'm very fond of Siu."

He smiled, breaking the set of his expression. "That's what I thought. You've never let prejudice stand in your way."

"I should hope not!" Ketti retorted, wondering where he was leading.

"And you've done a wonderful job teaching Siu English. I see an improvement since my last visit."

"We spend time together, and she's a fast learner," Ketti replied, still waiting.

"And you're a good teacher."

"Thank you, Char." Ketti glanced away, for a moment reminded of how much she had enjoyed her job in San Francisco, and how much she missed it. Although she'd been home for several weeks now, she was no closer to finding a goal, aside from Char's remark about a possible teaching position the last time he visited. There were not many people her age on the north end of the island, and not much future for her in the way of work...or marriage. Char's next words brought her thoughts back to the present.

"You've heard the whispers about an impending revolution?" he asked, his tone serious.

She nodded. "I've overheard several conversations, and I couldn't believe it. Is it really true? Are there people who want to overthrow Queen Liliuokalani?"

"It's true." Char glanced around, as though he feared eavesdroppers even now. "The Hawaiians want to keep the monarchy, as do the descendants of the early missionaries, who own most of the major industry in the islands. But another group—mostly sugar planters and small businessmen who are affected by our depressed economy—want it overthrown."

"But why?"

"So they can stay in business."

She inclined her head, interested in the political ramifications, but curious as to what Char was leading up to. That he discussed such topics with her, a thing most men didn't do with women, wasn't surprising. Although he was older, they'd had an open friendship since childhood, one based on mutual respect, and it had continued during their years in San Francisco, enabling each of them to have a window on the other's world.

He lowered his voice. "You know the primary support of the islands is sugar, and sugar profits hinge on a reciprocity treaty with the United States. If we don't get that treaty, we won't be able to compete with foreign sugar for the American market."

"I know. I heard that," Ketti replied. "It's being said that annexation by the United States would guarantee the sale of Hawaiian sugar."

"And that means the end of the Hawaiian throne." Char's usually inscrutable face was cast into a troubled frown. "And it's going to happen, Ketti. Money, and the power it brings, seem to run the world. Even now there are rumors of a secret organization dedicated to overthrowing the queen."

For long seconds she was silent. Char's prediction was a troubling thought to Ketti. Long before the *haoles* came to the islands, there had been Hawaiian kings. She knew the situation was serious, but she also couldn't stand the thought that the monarchy could be gone forever. No wonder the old myths had warned the Polynesians against marrying the *haoles,* she thought suddenly. Maybe Ketti's ancestors knew it would ultimately come to this.

Char's hand touched her arm gently. "I'm sorry if I've upset you," he said sincerely. "But it's going to get worse. And that's where you come in, Ketti."

She raised her brows in a question, puzzled by his sudden shift of focus. "What do you mean?" she asked, knowing he was finally reaching the point of the conversation.

"The Chinese in the islands need to speak good English more than ever. Big changes are coming, and they must be ready, so that they have a chance to find their destiny, make a living in work other than toiling in the fields for others." He hesitated. "I represent a group who are organizing a school so these people can learn their new language—and we'd like you to be our first teacher."

"In Honolulu?"

"Yes. We hope to be ready to start by winter." When she didn't reply at once, he went on quickly, and she saw how important the project was to him. "I thought of you at once, since you worked with poor Chinese in San Francisco, and you understand a little Chinese yourself."

"Can I think about it before I give you an answer?" The thought of the challenging job stimulated her, but she knew her parents might not approve. Polite society maintained the attitude that the Orientals didn't need an education, a position she and her family had never agreed with. Many Chinese, and more recently Japanese, had been brought to Hawaii to do cheap manual labor. But although her parents would likely consider Char's plan a noble one, they surely wouldn't want Ketti involved in a situation where she'd lose her good name.

But I've never been all that concerned with the hypocrisy of polite society, she reminded herself. And the Chinese did need a chance for an education, even if the monarchy stayed intact. And someone, if not she, would teach them eventually. She wouldn't allow herself more than a passing thought that she had another reason for hesitating at the thought of leaving the Big Island—the man who even now was making his way through the crowd toward her.

"Of course," Char said. "But I'll need to know soon." He smiled then, and she was reminded that the brilliance of his mind would have been lost but for his good education in America. That alone was cause for serious consideration of his proposition.

Then a smiling, but less shy Siu was back at his side, and with a promise to see them later during the dancing, Ketti made her escape before John had quite reached her.

Annoyance pricked John, as he watched her go. He knew she was avoiding him, and he knew why. The Meads. He sighed, his eyes still narrowed on Ketti as she disappeared into the crowd.

Then he saw Sarah approaching, and his annoyance deepened into frustrated anger. He hadn't been able to say no when the reverend asked for a ride to the barbecue, pleading the bad condition of his own buggy. Suspecting he'd been manipulated, he'd brought them nevertheless, and now Ketti wouldn't give him the opportunity to explain.

A wry smile twisted his lips. "I'll find a way to talk to you, Ketti Foster," he murmured to himself. "You can bet on it."

And then he did what she'd done. He hurried into the crowd, so that he wouldn't be stuck with Sarah again.

Ketti had sat to eat with family at a head table, and her father had made a short speech, praising the courage and daring of the island's *paniolos*. By the time the long meal of roasted meats and fish, salads and hot dishes—even Hawaiian poi made from taro—was over, the evening torches were already being lit in preparation for the dancing. She'd gone immediately to her room to change clothes.

Now, as she stood before her open window and gazed out over the darkening land that fell away to the sea, she hesitated. She'd changed into a full cotton skirt that was splashed with a pattern of brilliant red flowers, and a scoop-necked scarlet blouse. Beneath her outer garments, she'd donned a wide petticoat trimmed in lace, and short cotton drawers, skimpy underclothing so that she wasn't constricted for the dancing. Her lei of exotic red and white blossoms matched the wreath of flowers on her head, and created an invisible cloud of perfume around her. Below her, the compelling music of the ukulele and Spanish guitar were complemented by the throbbing beat of Hawaiian drums.

The night was unusually warm for the high country; it was a perfect tropical night, with soft trade breezes carrying the fragrance of sun-kissed white-sand beaches, rolling waves edged in white froth, palms swaying and an aura of mystery and longing. Even as she watched, she saw the moon break free of the mountains to begin its gradual arch across the sky. To Ketti, drinking in the magic of the night, it was as if time stopped for long seconds, as if the very whisper on the edge of the wind were preparing her for something. But what? she wondered.

She broke off her thoughts, shattering the strange mood that had momentarily possessed her. She was only going to dance the hula, as were other Hawaiians, not give her soul to the devil, she reminded herself; though she knew many non-Hawaiians thought the hulas meant exactly that. She

wondered what the Reverend Mead and Sarah—and John—
would think.

She went to the mirror, feeling suddenly hesitant. She
hadn't danced the hula since she went away to school at fifteen. Even though she'd once performed with the other
children at each annual barbecue, she was no longer a child.
Although her family honored the custom, she knew there
would be people who would criticize her participating in the
dance, especially since her skirt was only ankle length and
her legs would be bare but for soft slippers.

Before she lost her nerve, she went downstairs, hoping she
didn't run into John until after she danced. But Panana was
the one who saw her first and, laughing gleefully, she pulled
Ketti to where small children were already dancing, their
small limbs moving in liquid movements to the beat of the
music. The musicians were all men, dressed in brightly colored shirts and wearing leis.

Panana wore the traditional dance costume as well, and
she confided that she and Charles would do an ancient hula
later on. "Did you know that we once performed the love
dance together?" she asked Ketti, and giggled. "It was right
after that that Charles proposed."

Ketti wasn't able to question Panana further, as the music paused and the children scurried back into the crowd.
Then the instruments struck up the familiar notes of her
childhood. It was her turn. She hesitated, suddenly unsure,
aware of John sitting in the torchlit circle of spectators with
the Meads.

Then her parents came up on each side of her. "Go
ahead, sweetheart," her father whispered. "You're the best
and there's nothing improper about our way of dance."

"Your father's right, darling," Mari told her. "Go on.
Everyone is expecting you to dance, now that you're back
home."

Her confidence restored, Ketti moved forward, her body
adopting the fluid movements without conscious thought.
As she began to dance, her hands and body communicat-

ing emotion in a language older than time, the crowd
hushed, and Ketti soon forgot they were even there. Then
she began the *mele,* the words blending with her gracious
movements. The song told the story of the Polynesians, who
came thousands of miles across the ocean in an open canoe,
guided by the stars and by the omens perceived by the
kahuna—their seer. As the story progressed, the exotic beat
of the drums rose and fell, gathering momentum; Ketti sang
of the ancient founding; their villages, paying homage to
their gods. When she got to the part about the eruptions,
and the recognition of Pele, goddess of the fiery volcanoes,
Ketti moved faster, lost in the *mele* she sang, her voice clear
and sweet above the throbbing music, for all the world Pele
incarnate.

And to John, who sat transfixed, she *was* a goddess. He'd
never seen such a performance. It was as if she'd bewitched
the crowd. Although he'd heard the Meads gasp several
times, no one else seemed offended that Ketti's lower legs
were bare, that her movements were seductive and so very
feminine. He'd felt a stirring within him, a growing desire
to possess her. Yet he wondered if anyone would ever possess Ketti. Although her name—Katherine—was so English, she was completely Hawaiian, the most enchanting
woman he'd ever known. She was unique, one time rescuing a slave, another time a wild dog, fearlessly doing what
her heart told her she must. But tonight she would no longer
avoid him, he reminded himself, even as he banked down
the fire she'd started in him. Tonight she would be his.

The *mele* ended in a crescendo of drums, the hula in a final submission to the old gods. For several minutes no one
spoke. Then everyone rushed forward, all complimenting
her at once.

"It was the best interpretation yet of the old *mele,*" her
grandmother told her, as Ketti stepped from the crowd.
Both of her parents were beaming. The music began again,
and her parents moved away for a better view, as this time
Charles and Panana were dancing a sedate hula together,

moving around each other without touching, their gazes
never wavering from each other.

"It's the fertility dance," someone whispered behind
Ketti.

"It's—it's pagan!" Ketti heard a man hiss and turned to
see the disapproving expression of the Reverend Mead.
Sarah stood beside him, looking equally shocked. John was
no longer with them.

Instantly annoyed, Ketti reminded herself of her manners and held her tongue. But when Sarah went on, insult-
ingly, and other people heard, she could no longer pretend
politeness.

"You aren't enjoying our music?" Ketti asked coolly, her
eyes level on the woman who seemed so drab in her prim,
high-necked gray gown. Although Sarah was fairly attractive, the clothes and colors she wore, her severe hairstyle and
pale blue eyes were not becoming to her. She was every inch
the disapproving *haole,* who thought the native ways should
be banished forever.

"It's barbaric—ungodly!" she retorted, directing her
criticism at the performances, and not allowing her own
jealousy to show, or her horror at seeing John's reaction to
Ketti's dance. "And your own exhibition was—was
unladylike!"

Ketti tilted her chin. "You may have forgotten that I'm
Hawaiian by blood," she retorted, her anger now obvious.
"And I take your words as an insult—to me, my family and
my heritage."

Ketti's directness took Sarah off guard, and her pale
cheeks flushed crimson. But her eyes narrowed for battle,
and she would have said more had not her brother's hand
stopped her.

"Hush, Sarah," he told her curtly. But his expression was
overly pious, which was even worse as far as Ketti was concerned. "This is a different culture, a foreign land we've
pledged to redeem with the Word." He smiled faintly at

Ketti. "My sister has yet to learn patience," he said, his tone condescending.

"And you, Reverend Mead?" Ketti began, her words dripping with outrage at his insult. "Are you also patient?"

He only stared at her, his thin face drawing into a pinched expression. But before he could reply, Ketti had the last word.

"Because you'd better be. You'll need it when you wait for us heathens to give up our *meles* and hulas." She whirled with a flare of skirts, and left them gaping after her.

The music had paused again, and Ketti, still fuming from her confrontation with the Meads, became aware that the low throbbing drums had started up once more. She recognized the notes of the ancient love dance. The musicians had thrown out the challenge for an unwed maiden to start the seductive hula, and legend said her future husband would join her. Heedless of the ramifications of the dance, she kicked off her slippers and plunged barefoot into the center of the open area. She'd really give the Meads something to gossip about.

For a moment she glimpsed the surprised expression on the faces of her parents. But it was too late. The dance had begun, and she was already moving to the rhythm of the drums, and the compelling, seductive sound of the ukulele and Spanish guitar. The music filled her, and her body moved gracefully, her colorful skirt flaring around her bare legs, her delicate quick steps giving the impression that her feet hardly touched the grass. Her arms reached out in fluid supplication, her hands and fingers beckoning, then withdrawing, only to entice again. Ketti felt consumed by the night, drawn into the fire that burned on the torches all around her. At that moment she was touched by the past, by the feelings of all the Hawaiian girls before her who'd danced the pagan hula, and become obsessed with its magic. The sounds around her became the voices of her ancestors, their hopes and dreams for future generations—and the de-

sire for a perfect mate—whispered on the eternal wind off
the Pacific.

The tempo changed then, and vaguely Ketti knew a man
had joined her dance. The perfume of his lei assaulted her
senses even more, but, as tradition said she mustn't look
upon him yet, she only glimpsed his tall, muscular body. He
matched his steps to hers and they began to flow together.
A powerful longing took hold of her, a need to move closer
to him, as though the *old ones* had really taken possession
of her spirit. For a brief second, reason reasserted itself, and
she knew it was madness—a force beyond her will, or even
desire, to control. The man was Hawaiian. No *haole* could
know the proper moves.

Facing him finally, she saw first his blue eyes, which had
also trapped the torch fire in their silvery depths. Ketti
would have faltered, but he suddenly took her in his arms,
steadying her as the music quickened. They moved together, and even if Ketti had wanted to stop, there was no
way to do so now. As they danced, they seemed to melt into
each other, a strange blend of flickering light, color and
motion. Even the crowd fell silent in awe. Then the music
stopped. For long seconds Ketti still clung to John, shaken
by the power that still held them as one, and by a throbbing
need that had to be denied while they stood surrounded by
people.

Abruptly, the *paniolos* began clapping, and were soon
joined by everyone. The mood was shattered and Ketti
quickly stepped back. Her breasts rose and fell rapidly, and
her agitation was not just from the exertion. Her eyes,
clouded by passion, were held by John's, and a message
seemed to pass between them. *Now we belong together.*

Then everything seemed to happen at once. Ketti's parents approached, looking nervous, her grandmother smiled
knowingly from her chair under a banyan tree, and the
Meads were vocal in their disapproval. Even though the
music began again, the magical spell was broken for Ketti.
Her childish need for showing the Meads had turned around

on her. She was the one who would suffer from her action, not they. Quickly she turned away from John, not able to face questions, or the reasons behind his joining her dance.

She contrived a weak smile, acknowledged the guests who complimented her dance, then grabbed up her shoes and edged through the crowd toward the house. She indicated to her mother that she was going to her room, and that she'd explain later. But before she got to the house Sarah stopped her.

"That was obscene!" the woman cried. "You're a disgrace to all decent women!"

Behind Sarah, the reverend was calling for the buggy, telling the Fosters that they would not be staying the night after all, that the moonlight was bright enough to allow them a safe journey home. But Ketti was only half-aware of Sarah's brother, and instant anger came to her rescue at the other woman's accusations. Realizing that she didn't trust herself to be drawn into an argument about dancing with John, she responded to the reverend's pious decision to leave.

"Our hospitality is too pagan for you? Too sinful?" Ketti asked coldly, and continued before they could answer. "In that case I think you should take the road over the mountains to the Hamakua coast." She hesitated, her eyes round and luminous in the torchlight. "But watch out for the Night Marchers. They'd like nothing better than to come upon the very people who discount the Hawaiians as heathens."

Sarah stepped closer, and in the second before Ketti turned on her bare heel to snub the woman, she thought Sarah would strike her.

"And John is leaving with us!" Sarah cried after her.

Ketti rounded the corner of the house and left the crowd behind. But at the kitchen door she hesitated to slip into her shoes, suddenly overwhelmed by the day's events. She knew John would be leaving with the Meads as Sarah had said. After all, they had come in John's buggy.

Then Ketti knew she was about to cry. And she couldn't bear to go to her bedroom, because she knew her thoughts would dwell on the desire still burning through her veins to the warm, secret place between her thighs. With a muffled, wounded animal cry, she ran down the trail to the barn, deserted now since the competitions ended. Her white dog, Lapu—she'd named him with the Hawaiian word for ghost—would console her. She'd closed him into a horse stall so he wouldn't bother their visitors.

He'll be glad to see me, she reassured herself. Lapu was devoted to her. Not like John, who even now was driving the prim and proper Meads home.

"Goddamn him!" she cried aloud. "Why did he have to dance with me!"

And then the tears came.

Chapter Eight

The stillness in the barn was an intangible presence, and Ketti hesitated after she'd closed the door behind her, allowing her eyes to adjust to the darkness. Gradually she was able to make out the shape of the horse stalls that lined one wall, and she wondered why Lapu hadn't noticed her approach. As she reached the place where she'd left him, he suddenly appeared before her, wagging his tail and licking her hand. She realized that he hadn't barked because he'd known it was her.

She knelt, hugging the dog close. "You didn't mind being locked up, did you, boy?" she crooned against his white coat. "Tomorrow when everyone's gone you'll be free again." Her words to Lapu helped her gain control of her feelings, so that her tears abated. She sat down next to him on the fresh hay, and continued to stroke his coat. When a low growl sounded in the dog's throat Ketti was startled. His body was poised for attack, and his ears pricked up, alert.

Ketti scrambled to her feet. Someone was coming. She glanced around for a place to hide. She didn't want to be seen, as it was obvious that she'd been crying. Then she remembered the ladder to the loft. With a quick pat on the dog's head, she moved to quickly climb the rungs to the upper floor. The sweet fragrance of hay seemed to welcome her, muffling her footsteps as she moved back from the opening in the floor.

Then she heard the barn door open below her, and someone stride across the wooden floor. Although Lapu had given a few sharp barks, the dog was now silent, and she wondered why, as he was usually excited and noisy when anyone approached. A stillness settled over the barn, and as the quiet stretched and expanded around her, Ketti tried to quell a growing unease. She'd heard someone enter and move toward her dog—so why hadn't he barked? And where was that person now? She strained her ears, but all she heard were the distant sounds of people and music, the pagan drumbeats echoing in the silence of loft. She suddenly thought of the Night Marchers and felt a chill run up her spine.

Ridiculous! she chided herself. The footsteps she'd heard belonged to a living person, not the ghost of an ancient Polynesian warrior. But she tiptoed to an opening in the loft floor above the stalls, where hay was tossed down to the milking cows. She knew that there she'd have a good view of the lower floor and might be able to see who'd entered the barn. The moon shone through an air opening near the peak of the loft, illuminating a path across the hay to the square hole in the floor, its silvery light streaming onto the area below. Carefully, Ketti peered into the shadowy chasm, her gaze traveling over the stalls she could see. Nothing moved.

Unmindful of making her presence known, she whirled around to flee, wanting only to seek the safety of her bedroom. It had been a disconcerting night, and her emotions were so ragged that only the oblivion of sleep would rejuvenate her. But she was brought up short by the man who'd just stepped from the ladder into the loft. Even though it was too dark to see features, Ketti knew that he looked directly at her. For long seconds neither moved, as though frozen in place by the reaction of each to seeing the other.

Then he stepped into the moonlight. She drew in her breath sharply. "John!" The word came out in a weak whisper.

He inclined his head. He'd known she was in the barn, had caught a glimpse of her as she slipped away down the path from the house. He'd followed her, as soon as he saw Sarah and the reverend on their way, both Meads angry that he'd refused to accompany them; he'd chosen instead to borrow one of the Foster saddle horses for his return to the plantation in the morning. After his dance with Ketti he could no more leave her without an explanation than stop breathing. But now, as he watched her, long hair shimmered by a beam of moonlight, dark eyes round with fright in her pale, delicate face, he could think of nothing but taking her in his arms, feeling her soft body safe against his. His breath seemed to stop in his lungs, and a low groan sounded from deep in his chest, shuddering upward to his lips. For another moment he stood there, then he could hesitate no longer. A few steps took him to her.

A shaft of moonlight struck his face as he paused just short of touching her, silvering his eyes with molten heat. Ketti began to tremble, a strange melting sensation seeping through her, taking away her will to flee. His mouth was firm, even hard, as though he fought a powerful emotion within him, as though he were afraid to touch her and unleash whatever it was he was trying to control. Still separate, they continued to watch each other, and the stillness in the loft thickened and intensified so that it, too, was a presence that waited, poised for what was about to happen.

Ketti took a deep breath, and she felt her pulse quicken, its beat pounding in her throat and echoing in her ears. She licked her lips but still no words formed on her tongue.

"Don't be afraid, my wahine," John whispered, the words low and throbbing. "This was meant to be."

"No, John," she said, her refusal a faint plea for understanding, for she knew exactly what he meant. "We mustn't—it's not right."

His hand came down on her bare upper arms, drawing her against his chest. He could feel the hardness of her nipples under the thin cotton of her blouse, and remembered how soft her breasts felt without the barrier of clothing, how their buds would harden instantly under only a feathery touch from his fingers. The thought of her naked, of her flesh so pure and lovely, her body so perfectly formed and so ripe to be fulfilled, turned him hot and hard. Unable to withstand his growing need, he buried his face in her hair, savoring the heady fragrance of her exotic perfume before kissing her neck. He nipped at her earlobes and felt her begin to respond, then feathered her face with kisses, and as his passion mounted, his movements became more fevered.

"Right or wrong, my darling, it's ordained—by the Hawaiian gods."

John's words did strange things to Ketti. Her eyelashes fluttered as she tried to protest, but her body swayed closer to him, denying any protests she might have had. A pleasant tingling began between her thighs, a warm sensation that seemed to have a life all its own. She was suddenly aware of the muscled length of his body, from his ridged chest all the way down his flat stomach, over the firm hot bulge of his crotch to his long strong legs. His hands moving over her, drawing her even closer, intensified the tingling in the soft folds between her legs, creating a moisture that felt strangely incomplete, that gave her a craving for a release she didn't understand. But she did know that it had to do with giving herself to John. She wanted him, she admitted to herself. More than she'd ever desired anything in her life.

And then his mouth took hers, gently at first, his tongue licking her lips, moving over her teeth until they opened for him. Instantly the kiss deepened and his tongue was suddenly thrusting and demanding. Ketti felt a surge of pure lust for him, and she wanted more. Her own hand crept upward to his neck, her fingers smoothing and combing through his crisp hair, while her other hand slid under his unbuttoned shirt to caress his hard male body. His muscles twitched under her touch, and he made a noise against her lips. It was a heady realization to know that she could affect him so drastically—that she had that kind of power.

But for a brief moment she hesitated. How could she be so wanton, so consumed by a need to be possessed by him? She'd never experienced such feelings before, certainly not with James. But what about her future? If she gave her maidenhood to John and then he didn't want her, what would she do? She knew she was risking future happiness should John spurn her after they made love. He had made no declaration of love, no commitment of a future betrothal. But her fears were fleeting. With brilliant clarity, Ketti knew she loved John, had loved him almost since the beginning, and would love him forever. And with the knowing, she gave up her fears about the future.

As though he sensed her surrender, he lifted his head and looked down into her eyes. She gazed upward, unflinching under the question she saw reflected in the silvery-blue depths. Although Ketti's whole body quivered from the heat of her desire for him, her flushed cheeks telling him that she was suddenly hesitant, even shy, in the face of such undisguised passion. She reached to gently touch his face, as though it were the greatest treasure on earth to her. Something flickered in his eyes, and his breath came short as he read the trust and anticipation in Ketti's expression.

For a second he closed his eyes, savoring the sensation her hand wrought in him. With sheer willpower, he opened them again, and spoke words that sent Ketti's senses soaring even higher.

"You know I have to make love to you, don't you?" he murmured, and his breath was warm and intoxicating on her face. "Do you want me, too, Ketti?"

She stared, her eyes filled with moonlight, unsure of her answer, although she wasn't unsure of her feelings. She wanted him to take her into the uncharted sea of love, where she would fly free of all earthly constraints, higher and higher in a crescendo of passion such as she'd never felt before, couldn't even imagine. Everything within her screamed yes, but somehow she couldn't give voice to the word, as her old fear surfaced without warning. A yes to him now, if his passion lacked love for her, could mean spending the rest of her life trying to forget him after he was gone.

John couldn't bear her hesitation; it contradicted what he'd read in her eyes, in the pliant submission of her body. Her finger glided over his cheekbone to outline his lips, tantalizing him with a tingling sensation that trickled into his blood, where it surged with the violence of a fiery eruption, spilling its flow into his groin with such force that he could bear the waiting no longer. A rasp of expelled breath escaped his lips before he lowered them to close over her mouth.

His kiss was long and deep. Ketti's lips moved under his, kissing him back, allowing his tongue to lick the corners of her mouth, while she did the same to him. She explored the inside of his mouth, sliding over his teeth and then back to his lips, tasting him as he tasted her. They pressed together, their kisses wild and frenzied, unable to satisfy the mounting passion between them. He feathered her face with both lips and tongue, teasing her earlobes with sharp little bites, then thrusting his tongue inside. Ketti's nerve endings tingled and every cell in her body longed for him. Her arms tightened around his back, feeling the taut resilience of his skin under his cotton shirt as he bent to her. She strained to feel him closer, his hard muscled strength against her soft, yielding limbs. When his lips trailed a path of flame lower to her throat, Ketti arched to him, as a low animal cry of surrender was wrenched from her very soul.

Then he was edging her backward onto the fragrant hay, his body hunched over her, his eyes locking hers in a look that intensified the sweet aching between her legs. "I want you," he groaned. "Oh, how I want you."

His mouth came down again on her lips in a kiss that was gentle at first, then, as it deepened with unleashed passion, he moved his hand with slow, tantalizing strokes to curve her breast. Instantly, her nipples hardened, straining their buds toward his touch. But even as her craving for him soared beyond any sensation she'd ever known, a little voice of reason suddenly asserted itself from the back of her brain, reminding her that John had never proclaimed his feelings for her. She turned her face, suddenly unsure.

John's movements stilled. "What's wrong, my darling?" he crooned. "Don't worry. I'll be gentle—I won't hurt you." A low sound was emitted from his throat, and she knew that he only restrained himself with sheer willpower. "But I must have you, now."

It took all of Ketti's control to repress, even for that moment, the wild ecstasy that throbbed within her, pounding like the pagan drums in the ancient love dance, licking its seductive fire into her whole being. Even though her pride would not allow her to prompt him into an admission of love, she could test his feelings in another way.

"Would you—" She broke off. Her voice had sounded too faint, too unsure. She gathered more resolve, then went on. "Would you stop, if I ask you to?"

The lines and planes of his face were suddenly sharp and intense, and his eyes glittered in the strange moon-silvered night. For a second he looked frightening, as though no power on earth would stop him from having her. "Is that what you want, Ketti?" he asked finally, his tone heavy with the weight of his need.

"Would you?" she whispered, answering his question with a return to hers.

His gaze searched her face, trying to read her motives, for she hadn't tried to flee, was in fact looking even more in need of him. Her face was stained pink with her desire, and her eyes were wide and filled with a need to be sated by a love only he could give her. The thought jolted his manhood, so that it throbbed painfully, as though it would burst if her softness didn't relieve it soon. But as he looked into her trusting face, John knew he wanted her love as well as the tempting curves of her body, her sweetness that no other man had tasted.

He drew in a ragged breath. "I would," he managed.

For a long moment she drank in his features, drowned in the pools of his eyes. He *would* place her above himself, and that knowledge was an aphrodisiac to her. "Oh, John," she murmured, and reached to pull his face to her, the gesture saying all he needed to know. And for a long time they were lost, as he claimed her lips once more.

John slipped her wide-necked blouse from her shoulders, then lower so the upper curve of her breasts was exposed to his devouring gaze, then her nipples, rosy and hard, straining to him as they begged for his touch. "How beautiful, how lovely and sweet," he murmured.

He started to lower his lips to her breasts, then hesitated, seeking out her eyes, needing to hear her say she was his. "Are you sure, my Ketti? Very sure?"

She swallowed hard. For a second her only thought was of how his mouth would feel on her breasts.

"Please, Ketti." The words were torn from his mouth. "Tell me now, before I lose my last shred of control."

"I want you, John."

Her words were hardly a whisper, but they soared up into the rafters, then out through the roof opening and into the infinite night, a night ruled by the drums, and by pagan beliefs, and by the mythical gods of the ancient Polynesians. Then, as John reclaimed her possessively, almost violently, his knowing hands playing her senses like those of a virtuoso, everything slipped away as she centered on the sensations of her flesh.

John knelt above her, his mouth moving over her face, his tongue licking as he went, downward to her lips, then lower to her throat, lingering on its silken hollow, tasting each part of her with infinite care so that he missed nothing of her sweetness. His fingers circled her nipples, gently squeezing them so that they tightened even more. Ketti moaned, her eyes closed as she lay on the fresh-smelling hay, her long hair spread around her, catching the moonlight so that its blackness was shot with silver—like Pele's hair, the volcanic glass threads that appeared on the land after an eruption.

Then his mouth closed over one of Ketti's taut buds, and the flavor and feel of her enclosed by his lips, sent a sizzling shot of fiery hot steam into his groin, and he had to move lower, toward the ultimate destination of love.

But her skirt lay between his hand and her lower body. With quick sure motions, John gently pulled Ketti into a sitting position so he could remove her blouse completely. Her gaze was fixed on him, her long lashes screening her eyes, heavy with longing. As he pulled off each of her slippers, he hesitated a moment, holding her foot so that he could kiss it too, his unexpected action so erotic, so accepting of every part of her, that Ketti's heart was jolted with sparks of intense sensations; every artery in her body seemed to crackle with its heat. And then her skirt and petticoat and bloomers joined the blouse on the hay, and she felt the cool night air on her hot flesh, which tingled and throbbed for the return of his touch.

John yanked off his shirt and threw it aside, and the sight of Ketti's gleaming body, so poised for his return, gave wings to his hands as he removed his trousers and boots. She watched him, aching for him, but when he finished, his fenzied movements ceased. It was as if he'd been turned to stone. He stood above her, looking down at her perfection, his eyes drinking in every curve and hollow and swell of her body. Her legs were long and shapely, her breasts more beautiful even than he'd thought before, trembling now under his gaze. The *V* of her private hair was as dark as the cloud of black surrounding her face, and the knowledge that he would soon possess her maidenhood, know its soft secrets, inflamed him, and his manhood thrust toward her, seeking the place that would enfold it.

Ketti stared up at him, unable to look away from his nakedness. She swallowed nervously. He was almost frightening in his bigness and obvious strength. Yet she wondered why he hesitated. Did he regret undressing her, now that he saw her naked body? Her heart was pounding so hard she feared he would hear it and know how much she wanted him, even if he shouldn't want her. He was so masculine, so lean with taut muscled ridges and hollows, so tanned. He was a perfect specimen of primitive man—a Polynesian god, she thought suddenly, remembering the old stories of human sacrifices to those gods. Was she to become one? she wondered. But she knew it was much too late to worry about that, when all she could think of was being desirable to the man who stood above her.

"So beautiful," he said. She heard awe in his tone, saw it reflected in the silver glint of his eyes. "And you're mine."

With a groan that sounded more like an animal growl, he sank to his knees next to her. He caressed the velvet softness of her breasts, gently kneading and stroking, while his tongue, teasing and nipping and licking, made up for the time lost by undressing. She pulled his bare chest to her breasts, the sensation of male against female giving her a strange feeling of security—of being protected by his strength. Again he nuzzled her mouth, already pink and swollen from his kisses. But they both yearned for deeper gratification now.

He lay over her, the hair of his chest rough against her nipples, his manhood hard, throbbing and hot between them, his legs entangled with hers. This time when he lowered his mouth to her breasts, it lingered only long enough to titillate her raging pleasure...and his. Then it trailed down over her stomach while she moaned and writhed in mounting anticipation. When he touched her inner thighs, and the warm folds protected by her curling black hairs, she arched toward him, her legs spreading of their own volition. Her wetness, the final proof of her hunger for him, snapped the last thread of his self-control. He couldn't wait another moment to possess her sweetness.

John raised himself so that he was poised above her. For a fleeting second their eyes met and joined in surrender to the moment. He nudged her legs farther apart, as Ketti whimpered, and then as her need tightened her muscles with hot flickering jabs of fire that trickled into her thighs and groin, she begged him to take her. "Oh yes—please, John— *now!*"

"Yes, my darling," he said hoarsely. And slowly, using every ounce of restraint so that his out-of-control passion wouldn't hurt the woman he knew to be a virgin, he pushed inside her.

A spasm of pain shot through Ketti as her maidenhead was torn open to welcome John's shaft of muscle and flesh. She gasped only once before she began to soar, higher and higher as the sensations intensified. She was filled by him, in every part of her being. She'd never imagined the kind of fulfillment a woman could only know with the man she loved.

And I love him, she chanted as he moved rhythmically inside her, each thrust giving her a sensation of exquisite pleasure edged with a tinge of pain. Then she began to match his movement, and together they accelerated toward a climax that was as yet unknown to her. He murmured love words in her ear—*"Aloha au ia 'oe."* She recognized the Hawaiian phrase, *I love you.*

The night beyond the loft, the drums beating their hypnotic Hawaiian music, the fragrance of summer blossoms and sweet hay, and a wafting freshness from the distant ocean, all faded into a wild, boiling sea of ecstasy. Time stretched into one long moment of rising sensation. He'd taken her maidenhood, filled her with himself so that they were one, and the power of their joining was awesome. She cried out his name again and again, her body caught in a whirlwind of sensual oblivion, so intense that she didn't know agony from ecstasy, only that she needed release.

And then something gave way, and her body shook from reaction. The hot, wet folds that held John so possessively involuntarily contracted in spasms of unbelievable pleasure. Her release sent John to his own peak, and he groaned and shuddered, as a warm sensation of his climax spilled into her.

They lay together after their passion was spent, their bodies intertwined. Ketti was utterly sated, too contented even to move. She'd never felt happier or more fulfilled, and she could think of nothing more pleasurable than to spend every night, for the rest of her life, with this man beside her.

Finally John propped himself up on an elbow so that he could look into her face. "I love you, Ketti. Do you know that?"

She swallowed, unable to lower her eyes from his. "I love you, John," she whispered back, but her words were clear and steady. "I love every part of you."

The sheen of his eyes darkened, and she suddenly knew how deeply her admission affected him. Even her words had power over him. But he has that same power over me, she reminded herself, remembering their past hour of lovemaking. His touch melted her resistance like wax over an open flame.

"And I hadn't meant to seduce you." His brows quirked in a familiar expression of masculine superiority. "That is, not until *after* I told you that I loved you." He gave a short laugh. "But things got turned around."

"Shh," she murmured, and placed a finger over his lips. "Later is time enough for talk." The slow burning of desire was beginning again. Even now she saw the banked-down embers ignite in John's eyes, felt his hands tracing the lines of her body.

And as she turned to him, John knew that the passionate, vital Ketti, as courageous in love as she was in life, was his forever. He could never let her go now. Never before in his life had he been so close to another person.

"We'll talk later," he agreed huskily, and pulled her next to his heart, stroking her, glorying in her instant response.

"I love you, my darling," he repeated, his voice hoarse with revived desire to explore her even further.

"Ohh, John," she moaned, and then they didn't speak again for a long time.

Chapter Nine

They hadn't talked about their future, after all. When they'd finally left the barn, the moon was low over the Pacific, and the drums had long since stopped beating the pagan songs of old Hawaii. The ranch was quiet, the family and their guests asleep. John had seen her to the back door, kissed her one last time and then gone off to the bunkhouse where he intended to sleep before starting back to the Hamakua coast in the morning. He'd promised to see her before he left.

Ketti awakened late the next morning, and her first thought was of John. She blushed just remembering the night before. But she wasn't ashamed; she was filled with a sense of joy. She loved John, and he loved her.

After seeing to her toilette, she dressed in her riding skirt and a long-sleeved, white cotton shirt and went downstairs to eat breakfast, although she felt almost too excited to be hungry. She ate in the kitchen while Siu bustled about, preparing for the midday meal. She listened while the Chinese girl enthused about the day before and how much she'd enjoyed the music and dancing... and being with Char. As Ketti finished her coffee, she recognized that Siu was in love with Char. After giving her friend a hug, she went to the front hall to see why the house was so quiet and no one appeared to be in it. She wondered where John was.

"Ketti," Mari said, coming from the salon. She smiled and indicated that her daughter follow her to the dining room where a pot of coffee rested on a warming tray, a candle flickering under it.

"Where is everyone?" Ketti asked, accepting a cup of coffee.

"All our guests have gone," Mari replied, unaware as she sat down that her words upset her daughter. "And your father is down at the corral, your grandmother already napping. You slept through it all," she added. She looked very attractive in her light blue morning gown, her blond hair pinned up in a simple but becoming style.

"Everyone is gone?" Ketti kept her gaze lowered, her long lashes obscuring her eyes.

"John, too, I think," Mari said, anticipating Ketti's unspoken question. She hesitated, and as Ketti looked up, went on slowly, her tone soft, concern evident in her expression. "Why did you dance the love dance, Ketti? Surely you know it's usually reserved for couples already betrothed."

"I can't really explain it," Ketti began and paused, gathering her thoughts. It was true she'd done it to spite Sarah. But was it also true that the first chords of the music had sparked in her a primitive urge to fulfill a secret longing in herself? Whatever the reason, she knew that she'd shocked her family, if not the whole island. And what were John's motives? she asked herself, the warm afterglow of his love-making ebbing away. He'd left without a goodbye, leaving her with a staggering sense of doubt. If he loved her, as he'd said, then wouldn't he be sensitive enough to know she'd need to see him today as he'd promised.

When she finally began to explain, she told her mother about how Sarah had confronted her for doing the hula, and that she'd danced the ancient love dance to spite her. But she couldn't mention John. She didn't know how to explain his action, now that he'd left the ranch. Was he suffering from remorse?

"And why do you think John joined the dance?" Mari asked softly.

Ketti shrugged and glanced away. "Perhaps he didn't know the significance of what he was doing," she offered. "He's not Hawaiian."

"But he is," Mari replied at once. "His mother was Hawaiian, descended directly from the early kings."

"What?" Ketti's startled gaze flew to her mother. "How do you know?"

"Because I once knew her, and John's father."

"But he has blue eyes, and light hair and—"

Mari interrupted her. "His father was from San Francisco, and that's where they lived after they were married—where John was born."

For a moment Ketti couldn't find words. Why had no one mentioned this before? And why did her mother look so...uneasy about it? she wondered.

"You knew them well?" she managed. "And they owned the plantation that John now owns?"

Mari nodded. "I suppose you could say that we knew them well," she said wryly, and again Ketti sensed something was being held back.

"Is there anything you aren't telling me?" Ketti suggested, and saw at once that there was. Her mother had busied herself with the coffeepot. "There is, I can tell." She allowed a few seconds to pass, and when Mari didn't respond, she pressed harder for an answer. "I need to know, Mother. Because I've come to—that is, I *like* John very much."

"I see," Mari replied, and wondered what her daughter meant by "very much." Had she fallen in love with him? "Then I suppose I'd better tell you," she said finally.

"Tell me what?" Ketti prompted when Mari still hesitated.

Mari met her daughter's gaze, her thoughts tumbling with fragments of earlier memories, of a time when she and Adam were fearful they'd never be able to marry—because of the ancient taboos concerning Hawaiians of high birth marrying *haoles*. But that problem had been resolved long ago, and she'd never thought the past would come back to haunt them—that their daughter would fall in love with the son of Stuart and Jane.

"John's mother was once engaged to your father." Mari's lashes fluttered nervously. "And his father once courted me."

"That's all?"

Mari's gaze flew to her daughter's, surprised that Ketti wasn't upset. "Well, not completely. Stuart was a bit of a scoundrel, more interested in dowries than love, and Jane was determined to marry your father, as their families had arranged, for position rather than love.

"I understand that Jane died shortly after John's birth, and Stuart within the past several years."

A silence fell between the two women, and Ketti could hear the soft rustle of wind in the jacaranda and bougain-villea shrubs beyond the open windows. From farther away, the breeze brought the sound of the *paniolos* down in the paddock. It was a glorious day, the sun already high in the sky and silvering the distant ocean like a thin coat of brilliant glaze.

"And you believe John might be a scoundrel, too?" Ketti's question seemed to tremble on the perfection of the morning.

"I—that is—your father and I like John," Mari began. "But we don't know him well. And he uses his grandmother's last name, not Morgan, which was his father's last name—we wonder why." She smiled, trying to lighten her words, sensing her daughter's involvement and not wanting to hurt her. "His father—Stuart—was also involved in some political intrigues of the times, and when he left the islands, it was under a cloud of accusations."

"I see." Ketti drained her cup and stood up. She knew that her mother would say no more about her wanton dancing last night, and for that she was grateful. But she didn't want her to guess that she'd been with John, either. And if they continued the conversation, she might let it slip out. She needed to be alone, to sort out her ragged emotions and get over her state of upset.

"John's Hawaiian grandparents were fine people," Mari added. "It was their money that saved Stuart's plantation for John."

Ketti swallowed, and managed a smile. Then after explaining that she was going for a ride, that she needed a good gallop to clear her head after sleeping so long, she blew Mari a kiss and left her mother contemplating their conversation.

"Oh, dear God," Mari said to the empty room. "Don't let Ketti become the next victim of the old beliefs and taboos." Then she got up and started up the steps to her mother-in-law's room. She needed someone to talk to, to confide her fears for Ketti's future.

Ketti sat on the outcrop, her horse tethered behind her, and gazed out over the panorama of the island and mountains and sea, finally able to feel the eternal peace of the high country settle over her. Her eyes lingered on the grasslands that spread away at her feet, and in the distance she saw several *paniolos* driving a small herd of cattle, the cowboys' cries wafting with the bleat of the steers up to her perch at the peak of a high hill. As they disappeared, taking their sounds with them, she was suddenly alone with only the wind as a companion. It sighed upward from the ocean, and across the desolate old lava fields before climbing the long incline toward her. Finally it touched the cluster of ironwoods nearby, waving the branches like the robes of the ancient kahunas. Even now, the whispering of the old ones seemed alive on the edge of the air currents, flowing over the unpredictable land.

"Did you think I'd left without saying goodbye?"

Ketti gave a start, and slid off the rock to face John, her heart pounding furiously. He stood several steps away, tall and lean in his thigh-molding riding pants, his Stetson tipped to the back of his head, the reins of his horse in one hand. She licked her lips and managed a nod. He was so damn handsome, so totally a man. *Such a skilled lover.* Her random thought brought an instant flush to her cheeks.

The reins slipped from his hand as he moved to her and took her into his arms, his mouth on hers before she could utter a sound. "I'd never do that, my wahine—my woman," he murmured against her lips. "Don't you know I staked my claim during the love dance—before I even made love to you?"

"But you were gone, and I thought—"

"That I had regrets in the morning?" John finished for her. He gazed into her face, the blue of his eyes as silvered by the sunlight as was the ocean. He clicked his tongue and shook his head. "Did you?"

"Oh John, I didn't know what to think."

"Did you regret last night?" he insisted, his tone low and demanding an answer, as though he were suddenly stricken with his own doubts about her feelings.

Slowly she shook her head, her long hair a soft shimmering curtain that framed the delicate beauty of her face. "I have no regrets, John," she began, then hesitated, knowing she was placing her fragile emotions in his hands. But her feelings were honest, and because they were, she could be open, even at the price of her pride. She tilted her chin, her gaze unwavering under the powerful intensity of his, and went on. "None, since I love you."

For long seconds he only held her in the circle of his arms, drinking in the beauty of her face, which shone with the courage he so loved in her. Some women might have fluttered their lashes and acted coy; but not his Ketti. Even now, as he didn't speak, he saw doubt flicker across her expression. And then he couldn't allow her to suffer his silence any longer.

"Oh, my darling, my love," he whispered hoarsely. "Last night held no regrets, only a promise of all the future nights we'll have together."

Then he was kissing her, and with little feminine gasps and moans, she returned his passion. They clung together, arms around each other, stroking and touching, feeling their flesh through the barrier of clothing, remembering how it felt to lie naked together, to be wedded in body so that they were one.

The wind intensified, gusting around them, and the crazy thought came to Ketti that the pagan gods were pleased. Then other sounds drifted on the fragrant currents of air, the staccato of hooves and the cries of *paniolos*. As they realized how exposed they were on the hilltop, they instantly moved apart.

"Jesus Christ!" John squinted as he gazed at a pair of cowboys driving more cattle along the distant trail. He wondered if they'd seen the man and woman embracing on the outcrop. The hell with it if they did, he thought, although he didn't want to create problems for Ketti.

"It's all right," she whispered, touching him lightly on the arm. "They're too preoccupied with those wild steers to be looking anywhere else."

He grinned suddenly. The flash of his white teeth reminded her of how dark-skinned he was, and she remembered her mother's revelations earlier.

He noticed immediately when her expression altered slightly. "What is it?" he asked.

She lowered her long lashes so that they shadowed the upper curves of her cheeks, completely unaware of how seductive she suddenly seemed. But the fact that she chewed at her lower lip told him that she was concerned about something. Then she raised her eyes to his.

"My mother told me that you're half-Hawaiian—that my parents once knew yours." ·

"That's true," he replied at once, hiding his surprise. But his voice was guarded, and he suddenly reminded her of the stranger who'd rescued her in Chinatown, the man who'd seemed worldly and . . . dangerous.

She licked her lips, but before she could continue, he went on.

"Did you also hear that my father fled the islands one step ahead of the law, taking my mother with him?" He wondered how the Fosters had known who he was, as he'd changed his name to try to free himself from the old scandals of his parents. He sighed inwardly. He should have known that island gossip kept up with the changes. It was known that his grandparents had maintained the plantation, and that their grandson had inherited it. He just wondered what the Fosters *really* thought of him—and what they'd think when they learned he meant to marry their daughter. I'll just have to show them that, unlike my father, I pay my own way, he told himself with a touch of bitterness. That I don't marry for money.

She stared, seeing the pain in his eyes, and wished she'd never brought up the subject. It wasn't important, after all. Neither of them was responsible for the deeds of their parents. She loved him and that was all that mattered. "I didn't hear the whole story," she said quietly. "But it doesn't matter to me. I hadn't realized you were Hawaiian, too, that's all."

He searched her face, and was satisfied that she spoke the truth. She couldn't help it that she had touched on the one thing that had always been painful to him. He was just grateful that before his father died, he'd finally become a decent person, and had been paying off all his old debts. John had continued doing so after his death, even though it had taken most of his own inheritance from his Hawaiian grandparents.

He grinned suddenly, and the brief tension vanished. But he'd been reminded of the one thing he needed to discuss with her, and he proceeded to do it.

"My sugar plantation is our future, Ketti," he began. "All my financial resources are there now. I have to make it go."

"I understand that," she replied as he paused. The lines and angles of his face had sharpened, his determination to succeed apparent in his whole bearing. She wondered what it was that drove him, gave him the aura of ruthlessness even. Was it the past of his parents, which was clouded with questions? Or was it just a fierce pride? But now wasn't the time to pry further, she decided. She'd wait until he felt safe to share those feelings with her.

"I want you to be my wife, Ketti." Little glowing embers smoldered in his eyes as he spoke. "But I can't formally propose to you until I know I can sell my sugar crop when it's ready for harvest in less than two years. Until the political crisis is resolved and the American market secure, I won't know where I stand. If I can't sell my sugar, I could lose the plantation."

"But John! I'm not in love with you because you have a sugar crop!" she protested hotly.

The corners of his lips twitched and his eyes crinkled, although he didn't quite smile. But she knew her retort pleased him. "I know, sweetheart. You love me for my prowess in bed," he said teasingly.

Her blush was fiery and instant, but she answered quickly. "True." Her eyelids lowered seductively. "But I do have one tiny problem."

"Which is?"

"I can't decide which part of me likes your kisses best."

He drew in his breath sharply, and reached to bring her back into his arms. "Should I give you another demonstration, my little nymph?"

Her lips parted and her lashes fluttered as the sweet sensations began to heat her veins, liquid fire that sent contractions into the warm inner region of her femininity.

"Oh Ketti," he moaned as he proceeded to kiss her again. "The old gods have surely smiled on me. How else can I explain such great fortune as you loving me."

"Or you loving me, John."

But to her intense regret, he stepped back, his gaze flickering over the distant *paniolos*. "Unfortunately this isn't the place or time for us to continue," he told her. "We must think of your reputation." Even though he spoke lightly now, he had to use all his willpower to resist taking her under the ironwoods and making love to her again.

"Come on," he told her. "I'll ride back to the ranch with you before heading over the mountains."

She hesitated. "I need to ask you something else, John? Something important to me."

He arched a brow, waiting. But when she spoke, her question was unexpected.

"Were you ever planning to marry Sarah?"

It took a second for him to shift his thoughts into a different channel. "God, no!" he retorted. "Well, that's not completely true," he went on, realizing he must be totally honest with her. She was too important to do otherwise. "The reverend approached me with the idea of an alliance with her once." He went on to explain. "They're only my neighbors, and friends, I suppose, so they sometimes ask for a ride when we're all going to the same place."

"So the island gossip is just that—idle rumors?"

"Good God! Is that a topic of gossip?" His tone hardened with annoyance and surprise. "I suppose I need to learn how fast news travels in a small community."

She nodded, and allowed him to help her into the saddle.

He stood looking up at her. "And James, do you still care for him?"

For a second she didn't know what he meant. San Francisco seemed so long ago. "No," she told him. "I never loved James—I didn't know then what love really was."

He'd been still as she spoke, and his sudden hoot of laughter startled her. Then he leaped up into his own saddle and they started back. But they hadn't ridden far when he reined in abruptly, and reached to stop her horse as well.

"Ketti?" The word vibrated with his passion. "Will you trust in our feelings for each other and be patient until I'm able to speak to your father about marriage?"

She nodded, too overwhelmed by the powerful emotion that throbbed between them even to speak. She could do nothing less than he asked. She loved him, and would wait forever if necessary.

His eyes, shaded now by the wide brim of his hat, glinted like brilliant jewels, as he took in her agreement to his wishes, and the wide darkness of her own eyes that said everything he needed to know.

They continued on to the ranch, both avoiding thoughts of the moment when they would have to part. It was only later that Ketti wished he'd told her when she could expect to see him again. Or if he could at least be her beau, if not her betrothed.

But she would trust, as she'd promised. And she wouldn't allow doubts. She belonged to John, as surely as he belonged to her. The consummation of their love proved that.

Chapter Ten

"It's the Reverend Mead," Adam declared late one afternoon as he and Ketti walked up the path from the barn.

"Again!" Ketti followed her father's gaze to the one-seated buggy that was approaching along their driveway. There was no mistaking the man garbed completely in black for anyone else than Samuel Mead. Ketti's heart sank. It was the third time in the two weeks since the barbecue that the reverend had stopped at the ranch on his way to or from the port of Kawaihae. And it was becoming obvious that his interest was in Ketti.

Her father grinned and glanced down at her, marveling that the lovely young woman was his daughter. It was apparent that Ketti didn't welcome the preacher's advances, and he didn't blame her. The Foster family was cordial to the Meads, but none of them subscribed to the rigid code of the Meads' religion. Although there were many good ministers in the islands, some were like the Meads: critical, disapproving and possessing an intense fervor to banish the old Hawaiian culture forever. He was glad that Ketti had no interest in Sam Mead; otherwise, as her father, Adam would have had to point out how confining and oppressive such an alliance would be for her.

But as Adam and Ketti went to greet their visitor, Adam's thoughts shifted to John Stillman, who'd also stopped by on his way to Kawaihae the week before. Although he liked

John and knew he was highly respected by the islanders, Adam was troubled by the obvious attraction between Ketti and John. He couldn't help but remember that John's father had been motivated by his own self-serving interests, and John's mother, Jane, who once tried to trap Adam into marriage, had been a spoiled, vengeful woman who would go to any lengths to gain what she wanted. John seemed different from his parents, but even so, Adam had been relieved that Ketti was out on the range and had missed John's visit. But he knew she looked forward to John's return from Kawaihae, when he'd stop again on the way to his plantation.

"Aloha," Adam said as the Reverend Mead brought the buggy to a stop.

Ketti inclined her head in greeting, and tried not to feel annoyed when the reverend's eyes immediately fastened on her. She wondered about his intentions; it had always been evident that he disapproved of her completely. And yet she sensed his attraction to her as well. Was it the kind a man has for a woman? she wondered. She realized that despite his manner of acting like a much older man, in reality he was probably only about thirty years old. Maybe he wants to save my soul, she thought suddenly, because he thinks I'm such a pagan that it's his duty to convert me away from heathenish practices like dancing the hula. A smile threatened the corners of her mouth, and she suppressed it, not wanting him to think she was pleased at his attention.

"Good afternoon," he replied stiffly, and climbed down, looking overheated in his dark clothing. "I wonder if I could impose upon you for a drink."

"Come on in," Adam said. "I'm sure we can offer you something refreshing."

Ketti led the way, conscious of disapproving eyes that hadn't missed the fact that she wore *paniolo* garb, and that she'd probably been riding astride. Well, she didn't care. What she did was none of his damn business—thank God for that!

They entered the wide cool hall, and their guest immediately whipped off his wide-brimmed hat, allowing their Hawaiian housekeeper, who'd come from the kitchen, to hang it on the coatrack. Ketti would have gone upstairs to bathe and change for supper, but the reverend made that impossible by taking her arm to follow Adam into the salon.

She felt like shaking him off, but good manners prevailed. Once inside the room, Adam asked for drinks to be brought from the kitchen, and then Ketti seated herself on a footstool, not wanting to soil the cushioned seats with her dusty clothes. Her father stood by the fireplace and the reverend took one of the nearby overstuffed chairs.

"What brings you past the ranch?" Adam asked cordially. "Just the need for a refreshing drink?"

The reverend's thin face creased into a rare smile, although it looked more like a grimace to Ketti. "Actually, I have a favor to ask of you," he replied. "The ship I'm to meet doesn't arrive until midday tomorrow, and I hope to prevail on your generosity to spend the night. Traveling the road downhill is dangerous in the dark."

Ketti and her father exchanged surprised glances, but before they could speak, Mari answered from the doorway.

"Of course you're welcome," she said, coming into the room. "I'll have another place set for you at the dinner table." She went to stand next to her husband.

Reverend Mead nodded. "My thanks, Mrs. Foster. I appreciate the hospitality. Breaking my journey here will give me a fresh start in the morning, so that I'll feel up to the drive home."

"Are you meeting someone?" Mari asked.

"Members of our fellowship from Honolulu," he replied. "With news of the legislative session." He hesitated, his expression tightening into the austere, humorless lines and planes Ketti hated. "We—that is all the brethren—are praying that the queen doesn't act foolishly, so as to plunge the islands deeper into this economic depression."

Ketti was about to excuse herself, when she was caught by the turn in conversation. The reverend was well informed about the tense political conditions in the islands, and there was even gossip that he might be a member of the secret society to overthrow the queen.

"I don't believe Queen Liliuokalani would intentionally harm the economy," Adam replied dryly. "But I agree that she could have a stronger cabinet. We need to reach an agreement with the United States on sugar tariffs. I hope that'll happen soon."

"I believe that can only happen if there is annexation," Reverend Mead retorted.

"Are you suggesting that the queen should be deposed?" Ketti demanded.

His pale eyes shifted to her. "I'm only saying that we need to save the Hawaiian economy—in any way we can." His reply was ambiguous, his tone pious. "Or sugar, our major export, will rot on the docks. And the planters, men like John Stillman, will be bankrupt."

"And John? Does he agree with your opinion?" Ketti's words were deceptively soft-spoken.

Sam Mead stared for a moment, as though considering his reply—and her reason for asking the question. He opened his mouth, then closed it again as he spread his hands in a gesture of stopping the conversation before it became any more heated. "I can only speak for myself," he said, and then changed the subject again, leaving Ketti with the impression that John was in agreement with the minister's views.

She stood and, after excusing herself, left the room, suddenly wishing that they'd refused overnight hospitality to the reverend. Now she'd have to sit through dinner with him as well, she thought irritably. He was a pompous ass as well as a religious fanatic!

The atmosphere at dinner was strained, and Ketti's grandmother excused herself when it was over, declining coffee in the salon. During the meal the reverend's gaze had often lingered on Ketti, and she'd felt uncomfortable, and glad that she'd put on a high-necked, long-sleeved dress of gray muslin so that not much of her was exposed to his view. She wondered what was on his mind.

As Mari poured coffee into dainty English cups, Adam was summoned outside to speak with his foreman. Then, seeing that the cream pitcher was not on the serving tray, Mari went to the kitchen to get it, leaving Ketti in the very situation she'd hoped to avoid—being alone with the reverend.

The minute Mari left the room, he moved to sit on the settee next to Ketti, placing his hand on hers where it rested on the cushion.

"My dear girl," he began. "I was hoping I'd have a chance to speak with you. There are many things we need to discuss."

She pulled her hand away. "I can't think of anything we need to talk about," she said coolly, and wondered why her mother was taking so long.

"But we do," he insisted, his thin lips pursed, and his eyes narrowed with determination. "I see redeeming qualities in you, qualities that need nurturing."

His voice grated, and it was all she could do to remain seated. He was the most unattractive man she'd ever met— and she didn't trust him, preacher or not.

"I fail to see what my 'qualities' have to do with you. Perhaps you should just get to the point," she suggested.

A flicker of annoyance touched his features and was gone. He nodded and went on. "Of course, you realize I didn't approve of you dancing the hula." He tilted his head backward so that he looked down his long, narrow nose—much as he must look from the pulpit, she thought inanely, and suppressed a wicked grin.

Ketti had no way of knowing how attractive the man found her. He felt she might be a suitable wife for him if he could bring her into the fold, so that she would give up her sinful ways—like wearing pants and pagan dancing. He knew she'd been educated by nuns in California and felt it shouldn't be difficult to channel her religious beliefs into those of his flock. That she was the daughter of Adam Foster would only enhance his position on the island, and he could use a little financial support as well, he reminded himself. "But then one can mend one's ways and—"

She jumped up. "Surely you aren't criticizing me, Reverend," she said coldly. "Because—"

He stood, too, interrupting her. "Certainly not," he lied, seeing that he was proceeding too fast. "I was about to propose that you accompany Sarah and me to a ball at the Iolani Palace in Honolulu, in early October."

Taken aback, Ketti could only stare. The reverend going to a ball? Then she realized why. Since it was at the palace, it was expedient for him to go. She blurted the first thing that came into her head. "But that's almost two months away."

He nodded, his chin again tipped upward. "I wanted to ask you early, my dear." His lips twisted into his version of a smile. "John may join us—as Sarah's escort. And, of course, I'll seek the approval of your father, but I'm sure he'd have no objections, as I'm quite above reproach."

"It's *my* approval you'll need." She picked up the skirt of her gown and would have flounced to the door, had he not stopped her with his hand on her arm in a grip that was surprisingly firm.

His eyes glinted angrily. "Surely you aren't refusing my offer?"

"That's exactly what I'm doing," she retorted, her face flaming with indignation.

"What is it you're doing?" her father asked as he and her mother stepped back into the room, taking in the situation with a glance.

Ketti moved toward the doorway they'd just come through. "I refused the reverend's *kind* offer to go to a ball—dancing, of all things," she added with contrived sweetness. She glanced back, her eyes on their unwanted guest. "And of course I had to refuse. I have no idea what I'll be doing two months from now."

Then, with a swish of skirts and petticoats, she left them, the reverend looking incredulous, and her parents hardly able to restrain themselves from laughing out loud.

But Ketti was angry. The nerve of that—that hypocrite! she fumed. Then as she reached her bedroom, the reverend's shocked face surfaced in her mind. And she giggled. In seconds she was laughing so hard that the tears came. How could he have thought she'd even consider going anywhere with him?

Then a sobering thought struck her. Would John really escort Sarah to that ball—after he'd made love to *her?* He wouldn't, she told herself. But the thought lingered.

Ketti avoided the reverend the next morning by riding out early with her brother and a crew of *paniolos,* driving one of the herds from sparse grassland to pastureland her father had recently bought at the southern end of the island. Ketti hadn't seen the spread, but knew it extended from sea level to almost eight thousand feet up the slope of Mauna Loa, consisting of more than a hundred thousand acres. Although many of the acres were worthless because of devastating lava flows, the small patches of pasture surrounded by the hardened black swirls of lava rock furnished extremely lush grazing land, grass needed for the expanding herds. Lapu trotted beside Ketti's mount, as was his habit whenever she went riding. The sun was only a blush on the horizon when they left the ranch behind and headed down the sloping land on the same route the herds had taken when she watched from the outcrop—the last time she saw John.

She shifted in the saddle, reminded for a moment of how much she missed him, longed for him, woke in the night in desperate need of him. With an effort she pushed such thoughts aside and glanced over the brightening landscape.

Far below tumbled the breakers, a border of frothy white between the rocky coastline and the deep blue of the Pacific. The high peaks of Mauna Kea and Mauna Loa, and wide expanses of bare, black cinder fields in the valleys below, were all within the vista before her. The sounds of hooves and creaking saddles and the occasional jangle of spurs were all that disturbed the silence of the awakening day. A mist hung over the highlands, veiling it with a diaphanous vapor that was silvered by the first rays of sunlight. A faint wind whispered through the ironwoods and koa tress.

They rode all morning. At noon they stopped to rest and eat, then left the lava fields between the two mountains behind, finally making camp for the night on the western flank of Mauna Loa. Ketti had planned to return to the ranch the next morning, but decided to continue farther; this was the first time she'd really been able to visit with her brother alone, and although he had to keep checking the herd, they were still able to chat. But when midmorning came, Ketti knew she must turn back if she were to reach the ranch before dark. Her parents would expect her, and worry if she didn't return as planned. She knew it was time to go.

The rumble of the earthquake was unexpected, and startled the herd. Ketti's horse skittered, and it took all of her strength to hold the reins. They were in a rocky area, having already started the gradual climb around the western flank of Mauna Loa. The *paniolos* were frantically shouting, "Hup, thaaaa! Hup, thaaaa!" as they rode, and dust billowed all around them.

The quake was brief, but as it faded away, a loud hissing could be heard, followed by more cries from the *paniolos*.

"Look out!" someone cried. "It's a steam vent!"

Ketti's eyes darted upward, and her heart thudded with instant terror. Her mount, still under tight rein, reared up, almost unseating her, as a line of sizzling steam ripped down the side of the mountain above them, venting volcanic pressure through a rift in the solid rock. The fissure was long, extending all the way to the herd, where it ended in a crack only a couple of inches wide, a formation that would have gone unnoticed but for the steam escaping it.

The steers scattered, but several were caught by the scalding vapor, and went down. The *paniolos* were everywhere, shouting and waving their sombreros, frantic to stop the impending stampede. Ketti lost track of her brother in the dust-filled din. It was all she could do to keep her horse from bolting.

In a matter of minutes the *paniolos* brought the cattle under control, but to Ketti's amazement, she found herself separated from the others by the steaming vent.

"Are you all right?" her brother called.

She waved. It was hard to hear above all the hissing, and she urged her horse as close as she dared to the rift. "I'm fine!" she called, and glanced down the line of steam to where it ended at an outcrop of rock set against a high sheer wall. There was no way to cross over unless the venting stopped, which it might not do for days. "Are you?"

Charles looked shaken, but in command of the situation. "We're fine here, but it looks as if we've lost a couple of steers." They talked briefly, both knowing the activity of the mountain was not uncommon in that area of the island—the disturbance they'd just witnessed didn't mean that Mauna Loa would erupt. As Ketti had been about to start back to the ranch anyway, they said their goodbyes. Charles went back to the men, and Ketti watched them out of sight around the curve of the terrain.

Then she started off, allowing her horse to find his own pace, a slow trot. Abruptly she reined in to glance around her. Where was Lapu? Her dog was no longer beside her, and she realized she hadn't seen him since the quake. Without a second thought, she turned her horse around and headed back toward the still-steaming vent.

"Lapu! Lapu!" she called, her voice almost drowned by the hissing steam. Then she heard a yipping and her dog limped from behind a cluster of underbrush—on the other

side of the vent. The white hairs had been burned off one
leg, and it looked badly scalded even from her position some
distance away.

Quickly she scanned the length of the rift, and noticed
that the steam was only spasmodic now at the end near the
rock wall. She urged her horse forward slowly. When she
reached the end of the vent she hesitated, and tried to gauge
the bursts of vapor that could seriously burn if they caught
her. She weighed the risk of crossing against what would
happen to Lapu if she didn't. As the venting subsided momentarily, she spurred her horse across, narrowly missing
the hissing spray of heat that shot up behind them. She'd
made it.

Ketti went immediately to her dog, examined him and
then ripped a strip of blanket from her bedroll to bind up his
leg. But she knew he needed the healing salve the *paniolos*
used on burns, or an infection could take his leg. She must
get him back to the ranch as soon as possible.

Just as when she first found the dog, she was unable to lift
him into the saddle. Another glance at the fountain of steam
told her the return route was now cut off. Then she saw the
crevice between the cliff and the outcrop where the steam
vent ended. Ketti led the horse and dog toward it, surprised
to see it was passable, and wondered if it was possible to get
around the rift. She didn't hesitate, but started forward,
carefully choosing her steps in the event of an unexpected
burst of steam. Sulfur permeated the air, and she covered
her nose and mouth with a bandanna. The path of sorts
twisted and turned, keeping with the formation of the cliff
that rose on one side of her. Then, as her route narrowed
into a cave, it suddenly opened into another passageway
perpendicular to hers. She paused, her eyes wide with
amazement. She'd stumbled upon a lava tube, a tunnel formation in the mountain, created by an ancient underground lava flow that had originated in the volcano at the
very core of the mountain—and they usually vented on the
surface of the land.

After a glance behind her to make sure Lapu was still there, she moved forward, more quickly as she veered onto the smooth floor of the tube. As a glimmer of light shone ahead of her, she knew she'd been right about where the tunnel would end.

Ketti paused at the opening, which was overgrown with vines and lush foliage. A flush of pleasure touched her with satisfaction . . . and awe. She suddenly knew that no one—unless an ancient Polynesian—had ever stood where she was standing. She doubted anyone even knew this particular tube existed. Dropping the reins of her horse, she began to pull at the vines, gradually opening a door through the foliage. As she stepped into the sunlight, Lapu beside her, she found herself in a little meadow fringed with wild flowering bushes and trees.

"Auwe! Auwe!" someone shouted.

Startled, Ketti's glance flew to an old Hawaiian man, who stood across the clearing. She hadn't noticed him in the shadows of the leafy branches, nor the little house and his wife who was standing in the doorway. Before she could say anything, he went on shouting, and from his waving arms and the woman's stricken stare, Ketti knew her sudden appearance had frightened them. It must have seemed to them that she'd materialized out of the air.

"Pele, Pele!" the woman cried, and both fell to their knees.

For a second Ketti stood frozen. But as she recognized their fear, she tried to calm them, speaking in Hawaiian. They were old and lived in a remote area, and they obviously believed in the ancient myths. Her appearance shortly after the earthquake had convinced them that they were seeing the fire goddess with her white dog.

But they didn't believe what she was saying, and as she stepped closer, they cringed.

"Aloha no!" The words were spoken by another man, who had heard the commotion, and ridden into the meadow to investigate. Now it was her turn to be stricken with a strong emotion—only this had nothing to do with mythical beliefs.

"*Mai maka'u,*" he told the couple. "There's no need to be afraid. The woman isn't Pele." As he continued in Hawaiian, Ketti was astounded by John's command of the language. He was always surprising her.

When he finally convinced the couple that Ketti was human after all, he turned the full force of his gaze on her. All of a sudden the reaction from the morning hit her: her legs shook, her heart pounded, and she only wanted to be in his arms.

"How did you find me?" she managed.

For a moment he didn't answer. The whole length of him seemed tense, as though he'd been badly frightened. His brown skin appeared tight over his cheekbones and his eyes hooded as he continued to stare.

"I returned from Honolulu yesterday," he said at last, "and stopped by the ranch on my way home. When I heard you'd gone with Charles and planned to return today, I spent the night and rode out at dawn to meet you—so we'd have a chance to spend some time together."

The Hawaiians had gone into their house, convinced finally that Ketti wasn't Pele. Then her horse trotted from the tube, pulling away most of the remaining foliage, and seeing the grass, was content to graze. John noted the tunnel and then returned his gaze to her face, holding her by the power of his eyes, which sent a surge of electricity along her veins, weakening her even further.

"So that's how you got around the steam vent," he said almost under his breath. "You were lucky it didn't lead you into something even worse—like boiling lava."

They had been separated by several feet as they stood, and now John moved closer to hold her against him. "Oh, my God, Ketti. When I saw the vent blocking the trail I didn't know what had happened, because there were several dead steers." His breath was ragged. "I was looking for a way around it when I heard the commotion."

Her heart felt as if it were soaring right out of her chest. The Hawaiians had thought she appeared mysteriously. But it was even more surprising to her that John had come when she so needed him. She lifted her face for his kiss, welcoming the jolt to her body when his lips claimed hers. She suddenly wished the meadow belonged to them alone, that the old Hawaiians lived somewhere else.

John lifted his eyes to gaze at her face, pleased that her lips looked desolate, bereft of his, that her cheeks were flushed with desire, and that her breasts trembled beneath her cotton shirt. He wanted her, but he knew it wasn't the place for lovemaking. As he watched her, a slow smile quirked the corners of his lips. It was no wonder that she'd been mistaken for Pele. Her long hair shimmered in the sun, framing her face with its silken cloud of blackness, and her dark eyes blazed with all the fires of a volcano goddess. And she was his goddess.

John reined in his thoughts at that point. She wasn't his yet, not legally. And he wasn't in a position to offer her marriage, wouldn't be until he felt secure about the sugar market, until he knew his plantation was a success. The last thing he'd want the Fosters to think was that he was a fortune hunter—as his father had once been.

Ketti saw his expression change, and didn't know why. Was he angry at her? As they mounted to start the ride back, she felt suddenly upset. She knew something was bothering John. She vowed she'd find out what it was before they reached the ranch.

Chapter Eleven

They didn't ride far. The meadow was only a short distance behind them when they reached a second grassy area surrounded by trees and wild shrubs, terrain typical of that part of the island. John reined in first and Ketti was already about to do the same. Lapu, who'd been following, had lost his makeshift bandage, and was limping badly.

"I'd better have a look at him," John said, and tied the reins to a tree branch, then tied Ketti's. Lapu immediately slumped on the grass, obviously in pain. But his tail wagged as John and Ketti squatted next to him. Gently John lifted the burned leg, frowning as he saw the extent of the injury.

"It's bad, isn't it?" Ketti was shocked by the swollen, inflamed flesh. "He'll have to ride with me. I don't want anything happening to him." She swallowed hard. She'd come to love the dog, and couldn't bear to think of him having the same fate as the steers who'd caught the full force of the steam.

John glanced up, a slow smile lighting his features. "Don't worry, Ketti. He'll be fine, so long as he doesn't develop an infection." He went to his horse and took a small box from his saddlebag, then returned to the dog. "I always keep bandages and salve with me when I'm riding, in case of an accident."

With gentle but sure hands, John ministered to the dog, and as Ketti watched she couldn't help but remember those same hands on her body—and how much she loved his touch. Lapu whimpered but allowed John to help him.

Finally John stood, pulling Ketti up with him. He was aware of her eyes caressing his body, of a throbbing need for her that had begun in his groin. Taking her hand, he led her away from Lapu, who was content to rest in the shade. The meadow was bright with sunshine, but the shade was cooled by a light breeze that carried the scent of sea and flowers and the faint smell of sulfur. But John hardly noticed the tropical beauty of the place, for he was shaken by the knowledge that Ketti had been very close to being caught in the steam vent—and if anything had happened to her, he didn't know if he could go on living himself. He'd never felt that way about anyone in his life, and the depth of his feelings was unsettling. Sometimes he didn't know whether he wanted to care so much... because it made him vulnerable, as he'd been as a boy living with an embittered father.

Ketti noticed the slight tightening of his features at once. Puzzled, as she'd been earlier, she resolved to get to the bottom of whatever was bothering him. She knew he was about to kiss her, and she felt suddenly unsure. She couldn't allow him to make love to her when she had doubts about his motives.

She stepped backward, her gaze caught by his. Long arms of sunlight stretched through the leafy branches to touch his eyes with the brilliance of spun silver, and dapple the ground around them with varying tones of shade. The place was secluded, possessing a strange enchantment that suggested an earlier time, a time when a Polynesian warrior might have chosen the spot to consummate his love with a beautiful virgin. Ketti gave herself a mental shake. This was no time for daydreaming. Before the mystical spell gripped her completely, she must know what was disturbing John's thoughts.

"John," she began, and faltered, suddenly unsure of her ground. He looked so tall and strong and broad shouldered...and so utterly male. His shirt was unbuttoned down his chest to reveal brown skin that matched the column of his throat and his face. As she hesitated, obviously trying to say something important to her, John's eyelids lowered to shutter his eyes. She was momentarily disconcerted, and her own lashes fluttered downward, but when she raised them her gaze was direct. "I feel that you're upset about something—and I—I need to know what it is."

A silence dropped between them, and then grew to form an invisible wall. It was as though John struggled with his thoughts, as though he was hesitant to reveal them. Somewhere in the trees behind them Ketti heard the faint rushing of water, and wondered if there was a little stream nearby.

Then John spoke, equally direct. "I was angry with you," he said tersely, his expression suddenly grim. She was reminded that the man before her wasn't always tender and loving; he could be hard, dangerous even. Hadn't he been the one to stop the highbinders that day... they'd been intimidated by him, and she suspected it wasn't just because he had the gun. There were aspects of John she didn't know, she thought with a jolt.

"But why?" she managed.

"Because I don't want you out riding the range—like a man!" His tone had risen. "It's too dangerous for a woman."

"What?" His response was unexpected, and so was her instant annoyance. She flushed as he held his ground, his disapproval reflected on his face. "You have no right to—"

He cut her off. "I have every right. You're just lucky you aren't burned like your dog, lucky you weren't horribly scarred—or worse."

His words vibrated between them as they faced each other. The mood in the meadow was altered, affected by their anger. Her thoughts whirled. Although she was thrilled at his concern, she was also put off by the dictatorial sound to his voice.

"You *don't* have every right!" she flung at him. "Not unless I were married to you!"

He drew in his breath sharply, and his eyes narrowed so that they were even more hooded. "You know why that's not possible now, Ketti. I have to make a go of my plantation first."

"But I could help," she retorted, her anger deflating with the air suddenly expelled from her lungs. "I love you, not the wealth you might have in the future."

For a long time he was silent, and she saw that there was still more bothering him. She waited, letting him wrestle with his own demons. She'd been completely honest about her feelings for him, *trusted him*. Now it was time for him to trust her.

"There's more to it than just being financially secure," he said, and although he was exposing his inner concerns, it didn't detract from his manliness, Ketti noticed. When he again hesitated, she prompted him by inclining her head. She had to know, her own pride demanded it, so that she would never feel demeaned by giving herself to him...loving him.

"Once my father wanted to marry your mother," he went on quickly. "And although I understand she was beautiful and high-spirited, he wanted her because of her dowry." He took a ragged breath, his eyes burning into hers, but he didn't touch her—couldn't until she heard him out. "So I'll never approach your father while I'm in a precarious financial position. Your father would be reminded of my father's motives, which have never been mine."

He finished with a rush, and Ketti knew how much his words had cost him, he being a prideful man. She went to him and drew his face to hers, kissing him tenderly, all her love reflected on her face. "Oh, John, I love you so. And I understand—but my darling, no one would ever believe you're a fortune hunter."

"But it's how I feel," he whispered against her lips, still resisting the soft feminine feel of her body pressing into his. "Will you be patient? Wait a little longer? Because the politics of the islands are coming to a head—good or bad."

"Forever," she murmured, and kissed him back, the undeniable flow of hot desire surging through her and into her soft, private place, which tingled for the feel of him inside her.

With a low moan, he swept her up into his arms, grabbed his bedroll as he strode past the horses and stepped deeper into the trees. The sound of bubbling water was a soft melody in the utter peace of the woods, like a benediction on their love. He set her down but didn't release her, holding her against the length of him as he feathered her face with kisses. Finally he lifted his mouth.

"Wait, sweetheart," he said, a rich thread of passion in his voice. Quickly he spread a blanket on the only patch of grass under the sweeping branches. For a second she glanced around, noting that the water sound was caused by an underground hot spring. It bubbled out of an opening in a short rock wall into a shallow bowl formed of ancient lava, overflowing to slide several feet over the smooth surface to another small outcrop, where it disappeared back into the earth.

"Are you still upset?" she asked him softly as he pulled her down onto the blanket, although his hands unbuttoning her blouse distracted her from her question. He shook his head, and she forgot all about their argument.

As he freed each breast, he lingered over her, his mouth closing on one nipple, his tongue teasing it into a hard erection, while he caressed the other. She lay under him, her desire blooming within her, as his practiced fingers stroked and tickled and coaxed her to higher pleasure. Then he removed her boots and her *paniolo* riding pants and her underthings—so that she lay naked in the pure light of the enchanted woods. He moaned softly, his eyes filled with her, the blood in his veins surging to his manhood.

He raised himself then to remove his own clothing, and his eyes never left her. First he pulled his shirt over his head, and Ketti's eyes lingered on the play of his muscles on his bare back. Then he fumbled with the buckle of his belt, flinging it aside before he lifted a foot to discard one dusty boot, then the other. And never did his gaze waver from hers. His intensity and sure movements, the confident set of his features and his total masculine control of her, thrilled her with a pulsating rhythm of pure, raw need to be taken by him, to climb even farther to the heights of passion than ever before. She didn't even flinch when his pants were cast aside with the other garments.

He stood naked before her, a golden-brown Polynesian god, whose divinity had bestowed upon him the added attractions of light hair and compelling blue eyes, filled now with all the fire of his ancient ancestors. The thickly matted hair on his chest, like that on his head, was tipped with gold from exposure to the sun. Ketti's heart pounded for him, and every cell in her body strained toward him, desperate for his touch on her feverish flesh.

But he surprised her again by lifting her in his arms and carrying her to the pool of water, where he set her down on the smooth rock floor, the water swirling around her waist. Before she could utter a sound, he climbed in beside her.

For a moment he hovered above her, his gaze all-consuming, the sunlight beaming down through the leaves to glaze him with a golden sheen. He was completely self-possessed, graceful and elegant in his nakedness. She felt a mixture of wonder, excitement, love and anticipation of what he would do next.

"You're so very beautiful, Ketti," he said softly, and pulled her next to him as he sat down.

She swayed against his chest, as the warm water swirled around them, soothing and cleansing their skin. Her long hair was spread on the surface of the sun-fractured pond. He began to touch her, his fingers light as feathers, bathing her as though she were a child—her breasts, her stomach, her thighs and then the soft folds between her legs, which spread for his tormenting, tantalizing touch. She and John loved each other, and their love was right. They were betrothed to each other, if not in the eyes of the world. She belonged to him—completely—and one day she'd be his wife.

Her hands found him, smoothing over his limbs and chest, and then lower still to the shaft that was big and powerful, and oh so male. They moved slowly: caressing, kissing and exploring even deeper sensations of their delicious love. The water, soft and sensuous, glistened on their bodies, giving their wet skin the feel of satin. He cupped her breasts, and stroked them again, while his tongue thrust into her mouth, tasting her sweetness. His fingers trailed lower, to the triangle of hair between her legs, and a wondrous aching contracted deep within her.

"Oh, John," she whispered, shakily. "Please, take me now."

"Not yet, my love, not quite yet," he murmured against her lips, but as she pressed closer, her body arching for him, he groaned. His mouth, almost savage, demanded even more, as though he were consumed by a magic potion in the hot springs, one brewed up by the volcano goddess herself. His touch became rougher, arousing her to a peak of sensual torment.

His eyes blazed with passion out of control, equal only to her own. He wanted her. He couldn't get enough of her, and somewhere in the back of her mind, she knew it would always be so.

Then he raised himself, so that she straddled him in their shallow pond. Carefully he adjusted her body so that she leaned against the smooth rock side, one of his arms holding her across the lower back, so that he could elevate her body to meet his. She clung, holding him tight, glorying in his rippling muscles as he began his rhythmic movement inside her. Then Ketti was flying free, outside of herself, soaring above the trees to the very peak of Mauna Loa that sheltered their secret place, and higher, to blend with the high-sailing clouds that scuttled across the infinite sky.

Ketti felt the oneness between them, a belonging to the man who'd freed all her inhibitions and made her a woman.

She knew that John was the only man in the world for her, forever. Then contractions spread from their joining into her whole body. Uncontrollable spasms of joy coursed through her veins, throbbed at her temples and in her throat, filling her with such wild abandon that she cried out in her ecstasy. She felt the convulsive tremors take hold of his body, and with a shudder and groan, he spilled himself into her. At that moment she felt an awesome sense of power over him.

They subsided together, legs intertwined, half in and half out of the smooth rock that formed the sides of the pond. The storm of passion was subsiding, their hot flesh gradually cooling to the temperature of the warm water.

John was content for a long time. The afterglow of possessing Ketti filled him with such peace that he wondered how he could leave her again. He wanted her beside him, always. So he would know she was safe.

He bent and nuzzled the fuzz on her earlobe before settling his mouth over hers in a long, kiss of commitment. "I love you, my sweet," he told her, his voice still hoarse from their passion.

She smiled lovingly, her eyes filled with everything he needed to see.

Abruptly, he stood and helped her up beside him. "Time to go. We don't want your father sending out the crew to look for you."

But still they lingered for seconds longer, holding each other, because they didn't know when they'd be alone again. After a while they dressed, and then mounted for the ride upland to the ranch. John carried Lapu in his arms as they rode away from the meadow. Ketti didn't look back, didn't regret that their interlude was over. There would be more times together, and she suspected each one would be better than the last. But for now she was content just to ride beside him.

Summer drew to a close without another opportunity for Ketti to be alone with John, and even though he stopped at the ranch whenever he could, someone was always present. He divided his time between his plantation, overseeing the first stages of his crop, and Honolulu, where he was active in the politics concerning sugar export. But Ketti had her hopes set on John's escorting her to the first ball of the social season in Honolulu, the one the Reverend Mead had mentioned. She tried not to be disappointed when he didn't. Although she attempted to be patient, doubt crept into her thoughts. Why couldn't John announce their intentions, even if they had to wait for marriage?

Early in the fall she rode down to Kawaihae with her father and a crew of men to bring back a prized bull that had been shipped all the way from Texas. He was a ferocious beast, pawing and snorting once the men finally got him ashore. He lowered his long, curved horns and would have charged anyone in his path but for the ropes that held him secure between two mounted *paniolos*. Adam ordered Ketti to stay out of the way when she would have helped.

On the ride home she was thoughtful, once more pondering her future. She missed John desperately, and wondered how long it would be before they could announce their intentions. She suspected that her parents had already guessed that she cared for John. But in the meantime she needed something to occupy her time. Her thoughts moved to Char's offer of teaching in Honolulu. I'd probably see John more often there than here, she told herself, only half-listening to the men talking, hardly aware that the day was cloudy and threatened rain. By the time they reached the ranch the sky had darkened further, and as Ketti dismounted, all hell broke loose. An electrical storm exploded over the mountains with terrifying suddenness.

The rain continued into the night, but by morning the sky had been washed clean, and the mountains and valleys sparkled with renewed freshness. The next few days were similar: storms in the afternoon and evening, followed by a bright morning. On the third such day, Ketti sat in the kitchen to drink her morning coffee so she could chat with

Siu. The Chinese girl would accompany her to Honolulu when Ketti went to the ball, and both of them were looking forward to the trip.

Their conversation was interrupted when Adam came in from outside. "What next!" he cried, looking upset.

"What's wrong?" Ketti asked. Her brother, Charles, came in behind Adam, and he looked equally disturbed.

"The new bull is sick—looks like he might die," Charles said.

"My God! What's wrong with him?" Ketti poured them both coffee, but they looked as if they needed something stronger.

"We don't know yet, but thank God we've had him separated from most of the herd," Adam replied. "It could be contagious."

The men took their coffee into the office with them; and a few minutes later she heard her mother join them. From the sound of their voices, Ketti knew how worried they were. Concern continued throughout the day. By evening Adam and Charles suspected the bull had anthrax, a virulent disease that could wipe out an entire herd and ruin the grazing land.

The next few days were a nightmare. The bull died and two more steers took sick. The whole family, except for Ketti's grandmother, worked from dawn to dark, burning everything the bull had come in contact with, including the grass. The sick steers were shot, and the others were watched closely for signs of sickness. The veterinarian came daily from Waimea to check the animals, and finally determined that the sickness was tick fever, a disease spread by ticks brought to the island on the bull. Adam decided the remaining exposed steers had to be shot as well, to prevent further contamination.

Exhausted, the family then waited another week before they knew with relief that the crisis was over. But it was followed immediately by another one.

The night before Ketti was to sail with Charles, Panana and Siu for Honolulu, she came downstairs for dinner and found her Grandfather Webster in the salon with her parents and grandparents. She hesitated on the threshold to listen to their conversation.

"It's bad," her grandfather was saying. "I could lose my ranch."

"Why in the world did you do such a foolish thing without discussing it first with me?" Mari demanded of her father. "I do own half of that ranch, after all!"

Ketti stepped into the room, feeling sorry for the grizzled old man, who was still handsome despite his age. For the first time in his life, Russell Webster was afraid—afraid of losing everything he owned. "Why is everyone so upset?" she queried. "Surely nothing is *that* bad."

Her father just shook his head in disbelief, while Mari looked angry. It was her mother who finally answered Ketti's question.

"Unknown to anyone, your grandfather invested all his ranch profits in a sugar venture—and now it looks as if he can't even sell the crop and break even."

"Why would you do that, Grandfather, when everyone is in a panic about the sugar industry?" she asked softly.

"I invested more than two years ago, after the Treaty of Reciprocity went into effect to drop the sugar tariffs for our exports into the United States." He slumped into a chair and buried his face in his hands. "How was I to know, two years later when my crops were ready, that the McKinley Act would remove *all* foreign tariffs on sugar into America— that Hawaii would have to compete without the advantage of being the only country that didn't pay the tariff. The McKinley Act will destroy our sugar industry unless the issue is resolved soon."

A hush fell over the room. Ketti's grandfather lifted his head, and after taking a long shuddering breath, said the words everyone had known were coming. "I need a loan to save the ranch—not for me, but for Agnes, and Mari, and my son, Seth, who's coming home now."

"A loan of the amount you need would deplete our capital," Adam said finally. As Mari started to speak up, he waved his wife to silence. "But we'll do what we can—and hope to hell nothing else happens to bankrupt us all."

Soberly, and with great relief, Russell stood to shake his son-in-law's hand. "You won't regret this," he said huskily.

Then they went to the dining room for dinner. Ketti turned her thoughts to her trip to Honolulu. She hardly heard the further talk concerning the secret annexation club, whose members advocated the overthrow of the queen. But she did wonder how deeply John might be involved in the political unrest; she'd now seen firsthand how serious the sugar tariff issue was, and how much harm the United States was causing to the Hawaiian economy.

Well, she'd find out when she saw him. She could hardly wait. She often wondered why he hadn't invited her to attend the ball with him. She'd ask him, she told herself. She knew there was probably a good reason why he hadn't. That night she went to bed early, so morning would come quickly—and she could be on her way to him.

Chapter Twelve

Honolulu bustled with an energy Ketti hadn't felt before in the city. After the interisland steamer docked, the Foster party was met by a man who would take them by carriage to the home of Panana's parents where they would be staying. A thrill of excitement raced along Ketti's veins, sending shivers into her lower stomach; she would see John soon.

Charles and Panana sat facing Ketti and Siu; their luggage had been strapped on the back of the carriage. It was Friday, and the streets were filled with merchants and stevedores, buggies and horsemen; everywhere Ketti looked, she saw things that hadn't been there four years ago. The city even boasted electric streetlights, telephones and horse-drawn trams. She felt pride in her homeland, and sensed that Siu was also impressed. Ketti glanced at her Chinese friend, and noticed her cheeks were flushed; she anticipated seeing Char as much as Ketti looked forward to being with John. John had told Ketti the last time he saw her that when he was in Honolulu, he stayed in a cottage on the ocean shore that was once the summer residence of his Hawaiian grandparents. The small house and the plantation were all that was left of their fortune.

Everyone was silent during the drive through the streets, each with his and her own thoughts. When they passed the palace, its six towers etched against the brilliant blue of the sky, Charles turned from the window. "Isn't the Iolani Palace impressive?" he remarked.

Ketti nodded, thinking that the palace was a wonderful setting for the elegant ball tomorrow night. The others continued talking, pointing out the balconies and ornate trimmings and the lush exotic flowers on the grounds. But Ketti's thoughts had lingered on the ball, and the worry that had been on her mind for days now. Why hadn't John asked to be her escort? Didn't he realize she expected that of him? He would explain, and clear up her doubts when she saw him, she told herself.

Then they were turning into the driveway of an impressive mansion at the high point of a hill overlooking the distant harbor. Panana's parents, Kilia and Martin, old friends of Ketti's parents, came out to greet them, instructing the driver where to take the luggage. Charles helped each of the women to the ground as they ducked through the carriage door to avoid catching the wide brims of their straw hats. Standing to one side watching was Char, who was taking Siu to stay with another uncle and aunt in the Chinese section, an arrangement that had been planned since Siu knew she would accompany Ketti to Honolulu. When the greetings were over, Char stepped forward to take Siu's bag.

He bowed his greetings to everyone, then placed the bag in a buggy hardly large enough for two people. After a brief conversation, the others drifted into the house. Ketti lingered, anxious to hear Char's account of the situation in the city, and to see her friends off.

Siu, no longer as shy as she used to be, was telling him about the steamer voyage and how impressed she was with Honolulu.

Char's whole face beamed with pleasure. "What progress, what progress!" he said. "It's amazing how well you are speaking English, and in so short a time."

His eyes were warm on Siu, and the girl was suddenly bashful again, her long eyelashes sweeping down to screen the pleasure his words evoked in her.

"She's a fast learner," Ketti offered.

"And you're a good teacher, my old friend," Char replied, looking serious all at once.

She opened her mouth to speak but he raised a silencing hand. "I want to remind you, Ketti, that my offer for you to teach is still open. You're exactly what we need, and Siu proves that."

"I still haven't decided," she said, somehow not wanting to close that door. She wouldn't allow herself to think that her other hope might not work out—her dearest wish in the world ... to be John's wife.

"The Chinese merchants behind me are willing to pay a huge salary, as they, too, know how important an education will be to our people in the future." He named the amount.

"But, Char! That's twice as much as the best teacher gets in San Francisco!"

"We believe you are the best." His words held his conviction on the matter.

"I'll think about it very seriously," she said slowly. If only she knew what the future held for her. If John was to spend so much time in Honolulu—leaving his young crop to his overseer, and if they weren't to be married for another year, then she could accept the post for that period of time, and be near John. Her thoughts whirled. "And I'll let you know soon," she added.

He inclined his head in a typical Chinese gesture. "We believe annexation is coming," he said. "It has to. Now that U.S. tariffs have been lifted to other countries, it doesn't even pay to ship our sugar—it's less of a loss to just let it rot."

Ketti had wanted to hear that somehow the situation was better, but Char's words dashed that hope. She wondered how it was all affecting John.

"And there's much rumor that the queen will be overthrown, and that it will happen soon."

Such rumors were hard to believe, for the social season was continuing as though nothing was wrong, as though there wasn't a secret society plotting the end of Hawaiian royal rule.

Then Siu, who'd been listening in silence, suddenly stood on tiptoe to hug Ketti, taking her by surprise. "Not to worry. Everything be fine for you—and Mr. Stillman."

Ketti hugged her back. Siu knew what she was feeling. As Ketti watched the buggy disappear, she was thoughtful. Char and Siu were good friends; she wished them happiness. Just as she wished it for herself.

The carriage came to a rocking stop in front of the palace. Two attendants sprang forward, one to hold the horses and one to help the ladies step to the ground. Panana went first and then Ketti, followed by Charles. The palace was ablaze with lights, and the grounds twinkled like a fairyland, Chinese lanterns and electric lights having been placed in the trees and shrubbery.

Ketti's heart thumped with anticipation. She was not in the least mindful that she'd refused the kind offer by Panana's parents to provide her with an escort, a visiting American. Ketti had no intention of creating a problem between her and John.

Carriages arrived in a continuous stream, and Charles offered an arm each to his wife and sister. He led them up the wide stairway to the huge veranda of the plastered brick palace, which was trimmed in concrete block and iron. As they approached the entrance, the familiar music from the Royal Hawaiian Band drifted out through the open double front doors to add enchantment to the fragrant warmth of the night. Once inside the large entry hall, Ketti paused, amazed by the splendor before her. A long staircase swept upward to the second floor, dividing the hall. On her right was the huge throne room, and to the left, the drawing and dining rooms. Huge, ornate chandeliers hung from the ceiling, and everywhere people were clustered in small groups talking. The queen herself was nowhere in evidence.

Panana, who'd often been a guest at the palace, her father holding a government post, led Ketti to a powder room upstairs where they would leave their wraps. Once inside, Ketti expelled her breath, and only then realized how impressed she was with what she saw. And proud. The monarchy represented the culture of her Hawaiian heritage. It would be difficult to see it overthrown, if indeed that happened.

"Did I tell you how beautiful you are tonight," Panana said, catching Ketti's glance in the mirror. "I haven't seen your gown before—is it new?"

Nodding, Ketti glanced at her image. "I had it made for a special occasion in San Francisco, and then never wore it." She smiled wryly. "Because I came home instead."

"And we're all happy you did." Panana grinned back, herself lovely in navy silk, and then turned toward the door. "Ready to go back downstairs?"

Little wings of nervousness suddenly fluttered in Ketti's stomach. "I—I think I'll just touch up my face. You go ahead. I'll join you shortly."

About to say she'd wait, Panana changed her mind. She could see her sister-in-law was anxious, and she knew why…John. So she agreed, and left Ketti to calm her nerves.

After Panana shut the door, Ketti examined herself in the glass, and wondered if she should have chosen another gown after all. Her doubts spun in her head. The soft black velvet might be too clingy and sleek—and the low neckline might be too revealing. Though the style was all the rage in San Francisco, Ketti worried she would appear too brazen. The wide hem of the bell-shaped skirt accentuated her tiny waist, and obscured her matching satin slippers, while the sleeves were puffed voluminously. Her hair was swept up into an elegant coiffure of shimmering black curls and waves, several of which lay against the delicate skin of her neck, and she wore her mother's diamond aigrette that matched the necklet and earbobs that complemented her gown. As she examined her face, tinted with a natural pink, she was glad she'd not worn rouge, although she had used a little red lip salve and some charcoal shadow on the lids of her eyes.

Oh Lord! she thought. Why do I feel so unsure? It's silly, she told herself sternly. With a final glance in the mirror, she left the room and went to the open staircase, hesitating before she started down to join Panana and Charles. Then she straightened her shoulders and, holding her skirt, went down the steps.

James Rawlston, who stood among the crowd below her, caught his breath, recognizing the exotic, beautiful woman whose bearing denoted her high Polynesian lineage. She was magnificent, easily the best-looking woman there. Then others noticed her, and a brief hush fell over the hall. Ketti didn't falter, although she'd noted the attention, and wondered if those staring were shocked, or admiring. Head high, she continued down to the hall.

The first notes of the Hawaiian national anthem signaled the entrance of the queen, and Ketti moved with the others into the throne room, where two red-cushioned, ornate golden thrones sat on a dais. When the formalities were over, a small Hawaiian band replaced the large one, and as the first dance began, someone touched Ketti on the arm.

"Hello, Ketti," a familiar male voice said. "May I have this dance?"

For several moments she could only stare incredulously at the impeccably dressed man whose well-built body suited the black formal attire. "James!" she managed finally. "I can't believe it." Although surprise registered on her face, there was no warmth in her tone. She remembered that James was related to one of the old and powerful missionary families in the city, that the Rawlstons were closely associated with the Hawaiian economy, as they had business interests in the Islands.

He put out his hand, indicating that he wanted to partner her. Behind him she saw several young men turn away in the belief that her dance was taken. Annoyance pricked her; he'd put her in an awkward position—and he knew it. She could hardly refuse. She allowed him to lead her onto the dance floor where the musicians were playing a waltz, and in seconds she was in his arms, joining the swirl of colorful dancers.

"Hmm," he murmured against her hair. "It's been too long since I held you." His arms tightened, pulling her closer—too close—so that her breasts were pressed against his waistcoat.

She strained, and tried to arch away, but his arms only tightened more. "Hold me right!" she whispered angrily, "or I'll walk off the floor!"

"Come now," he said in a coaxing tone. "Surely you've come to your senses by now, and realized I was only fooling around that night in San Francisco. The girl didn't mean anything to me."

"I said let me go! We have nothing to discuss. I'm no longer interested in you. Everything is different now."

He loosened his hold so he could look directly into her face. He was silent for so long that Ketti finally lowered her eyes, unsure of what she saw reflected in them. They hadn't missed a step, but Ketti felt stiff and moved automatically in the sways and dips and whirls of the dance. Finally he spoke, his voice edged with jealousy and a touch of anger.

"You *do* look different," he began slowly. "Is there another man?" His brown eyes glinted.

"That's none of your damn business!" she retorted.

"But it is." Abruptly he pulled her to him again, his arms so rigid that she missed a step. "I don't give up what I want—what I intend to have." His tone was harsh with anger.

"You don't have a thing to say about me!" She tried to keep her voice down but she stopped dancing. To her horror, he stopped, too, and with a quick movement, bent and kissed her on the mouth.

Her face flaming with embarrassment, she jerked away. "You're—you're despicable!"

James still held her hands, a sardonic smile twisting his lips. "Perhaps. But now everyone knows who you belong to," he told her, so low that the couple who'd stopped dancing behind them couldn't hear.

Ketti glanced over James's shoulder, at the tall man, who in his dark formal suit was easily the most handsome man in the room. Her gaze was caught and held by steel-blue eyes, eyes that also registered outrage. Her heart sank. John had seen James kiss her, and by the look of him, he believed she was a party to the kiss.

"I see you're up to your headlong ways, Miss Foster," the woman beside John said.

For a second Ketti forgot about the kiss, about James and about her fear that John misunderstood the incident. *He was with Sarah!* Sarah looked transformed with her upswept hair and peach silk gown; her eyes were shining in triumph as she stood beside John, her arm linked through his. Ketti's eyes widened with shock, and she swallowed back the involuntary choking sensation in her throat. That was why he hadn't asked her to the ball—he'd asked Sarah instead! Shattered, all she had left was her pride. As the dancers waltzed around them, Ketti tilted her chin, her cheeks redder yet, and fluttered her lashes at the other woman.

"Yes," she managed with contrived dignity, "I do seem to have a penchant for shocking people like you, don't I?" She didn't realize that she'd taken a step closer to James, strengthening the impression that she was not averse to his kisses.

John's eyelids lowered and his face muscles went rigid, as though he only controlled himself by sheer willpower. Then those glittering eyes turned on James. "I see you bring problems wherever you go, eh, James?" He spoke coolly,

but Ketti had a sudden flash of intuition: John wasn't a man
to trifle with. He had a dark side to him—a side that reminded her he would be a dangerous enemy. "First San
Francisco, then to the political situation here in Honolulu,
and—" his eyes, as cold as an arctic wind, shifted to her
"—even to the palace."

"Now see here," James began hotly, "this isn't the place
to debate annexation. And I resent being insulted just because I'm against it."

Neither man looked at her, but Ketti knew she was part of
their anger. She suddenly realized why James was in Honolulu. His family interests wanted to keep things as they
were, so that they could be one of a few to control the whole
Hawaiian economy—and reap the profits. Yet, wasn't John
wrong, too? How could he even attend the ball at the palace if he wanted the monarchy overthrown? His next exchange with James clarified her questions.

"Your interest is self-serving!" John retorted.

James gave a snort of laughter. "Ha, don't tell me that!
Not when your concern is selling your sugar!"

"*My concern* as you put it, is retaining the monarchy, but
in a nonpolitical function under annexation."

Sarah glanced around, fearful of causing a scene, and
Ketti felt a brief satisfaction. But when the other woman
pulled on John's waistcoat, and reminded him that they'd
interrupted their waltz, Ketti's fury flooded back. Too upset to worry about proprieties, she whirled around with a
faint rustle of petticoats against her silk stockings, and left
them all. Damn them to hell! she swore, trying to fuel her
anger so she wouldn't cry. Once out in the hall she ran upstairs to the powder room, relieved that it was empty.

After a while she was able to restore a semblance of calm,
and went back downstairs. But she hesitated again, and
stood behind an ornamental trellis decorated with fresh cut
flowers, bracing herself to face John—or James. Then on
the other side of the floral wall, she heard the voices of two
women who were passing on their way to the powder room.

"Yes, I hope to announce my betrothal in the near future," one woman said. Ketti couldn't hear the other woman's reply, as they had already passed her hiding place.

But the woman she'd heard was Sarah!

Strangely, the words had an odd effect on her. She straightened her shoulders and marched into the ballroom. Immediately her smile dazzled several young men, and she was soon besieged for dances. She carefully avoided the angry eyes of two other men in the room.

The night passed in a blur of color and motion and sound. Ketti accompanied her brother and Panana to the buffet in the dining room, then pushed her food around her plate in a pretense of eating. When they returned to the ballroom, the first notes of a Brahms waltz were already beginning the next dance.

Charles swept Panana onto the floor, leaving Ketti surrounded by anxious suitors. Her smile felt forced and she wished for the night to end; she would have left earlier had that been possible. Although she'd successfully avoided both John and James, the constant stress in doing so had exhausted her. John had danced with Panana but she hadn't noticed him partnering Sarah again. To her surprise, it was James who'd danced with the reverend's sister several times. As Ketti was about to accept a young man's arm for a dance, John suddenly appeared at her side, his eyes unreadable, his face set, and took her arm instead. She had no choice but to submit or cause another scene.

After the first glance, Ketti kept her eyes averted, chilled by the cold glint in his. He held her close, one hand flat against her back, as though he was ready to keep her should she try to flee. She felt his breath on her hair, but he didn't speak, and she couldn't think of anything to say, either. Somehow neither wanted to explain; it was enough to be close, the velvet over her breasts crushed against his white shirt and waistcoat. Slowly, her head came to rest against his chest, and she heard the powerful beat of his heart under her ear. The room's colors—the flowers, the brightly gowned women and their black-coated partners—blended together like the view through a kaleidoscope.

The music ended abruptly and they moved apart, but John didn't release her. "We have to talk," he told her tersely.

Before Ketti could gather her tattered feelings around her again, he was leading her across the floor among the dancers, his expression set determinedly. "The Blue Danube" waltz was playing when they went out through the door to the veranda. At first she protested going, but he'd only looked more intent on getting her alone. Once outside he led her to a secluded area at the very end of the long, wide porch, and then turned her to face him.

For long seconds his gaze burned into her eyes, and she wondered why he was finding it so hard to speak. A pulse beat furiously in his temple. Was he about to tell her that he'd changed his mind—that he no longer wanted her? They stood in the shadows of a heavily fragrant shrub, and behind it a half-moon hung in the sky, sending narrow beams onto the palace grounds. She licked her lips and waited, puzzled by her own curious lack of anger with him. She feared his next words, and wanted to hold them back.

But he surprised her again. His grip tightened on her arms, and he pulled her against him roughly, almost with desperation. Then his mouth closed over hers, demanding and lacking in gentleness, as though she were not the same Ketti he'd loved with such passion and tenderness. His lips were bruising, his tongue thrusting, as though he couldn't take enough of her. His hands moved over her, cupping her breasts, feeling her body through its covering of lacy underthings and soft velvet. Although she wanted to resist, knew she should until he explained about Sarah, she couldn't. Her own hands were clutching at him, her breath quickening to match his ragged breaths. Despite their anger, disappointment and misunderstanding, their bodies still screamed for fulfillment. Vaguely, the sound of voices came through to them, and they jumped apart at the same time.

She adjusted her clothing while John watched. Still they didn't speak, and somewhere in the back of her mind she wondered about the oddness of the situation. Then she heard her brother's voice. "Ketti? Is that you?" He strode up to them while Panana waited by the front entrance.

"Yes," was all she could manage.

"We've just been talking," John said coolly. Ketti wondered how he could seem so unaffected—so in control, when only seconds before he'd seemed ready to tear her clothes from her body.

Charles nodded and was cordial. But something was troubling her brother, Ketti could see. After he'd excused himself for interrupting them, he turned to her. "Panana isn't well since the buffet, and we'll have to leave."

Ketti hesitated a moment, but her brief hope that John would offer to escort her home was dashed by her next thought. There was Sarah. It appeared that the reverend hadn't attended, after all, but he had been right about John escorting Sarah.

Her goodbye to John was cool, and so was his to her. It wasn't until she was in the carriage that she realized that John hadn't said what was on his mind. As usual, when they were alone, their emotions quickly took them beyond talking. Now she didn't know if he'd been about to clarify their relationship...or end it.

Chapter Thirteen

"Where are you going?" Charles asked the next morning, as Ketti was about to go out the back door on her way to the stable. She'd been up early and had already made a pretense of eating breakfast with Panana's parents, who'd given her permission to ride one of their saddle horses.

"I'm riding out to Waikiki to take a walk on the beach," she replied. For a second she thought he might offer to go along, and her heart sank. She needed to be alone.

"It's a good thing I caught you then," he said. "Panana is still not well and we've decided to leave for home on an evening steamer. I assumed you were ready to go as well." His dark eyes probed hers, trying to determine if his sister was all right. He knew she was fond of John, and he worried that she might be setting herself up for heartbreak. Charles had also heard the rumors about a possible alliance between John and Sarah. "You could stay longer if you wish, Ketti," he added.

She shook her head. "I'll return with you." She contrived a smile. She didn't want anyone to know how upset she felt, and she welcomed the thought of leaving Honolulu. "I'll be back by midafternoon. Is that time enough?"

He dropped an arm around her, walking with her to the door. "That'll be fine."

"But we'll have to send word to Siu," she reminded him.

"I'll take care of it," Charles assured her.

After a few more words Ketti went outside, and crossed the beautiful grounds to the stable. Several minutes later she was mounted on a black stallion and on the street headed toward the beach. High clouds checkered the sky, while low-flying ones scuttled beneath. A stiff breeze off the ocean reminded Ketti that it was the time of year for storms, and she hoped they made it back to Kawaihae before the weather changed. Rough water wouldn't help Panana's sickness.

Ketti was relieved to leave the house behind. She'd already considered the possibility that James would stop by to visit, especially after Panana's father had announced at breakfast that James was the American who'd wanted to escort her to the ball. She didn't know if John even knew where she was staying.

She rode astride, wearing a forest-green riding skirt and a formfitting, matching jacket that finished above the waist. Since she wasn't on the range, she'd omitted a hat, and allowed her long hair its freedom. The streets were busy with carriages and horsemen, and she was aware of many admiring glances. Once she left Honolulu behind and the road traffic thinned, she gave her horse free rein. The stallion leaped forward, and Ketti felt a rush of pleasure. She'd chosen well; her mount was fast.

The terrain flashed past: green rice fields, the mountains behind them, and the occasional house nestled among the thick tropical foliage. As she rode, her spirits lifted, as they always did when she gave herself to the mood of the land. The palm-lined beach loomed ahead sooner than she expected.

They slowed to a trot when they reached the sand, and without hesitation Ketti signaled the horse toward the distant point of Diamond Head around the curve of beach. The breakers were huge, rolling with great force to crash ashore, finally subsiding in frothy foam. The size of the waves was another sign of an impending storm.

She noticed a few summer residences nestled among the palms, owned by the rich people of the island, as the beach was one of the best in all of Hawaii. Reaching a more deserted part of the beach, Ketti reined in and dismounted. She decided against a walk, and instead tied her horse to a tree trunk, then climbed up on a rock that jutted into the surf. She sat on a flat area, her eyes on the distant ocean. An occasional burst of airborne spray tickled her face, and the pounding roar of the ocean isolated her completely. Her thoughts drifted, and after a while the wild turbulence at her feet lulled her even further into melancholy.

She turned into the wind and her hair streamed behind her. Pulling up her knees, she rested her chin on them, her mind going over the night before. That James was in Honolulu didn't help her mood; she was reminded of how he'd cheated on her, a thought that strengthened her fear that John was doing the same thing now. There was no denying he'd chosen someone else to escort to the ball.

After a while the sun disappeared behind a bank of clouds, and Ketti suddenly noticed that the whole sky was darkening. A storm was on its way, and she knew it was time to start back if she was to be ready in time to catch the steamer. But she sat on for a few minutes longer, somehow loath to leave.

John looked up from the ledgers spread on the table in front of him. He was sick of going over the accounts for the plantation, trying to make the numbers less unfavorable should he lose money on the first crop. Even though it would be many months yet before his sugar plants were ready to harvest, his financial picture was not conducive to his continuing that long if he wasn't guaranteed to sell the sugar. He sighed and lit a cheroot, pondering the dilemma. Either he had to gamble that annexation would happen, and that being a part of the United States would then ease the current tight market, or he had to get out now, before he lost the plantation.

Unsettled, he went to the window and looked out over the Pacific, instantly feeling the ocean's calming effect. That was what he loved most about the little house, its proximity to Waikiki Beach and the ocean. He loved the cottage where he'd come as a boy to spend a summer with his mother's parents. That summer held his fondest memories, when he'd discovered his Polynesian heritage, and realized that Hawaii was home. He vowed he'd never sell the cottage at any cost. Someday he wanted his own children to have it for a summer retreat. He smiled wryly. And the plantation on the Big Island as their main home.

The switch in thoughts brought the image of Ketti to mind, and his stomach immediately knotted with fear of losing her. When he'd seen James Rawlston kiss her, he'd had an urge to strangle the man. It was only later that he'd realized that Ketti hadn't come with James, had in fact only danced with him once.

John blew smoke, regretting that he hadn't been able to escort Ketti as he'd planned. Instead, he'd been traveling throughout the islands, talking to the planters about annexation. Almost all of them agreed with his position, differing only in that they favored overthrowing the queen. That was the very thing John was trying to avoid. He was convinced that the monarchy should remain, but under the political umbrella of the United States—that the queen should not be involved in economic policy making. But his was a losing battle, and the meetings had taken longer than he'd expected. He hadn't been able to return to the Big Island in time to make sure Ketti was going to the ball with him.

James had added to the problem. He'd come from California to represent his family in the fight to maintain the throne; the Rawlstons, like some other old families who controlled the economy, didn't want change to upset their profits. John knew James was trying to influence some of the planters with offers of cheaper shipping charges for their sugar if the queen stayed in power. John feared some planters would fall for the ploy, which he suspected was misleading. People like James didn't give a hoot about the monarchy; they only needed it intact to guarantee their own profit margins. John still hoped both sides could come to a compromise. He sighed. He feared both sides felt they had too much at risk to consider the bigger issue of retaining their unique Hawaiian culture.

He went out to the veranda, too unsettled to continue working on the ledgers. His thoughts moved to Ketti and lingered there. He wondered how she felt about him. She believed he'd escorted Sarah rather than her, and that wasn't completely true. The reverend had intended to attend but had come down with one of his bad headaches, and had prevailed on John to take Sarah in his place, or she'd have had to miss the ball she'd been so excited about attending. John hadn't been able to refuse doing his neighbor the favor.

Then, as his gaze moved up the beach, he saw the figure of a woman sitting on his favorite rock. He stared. There was something familiar about her, the way her hair flowed in the wind, and the set of her shoulders. With a jolt of surprise, he realized it was Ketti. Had he conjured her up out of his thoughts? he wondered in amazement. He was striding down the path before he even paused to consider his next move. As he reached the beach he tossed his cheroot into the surf, and continued at a fast walk toward her. Her back was half-turned to him and she didn't see his approach.

"Hello, Ketti!" he called above the sound of the breakers. He saw her startled reflex, and then she twisted around on her perch and her eyes met his.

For a long moment their gazes locked, while the ocean played its thunderous music. A seabird wheeled on the quickening wind currents, and out on the horizon a ship moved toward Honolulu harbor. The brisk weather had stained her cheeks with a rosy glow, and her windblown hair and wide-eyed stare gave her an artlessly seductive look. He didn't know how she came to be there—how she knew where he lived—but he didn't care; he was overjoyed that she was close enough for him to touch.

As the silence between them stretched, her long silky lashes fluttered nervously, as though she couldn't believe her eyes. He saw her mouth form his name, but the wind snatched it away before the sound reached his ears.

Then she scrambled to her feet and slid off the rock. He moved quickly, so that she slipped right into his arms. Immediately, her heartbeats were so fast that she could hardly catch her breath. But as he held her close, her breasts against his chest, her stomach pressed into the hardness of his thighs, she felt the sweet awakening in the softness between her thighs. She swallowed hard, disbelief still surging through her. Had she gone mad from her need of him? Was she only imagining his touch that sent shivers racing through her veins, and a tingling into her most secret place?

"How did you get here?" she managed in a shaky whisper.

He inclined his head toward the cottage that was almost hidden among the palms. "It was my grandparents' place," he told her in a low tone. "It's mine now."

"I didn't know it was here," she began and faltered. "That is—"

"You were sent by Providence, perhaps—the will of the old gods?"

She couldn't answer. Her thoughts were consumed by the implication of his words. They were alone. She ran her tongue over her lips, and his gaze lowered to her mouth. When he looked up, the banked-down embers in his eyes had blazed to life. Then his lips were on hers.

Again they hadn't taken time to talk, their bodies communicating in a language far more important. Ketti strained to him, opening her mouth to his thrusting tongue. Her senses reeled, and she knew that he would take her to his cottage in the trees. When he lifted his head briefly, a distant movement behind him caught her glance.

"Oh, my God!" she cried, and arched away. "There's a rider coming."

John dropped his hands at once, and they stepped apart.
Then, to her horror, she saw that the man on the horse was
James. In seconds he reined in, bringing his mount to a
shuddering stop. His glance flickered between Ketti and
John, and Ketti saw glints of anger in his brown eyes. But
his tone belied his feelings. He'd been far enough away that
he didn't know if Ketti had been in John's arms or not.

"I came to meet you," he told Ketti with a forced grin,
and after a curt nod in John's direction, ignored him.
"Charles said you were here, and that you'd better hurry or
risk missing the steamer."

Ketti's eyes widened. She'd forgotten about catching the
evening steamer! She glanced at John and was about to explain, but met sudden anger in his eyes instead.

He fumbled in his shirt pocket for another cheroot, and
lit it, blowing smoke so that it obscured his gaze. "You'd
better hurry then, Ketti. You'll hardly make it."

"But John," she began, wanting to explain. He put up a
silencing hand, indicating he already did. Then he turned on
his heel and strode to her horse, untied him and brought the
stallion to her. "John, we need to talk," she said, her voice
shaking.

He arched a brow, as though to suggest James's presence
said it all. Before she could protest, he'd boosted her up into
the saddle while James looked on gleefully, realizing that
whatever had been going on between them had been altered
by his arrival.

John watched them ride off, more upset under his cool
exterior than he'd ever been in his life. She was his woman,
and yet his financial situation—and his pride—wouldn't
allow him to propose. But he knew one thing: that bastard
James wouldn't have her! But what if she wanted him? John
asked himself. She'd once hoped to marry him.

He went back to his cottage, suddenly seeing how run-
down it looked, how in need of paint and repairs it was,
which cost money—and his money was invested in sugar.

But he sat down with his ledgers anyway to go over his possibilities once more.

They rode back in silence, Ketti refusing to speak to James. When she reached the road, she allowed the stallion his head, and he quickly outdistanced James's mount. Upon reaching the house, she barely had time to bathe and dress before it was time to leave. Char brought Siu and soon they were on their way to the harbor. Once they were on the steamer, the weather turned foul, as Ketti had expected. Charles came to the cabin Ketti shared with Siu, and asked his sister if she would see to Panana, who was lying down in the couple's cabin.

"Thanks for coming," her sister-in-law said as Ketti closed the door behind her. "I've such an upset stomach that I'm afraid I've scared Charles. I thought it would be best if you would sit with me."

"How can I help?" Ketti asked, concerned for the young woman in the bunk who was so white and drawn.

"Don't be so upset," Panana said. "It looks bad, but it's not really. That is, I'm sick, but it's a natural sick."

"What do you mean?"

Panana smiled wanly. "Remember the barbecue? And the fertility dance?"

"Of course."

"Well, it worked—I'm pregnant!" Panana's smile was wiped away by another bout of nausea, but Ketti could see that nothing, not even being sick, would dampen her thrill of impending motherhood.

Ketti stayed with Panana until they finally arrived at Kawaihae, and during the long vigil her thoughts kept returning to the night they'd all danced the hulas. The magic of the fertility dance worked for Charles and Panana, she told herself. But what about the ancient love dance? It was true she loved John. But would she be his forever, as the legend promised?

And then she had an awful thought.

She *was* his forever, would love him for the rest of her life. But what if she were never to be his wife? The old myth said only that they would belong to each other; it didn't necessarily mean marriage—or even being together.

Ketti went back to the ranch wishing she'd never gone to Honolulu. When she saw John again, she'd control her wanton desires—at least until they'd had a chance to talk and explain what had happened at the ball and on the beach. But all her reassurances to herself didn't help. She knew he believed she was involved with James, and she wasn't.

Then she had yet another thought. Was it possible that John wasn't involved with Sarah? Appearances could be deceiving, as she was learning. Despite feeling so bad, she suddenly had a new flicker of hope.

Chapter Fourteen

Once back at the ranch Ketti felt an anticlimax after all her
expectations of Honolulu and the ball. But she hid her feelings. The family was delighted about Panana's being pregnant. Ketti's sister-in-law had gone at once to the doctor and
he had confirmed that a baby was indeed on the way. "An
heir to our empire!" Adam had exclaimed, and Mari had
given a special dinner in celebration. Although Ketti was as
happy as the rest of the family, the impending event only
pointed up her own situation. She needed her own goals,
especially if she didn't marry.

She hadn't heard from John, although he'd stopped by
the ranch on his way back to the plantation. She'd been out
and he hadn't stayed, as another storm threatened and he
wanted to be across the mountains before it hit. Now, riding in the buggy with her parents and Charles on the way to
her grandfather's ranch, she wouldn't allow her fears about
their relationship to mar the beauty of the afternoon. As
they reached the driveway to the Webster ranch, she noticed that there were many buggies and saddle horses tied up
in the yard. She hadn't realized that a meeting to discuss
annexation would bring out so many people. But then it was
Sunday, and most of the ranchers took that day off.

The buggy was reined to a stop just as a horseman rode up
beside them, and Ketti's heart sank when she saw it was
James. He tipped his hat to her parents. "Afternoon, Mrs.

Foster, Mr. Foster." He nodded at Charles, then looked directly at Ketti. "You're looking pretty as ever."

She thanked him coolly, and was about to descend from the buggy, when he quickly dismounted and put out his hand to help her. From the corner of her eye she saw her parents exchange glances, and she hoped they didn't have the wrong idea of the situation—that she might be interested in him.

The meeting had been organized on short notice; the situation in Honolulu was worsening, and people were confused. Ketti's grandfather had arranged the gathering, so questions could be raised, and each man given the opportunity to air his views. To Ketti's annoyance, James stayed beside her as they made their way toward the barn, where there was room enough for the crowd. Then another buggy turned into the driveway. Ketti's pulse accelerated the instant she recognized John as the driver. Two men sat beside him, one the Reverend Mead. As they drew closer, she saw two more men on the back seat . . . and Sarah.

Her face flushed with anger. If there was nothing between him and Sarah, as John had insisted, why was she always with him? Actions speak louder than words! she fumed. Well, she'd show him. She didn't even have to acknowledge him.

The bright yellow ribbons of her straw hat flying behind her, she strode as quickly as her cotton dress and petticoats would allow, finally lifting the yellow floral skirt so that she could walk even faster. James kept up, and for a moment she wanted to tell him to leave her alone, then thought better of it. Let John see that other men found her desirable—and weren't afraid to make their feelings known. When James took her arm, she didn't protest.

She sat with the family, James beside her, and listened as the meeting got under way. Both sides of the issue were presented. The men who raised sugar were outspoken in their belief that annexation was the only way of saving the Hawaiian economy. Then James stood to state the opposite side of the question, that the Hawaiian people would lose their culture, their independence and their unique way of life, along with losing the monarchy. Ketti was impressed, and for the most part agreed with James, wishing that she could trust he was speaking from his heart, and not his bank account. But she also believed that a compromise might be the solution. Then John, tall and bronzed in his white shirt and riding pants, stood and suggested that very thing.

Despite her hurt and anger, she *knew* he spoke honestly, and she was pierced by the depth of her love for him. She watched him speak—and thought of his lips on hers, his tongue probing with a fiery touch that sent spasms of desire all through her body. She saw his hands gesture—and remembered his fingers tracing ecstasy across her flesh. Oh, God! she thought. Why can't things be right between us? As he gave his views, explained that Hawaii must move forward and take a place in the world market, his eyes touched hers. But even before she had a chance to react, he looked away—as though she were a stranger. *He'd ignored her!*

She sat numb, hearing the voices but not what they said. She smiled or nodded responses when spoken to, even to James, who took it that she was no longer upset with him, and to the reverend, who was happy to see her more decorous manner, which boded well for his future plans. Refreshments were served by her Grandmother Agnes after the meeting ended, and John and his group left immediately afterward. Ketti was glad when she was finally on her way home again. She kept up a front of good spirits until she finally reached her bedroom. And then she fell on her bed and cried into her pillow.

The next morning she washed her swollen eyes with cool water and went downstairs, but only after she knew her father was gone and her mother and grandmother were already busy for the day. She didn't feel like discussing the day before. She ate a light breakfast, and then she began her hour-long teaching session with Siu. The time went quickly, and when she closed the English primer, she smiled at her friend. "You grasp the language so fast I can hardly keep up with you," Ketti said.

"You too learn Chinese—real good," Siu replied, her cheeks pink with pleasure. "When you teach in Honolulu, good to know some Chinese."

"*If* I teach in Honolulu," Ketti corrected.

"Char hopes—real hard—that you work to help Chinese." Siu suddenly looked radiant, her feelings for Char written on her face. "He says you perfect teacher. I agree."

She sat, looking so sweet and appealing with the bloom of love softening her expression, her pale pink dress accentuating her dark beauty. She'd begun wearing Western clothes shortly after arriving in Hawaii; Ketti guessed it was to please Char, who had also adopted the Western way of dress years earlier when he started school in America.

She'll be the perfect wife for Char, Ketti thought, but didn't dare mention the subject, for she knew it would embarrass Siu, who still felt she wasn't free. No matter what Ketti said, no matter that she was paid wages, Siu still believed she owed her life to Ketti, who'd saved her from the highbinders. When the time is right, I'll just let Char convince her, she told herself.

But the thought of teaching in Honolulu was growing in Ketti's mind; she couldn't continue forever at the ranch, running errands into Waimea or down to Kawaihae. Although she knew she'd be welcome with her family forever, she also knew she must make a decision about her own future soon.

She pushed back her chair and stood. It would soon be time to change for lunch. Her parents had invited James for dinner. Ketti wasn't pleased, and wished she hadn't adopted such a childish ploy the day before—allowing James to think she still cared just to make John jealous. Now he was taking advantage of that, and of the fact that his parents knew hers. After a few more words with Siu, Ketti went upstairs.

Ketti felt restless, and had been unable to concentrate on any of the chores she'd done during the day. So she'd gone to her room to have a bath, and had soaked for a whole hour. She was still in the tub when Siu came to clean up the bathroom. She grinned at her friend, but Siu realized from the sad expression underlying the smile that Ketti was upset. She knew the reason was John, and she wondered what possessed the man that he didn't claim the beautiful Hawaiian girl at once. It was a puzzling situation. The Chinese girl sighed. She didn't as yet understand the Western culture, and why there was such restraint in some matters, and none in others. But even as she had the thought, it occurred to her that Orientals were not so very different, after all.

Siu handed Ketti the towel and Ketti stepped from the cooling water. Her body was refreshed and scented with perfume, but her spirit still sagged. She slipped into her wrap and then glanced at Siu, who lingered, her expression concerned.

"Can I help?" she asked hesitantly. Ketti knew she was referring to her mental state, not her toilette.

Slowly Ketti shook her head. "Thanks, Siu. I appreciate your asking, but no. I'm still trying to understand what I should do—if anything."

The other girl's lashes fluttered. "Maybe Char could help? He is coming to visit," Siu went on. "And to speak to you again about his offer."

"When?" Ketti regarded her thoughtfully, and again realized how much Siu loved the Chinese lawyer. Ketti wouldn't have been surprised if Char asked for Siu in marriage. Ketti dismissed the thought of her own hopes and contrived a lighter expression. She didn't want to mar Siu's joy with her own unhappiness.

"Tomorrow morning—before he leaves on steamer."

Ketti nodded agreement, and then, after assuring Siu that she didn't need her help, went to fetch an appropriate gown for the evening with James. Siu finished cleaning up and returned to the kitchen.

Ketti made quick work of her preparations, pinning her hair up in a prim chignon, then stepping into a high-necked, long-sleeved navy polka dot dress that hung in a graceful sweep of skirt. Then, with a final glance in the mirror, she went downstairs to the salon. It was still early and no one was in the room, so she went to the cabinet grand piano and sat down to run her hands over the keys. Although she wasn't a great pianist, she did play with some feeling, and her feelings suddenly escaped through her fingers into the music of Mozart. She didn't hear the knock at the front door, or see the man who stepped into the hall when no one answered.

He stood in the doorway, like a great black hawk, his gaze fixed on the woman who played with such emotion. The Reverend Mead was moved by the music, and by Ketti who looked so lovely—and proper—in her dark dress and no-nonsense hairstyle. He could see her in another setting, as the wife of a minister, primly playing the piano for the congregation. A rare smile touched his lips. He hadn't been wrong; she was the woman to be his wife and help him minister to his flock, Hawaiians who'd still be heathens but for him.

Ketti ended the piece and was about to begin another, when she sensed his presence. She turned on the piano bench and met his admiring eyes. Immediately she stood, conscious that he'd been watching for a while, intruding on her privacy.

"I knocked, and no one answered," he said, his tone still reflecting his pleasure at recognizing her potential. He stepped farther into the room. "I'm on my way to another ranch, and I decided to stop. I'm glad I did. God works in mysterious ways," he added, unaware of how pious he sounded.

Ketti wondered what he meant, but decided it was best not to ask. "Um . . . would you care for refreshments—before you go?" she asked, making the point that she didn't expect him to stay long.

"That would be nice."

He had an odd glint in his eyes that she didn't like, and Ketti was suddenly uncomfortable. She walked to the hall and called for Siu, hoping that another family member would appear as well. But only Siu answered her call, and so Ketti asked her to bring tea to them. Then she indicated that the reverend take a seat, which he did at once on the settee. She sat on the chair opposite him. Then Siu brought the tea tray and placed it on the table between them. Ketti poured, then offered him a cup, anxious for him to drink it and be gone. She certainly didn't need his dour personality to further depress her day. She just hoped he hadn't felt encouraged by her friendliness at the annexation meeting. But his next words told her how wrong she'd been.

"You've occupied my mind these past weeks," he said. "And I've come to see it as a sign from God."

Ketti straightened her back. "I don't understand why...." She faltered, ill at ease under his intense regard.

He gestured with both hands for silence, very much the stern preacher that Ketti didn't like. "When I saw you playing just now, His plan came clear to me." He took a deep breath, and then moved around the table to her so quickly that she didn't have time to react before he pulled her out of the chair. Then his narrow lips came down on hers in a kiss that was both cold and lacking passion. She was repelled.

Jerking away, she stumbled backward, her cheeks fired with anger. "How dare you kiss me!" she cried. "What do you think you're doing?"

He smiled patiently. "Just sealing our betrothal," he said, fully convinced of her ultimate acceptance. "I need a wife, and you are my choice."

For a second Ketti was too stunned to believe her ears. Then, as the words sank in, she shook with outrage. The pompous ass! But before she could even speak, he was going on, telling her of all the changes she must make after their marriage.

"There'll be no more hulas and fancy gowns and trips to Honolulu—unless it's for church work, of course. And—"

"I'll hear no more!" Ketti cried, backing even farther away. "You have no right to expect anything from me be- cause—because—I wouldn't marry you if you were the last man on earth!"

His eyes narrowed, and his features tightened so quickly that his face seemed to purse into a point. He worked his mouth, and finally something dropped out. "Now, see here, my girl. These things are decided for us, and—"

Again she cut him off. "*I* decide who I will marry, no one else! And it will never be a critical, unbending man like you!" She turned in a huff and almost ran to the door. But she was stopped by James, dressed for dinner in a brown frock coat and trousers, who was suddenly in her path. It seemed he could hardly control himself from laughing.

It was more than Ketti could stand. He'd overheard—and thought it was funny! Her eyes flashed at him. "Please let me pass, James," she said through clenched teeth.

The corners of his lips quirked, but he still managed to keep a straight face. Instead of letting her go by, he took her arm and led her back into the room. When she tried to shake loose, he only tightened his grip painfully.

"Now, Reverend Mead—that's your name, isn't it?" James began.

The reverend nodded, but a flush of anger stained his pale cheeks. "Take your hands off Miss Foster," he demanded in his best pulpit voice. "She is about to be betrothed."

"Betrothed?" James asked in a deceptively calm voice.

The reverend nodded. "To me. Of course, there are some things to be worked out."

"That's impossible," James said in the same soft voice.

"Hardly impossible, not if Miss Foster accepts the teaching of my church!" the reverend thundered.

Ketti was astounded, so fascinated by the interplay be- tween the two men that she was momentarily struck mute. But one thing was for sure; they were equally obnoxious each in his own way. She wondered how she could ever have thought she might be in love with James. He was almost as repulsive as the reverend. Deep in thought, she missed some of their conversation. She came back to it with a jolt of shock.

"It's impossible because Ketti has consented to be my wife!" James was saying, his voice raised to make sure his point hit home.

"Now just a minute!" she cried. "This has all gone far enough! I'd—"

"Like the reverend to leave?" James flashed her a glance as he finished her sentence. Then he took the minister's arm. "I think it best you do go. You've upset Miss Foster."

The reverend shook him off, and after a dark look at Ketti he strode to the door, where he turned back to face them. "I have to go anyway. But you haven't heard the end of this matter. The will of God will not be denied." Then he was gone and the front door banged shut behind him. A minute later his buggy could be heard creaking away from the house.

Ketti faced James, her anger now directed at him. Although she was glad to see the last of the reverend, she resented James's interference. "Why on earth did you tell him that I agreed to marry you! I did no such thing!"

He shrugged, amused. "It got rid of him, didn't it?"

"You—you—" she sputtered. "That lie will be all over the island within a week."

"So?" He lowered his eyelids to shutter his eyes, which suddenly burned with his determination to do just that—marry her.

"I'll never marry you, James!" she flung at him.

"We'll see." His smile chilled her. "We'll see."

She left him then, unable to endure his presence any longer. It was the final straw that she would have to sit with him through dinner—and be polite. She went to the kitchen where she knew the presence of the cook and Siu would prevent him from harassing her. She would only return to the salon after the family had assembled. But it was a long time before she was able to leash her anger and frustration. She knew that both James and the Reverend Mead were problems that weren't about to go away. So maybe *she* would, she thought suddenly.

The thought that she might get away sustained Ketti through supper and the long evening until she excused herself for bed, accompanying her grandmother upstairs. She planned it that way to offset any plan James might have to waylay her on the way to her bedroom. But she didn't sleep well, worried that the reverend would tell John she was engaged to James. Why didn't I clarify it at once? she asked herself many times during the long night. But she realized that if she had, the reverend would only have taken it as another sign that she was interested in him.

A damnable mess! she fumed on the way to the kitchen the next morning. She used the back stairs to avoid James, should he still be lurking in the house. She burst into the kitchen, surprising Siu in Char's arms. Ketti just stood there, for a moment stricken that she should have caught them together, perhaps embarrassed them.

Char dropped his arms at once, and grinned over Siu's head at Ketti. "Don't look so upset, Ketti. It's all right. I was only kissing Siu. I don't mind that you saw—and I'm sure Siu doesn't, either."

Siu nodded, but her cheeks were pink and her eyes downcast. Ketti still felt awful to have intruded on their private moment. "I can come back later," she began. "I—"

Char waved away her words. "Nonsense. We were just waiting for you and..." He grinned down at the girl he was so obviously in love with. "And passing the time until you arrived."

He was so natural about his feelings that Ketti's awkwardness passed and was replaced by fond amusement. Char, raised in the old Chinese traditions, was becoming so

Western in his reactions, she thought. Times really were changing in Hawaii.

They sat down to coffee and discussed again the possibility of her taking the teaching position in Honolulu. And as they talked, Ketti's mind whirled with other considerations. Like John. She'd written him a note earlier, and then torn it up when she remembered how he'd ignored her at the annexation meeting. Her pride wouldn't allow her to go crawling to him—when she didn't even know if he really loved her. Of course he'd told her so many times; but that was during their lovemaking, she reminded herself. Maybe men lied at such times, to have their way with women foolish enough to make love without the security of a wedding band. For a time she'd even worried that she might be pregnant, like Panana, and it was a relief when she knew she wasn't.

"I need your answer now," Char said. "I've taken care of all the arrangements for the classes, and if you can't do it, Ketti, then I'll have to find someone else."

"I understand," she replied. "I've given it much thought—and I accept."

He grinned, his expression so pleased that it made Ketti feel good. But when he would have spoken, she stopped him. "I do have two conditions."

"They are?" he asked, and hoped they didn't mean she might not teach after all.

"First, I have to discuss this further with my parents, but I believe they'll agree to my wishes, so long as everything is done properly." She gave a laugh. "Where I'll live, for instance."

"And the second condition?" He braced himself, seeing the determined expression on Ketti's face, one he'd come to respect even when they played together as children.

"I'll need an assistant, someone who can speak some English as well as Chinese, someone who can help me and also the people to understand the meaning of the words."

She paused, and kept her gaze level. "You would also have to pay my assistant a salary."

"Agreed," he said immediately, relieved. "And do you have someone in mind?"

Ketti shifted her gaze to Siu, who'd remained silent during the whole interchange. "Yes—Siu."

She'd managed to surprise them both, but in seconds she watched anticipation dawn on Siu's face, and approval on Char's. They talked for several more minutes, arranging dates, and then Ketti pushed back her chair and stood. "So if you don't hear to the contrary, I'll be in Honolulu well before the first class."

Then she left them to a few more private minutes before Char had to leave. But she knew they were both pleased. And she was pleased, too. She would see to it that someone had a happy ending. And that thought brought John to mind, and all of her anguish over their own situation. She went to find her parents, and hoped her father hadn't ridden out on the range yet. She wanted the matter settled.

"I hate to see you go, Ketti," Mari was saying. "You've hardly settled in from your years in California."

"I know, Mother, but times are changing. I need to occupy my time with real work, and teaching is my strong point. And in any case, Honolulu isn't California. I'll come home often."

She'd already explained about James and the reverend, and although both Adam and Mari were relieved that she hadn't taken up with James again, and were angry about the minister, they hated to see her go. But they tried to understand her feelings.

So it was decided that Ketti should go, that a letter would be written at once to Panana's mother, Kilia, who was Mari's best friend. Ketti and Siu would stay with Panana's parents.

For the remainder of the day Ketti occupied herself with thoughts of how she would conduct her classes, and how she would prepare for them. She managed to keep her thoughts from dwelling on John. And that was what she was striving for. She couldn't allow herself to die of grief, have nothing else, should they never resolve their differences.

But when night came and she closed her eyes to sleep, all she saw was John. She tossed and turned, and finally told herself that the move to Honolulu would solve that problem, too. She just needed to stay busy....

Chapter Fifteen

The air in the mountains was cold, and Ketti tucked the lap robe tighter around her legs to keep out the chill. It would be a relief when they finally reached the ranch, as the journey from the Hamakua coast seemed endless in bad weather. It had been a wasted journey; she hadn't seen John, after all.

She glanced at her Grandfather Webster, who drove the pair of bays. He looked drawn and older than his years, and she felt a tinge of fear. She loved the old man, understood him in a way that even her mother didn't. She'd visited the Webster ranch often when she was a child, which was how she'd come to be such good friends with Char, who was the son of her grandfather's cook. She hoped that the present crisis wouldn't affect her grandfather's health, as he was in his mid-sixties and had already suffered some medical problems in the past.

He glanced at her and smiled wryly. "Guess we didn't really gain anything from the trip," he said. "Half of the planters were in Honolulu."

Ketti nodded, staring at his profile, and in her mind's eye she visualized how he must have looked in his youth: tall and powerfully built, blond and ruggedly handsome. He'd been a whaler before he finally settled in Hawaii and married Agnes, his second wife. His first wife, Ketti's grandmother, had died many years earlier, and their daughter, Mari, had been brought up by his parents in New England. Ketti knew her mother hadn't been close to him, having never really gotten over the feeling that he'd abandoned her as a child.

"Maybe they're having some success in securing reduced shipping costs," Ketti offered. "That could mean at least breaking even with the current crop, so that the plantations won't go bankrupt."

"I hope so," he replied, worry edging his tone. "It would help." He hesitated. "But I fear the only real hope is in annexation, so that we have a voice in the American Congress."

"You favor the overthrow of the queen?" she asked, not really clear on her grandfather's position.

"Of course not," he replied. "I agree with John Stillman. We should be able to maintain the monarchy, if the governing power was under the jurisdiction of the United States."

For a while they rode in silence, and for once the peace of the high country failed to soothe Ketti's troubled feelings. She'd gone to the gathering of sugar planters with her grandfather because Mari had worried about him going alone when he looked so troubled and upset, and because Ketti had hoped to have a chance to talk with John before she left the island. But John had gone to Honolulu once again. He was outspoken in his position, and, as the situation worsened and moved closer to a final confrontation between the two political factions, John was travelling even more, from group to group, trying to instill a sense of unity among the panic-stricken businessmen. Even today, Ketti had heard that other businesses were failing in Honolulu; when there was no money to spend, business suffered. And worse yet, an American troop ship was anchored in Honolulu harbor, ready for action should there be an uprising.

"I just wish Seth wasn't still in New England," Russell was saying, bringing Ketti's thoughts back to the buggy that was creaking and bouncing over the rough road. "I could sure as hell use his help."

She glanced at the grizzled man at her side, and glimpsed pain on his face. She suddenly felt sorry for him, not because he'd been wronged by his two children, he hadn't. He simply had never understood either Mari or Seth. Ketti hardly remembered her uncle, who'd gone to live in New England with his grandparents so he could be educated in America. He'd become a lawyer. Russell had given up hope that he'd ever return, when he received word that Seth was finally coming home. But from what Ketti knew of Seth, she doubted he would be taking over the Webster ranch as her grandfather hoped. That job would fall to Charles, Ketti thought, and one day the Foster and Webster ranches would be combined.

"You know, Ketti," he went on, "if I'd known Seth would stay so long, I wouldn't have let him go."

Her grandfather was in a strange mood; it was unusual for him to reveal his feelings. And now, as they rode through the still mountains, he shared even more of his past. He explained the estrangement with his parents over his marrying a woman they felt was beneath them, and how, even as a boy, he had never been able to please his stern father. "When I learned there was a secret about my birth, that he was only my stepfather after all, I began to understand," Russell finished. "And that's when I ran away to sea."

Ketti didn't know what to say. She was glad when another silence fell over them. Her own concerns soon took hold of her, and she felt like crying all of a sudden. She'd put such hope in seeing John, and having a chance to explain, to hear him tell her once and for all whether or not he was involved with Sarah. But it's not meant to be, she told herself. Maybe it was just too late. After all, John had made no further attempt to see her and explain.

By the time they reached the ranch Ketti was chilled to the bone, for a cool evening breeze had come up from the ocean. She invited her grandfather to stay for supper, but he said Agnes would be expecting him home for the meal. So

Ketti kissed her grandfather goodbye, and went into the house.

With her new discipline, she forced any thought of John from her mind. Instead, as she went upstairs to freshen up for supper, she concentrated on the English lessons she had been preparing for the past two weeks. But the hollow spot in her stomach had grown bigger, and she wondered if it would ever begin to heal. She doubted it.

"Am I really doing the right thing?" Ketti asked herself late the following afternoon, and the words seemed to echo in the empty dining room. She sat alone at the table, her lessons spread like a fan in front of her, and pondered that question. The sun shone through the long windows, swaths of golden light on the Oriental carpet.

But, as she looked at all the work she'd done in the past two weeks, preparing for her English classes, she knew she was. Although going away might mean she'd never have a chance of seeing John, she also knew she couldn't just wait for that chance to happen, while she did nothing about her own future. There are no guarantees, she reminded herself. Her happiness was up to herself alone; no one else was responsible for it.

She stood, pushing back the chair, and began to gather up her papers. She felt good about teaching, and she was grateful she had the ability to do it. It'll be my salvation, she told herself. If she were busy enough helping others, her feelings for John might begin to fade.

"Ketti?" her mother said from behind her. As Ketti turned, Mari went on. "I wanted to talk to you—just us—before you left in the morning. Are you finished?" She glanced at the papers in Ketti's hands. "I don't want to interrupt."

Then Ketti noticed that her mother carried a tea tray with two cups. As she assured her mother that she was free, Mari smiled and moved into the room to place the tray on the table. Then she indicated that Ketti sit back down.

They sat quietly while Mari poured. Then as they sipped the hot tea, Mari's gaze was suddenly direct, although Ketti saw something else in her eyes. Concern? she wondered.

"Ketti," Mari began and hesitated, as though she didn't know how to go on.

Ketti patted her mother's hand. "Just go ahead and say whatever it is, Mother," she said gently. "I don't bite, you know."

Mari smiled, and Ketti marveled at how lovely her mother was, how unlined by the years. "All right, I will—and trust you won't be upset with an interfering mother."

"I'd never be upset with you," Ketti said, her smile warm and sincere. "I love you, don't forget. And I'm sure that whatever is on your mind, it has to do with what you believe is best for me."

Her smile broadening, Mari took a deep breath before continuing. "You're very perceptive, Ketti. I do have some fears for you, some questions in my mind about your future, and I wanted us to talk about them."

Ketti inclined her head, waiting.

"Something is bothering you, Ketti, and I think I recognize the symptoms." Again she paused. "Are you in love with someone?"

For a second Ketti was taken aback. She'd expected her mother to express worry about her going to Honolulu, or teaching the Chinese in Chinatown, or about how her reputation might suffer for working with people who were discriminated against by many, especially the *haoles*. Ketti glanced down, unaware that her knuckles had gone white on the cup she was holding.

But Mari noticed, and felt a thrill of fear along her spine. Ketti was in love with John, the son of the man who'd once pursued her. Although she liked John, she couldn't entirely forget that his father had been dishonest, even dangerous. She wondered what John's motives were, as he hadn't openly courted Ketti. She'd watched Ketti and John do the ancient love dance, and had seen her daughter's expression when she looked at the man. There was no doubt about it; Ketti was deeply in love.

"Is it John?" she prompted softly.

Mutely, Ketti nodded.

"Can you talk about it, dear?" Mari remembered what it felt like to love a man she thought she couldn't have, as that was what had happened between her and Adam. Thank God we resolved it, she thought, as even now, so many years later, the memory of that time sent a stab of fear into her very soul. "Perhaps it would help," she added gently.

Still Ketti hesitated. Although she felt empty with loss of John's love, and didn't understand his motives, she didn't want to say anything to cause her parents to dislike him. It wasn't really a surprise to Ketti to finally admit to herself that she loved him more than ever. All her avoidance of the issue hadn't changed that.

With a long ragged breath she began, explaining his part in rescuing Siu from the highbinders, then how she'd gotten to know him on the ship, and finally how her feelings had grown into love. She omitted the fact of her intimacy with him, fearing her mother's disapproval of her... and John. When she finished, her mother looked thoughtful for long moments.

"I don't know what to tell you, darling," she said. "I respect John's judgment in not becoming betrothed until his financial picture is stable, but I, too, am puzzled by his involvement with Sarah."

Ketti's throat tightened, and she quickly looked out through the windows where she could see the sun had slid farther down the sky toward the ocean. A brilliant sunset was only a couple of hours away. A mountain range of clouds was spreading from the horizon, and Ketti had a fleeting worry that they might herald a winter storm by sailing time in the morning. Finally she met her mother's eyes, which were filled with compassion.

"Thanks for your concern, Mother," she said, her voice hardly more than a whisper.

"All you can do is go on with your own life, Ketti," Mari said. "And if your feelings for John are meant to be—then they will be." She got up and, moving around the table, she hugged her daughter. "I—your father and I—" she corrected herself "—want you to know that this is your home, and although you're off to teach in Honolulu, we welcome you back with us any time. And that means for always," Mari added, her voice lowered with emotion. "Because we love you very much."

They clung together, each one near tears. Ketti was the first to pull away. "Thank you, Mother. I love you and Father, too. And I appreciate that you care so much."

They walked to the doorway where Ketti paused. "And Mother?" As Mari waited, Ketti continued. "You won't say anything to anyone—about our conversation?"

"I promise."

Then Ketti went to play the piano one last time. Mari watched her go, her heart heavy. Please let things work out for Ketti too, Lord, she prayed to herself. But another random thought disconcerted her suddenly. No, she told herself. Ketti was *not* another victim of the old taboos.

But as she went to the kitchen with the tray, she was reminded that Ketti was more *haole* than Hawaiian. She shook off the morbid thoughts. The gods had been satisfied long ago.

Ketti stood next to the rail beside Siu, and they saw Char standing on the wharf long before they docked. Once the steamer was tied up, they went down the ramp to the grinning Char, dressed in a black suit, his hat in his hand.

"You look like a successful lawyer," Ketti joked. She took a deep breath of the fresh salt air, and glanced around the waterfront. Several stevedores looked back, admiration reflected in their eyes. It wasn't often that a beautiful girl in a blue velvet traveling suit that enhanced her slim, but curved figure, stepped off the steamer to brighten their day, if for only a few minutes. But Ketti didn't notice them, her attention on Char.

"Not successful yet," he replied seriously. "But I intend to be one of these days—with some help," he added, his glance warm on Siu, who was lovely in a new forest-green suit Ketti had insisted she accept. The Chinese girl was proud, but after Ketti explained Siu would need a few more clothes for her new job, she'd accepted gracefully, under the condition she repay Ketti when she could. Mindful of Siu's fierce pride, Ketti had agreed.

Char led them to his buggy, and helped them onto the seat. As he clucked at the horses and jerked the reins, Ketti realized that Char was already started on his path to success. The carriage was new.

Char detoured through Chinatown, pointing out the building where he'd rented space for his practice, then explained that the school was in the same building, one large room on the second floor. He told them that he would pick them up each morning, and either he or someone else would return them in the afternoon.

"I wanted the school near me, so I could help with any problems that might arise," he added in a tone that told Ketti what he really meant was that he'd be there to protect them.

They arrived at the home of Panana's parents, the stately two-story house with a sweeping view of the Pacific Ocean where Ketti had stayed with Charles and Panana to attend the ball. Kilia, Panana's mother, immediately came out to greet them, a matronly-looking woman dressed in black silk, whose once slim body had thickened with the years, whose black hair was now streaked with gray, but whose dark eyes still shone with all the vigor of youth. Kilia was cordial to Char, and Ketti again realized how kind most Hawaiians were, equally so to Oriental or white. After they said good-bye to Char, he left them, promising to return on Monday morning to take them to the first day of school.

Kilia showed them to their rooms, again treating Siu in the same manner as Ketti, while a servant brought their baggage. Once settled into her room, which was decorated in pale greens with dark furniture from France, Ketti went downstairs for afternoon tea, knowing Kilia wanted to hear all about her daughter's pregnancy. While Siu chose to unpack, Ketti sat in the formal drawing room, which was amazingly French, from its satin wallpaper and red velvet cushioned chairs and matching drapes, to its Louis XV furniture and porcelain lamps with fringed shades. Ketti filled her in on everything she could think of, and as she finished, Kilia smiled whimsically.

"It's such a blessing—I can't tell you," she said. "Your mother and I have been best friends for many years, and it's a special joy that our children are now joining us by blood. Mari and I will both be grandmothers to the same baby."

Ketti's own smile felt sad. Kilia's words about the baby had brought all her own hopes for family and children to the surface of her thoughts. And with them had come John. But she managed to finish her tea without revealing her upset, and was just about to return to her room for a bath when Kilia suddenly jumped up and ran to the mantel, where she took down several little envelopes.

"These came for you," she said, and handed Ketti the letters.

"But how on earth does anyone know I'm here? I only just arrived."

"News travels fast—with a little help." She grinned and arched her brows. "I let it out that you would be in Honolulu for the social season."

"And the social events are continuing? Even with all the political unrest, and the poor economy?"

For a second Kilia sobered. Then with a visible effort, she put the troubling thoughts aside for the moment. She nodded. "The queen believes that social life is important too. So it continues, even though times aren't as good as they could be."

At Kilia's urging, Ketti opened her mail to discover that each little envelope contained invitations to social events, the most important being a party at the palace on the following Saturday night. "I'm overwhelmed," Ketti told her hostess.

Kilia beamed. "I hope you don't mind, but I accepted on your behalf. It will be good for you to meet other people your own age, now that you'll be living in Honolulu. You'll go with us, that is, Martin and me. Alfred will be your escort."

Ketti only smiled agreement. She was fond of Panana's seventeen-year-old younger brother.

And despite her qualms about the political situation, which had reached a crisis point, and her sense of loss over John, Ketti found herself looking forward to the party. She had a perfect gown, one that she'd never worn before. And maybe she would meet people her own age, new friends who'd be a help in keeping her thoughts from John. Maybe she'd even get over him, she told herself. Because she knew she must, if she were never to be his.

Chapter Sixteen

John stood in the wide hallway and watched as the guests arrived. He'd been surprised by the invitation to the party, but in retrospect he realized that being included in the season's social events was only protocol; his mother had been of high birth and his Hawaiian grandparents had been highly respected in their day. A sad smile touched his lips. Jane, his mother, the woman he'd never known, had once been the belle of Honolulu society. Although a spoiled, only child of doting parents, she'd had a loving side as well, according to his father.

He sighed, and glanced around the small gathering of jeweled and gowned women and men in black formal attire. He'd glimpsed James, and figured the Californian was Ketti's escort, even though he hadn't as yet seen her. His invitation had included a guest, but he wasn't interested in being a partner to any woman other than Ketti. A terrible ache tightened his stomach, one that had become chronic since he'd heard from the reverend that she was engaged to James. He still couldn't believe it, although all indications had pointed to that happening. He'd believed that she loved him—only him—and would be patient until he was in a financial position to marry her. But she obviously still cared for James, after all. John's face suddenly felt tight from the depth of his anger with her for fooling him—for playing with his emotions.

A moment later he was able to leash his feelings, so that his expression was a correct one for socializing with the most important people in Hawaii. He knew Ketti was in Honolulu, and why, and that she would be in attendance tonight. That was the reason he was here. He meant to show her whom she loved—and then send her back to James, a family puppet who was contributing to the political unrest in the islands. When he was done with Ketti, she'd never forget him. He meant to show her how it felt to lose the only person she'd ever love... him. And then he saw her.

She stood at the top of the steps, every inch a Hawaiian princess, although her delicate features and pale skin were so like her mother's. The lights from the chandeliers shone on her hair, which was swept up into a confection of curls interwoven with a garland of tiny red flowers. Diamonds and rubies sparkled on her neck and wrist, but it was the dramatic splash of her crimson silk gown that drew the eyes of the people below. Low-cut and sleeveless, it revealed the upper curves of her full breasts, molded her bodice and tiny waist and swept to the floor in a wide bell shape of shimmering material. She was the most beautiful woman present, and a glance at the admiring crowd told John that everyone realized that at once.

Ketti was unaware of the sensation she was creating. Alfred, her young escort, stood waiting for her at the bottom of the steps. She smiled at him. Although he was almost three years younger, she and Panana had often included him in their childhood games. He was good company, if a bit immature.

About to start down the stairs, she hesitated, her gaze moving from the tall man leaning against the wall to the one who looked up from a conversation with Kilia and Martin. John and James, and neither had a woman at his side. A flood of confused emotions struck Ketti, and she shivered nervously. She hadn't expected to see either of them, and she was suddenly unsure how to react. So she lifted her chin, then her skirts, so that she could move down the steps without tripping. She kept her eyes on Alfred while she tried to gather her ragged feelings and decide on a course of action.

She was saved having to do anything by the announcement that dinner was served. Small tables had been set all over the dining room, and Ketti was relieved when she was seated with Alfred and his parents at a table across the room from both James and John. But all during the long meal—which began with mock turtle soup, then proceeded through fish, poultry and meat courses with potatoes and vegetables, pudding, ice cream and fruit, and ended with coffee and liqueurs—Ketti was conscious of their eyes on her. She kept her own gaze averted, and only picked at the feast everyone else found delicious. She wanted no part of James, and her feelings for John were so close to the surface that she feared he'd see them reflected in her eyes.

At last the long meal was over and Ketti moved with the other guests to the ballroom. A small string band was already playing, and she couldn't help but notice that the room was not elaborately decorated as it had been for the ball. Nevertheless, it was lovely with garlands of flowers and greenery draped along the walls. She and Alfred were immediately surrounded by young people—men who wanted to secure a later dance with her, and a few girls who glanced shyly at her young escort. But before she and Alfred did their first duty dance, John appeared at her side, his eyes glinting silver fire, his expression unreadable. In silence he drew her arm through his and led her onto the dance floor. Several steps behind him James paused in midstep, anger distorting his features as he saw John claim her.

The situation seemed unreal to Ketti. It amazed her that she hadn't even uttered a protest at John's boldness. He pulled her close, and they began the slow waltz. She felt his leg muscles move against hers, felt the strength of his shoulder under her hand, and heard the steady beating of his heart as the top of her head lay against the hollow of his throat, her breasts crushed against his chest.

"Oh Ketti, Ketti," he murmured against her hair. "Why did you do it?"

She lifted her head to meet his eyes, for a second puzzled by his words. "What?" she whispered simply.

He looked into her sweet face, and wondered at her deceit. Although he realized she wasn't with James tonight, had indeed snubbed James, he couldn't figure out her motives. He'd seen her at the annexation meeting with the man, knew he was a frequent guest at the Foster ranch and had heard she was engaged to him. What puzzled John was why she wasn't with James tonight. Was it possible that she was fickle? A temptress who lost interest in a man once she had his commitment of love? But that description went against all his instincts about her, he argued. But then, what was he to believe? The Reverend Mead, for all his narrow-minded ways, didn't lie.

His eyelids lowered to veil his eyes, and he stiffened his resolve. "James," he said, and his tone dripped ice. "And your alliance to him."

She was stung by the harshness in his voice. "What about yours to Sarah?" she flung at him, so upset all at once that she missed a step.

Instantly his arms tightened, steadying her, but his words retained their censure. "I have no alliance to Sarah!" he retorted. "I don't love Sarah, as I once told you, and I've never encouraged her feelings—I'll never marry her!"

"But I saw you with her and—"

"And nothing," he interrupted. "There's nothing more to it. Not like you and James," he added hotly.

"James and I?" Ketti began to explain but he cut her off again before she was able to tell him that he misunderstood. She suddenly knew that the awful reverend must have told John what James had said that day—that she was engaged to him.

"Shh," he whispered, and pulled her even closer, as though he didn't want to hear any more upsetting news.

"Everything has already been said," he murmured against her hair, and she couldn't see the pain in his eyes.

"No," she protested, and knew that she must pin him down to a time to discuss everything, or she might never have a chance to explain. "If not now, then when can we talk—when we won't be interrupted?"

For seconds he was silent, digesting her words. He wondered what kind of game she was playing. Well, he could play, too.

"Tomorrow is Sunday. Can you meet me on the beach by my cottage at noon?"

She was quiet in his arms, for a great load of sorrow was suddenly lifting from her spirit. She would be there if she had to walk. She nodded against his chest, unable to lift her eyes, which threatened tears of relief. He wasn't involved with Sarah, and now everything could be made right between them.

As the music slowed and stopped, he dropped a kiss on her nose, gave her a long searching look and then escorted her back to the men awaiting their turn to dance. "Until tomorrow then," he said, and strode off.

But his final glance troubled Ketti. It had almost seemed calculating, as though he believed she had lied to him. And all during the evening it haunted her. He, like James, had left early. She'd managed to avoid James, and knew he was angry, but she didn't care. She owed him nothing.

Then it occurred to her what might be troubling John. She'd forgotten to clarify her relationship to James. Good God! she thought. John still believes I'm engaged to James.

Her upset was only calmed by the knowledge that she would have the chance to explain everything tomorrow. Her body tingled with the thought of being with John. And she didn't doubt for one minute that she'd soon be back with the man she loved.

It wasn't difficult to find an excuse to be gone for the afternoon, as Kilia knew how much Ketti loved to go riding.

The day was cloudy, with a storm threatening on the horizon. As she rode, the wind came up with a vengeance, whipping at her hair and flapping the green material of her divided skirt. By the time she reached the beach, the surf was high, driven by the wind off the ocean, and its thunderous pounding filled her ears. She headed along the curve of Waikiki, and as she approached the rock where she'd met John that day, the first drops of rain splattered onto the sand.

As she reined up, John suddenly appeared, and it was obvious that he'd been watching for her. He led her and the horse along the path to the cottage. Once there he helped her dismount, then put the stallion in the stable a short distance away. In seconds he was back, just as the sky opened in a downpour of rain. He grabbed her hand and they ran toward the veranda, getting there before they were completely soaked.

He hesitated by the front door, and then looked her full in the face for the first time. She stared back, liking what she saw: his tan shirt was wet and clinging to his broad shoulders, and his snug brown pants molded the long muscled length of his legs. But it was his eyes that held her, blue and intense in the dark afternoon. And something else was reflected there, she thought. There was something about the quality of his look she couldn't identify—something that verged on . . . hostility? She dismissed the random thought as being a sign of her own nervousness.

"Come in, Ketti." His tone was low, as though he held his feelings in abeyance by sheer willpower. His eyelids shuttered his gaze so she couldn't read his thoughts. He held the door for her.

She nodded, suddenly shy, because he seemed somehow different. But how? she asked herself as she preceded him into the cottage. Maybe he, too, felt awkward, she thought. The tiny entry immediately opened into a large room overlooking the furious ocean, and it was comfortably furnished with chairs and end tables and a settee, all worn from years of use. A deep-piled Oriental rug covered the floor, extending all the way to a lava-stone fireplace where John had lit a fire. A tray containing brandy and two glasses stood on a side table nearby.

"Take off your jacket," he told her, and his voice sounded vaguely different, too. If Ketti hadn't known better she might have thought he was about to seduce her. "So it can dry out."

He went to her, his eyes unwavering from hers, compelling, with something in their depths that was hard to define. He helped her out of the jacket, and his hands seemed to linger on her upper arms, and accidently brush over the points of her breasts, which were suddenly trembling under her blouse.

"And the hat?" Before she could remove the perky little toque she'd fastened in place with two long gold hatpins, he'd pulled them out, and somehow loosened her hair, which had been pinned up into a Grecian knot. It tumbled down her back in soft waves. Ketti stepped away from him, and managed not to look startled.

Then he motioned her to the settee, and took the chair opposite where he could watch her. She licked her lips nervously. Although he was the perfect host, there was an intangible barrier between them, something she'd never felt before—something almost dangerous. And then she remembered how she'd felt that day in San Francisco—that he was a dangerous man if crossed. But I haven't crossed him, she reminded herself.

Ketti forced herself to remain unflustered by his regard, which took in every curve and angle of her, each change of expression; he even watched her tongue when she licked her lips. She knotted her hands in her lap, and tried to think of how to begin the conversation. She hadn't realized it would be so difficult, but then she was seeing a side to John she'd only glimpsed in the past. Why was he making it so hard for her? she wondered suddenly.

A slow smile quirked the corners of his lips, as though he sensed her discomfiture. But before she could examine his expression further, he turned away to pour brandy into the two glasses.

"I—I don't care for any," she said, horrified that she stuttered.

"Nonsense," he replied, his lowered eyelids belying his cool tone. A second later he handed her the glass of amber liquid and sat down next to her.

Completely disconcerted now, Ketti took a quick sip, and as the brandy burned her throat, she managed to stifle a choking sensation. The fire crackled in the fireplace, sending its sounds to fill the room, and the silence between Ketti and John. She was aware that his eyes never wavered from her, and a glance at him brought the color to her cheeks. The blue of his eyes reflected the fire, and gave him the look of a man filled with desire for his woman—blazing with the passion that suddenly trembled on the still air between them.

John tossed back the brandy in one swallow and placed the empty glass on the table. Then his hand covered Ketti's, urging her to finish. "Drink it, sweetheart," he crooned, and his voice seduced her. "It'll warm you."

She sipped until she finished, aware that he watched, that he'd moved closer, until their legs touched. He took her empty glass and set it with his. When he turned back he was even closer, and then his hands were on her arms, drawing her to him. She leaned back, suddenly unsure. She'd come to talk first, and then—maybe—make love, she admitted to herself. But John didn't seem inclined to talk, and again she wondered why he was so different.

"John—wait. We must talk. I have things to tell you."

For a second he stiffened, the infinite blue of his eyes probing her brown ones, as though he were trying to make up his mind to something important. Then it was as if a curtain dropped over his doubts, and his face set determinedly.

"Not now, my darling. Later is soon enough." Now was not the time to hear her tell him that she was betrothed to another, John decided grimly. First he had to have her one more time. He wouldn't allow the afternoon to be spoiled by her confession of changed feelings.

Abruptly a fork of lightning lit the room, and the crash of thunder that followed was deafening. She jumped, and instantly she was pulled into John's arms. He whispered soothing words against her hair, quieting her fears, letting her feel his strength, while he held her softness. When his lips moved lower to feather her face with kisses, and when his mouth claimed hers, his tongue thrusting inside between her lips, her whole body felt as if it ignited in flames. The slow throbbing sensations were already beginning in the warm place between her thighs.

With a cry of surrender, she knew she was lost, that she could deny him nothing. As in times past, the talking was forgotten in the indistinguishable sounds of love and mounting passion. They clung, caressing and stroking, their mouths hungry for the taste of the other. The settee was awkward, so they slid to the carpet in front of the fire, adding their shadows to the reflected flame patterns that licked and flickered outward from the hearth.

Slowly, John unbuttoned her blouse, gazing in wonder when the white globes of her breasts were free to his eager eyes, and to his tongue that nibbled and licked each nipple into an erection. Ketti moaned, her flesh on fire, her veins tingling with remembered sensation. He gently removed her skirt and underthings, so that she lay naked before him, her long lashes drooping with desire, and her breath quickened so that she could only pant with an undeniable urge to enfold him, to be one with him. When he touched the *V* between her thighs, she felt the warmth of her own wetness. She grasped his head, pulling him to her, touching the crispness of his hair under her fingers, crying out when his lips once more took her to heights of ecstasy.

"John, John," she moaned. "Oh, dear God, it's been too long."

Her plea for his love was more than he could stand. His urge to possess her completely took hold of him. He stood above her, staring down with an intense all-consuming gaze, as he tossed aside first his shirt, then his boots and trousers. For a moment he hesitated, his powerful form, his primitive masculine beauty, his taut muscles and male hardness illuminated in the glow of the fire behind him. But the urgent need that clouded Ketti's eyes, that begged for his manhood, took John's final compunction from what he was about to do: make love to another man's woman.

"You belong to me, Ketti." His voice, husky and low, was colored by his intense need. "For now, you are only mine."

He lowered himself to cover her body with his own. He felt her arch to him, so that she pressed her breasts into his chest. He wanted to possess her more than he'd ever wanted anything, but he found himself prolonging the act, wanting it to last. He licked her, from her mouth to her feet, until she writhed and twisted and squirmed with a desire that could not be contained. Her own tongue moved over him, stroking and flicking down his neck, to pause where his pulse throbbed in his chest. Then lower to the hard buds on his chest, enticing and seducing, and when John could hardly catch his breath, Ketti continued to move down, tracing fire over his belly to go lower still.

Outside, trees and bushes twisted in their own agony, from a wind that ebbed and flowed through their branches. Rain lashed the house, pounding the roof and dropping down the chimney to sizzle in the leaping fire. But the storm outside was only background to the crescendo of rising, ever rising passion, between the man and woman.

John could stand to wait no longer. His mouth returned to Ketti's, savage now, as though he'd become a part of the elements raging outside. Her legs moved apart from him, and he thrust himself inside her. They moved together; she held him with her tightness, and her heat only drove him faster. Each thrust took her higher, higher than he'd ever taken her before. Her mind slipped into an oblivion where there was only sensation straining for release. She shook with it, until she felt the high pitch of her essence—the place that reminded her of how the highest note on the scale would feel if it were translated from sound to sensation. She throbbed with sudden contractions that flowed into her upper legs and lower stomach, followed by a rush of wetness. Her cries were muffled under John's lips.

And then he, too, shuddered and groaned with his own climax, spilling more wetness into her. Spent, they lay together, their bodies still joined by the intense experience. Ketti was the first to speak, her voice low with the passion that had gentled into peace and total fulfillment.

"I love you, John. Only you. I'm not betrothed to James, and I never was." The words that had been so hard to say earlier now dropped from her lips naturally.

He propped himself on one elbow, his eyes filled with wonderment—and something else. Surprise? she wondered lazily, and reached to trace his beloved features with the tip of a finger.

"Why didn't you tell me?" he demanded, but he realized that his anger with her was gone. He'd made love to her believing she belonged to James, so he could make her sorry, so she'd remember him always…with regret. And it was all unnecessary. There was no need for a talk after all.

But as they lay side by side, the heat of the fire warming them after the heat of passion passed, they did talk—for a whole hour—until all questions between them had been answered. He even admitted his motive had been to seduce her today, one last time. Ketti only smiled, too sated to be angry about anything he said.

"We still can't marry for a while," he told her finally. "Until this thing is settled about annexation."

"But I'll have a dowry," she said softly.

"I want you, not your dowry." For a second his eyes glinted with conviction. "That was once my father's goal, but it's not mine. And since it's not, I won't accept a dowry from you. If it's traditional in your family, then you'll just have to put it in trust for our children."

God, how she loved him, this proud, independent man. Her mouth parted seductively, and she pulled his lips onto hers. He groaned, his desire for her growing in him again.

"Earlier I believed I was making love to another man's woman. This time I'm making love to *my* woman."

And he proceeded to do so.

Chapter Seventeen

"To our future," Adam said, and lifted his glass of brandy.

"And to the future of Hawaii," Mari added.

Ketti's family and John all drank to the toast. It was New Year's Eve, and the cabinet clock on the mantel had just gonged midnight. Even her grandmother had stayed up to welcome 1893, a year everyone hoped would resolve the political unrest and economic depression in their country.

Placing her glass on a table, Ketti glanced at John, and smiled. He'd come to their holiday dinner and spent the evening, but he had to leave again the next morning. Although they'd straightened out their feelings for each other, they were still not formally betrothed, even though John's private conversation with Adam had clarified their intentions for the future—that he and Ketti planned to marry after John knew he was on more secure financial ground.

Glancing around her family, Ketti silently reaffirmed her devotion to all of them. Panana and Charles were so obviously in love, so thrilled that they would soon be parents. She couldn't help but think the love between her parents had set a good example for their son and daughter, who had both chosen a mate out of love, not for any other selfish motive. Ketti could hardly wait for the day when she, too, would be a wife, John's wife. And be with him each day...and night. She scolded herself lightly for allowing her aching need of him to fill her every thought. She'd only seen him once since the afternoon at his cottage, on Christmas when he'd brought her a present—a cameo brooch that had belonged to his mother. He'd spent the day with the Fosters, and that was when he'd spoken to Adam. He'd left with a promise to return for New Year's Eve.

Even though she hadn't seen John again in Honolulu, she'd been so busy with her classes during the day and correcting papers at night that the time had passed quickly. John had written several times, and his letters, filled with news of his meetings and progress on his plantation, had sustained her. All John needed was a stable economy for his business to warrant his investment. She'd looked forward to the holidays on the Big Island with her family, and John, who'd fulfilled his promise to see her then—and have a talk with her father. Siu had stayed in Honolulu, planning to spend her free time with Char and his relatives, who'd grown fond of the Chinese girl.

The talk swirled around her as her thoughts spun through her mind. She stood up with the others as her grandmother went off to bed, and her brother and sister-in-law left for their own house. Her parents lingered for a few minutes more, and then they too said their good-nights and went upstairs, leaving Ketti alone with John.

The flames in the fireplace had burned down to embers, and the gas lamps were on a low wick, so that the light in the salon was soft. John moved next to her on the settee and took her hands in his. He'd noticed that she wore his brooch on the high neck of her green velvet dress, and as she sat in the flickering light, with her upswept hair, her cheeks tinged with the heat of the fire and her long lashes lowered, he was reminded of how much she'd come to mean to him.

"You know I talked to your father."

She met his eyes, and nodded. "Yes, and whatever you told him, he seemed impressed." She hesitated. "I think both of my parents approve of you."

He grinned, his eyes crinkling with pleasure. He'd never looked more handsome, she thought. So completely a man who knew what he wanted. "They'd better. Or we'll just have to elope when the time comes to marry."

Her smile stiffened despite her resolve to be patient. "And when will that be, John?"

"By spring, perhaps, no later than summer, whatever happens."

"I do have a dowry."

He pulled her into his arms and kissed her lightly on the mouth before murmuring against her lips. "But you remember what I said about that, darling. If the family insists on the dowry, then it either stays yours, or goes into trust for our children."

Her lashes fluttered as his words sent a wave of pleasure through her. "Our children," she said, her tone filled with wonderment at the thought of it. "Half you and half me."

His eyes darkened in a way that quickened her pulse. Then he kissed her until she could have swooned in his arms, weak with the longing his touch always evoked in her. She couldn't resist him. Ketti forgot that they were in the salon of her parents' house, that anyone could walk in on them. She wanted only the completeness of their love. It was John who broke away first.

"This is not the time," he told her. "I don't want your father to throw me out, not after our frank talk where I convinced him my intentions were honorable." He dropped another kiss on her nose, a playful kiss that took some of the sensual tension from the room.

Ketti straightened her skirt and stood up with John. He was quite right; it wasn't the time or place. But it was so hard to wait. She walked with him to the front door, and lifted her face for his kiss good-night. After a long meaningful look that held all the promise for their future, he went out to the bunkhouse where he'd chosen to stay, rather than in a guest room. He'd explained he felt it more appropriate, and her father had agreed. Ketti could tell that her father's respect for John was growing each time the two men were together.

As Ketti turned off the lights in the salon, she was thoughtful. John was a great deal like her father, she realized, a man with pride and honor and a sense of propriety. Then her mind shifted, and she pondered a possible time for her marriage. No date had been set, and once she was away from John, a niggling fear set in. Maybe the sugar crisis would never be solved—and then what? Shouldn't they set a date anyway? She couldn't completely understand why not. Didn't he realize that she'd marry him even if it meant living in a shack?

She sighed deeply, and slowly mounted the steps to her bedroom. She knew John loved her. But what if they never married after all? The thought shook her, and she forced it away. The day after tomorrow she was returning to her school in Honolulu. She'd concentrate on that—and the spring as John said. That was still several months away, and everything could be settled by then.

"Queen Liliuokalani has been overthrown!" a man's voice cried from the street below where Ketti stood in the classroom. The Chinese students, mostly men, glanced up from their studies; even if they did not understand the English words, the urgency in the tone was unmistakable.

"Sanford Dole has been named president of the new provisional government!" someone else hollered back.

Ketti ran to the window and saw there was a crowd of Chinese men in the narrow street, clustered around five white men on horseback. As she watched, Char strode out to join them, explaining to the Chinese in their own language what had happened. Then everyone was talking at once.

Ketti couldn't believe it. The queen couldn't have been overthrown. What that would mean was unimaginable—Hawaii without the monarchy? She, like everyone else, had been fearful that a revolution was unavoidable, especially after the queen had proposed a new constitution, and had reinstated the hotly debated licensing of opium.

Her sixteen students and Siu joined her at the windows. "Is it true?" Siu asked, putting into words what everyone was thinking.

"I don't know," Ketti replied, nervously fingering her cameo brooch on the ruffled neckline of her white blouse. But she secretly feared it was. Hadn't American troops come ashore from the *Boston,* which was anchored in the harbor? She'd heard that 162 marines had landed by five o'clock last night, and that they'd been quartered at Arion Hall near the palace.

It's really happened, she thought in dismay. She'd hoped that Queen Liliuokalani could continue to reign, if not rule. Suddenly the full impact of the event hit her. She whirled away from the window to face the class. She clapped her hands for attention and quickly dismissed her students for the day. Then she and Siu went downstairs and out onto the street.

By then people were swarming everywhere, and more riders had appeared on the scene, but the newcomers were obviously opposed to the revolution, whereas the first group had been jubilant about a new regime. She explained to Char that she must return home, so she could learn what had happened.

"Don't go yet, Ketti," he told her. "Not until I can find out whether it's safe to do so." Although Char had been in favor of political change, even he looked worried. He took her arm, gently restraining her, while he spoke to several of the men, who gave him the information he was seeking.

"It's a bloodless coup so far," he said tersely, dropping his hand. "But I think you should wait until I'm able to drive you back."

She shook her head, and knew she had to go at once. Her whole world was upside down. And there was her family, Kilia and Martin . . . and John, who'd sent word he was arriving today. She had to know everyone was safe.

"I don't want either you or Siu to go," he said, his tone hardening when he saw the determined expression on Ketti's face. He dropped an arm around Siu's shoulders. "It would be dangerous for Siu, at least. Many people are blaming the Chinese for some of the trouble, that immigration from China should have been limited and thus legalizing opium wouldn't have been an issue."

"Siu must stay with you," Ketti replied at once. "But I have to go."

Seeing that he couldn't stop her, Char finally nodded. "But you'll never get through the crowd on a horse."

She glanced around wildly, and saw that he was right. At least in Chinatown the streets were packed with people. "I'll walk then," she said, and before he could say anything else, she'd turned away in a swirl of her black woolen skirt, and was soon swallowed by the crowd. She didn't fear being unescorted in Chinatown. She felt accepted there, as the people had come to expect seeing her. Often the women would smile, the men bow respectfully with a polite "Tee-chur" as she passed, their usually enigmatic faces showing their appreciation.

She'd gone only a short distance before she was stopped, this time by two roughly dressed men who'd been drinking. They came out of a saloon and almost bumped into her as she hurried along the walk.

"Hey, lookee here!" one of the louts cried, grabbing her arm. "It's that schoolmarm who's been teaching them Chinese!"

"Yeah," the other one chimed in. "Helping 'em get uppity. Next thing we know, they'll be taking over the islands."

"Let go of me!" Ketti tried to twist away, but the man's fingers only tightened. Several Chinese people watched, startled and undecided about how to help her. Then she saw one of her students, a young man in his early twenties. As their eyes met, she saw the resolve form on his face a second before he stepped forward.

"Leave Miss Foster alone!" he told the bullies.

"Go to hell!" the bigger man retorted, and elbowed the slightly built young man so hard that he fell.

"Damn opium eaters!" the other man chimed in. "We don't need their kind in Hawaii."

"You—you louts!" Ketti cried angrily. "Unhand me at once!"

The man sneered into her face, his breath strong with the stench of rum. "Says who, little lady?"

"I say!" Another man's voice rang out behind them. Then John, head and shoulders above the crowd, strode forward, the Chinese gladly stepping aside to let him pass.

"Ain't none of your business!" the man holding Ketti retorted. "This here woman has no business teaching Chinese peasants how to read and write. It ain't proper!"

John hesitated only a second, and when the man didn't respond, he grabbed him and shoved him aside. Instantly the Chinese men crowded closer, and the two troublemakers realized they were outnumbered. They muttered under their breath and glared at John, but they backed off, and soon disappeared into the crowd.

Ketti ran to her student who was struggling to his feet. He smiled weakly, and assured her that he was fine, if shaken up. Then John took her hand, and she turned to face him, a grateful smile already forming on her lips. But it froze. His eyes glinted like sun on ice. His anger was hardly contained—and it was directed at her.

"Come on," he said, as he pushed his way back through the crowd, pulling her along behind him. "Let's get out of here."

"Wait!" Ketti cried, suddenly annoyed by his highhanded attitude. She pulled her hand free just as they reached his horse, which was tied to a hitching post. "There's no need to rush like this. What's the matter with you?"

His body went still, and then he slowly faced her. "For God's sake, Ketti! Don't you have sense enough to know that you were in danger? Those men wouldn't have let you go if I hadn't caught up with you."

His tone was harsh and cutting and she resented it. He was treating her like a child. She tilted her chin. "The Chinese people would have stopped them." But even as she said it, she knew it wasn't true. They wouldn't dare, for fear of bringing down the law on themselves, perhaps landing in jail, or worse yet, being sent back to China.

"Don't be a child, Ketti." He still sounded upset, and she suddenly realized he'd been afraid for her. Her annoyance slipped away, but it returned in force at his next words. "You should know better than going unescorted on the streets of Chinatown. It was a stupid thing to do!"

Her face flushed with indignation. "I was only—"

He suddenly grabbed her shoulders and pulled her to him, the unexpected action stopping her protest. "If Char hadn't told me that you'd left, God only knows what could have happened to you...." John's words trailed off.

"Jesus! What am I to do with you?" He tightened his hold, until she was pressed to him, his face only inches away from hers. "Do you know that I worry constantly about what you'll do next to land you in trouble. I swear, Ketti Foster, you need a keeper."

His tone had softened, and the stiff set to his body had relaxed. A hesitant smile touched her lips. "Then you're not still angry?"

Little flames ignited in his eyes, silvering them with an emotion that sent that same fire licking through her veins. And then he did something in total defiance of social convention—he kissed her in public. For a second Ketti's eyes widened in shock, and she saw the expression reflected on the Oriental faces around them. But a moment later her lashes fluttered down, and she gave herself to the pleasure of his mouth.

As quick as his action was, his next one was even faster. With a swoop of motion he placed her on his horse, then leaped up behind her. A moment later the animal was headed away from Chinatown. Ketti leaned her head back against John's chest, content for the time being. But she couldn't help but wonder what would happen next for her beloved islands.

Her musings brought another thought. Annexation could make all the difference in the faltering sugar industry. And if that happened, John would feel free to marry.

They'd hardly dismounted at Kilia's house, when another horseman turned into the driveway. As the hatless rider drew closer, Ketti saw it was Char. His mount came to a sudden halt, almost unseating her Chinese friend, who immediately dismounted too.

"What are you doing here, Char?" Ketti cried. "Siu is all right, isn't she?"

He nodded, his black hair mussed from his headlong ride. "I had to make sure you'd gotten home safely," he informed her. "I was worried." Then, realizing Ketti's concern for Siu, he went on, "I left Siu with my family. I didn't want her on the street. We don't know what will happen next—or if some people will be angry with the Chinese."

"Why would they be?" Ketti retorted at once.

"Because there are people who get frustrated when things turn out badly for them—and they pick on those who can't fight back," John replied for Char.

Char nodded. "Exactly."

A silence fell between them, and Ketti suddenly realized that no one had come out to greet them. Then the housekeeper appeared in the doorway. "The mistress has gone with her husband to the queen's private residence," she told Ketti, and held the door for them to enter the house.

"Please bring tea to the drawing room," Ketti told her, and the woman immediately went to the kitchen. A few minutes later she brought the serving tray, and Ketti poured for the two men, who'd taken chairs opposite her.

Char was the first to speak. "The revolution today has left a big impression on me," he began. "Although I believed it would happen, the reality is shocking."

Both Ketti and John only nodded, feeling much the same.

"And I know it can mean a better future for my people, give them greater opportunities—education, even professions like medicine and law," he went on. "But change is also frightening." His gaze met Ketti's. "And it makes me realize the importance of some things, like the issue I wish to speak with you about now."

Momentarily startled by Char's sudden shift in the conversation, Ketti could only incline her head, and wait for him to continue. But he hesitated, and she suddenly realized he felt awkward. Puzzled, she prompted him gently. "What is it, Char?"

Ketti was aware that John shared her interest in what Char was about to say. As Char still hesitated, John finally spoke. "Perhaps you'd like to speak in private, and I—"

Char waved a hand. "No, John. I don't mind that you hear—you were involved in the beginning, too."

As Char glanced down, Ketti and John exchanged glances. Abruptly, Char looked up, his dark eyes direct on Ketti. "I want to buy Siu. So I can ask her to be my wife. I need to know she is safe in my own home."

For a second Ketti was taken aback by Char's words; sudden anger pricked her that he could ask such a thing. "Siu isn't for sale!" she retorted.

His eyes widened in disbelief. He'd thought he knew Ketti, that she would understand his love for Siu, especially since she was so obviously in love herself—with John, who looked equally incredulous.

"My God, Char!" she went on indignantly. "You've known me since I was born. How could you ask such a thing?" She took a quick breath. "I can't *sell* Siu because she's a free person, and whether or not she marries you is up to her!"

Char only stared for a moment, and as her explanation
sank in, he grinned. Then he let out a whoop of joy, so unexpected from the usually serious Char, that both John and
Ketti laughed, too, breaking the tension that had briefly
settled over the room.

"A new day has really come!" he cried, hugging Ketti and
shaking John's hand. Then he took his leave and hurried
outside. He jumped back on his horse, wheeling it around.
As he jerked the reins and the animal leaped forward, he
called over his shoulder. "You'll both be invited to the
wedding!"

A private Chinese ceremony was held in the parlor of
Char's uncle's house a week later, followed by a Christian
wedding that evening. Char wanted to adhere to family traditions, but he also recognized the changes coming to his
people, and therefore wanted his marriage to be in accord-
ance with Hawaiian law. Ketti and John attended the second service, John acting as best man and Ketti as
bridesmaid.

As Ketti listened to the minister she glanced at John, who
stood tall and handsome in his formal black suit. Candlelight glinted on his sandy hair and cast his strong features
into shadowy lines and hollows; his startling blue eyes reflected the glow. Ketti longed for her own wedding, and
wished John would act in as sudden a manner as Char had
done with Siu. But then, she also recognized that Char saw
his future as secure, whereas everyone in the sugar industry
was still waiting for word that the United States would an-
nex Hawaii as a territory.

The minister, a slight man in black, his Bible open in his
hands, spoke in a low drone, but the bride and groom
seemed oblivious of his joyless manner. Siu was radiant in
a white satin gown trimmed with lace and a matching veil
ornamented with ribbons and a circle of delicate white
flowers; Ketti had given the apparel as her wedding gift to
her friends. Char was dressed in the traditional black.

Then the minister pronounced them man and wife. As the groom kissed the bride, a pleased smile touched Ketti's lips, and she was unaware that John's eyes caressed her approvingly. She stood in a pool of candlelight, her eyes sparkling her pleasure. Her pink silk gown, simple in its cut, molded her breasts and waist, and fell in soft folds to the tips of her pink satin slippers. The color of her gown was reflected in her cheeks, and in the garland of flowers around her head. Her black hair hung in a shimmer of waves down her back. John had never seen her look so lovely—or so desirable. He only wished it was their wedding, that Ketti was his to have and hold forever.

Soon, he told himself. As much as he grieved for the lost monarchy, and hoped the United States would reestablish the queen, if only in name, he longed for annexation, which would guarantee the Hawaiian economy—and his plantation's success.

After the ceremony, the wedding party moved into the small dining room where refreshments and toasts were to take place. A short time later, as the bride and groom were being congratulated, John pulled Ketti out into the garden and led her to the far end near the high board fence, where they were sheltered by a fragrant tree heavy with lush white flowers.

He turned her to him, the light from the Chinese lanterns that had been strung throughout the tiny, formal garden burning in his eyes; Ketti was caught by their fire, by the passion she saw reflected in his expression. Above him, a moon lit the sky, gilding frothy, high-flying clouds with a magical brilliance. But the night and all its beauty were only passing thoughts to Ketti. It was John and his thrilling touch that occupied her mind with the promise of more.

"You're so beautiful," he whispered. "I love you... everything about you. Your courage, your loveliness and your generosity of spirit."

"Oh, John," she murmured. "And I love you—so much it makes me ache with it."

He pulled her closer, but he tried to hold his desire in check. His hand had begun to caress her bare arm, though; he couldn't help himself. "You made the wedding so perfect for Siu."

"But I did nothing," she protested.

He smiled, his eyes moving over her face in a way that tightened her thighs, and rippled little sensations into her groin. Slowly he shook his head, his well-defined lips curving into a smile.

"You saw to Siu's wedding dress and other clothes as well. Not to mention arranging for the minister and helping Char's family with the food."

Her eyes widened. "How did you know?" she whispered.

"Char," John replied. "He and Siu love you very much." He dropped a kiss on her nose. "Loving you seems to be contagious."

She swallowed hard. "I love them, too. They're very special, and I've been told that their first child is to be named after me."

John couldn't wait any longer. He lowered his mouth to hers, and for a long time they clung to each other. It was only the advent of other guests in the garden that finally separated them.

Later John drove Ketti home through the quiet streets of Honolulu. More than anything, she wanted him to take her to his cottage on Waikiki, but he didn't suspect it. And she knew it wasn't possible, anyway. Kilia had promised to wait up, anxious to hear the details of Siu's wedding. She and Martin hadn't been invited to the ceremony, as the house of Char's uncle was too small to accommodate more than his large family.

John halted the pair of bays in the driveway near the front entrance, and immediately the door flew open. Kilia stood framed in the doorway, a gas lamp in the hall backlighting her. Both Ketti and John answered her greeting, but Ketti was disappointed. Now she wouldn't even have a good-night kiss.

John jumped down and went around the buggy to help her to the ground. As she jumped the final step, he caught her in his arms and pulled her to him.

He hesitated for only a second, and then he kissed her, long and hard. "Sleep well, my love," he whispered as he lifted his head and put her away from him. "I'll see you soon."

And then he bounded back into the buggy, and with a cluck of his tongue and a jerk of reins, the wheels were once more moving on the rocky driveway, this time toward the street.

"Oh, my dear," Kilia said. "I'm so sorry I came out to greet you. Forgive a woman who's forgotten how young love feels." She dropped an arm around Ketti's shoulders, her eyes warm with affection, and they went into the house.

Over a cup of warm milk, Ketti described every detail of the wedding, but her thoughts were with John. He'd kissed her even though Kilia watched. Was it a foreshadowing of his proposal to her? she wondered. Because John would never compromise her before family or friends unless he was confident of their own marriage announcement, she told herself.

She seemed to float up the steps when she went to her room a short time later. And her heart was still singing when she finally went to sleep.

Chapter Eighteen

"I'm asking you to marry me."

Seconds before, James had gotten up from the chair where he'd been sitting across from Ketti, and moved to stand at the fireplace. He'd fixed her with a glazed stare before uttering his proposal. All Ketti could think of was her wish that Kilia and Martin had not left them alone in the drawing room, mistakenly allowing Ketti privacy to visit with the man they believed was an old family friend from California.

"C'mon, Ketti. I asked you to be my wife, to return to San Francisco with me." His words were edged with impatience. "Once you would have said yes immediately."

"That was a long time ago. Everything is changed now. I'm no longer a girl."

His eyes narrowed. "And now you're a woman?"

She glanced away, not bothering to answer. She didn't like the look of his rumpled suit and drawn face—as though he'd been wearing the same clothes for several days, and hadn't slept for as many nights. He'd already told her that he, along with several prominent businessmen, had been detained by officials of the new government, as they were suspected of plotting to restore the throne. He'd been released from lack of evidence, but had been ordered to leave Hawaii. Although he denied involvement in a plot, Ketti suspected he lied, as his family business interests would no longer monopolize the Hawaiian economy now that the monarchy had been overthrown.

With a quick motion, he pulled her out of the chair, holding her at arm's length so she had to meet his eyes. "Tell me why you're suddenly a woman?" he demanded angrily.

"None of your damn business!" She jerked herself free. "Please leave. We have nothing left to say!"

He stood glaring at her, conscious of the other people in the house, knowing that she had the upper hand. "It's John Stillman, isn't it? You're in love with John." His words were hardly more than a hiss.

She tilted her chin, her eyes filled with anger and disgust. "I asked you to leave, James," she told him coldly. "Am I to have you thrown out?"

Their eyes locked, and Ketti was determined not to look away first. She meant what she said.

He turned on his heel, grabbed up his hat and strode to the door, where he hesitated, his gaze darting back to hers. "You haven't heard the last of me," he said. "And neither has John Stillman!"

He left her then. Ketti slumped back in her chair, her bravado spent. Long after the front door slammed behind him, the image of his final vicious look stayed with her. She was glad he'd been ordered to leave Hawaii.

Char and Siu had gone to the Big Island on their wedding trip to visit Char's family, and had already been away for ten days. Ketti missed Siu's help in the classroom, and was glad that she and Char were due back any day. It was the end of the week, and as she dismissed class, she looked forward to the weekend ahead. John was taking her with him to a sugar plantation on Sunday, and she could hardly wait. Kilia had invited him for dinner tonight, and they would finalize their plans then.

Her students gone, she hurriedly gathered up her things and was about to leave, when someone spoke behind her.

"Hello, Ketti."

She turned from her desk to see James standing just inside the door. Instant alarm sent fear rippling down her spine. They were alone now that her students had left, and Char's office below had been locked up for a week. She managed a cool nod, and went on stacking her papers and books, pretending a nonchalance she was far from feeling. She heard him move forward until he was right behind her.

Her books in her arms, like a barrier to keep the distance between them, she faced him again. She contrived to stay expressionless, not allowing him to guess her discomfiture at his sudden appearance in her schoolroom. But the questions whirled in her mind. How had he known where she taught? And what on earth could have brought him there? She'd not seen him since the night he proposed almost a week ago. She was surprised that he hadn't left Hawaii yet. He was no longer the James of her girlish infatuation. The man before her looked desperate... and dangerous.

"You're looking well," he said, his tone low and controlled. But his eyes searched her up and down, from her hair knotted primly on her head to her high-necked, long-sleeved yellow print blouse, and down the length of her brown serge skirt that flared in a slight bell just above her feet.

Despite her resolve, Ketti's cheeks flamed in indignation, and she didn't respond to his dubious compliment. "I'm surprised to see you, James," she said coolly instead. "What brings you into Chinatown?" She glanced down to pick up a stack of papers on her desk. "I hadn't realized your family had business interests here."

In a flash he grabbed her, and the books and papers tumbled from her arms. He slammed her up against his chest. "Don't play games with me, Ketti!" he snarled. "It's far too late for that."

She twisted in his arms, but she couldn't free herself. "Let me go, James!" she cried, "or I'll scream for help."

His laugh was hardly more than a growl. "Go ahead," he taunted. "There's no one to hear you."

"What do you want?" Ketti's fear was growing. She wondered if he'd become unhinged; his eyes were wild, as though his darting glance couldn't settle anywhere for long.

His lips twisted into a smile and his eyelids lowered, repelling Ketti even further. "You," he replied hoarsely, and started moving with her toward the door.

"Let me go!" she cried again. "I insist that you take your hands off me."

He paid no attention to her demands, which continued all the way out to the hall and down the stairs. When they reached the front door, he paused. "You're going with me. My buggy is right outside the door."

"No, I'm not. You can't make me!" Her arm ached where his fingers dug into her flesh, and the more she struggled, the tighter he held her.

His brown eyes glinted with anger. "Yes, I can," he snapped. "If you cause a scene, and one of your little friends comes to your rescue—I'll shoot him!"

She drew in her breath sharply, as he showed her the handgun holstered under his coat.

Satisfied with her reaction, he continued on through the doorway, half dragging her beside him. Her blouse was pulled out of her waistband, and her hairpins scattered on the floor as her hair fell out of its chignon. Once outside, Ketti noticed three of her male students talking on the corner. They saw that something was wrong, and after a brief discussion, they started toward Ketti and James.

James came to an abrupt stop, his eyes on the men. "Tell them you're just fine," he whispered to Ketti. "Or they'll get hurt." When she hesitated, his tone hardened. "I'm not fooling, Ketti. I've got nothing to lose. The authorities are already looking for me."

She glanced at him, and realized he meant what he said. Already his hand was on the gun under his coat. Trying to control the tremor in her voice, she told the men that James was an old friend from California—that they'd just had a misunderstanding, but that she was going with him, and she'd see the students in class on Monday.

They paused, uncertain, their gazes darting back and forth between Ketti and James. For a second Ketti thought they would come forward anyway. She knew the pigtailed men had become very fond of her, one or more of them always making sure that she was safe in Chinatown.

"Please, it's all right." Her eyes beseeched them to stay back. But she caught a word or two of their language, and knew they had their doubts. Finally they stepped back, as though they knew James could be dangerous to Ketti as well as to them.

Then James pushed her into the buggy and climbed up beside her. He gave her another terse warning not to make any quick moves, like trying to jump out. "Or I'll shoot the closest person on the street," he told her. "Man, woman or child. And their blood will be on your hands."

With that final threat, he cracked the whip over the back of the horse, and the buggy lurched forward on the narrow street. A cold lump of fear settled in Ketti's stomach. Where was he taking her? She vowed to escape—as soon as they were beyond any human targets for James's gun. She just hoped she could, because she dared not imagine what his intentions were.

"John won't stand for this," she told him, dismayed that her voice shook. "When he catches up with you, you'll wish you'd never forced me into this buggy!"

He let out a whoop of laughter, so purely evil sounding that a chill ran down Ketti's spine. "Don't worry your pretty head about John riding to the rescue. He's not going anywhere for a while."

"You've hurt John!"

He shook his head, and darted her a glance filled with sadistic delight at her fears for the man she loved. "Not physically—although I'd like to get my fists on him." He shook his head. "No, John is quite safe, probably in jail even as I speak."

"You're a liar!"

His jaw tightened. "Perhaps you're right," he said, surprising her. "But not in the way you think. John was taken into custody, that's true. He's accused of being the person behind the plot to restore the throne. That was a little lie I told the authorities, confessed in a way they all believed. So I'm to leave on the next ship, while John is left behind to rot in jail."

"You—you bastard!"

He clucked his tongue, and rested one hand on her thigh. Immediately she flung it off her. "Keep your dirty hands off me!" she cried.

He glanced at her again, his expression so grim she hardly recognized him. "I can be patient, my love. I have no doubt that I'll have you licking my feet before we get back to California."

A new fear shook her. He was taking her to the ship. He meant to kidnap her!

Ketti knew it was now or never. They'd reached the wharf where the ship to California was docked. She braced herself, and when James jumped down to tie up the buggy, Ketti leaped to the ground on the opposite side. She was running toward the street before James realized what she'd done. Immediately he was after her. She screamed for help, but for once she saw no one on the waterfront, the ship being docked away from the main harbor traffic.

James grabbed her arm as she reached the street, and slammed her against him so hard that it took her breath. "You spitfire!" he cried, and slapped her face hard. "Don't try that again!"

Stunned for a second, she went limp in his arms. Vaguely she became aware of the sound of approaching horses, but couldn't command enough wind to even speak, let alone shout for help.

Then the horses were almost on top of them, and were reined in so fast that two of the riders were out of the sad-

dle before the horses had come to a complete stop. Ketti
hardly had time to blink before hands came down on James,
yanking him away from her, and then a fist connected with
his jaw and knocked him to the ground.

"John," she managed weakly, blinking back the tears
that came unbidden. "You came." As she swayed on un-
steady feet, John grabbed her and held her secure against his
body. She recognized Char and her three Chinese students
who'd watched James abduct her. Both John and Char
looked grim with anger.

James propped himself on an elbow and glared at John.
"You have no right to interfere. Ketti is mine," he whined.

She felt every muscle in John's body tighten. "You goddamned bastard!" John retorted dangerously. "I have every
right to interfere. Ketti is *my* woman—*my* future wife."
Ketti sensed that it took iron control for John to restrain
himself, for the angles of his face were set in hard lines, revealing the formidable side of his nature she'd seen several
times in the past. And his next words proved it. "I ought to
kill you for this. And I will, if you ever come within a mile
of Ketti again!"

"You won't have the chance!" James retorted. "You'll
be rotting in jail!"

John's face went white with anger, and again Ketti sensed
his momentary impulse to yank James up and hit him again.
"So it was you who accused me of plotting to restore the
throne." John hesitated, his eyes narrowed to slits. "I'm
sure you'll be pleased to know the matter has been resolved," he said coldly. "And no one believed you for one
minute, your own character being in such disrepute."

As Char and the other men helped James up and then
held him secure, Ketti snuggled closer to John, so relieved
that she wanted nothing more than to feel herself in his arms
forever. He'd announced his intentions toward her in front
of her students and Char. She belonged to him, and the
thought thrilled her with desire for him. And there was no
doubt in anyone's mind that John meant what he said to

James about staying away from "his woman." She'd always known he wasn't a man to back down to anyone. He was strong and sure of himself—and he was *her man*.

While she allowed herself to daydream, John was giving orders and Char was nodding agreement. Char and the other men would escort James to the ship and make sure he stayed on it until it cleared the harbor. Then John lifted Ketti into his arms, his eyes steely with resolve, and carried her to the buggy James had driven to the wharf. Once she was deposited on the seat and John sat beside her, he took up the reins and signaled the horse toward the street.

"James won't need the buggy," he told Char as they passed the men who'd disarmed James and were leading him to the ramp. "Would you take care of my horse? And please tell Kilia that I'll bring Ketti home later."

Char nodded, and Ketti glimpsed something else in his black eyes. Approval? she wondered. Of what John was about to do? Instantly her veins were singing with an ecstasy she'd been longing for... she welcomed it.

At that moment John drew her next to him. She realized where they were going... to his cottage.

The sound of wheels and hooves lulled Ketti; she was content to ride in silence, as John didn't appear in a mood to talk. The sun hovered just above the horizon, building toward a spectacular sunset. Brilliant ribbons of red and crimson and purple stretched across the western sky from the sinking globe of light, as the road took them along the ocean. At last they turned into the long driveway that twisted among the palms and shrubbery to the cottage. As the buggy stopped, John turned the full force of his eyes on her.

The ebbing day was suspended in the stillness of approaching night. Even the gentle trade wind had subsided in the palm fronds. It was as though everything around Ketti waited with her for John's next words.

"I didn't bring you here to make love," he said softly. "But to discuss our future."

For a second she was taken aback. Before she could ask any questions, voice a sudden fear that maybe he was angry with her after all, he jumped to the ground and helped her from the buggy. He led her onto the veranda and then into the house. The main parlor was much as she remembered, although there was a chill in the room. John motioned her to the settee, then bent to light the kindling under the logs in the fireplace. A few minutes later the flames crackled and light flickered into the shadowy room.

John poured brandy into two glasses and gave her one. He then sat on the other end of the settee. "It'll help calm your nerves," he told her.

His tone was low and controlled, but she sensed more behind his words. Did he blame her for being with James? Was he upset with her? A wave of doubts flooded her mind. Tears threatened and she realized she was still in shock over what James had tried to do—abduct her and force her to submit to his sexual advances. She shuddered, and then couldn't stop the little tremors that had taken hold of her whole body. She quickly sipped the strong liquor, and willed it to calm her nerves, and her fear of losing John. Oh Lord, she thought, she loved him so much, but there had been so many obstacles in their relationship that she couldn't stifle her sudden doubts.

John watched her changing expressions, trying to read her thoughts. Her black hair hung in disarray, framing the paleness of her face. Her long lashes were half-moons on the upper curves of her cheeks, and to him she'd never looked more vulnerable, more desirable. But he resisted taking her into his arms, knowing he and she had to talk. If he touched her, he'd be lost in a torrent of passion, and forget all of his good intentions.

"Ketti?" he said, and the word sounded like a caress.

She'd been staring at the amber liquid in her glass, and now she darted a glance at him. Brown eyes locked with blue, and she couldn't look away. Finally she gave a slight nod, and waited.

He put down his glass and slid along the velvet cushion to take her cold hands in his. "I can't go on like this," he began, and as her eyes widened in instant fear, John continued quickly. "I'm asking you to marry me—because I'm too damned afraid of what'll happen to you if we wait."

"Marry?" She was incredulous. She'd wanted that for so long, and now when he finally said the words, she hadn't been expecting them.

His tone hardened. "If James had gotten you on the ship, you would have been at his mercy until I caught up with him and—"

"Shh." Ketti placed a finger over his lips, her senses reeling, her pale face brightening with color, and her tremors changing to sensations of a great throbbing need to feel herself in his arms, his lips on hers.

His eyes burned with banked-down fires. "God almighty, but you've given me some bad times," he groaned. "You're always doing something, going somewhere or saying something that places you in dangerous situations." He took a long shuddering breath. "So all I can think to do is what Char did: marry the woman he loves to make sure she's safe."

"What about your plantation, your fears that my family will think you're only after my dowry?"

He hesitated, gathering his thoughts. "I still feel the same about it, but now it looks as if the sugar industry will eventually be saved. But I won't accept a dowry...ever. That still stands."

"And would you still marry me even if my family disapproved—which I know they won't?"

He nodded. "If you still wanted me. But before we announce our betrothal, I want to speak to your father."

"Announce our betrothal?" She couldn't help but tease him. Her joy was bubbling up inside her. "I haven't even accepted your proposal."

He took her seriously and suddenly looked stricken, as though he didn't know what to say.

"I accept," she said at once, horrified that she might have hurt him. Then her lashes lowered seductively. "So—can I have a kiss now?"

John sucked in his breath, as though he could no longer contain the feelings he'd been suppressing so that they could have a sensible talk, without their passion for each other surging out of control.

He picked her up and carried her to his bedroom. She couldn't help a delighted giggle. He'd be taking her to his bed for the rest of their lives, she thought, as he laid her on the cotton spread.

He quickly removed his shirt and threw it over a chair. It was followed in seconds by the rest of his clothing. Soon he bent over her, his fingers sure, then urgent as he undressed her. Then she lay under him, her nakedness straining to his.

"Lord, but you're beautiful, so perfect," he murmured, his gaze moving over her, lingering as he drank in her loveliness.

She smiled into his face, only inches above hers. "I love you, John," she said simply. "I love you now, and I'll love you when I'm old and cranky, and for the rest of my life."

Then he kissed her, again and again, from her mouth to her breasts, and lower still. Unable to control herself, Ketti moaned his name, and finally cried out. "Love me, John . . . love me now!"

He groaned, and entered her. She forgot everything but his exquisite touch of love. She was soaring higher, and higher still. The surf crashed on the beach outside their window, and then even that faded away. Only ecstasy remained.

The moon had traveled its arc across the sky and hung low over the ocean when John brought Ketti home. He helped her down, but for another moment he couldn't let her go. They clung together in a long kiss, and then he gently put her away from him. Even after their lovemaking he could feel a new rise of desire for her. A kiss must be enough for now, he told himself. He didn't want Kilia and Martin upset, and he hoped they wouldn't disapprove of Ketti's late arrival home.

"Remember, darling," he whispered. "I'm speaking to your father when I return to the Big Island. After that we can have the banns read in church."

She only nodded, wishing they could do it tomorrow. Yet, as they'd discussed sometime during the night, she had to finish her classes; she couldn't leave Char and Siu without a teacher until they found a replacement.

"And *please* stay out of trouble," he added teasingly, but his eyes glinting in the moonlight, were serious.

"I'll try," she said, and then offered her lips for one last kiss before he got started on that topic again. She really didn't think she was inordinately prone to trouble, but she understood his worry. Didn't she worry about him when he was gone?

She watched him start down the driveway before she went into the dark house. Everyone was asleep, and she somehow knew that Kilia wouldn't mention her late return in the morning. Kilia and Martin liked John.

She tiptoed up to bed, and then lay awake remembering John's bed. She fell asleep with a smile on her face.

Chapter Nineteen

"My Uncle Seth is arriving next week from New Bedford," Ketti told Kilia as she glanced up from the letter. "My mother and grandparents are coming to Honolulu to meet his ship, and they want me to accompany them back to the Big Island."

Kilia nodded, her hands coming to rest on the sewing in her lap. Her dark eyes were bright with anticipation of the impending visit of her old friend Mari. Dressed in a floral silk afternoon dress, the lace fluffing like foam at her neck and wrists, she looked more like a young girl than a middle-aged woman. "I know. I had a letter from your mother, too," she told Ketti. "They're arriving two days ahead of Seth, and I've invited them to stay here."

Ketti had arrived from school only minutes earlier, to find the letter waiting for her. Although it was happy news, she was disappointed that there had been no word from John. She walked to the long windows, which were open to the fragrance of the garden, where bougainvillea, oleander, hibiscus, jasmine and jacaranda blended to perfume the fresh salty air that wafted off the ocean. Beyond the palms and shrubs that lined the edge of the grassy area, the Pacific Ocean lay placid under the afternoon sun.

"Isn't it strange how things happen?" Ketti said thoughtfully. "I was planning on going home next week anyway." She turned back to face Kilia, and a streamer of sunlight stretched down through the fronds and branches to gild Ketti with a golden aura, the impression magnified by the fact that her cotton dress was also a deep yellow color. "John and I want to announced our engagement—after John talks to my father."

"Oh, my dear," Kilia replied, going to the girl she loved like a daughter and hugging her. "I'm so happy for you! Both Martin and I like John very much. He'll make a fine husband."

Ketti's smile was hesitant. "I just hope my parents have no objections, as I've sensed that they've had some reservations about John in the past. They knew his parents, you know."

"That was a long time ago," Kilia said, but she glanced away. "And John is very different from his mother and father."

Scanning her letter again, Ketti felt uneasy, but she suddenly realized that the feeling had nothing to do with John. There was a tone to her mother's writing that seemed odd— as if there was something wrong. But she couldn't put her finger on what it was, aside from the fact that Mari had mentioned many extra ranch expenses, starting with the sick cattle before Ketti came to Honolulu. She met Kilia's eyes.

"Did you get the impression that Mother was worried about something?" she asked slowly.

Kilia was thoughtful. "Now that you mention it, her letter was very brief, and she usually writes a book," the older woman agreed. "But I just thought that was because she'd be here in person next week for a visit."

"Maybe so." Ketti hesitated, remembering other things her mother had failed to mention, like how her grandmother was, and Panana's advanced state of pregnancy. "No, I think something isn't right," she said finally.

"Well, there is one thing," Kilia began, and hesitated, wondering if she should even bring it up.

"What?" Ketti's gaze was direct, and Kilia knew she had to finish.

"There's been talk—political talk—about the American economy, which directly affects ours." She gave a slight smile, as though she didn't really believe what she'd heard, but Ketti could see that she did.

"And?" Ketti prompted.

"It's being said that the gold reserve is too low, that if something isn't done, there could be a panic later in the year, which could mean bank and business failures."

"My God!" Ketti cried. "How do you know?"

"Everyone in the business community knows, and even the banks here aren't lending unless there's plenty of liquid collateral to guarantee payment."

"Liquid collateral?"

Kilia nodded. "Money, rather than land or buildings that wouldn't sell in an economic panic, which is usually followed by a depression."

Then the subject changed to Panana and the new baby that would bind the two families by blood, and after a while Ketti wandered out into the garden, where she sat on a bench by the fountain. Her mind was still on the earlier conversation about the economy. Was it possible her father needed to borrow money from the bank to see him through his expenses, until he shipped more cattle? Thousands of dollars of ranch reserves had already been spent to keep the Webster ranch from bankruptcy. Her thoughts whirled with what that could mean: both ranches could fail.

It's my overactive imagination, she told herself firmly. No one had ever even indicated that the Fosters could be in financial trouble. But as she went back inside to correct papers, Ketti couldn't forget the day her grandfather had come for the loan. She and the whole family had known they were dependent on future cattle sales to replenish the family coffers. And then, after the loan, the ranch had suffered heavy losses.

I won't worry about it now, she thought. Next week is time enough—if there is, in fact, something to worry about.

* * *

Ketti liked Seth from the moment he stepped off the ship, a slim, brown-haired man who wore glasses. His intelligence was immediately obvious, as was his niceness. After he hugged his parents—Agnes and Russell—he embraced Mari, and then turned his pale blue eyes on Ketti.

"Katherine, or are you still called Ketti?"

"Ketti," she replied, returning his smile. He looked so much like his mother, so youthful for his thirty years, not at all like Ketti's big, rough grandfather who'd once been a whaler on the high seas.

After he gave Ketti a hug, he held her at arm's length, examining her face. "My, how you've grown up," he said, his voice highly cultured, with a New England accent from his years of schooling. "Nineteen now?"

"Twenty," she replied, and grinned wider. "You're only ten years older, remember?"

They all laughed, and with Agnes and Mari on each of Seth's arms, they walked to the carriage. Ketti followed with her grandfather, who had never looked happier. All the worry lines seemed to have vanished from his face, and Ketti was reminded of how he'd always put so much hope in his son, and how disappointed he'd been when Agnes was unable to have more children. Russell's attitude that sons carried on the family tradition, while daughters just got married, had always been a sore point to Mari. Ketti knew that her mother had resigned herself to his ways long ago, had overcome her disappointment that Russell had never completely recognized his own daughter's abilities . . . simply because she was a daughter and not a son.

But that all happened long ago, Ketti reminded herself as she and the rest of the family listened to Seth recount his years in New Bedford, and his adventures during his long journey back to Hawaii. The carriage ride passed in a flash, and they soon reached Kilia's home. A special Hawaiian supper was served in the dining room, and the conversation continued until bedtime.

The next morning the three Websters, Mari and Ketti caught the steamer for Kawaihae, and Ketti was happy that her arrangements allowed her to accompany the others. Siu would look after her classes for the ten days Ketti was away. *Besides,* she told herself as they left Honolulu harbor behind, *I'll soon see John.*

Adam and Charles met the steamer, and the talk didn't stop all the way up the road to the ranch. Ketti's grandparents and Seth were spending the night with the Fosters before they continued their trip to the Webster ranch. That night the cook served a special dinner, another celebration of Seth's arrival. Afterward coffee and brandy were served in the salon. It was only then that a silence fell over the family for the first time since Seth's arrival in Honolulu.

Seth glanced around and grinned. "I've talked continuously, now I'd like to hear about Hawaii. How's ranching?" He sipped his coffee. "Everything I've seen certainly looks prosperous."

For several seconds no one said anything, and Ketti saw her parents exchange glances. Her grandfather shifted in his chair, and looked uncomfortable, but finally he spoke.

"Uh, not so good, son. We've had a few problems," Russell replied. Ketti saw that his strained expression was back, and felt sudden alarm. She'd been right. Something was very wrong. She could see it in the averted eyes of her parents. Even her Hawaiian grandmother was keeping her gaze on the burning logs in the fireplace.

"What's wrong?" Seth asked, and glanced from one to another of them. Only Ketti met his eyes, and he saw that she was equally puzzled by his father's announcement.

"Come on," Seth prompted firmly, and suddenly a resemblance to his father was apparent. "Ketti and I are part of the family, and we want to know what's going on."

"There's a financial problem," Russell said at last. "And it's all my fault."

"Not completely," Adam added.

"Yes it is," Russell said, contradicting Adam. "If I hadn't invested in sugar, none of us would be on the verge of bankruptcy."

"Bankruptcy! Both ranches?" Seth asked sharply.

When Russell could only shake his head, Mari took up the conversation. "You know what's been happening in Hawaii—the overthrow of the monarchy and the annexation issue. Well, long before that, several years ago when the American sugar tariffs favored Hawaii, Father wanted to expand his interests and invested everything in sugar. But by the time the sugar was ready for export, the laws had changed and the planters couldn't break even. Adam and I gave him a loan to save his ranch, but now we need a loan to keep our own ranch going, and the banks won't give it to us."

"I understand," Seth said seriously. "The economic indicators in the United States suggest a financial panic is imminent. Bank loans are hard to come by these days."

Seth got up abruptly, and poured himself more brandy. Then he took another chair nearer his parents on the settee. "It sounds like a family financial panic," he suggested lightly. Then his tone hardened. "Father, I had a matter to discuss with you—a personal matter that has to do with finances. I was going to wait until later, when we could talk in private, but now I believe this might be a better time."

He had everyone's attention. Ketti couldn't help but admire her uncle. He might be a slightly built man, whose appearance wasn't that of a tough cattle rancher, but he had his own strength—a strength of character that commanded respect.

"As I said, it's a personal matter that has to do with your family in New Bedford. Do I have your permission to speak?"

Russell nodded, puzzled but curious.

Seth took a deep breath, then began a story that kept the listeners in silence, waiting for his next word. "Years ago you left New Bedford—we all know why—and took to the sea. Your parents didn't approve, and in fact, you believed yourself disinherited.''

"That's right!" Russell retorted. "You might as well add that my father was really my stepfather, and the family wealth went to my younger half brother."

"There's more to it, Father," Seth said. "The fact is that you aren't a stepson at all, but the first son of the man you believed was your stepfather." As Russell opened his mouth, astonished by Seth's words, Seth waved him to silence.

"That was the great family secret, and, I'm sorry to add, shame." Seth lowered his tone, sympathy for the wrong done to his father evident in his whole bearing. "You were born out of wedlock. Your mother learned she was pregnant with you after your father had sailed for England to buy a ship. By the time he returned you'd been born in secret, and a story made up about a supposed husband who'd been lost at sea. Your parents were both from good Christian families, and had always planned on being married. So when this happened, your father felt it best to continue the lie to avoid scandal."

Seth's final words fell into a silence so deep that even the flames in the fireplace sounded loud. Then Russell, his face incredulous, broke the quiet.

"That bastard! All those years—when I tried so hard to make him proud—and he wasn't even man enough to tell me I was his son."

Soberly, Seth nodded agreement. "It was a terrible thing to do, and he was contrite about it before he died, I'll have to say that for him."

Mari sat like a statue, memories circling in her mind, remembering how she used to think her grandfather and father were so alike, despite believing they were not related. What a horrible thing to do to your own son, she thought. "Yes, he was a bastard," she told her father. "And a coward."

"But he didn't take the secret to his grave," Seth reminded them. "He told me everything before he died, and he left half of his vast shipping empire to you, Father, and the other half to your brother, who manages it now." When there was no reaction, Seth went on. "You're a very rich man, Father. You can pay off everything you owe, including your loan to Mari and Adam."

Finally the realization of what it all meant struck the old man. "Thunderation!" Russell exclaimed. "It's a damned miracle!" Abruptly he sobered, his eyes narrowing on Seth. "What does this mean for you, son?"

Seth raised his brows. "How do you mean, Father?"

"Will you be staying in Hawaii—or returning to New Bedford?"

"My roots are here, even if I'll be practicing law, not tending cattle." He hesitated, a serious cast to his features suddenly adding years to his age. "I feel that you should allow your brother to buy you out, as your life is here, and his is there." Seth paused again. "I've already discussed this possibility with him, and he agrees."

Slowly Russell inclined his head in agreement. A sad look touched his face, as though he were remembering the distant past . . . and what might have been. Then he gave himself a mental shake, and again a big grin curved his lips.

"What's past is over and done with. I agree with that plan, son. Later we can draft a letter to my brother," he said, his eyes bright with pride in his son.

And then everyone was talking at once. Seth explained further details, winking at Ketti when the excitement got out of hand. But Ketti's thoughts moved elsewhere after the news finally sank in. She pondered the great-grandparents in New Bedford whom she'd never known, except for the faded picture her grandfather kept in his office at the Webster ranch. Somehow she sympathized with them. They'd been trapped by circumstances, and an unforgiving townspeople who firmly subscribed to strict puritanical principles. Even though it was wrong that the lie had continued through the generations, she could understand why they had perpetuated it.

What if John had to go away, and we weren't married, and I found myself pregnant? she wondered. Would I have done the same thing as my great-grandmother? And after the deed was done, would I have the courage to bare my soul to a critical society?

Love, and being in love, and making love, are the same in all generations, she thought later when she was alone. But everyone isn't fortunate enough to have things turn out right, she told herself, as she got ready for bed.

I'm one of the lucky ones, Ketti mused, and remembered that John had sent word that he would arrive at the ranch tomorrow afternoon. He intended to speak with her father before supper. She smiled to herself. She would soon be married to her beloved John. I'll never be in my great-grandmother's predicament, she reminded herself. And then she went to bed.

John arrived a little early, and Mari met him at the door to invite him inside. He was informed that Ketti was upstairs getting ready for dinner, as was the elderly Mrs. Foster.

"And Adam is still in his office going over the ledgers," Mari said with a smile, but John thought she seemed a bit ill at ease. He wondered if Ketti had already mentioned the reason behind his visit—that he was now in a position to set a date for their wedding—or if her parents had only guessed.

After he'd been shown to the guest room and had freshened up, he went back downstairs, lean and bronzed in his white piqué shirt and casual, light blue lounge suit. John glanced into the salon and saw that he was the first person there, but he heard the faint murmur of voices from the kitchen. Then Adam appeared in the doorway of a room at the back of the hall and motioned John to join him.

"Come in, John." Adam stepped aside so John could precede him into his office. After he closed the door, Adam went to a wall cupboard and took a crystal decanter of whiskey and two matching glasses from the shelf. "Will you join me?" He raised black brows.

John nodded. "Please." He watched as Adam poured, measuring the older man's dominant presence with his own. Adam was still lean and muscled and was as tall as John. Although his black hair was silvered at the temples, and his face lined by his years in the saddle, he was an imposing man in both looks and bearing. He was well-known for his fairness, and equally recognized for his willingness to stand up for his rights. The man before him, already dressed for dinner in a tan waistcoat and trousers, wouldn't be an easy man to cross, John thought suddenly, and hoped he'd never have to. After accepting the glass, John sat down in the chair Adam had indicated opposite his desk.

"I understand you wanted to talk," Adam said, and swirled his whiskey in the glass. He'd guessed what John was about to say, but he wasn't going to broach the subject himself. That was up to John.

"Yes," John agreed. "You already know that Ketti and I had plans for a future together, but that my financial situation forbade me from being formally betrothed. Now that's changed."

"In what way has it changed?" Adam's gaze was direct.

John's was equally straightforward. "I didn't approve of the monarchy being overthrown. It went against my Hawaiian heritage. But I do believe annexation is a must for the islands if our economy is to survive. However, I still hope the throne is reinstated, under the jurisdiction of the United States." He hesitated, and when Adam didn't comment, John went on. "Annexation means averting financial ruin for sugar planters. And for me it means I'm solvent enough to propose marriage to the woman I love."

A brief silence fell between the men as John finished, their eyes locked. John didn't flinch, but held his ground. Finally it was Adam who spoke. "You're referring to Ketti?"

John inclined his head and waited, taking a swallow of whiskey. He respected Adam, but he'd be damned if he'd kowtow to him. "I love her, and want her to be my wife."

The words, although expected, held Adam suspended in his thoughts for a few moments. It was hard for him to believe his little girl was all grown-up, ready to be a wife. He'd known this day was coming ever since the barbecue last summer when Ketti and John had performed the ancient love dance. He'd recognized their passionate young love, for he had once felt the same, when he'd fallen in love with Mari.

Adam tossed back his whiskey, then went to the cabinet and poured more for them both. He remained standing, feeling the moment was too important to sit. Other faces surfaced in his mind, ones he hadn't seen for more than twenty-five years—the faces of Jane and Stuart, John's parents. Jane had been a spoiled girl of high birth who'd been chosen by Adam's mother and her parents for him, and Stuart had been a scoundrel searching for money and position, who'd courted Mari. Jane and Stuart had ultimately gone to California together and married.

Watching Adam, John guessed what the older man was remembering. He put down his glass and stood, too. "I'm not interested in Ketti's dowry," he said dryly. "If I were, I wouldn't have waited until now to propose marriage. And I'd like to remind you that my mother's background was respectable, as was my father's." He hesitated, and felt the old pain of being the son of a man who'd been thought a dishonest scoundrel. "However, I make no excuses for my father's past behavior. I only remind you that I'm a different type of man entirely."

Impressed by John's bluntness, and by his refusal to back down, Adam conceded to himself that the man was his equal, and wasn't at all like his father. It was true that Jane, his mother, had come from a good family, and he'd heard that Stuart had as well, if an impoverished one.

"And Ketti? How does she feel about marrying you?" Adam asked finally.

"She's accepted," John replied at once.

"And if I refused my blessing on this?"

"Then it would be up to Ketti to decide." John's eyelids were half-lowered, as he tried to read the other man. "I would prefer your permission—and the blessings of both you and Mrs. Foster—which is why I spoke to you at Christmas concerning my future intentions, but if not..." He shrugged. "I still want her for my wife."

Adam couldn't help but admire John. He had a backbone and the courage of his convictions; he was the type of man he wanted for his only daughter. And John had reacted exactly as he would have done. There was no one in the world who could have kept him from marrying Ketti's mother.

"Then I offer my approval of your proposal, and I speak for Ketti's mother also."

They'd been standing almost toe to toe, and suddenly the tension went out of the room. Adam grinned and held out his hand. "Congratulations, son!" he said.

After they'd shaken hands, they tossed off the whiskey in their glasses. Then they went to join the women waiting in the salon. John felt as though he'd just gone through the most intense minutes in his life. If Adam had refused, he wasn't sure what he would have done...or what Ketti would have done. She loved her father, and John didn't know if he could have made her choose between the two men she loved most in the world.

But it's all immaterial anyway, he told himself as he feasted his eyes on the very woman he was thinking about. She stood in a pool of light by the fireplace. She wore a simple gown of emerald-green velvet with leg-of-mutton sleeves; her hair shone from the lighted gas lamps, and as the men stepped farther into the room, she lowered her long lashes shyly. She glanced at her father, and then met John's silvery gaze. And then she knew. Everything was all right.

After dinner, when John and Ketti were alone with her parents, John explained further about his plans for the plantation, and the future; he felt the economy would be strong by the time his sugar crop was ready to harvest in a year and a half. The conversation was frank and, after all questions were answered, both Adam and Mari gave the couple their blessing.

"So I'll have the banns read in church," John said, after a toast had been raised to their betrothal.

Ketti smiled happily. "We're really engaged. I can't believe it."

John grinned. "I'm afraid it's true. And now you're stuck with me." His eyes brimmed with his own joy and, unbeknownst to the young couple, Ketti's parents were pleased by the display of genuine affection.

"It might be nice for Ketti to visit my plantation," John suggested, "as she might want some changes to the house before she moves in."

"That's an excellent idea," Mari agreed. "Perhaps Ketti and I could accompany you on your return trip."

John agreed at once, and didn't allow his smile to show. Now that they were formally engaged, he meant to adhere to all proprieties. Having Ketti was too important to risk disapproval.

Ketti and her mother left with John the next morning. During the buggy ride across the mountains and during their stay at the plantation house throughout the next several days, both John and Ketti were circumspect in their behavior. They were rarely alone, but Ketti consoled herself with the thought of how it would be when they were married and living in the large two-story house. Although it was a little run-down, she loved the large rooms, and the upper and lower verandas, and the huge lava-stone fireplace in the drawing room. She and her mother had gone through the rooms, making notes on improvements and minor repairs to be made, walls that required paint or paper, and furniture needed.

"There is your dowry, you know, dear," Mari reminded her.

Ketti shook her head and explained John's view on her dowry. "So the only way a dowry is acceptable to John is if it's placed in trust for our children."

Mari raised her brows and smiled. But she was secretly relieved. John certainly wasn't like his father.

John did kiss Ketti goodbye when it was time to leave, and again she reminded herself that a few weeks would pass quickly. She had to return to Honolulu and finish out the term of her classes, and then she would have more than John's prim kiss. The thought sustained her all the way back to the ranch. Once home, she and her mother went over their list again, describing the house and the needed changes to Ketti's grandmother the next day.

Ketti glanced up from where she sat opposite her mother and grandmother at the dining room table. She smiled lovingly at the two dearest women in the world to her. "You know," she began slowly, "I was just thinking how everything—grandfather's old grudge against his New England family, the Webster and Foster ranches out of debt, Seth being home and me getting married to the man I love—and all our good health—has been resolved. We're so very fortunate."

She took a deep breath and went on. "I believe all the old taboos must be satisfied now, the ones that forbid Hawaiians to marry *haoles,* and *haoles* to live on the sacred land that once belonged to the ancient kings."

A heavy silence ensued, suddenly cloaking Ketti with a chill of foreboding. Her mother looked upset, but her grandmother was completely stricken. "Oh, my dear!" her grandmother said, and her voice shook. "You mustn't tempt fate by saying such things."

"Your grandmother's right," Mari chimed in. "Here in Hawaii, we don't talk about the ancient superstitions. That in itself is almost a taboo." When Ketti looked deflated, Mari gave a nervous laugh and tried to lighten the mood. "We'll just pretend you didn't say it."

But Ketti felt awful, and for the rest of the day her words kept coming back to haunt her. She wished that John were there to console her and not on his way to Honolulu for supplies.

The very next morning, when the Reverend Mead and Sarah made an unexpected visit, Ketti knew she'd spoken too soon about old taboos.

"I have come to prevent a terrible sin from being committed," the Reverend Mead announced piously in a thunderous voice. "There will be no wedding between Ketti Foster and John Stillman. That I promise you!"

Chapter Twenty

"What?" Ketti jumped up from where she was sitting near the open windows in the salon to face the man and woman in the doorway. "How dare you come into my home to say such a thing!"

The housekeeper had shown the Reverend Mead and Sarah into the house, and the two had followed the voices of Ketti, her mother and grandmother to the room where they were discussing the upcoming wedding. At the reverend's words, they'd all been startled, and Ketti had been the first to react.

"I would dare much more under the circumstances, my dear Ketti," he retorted. His black suit and hat gave him the look of a great, black bird of prey hovering in the doorway. "As a messenger of God, I have a duty to put a stop to this—this obscenity!"

"My brother is only doing what must be done, for everyone's sake," Sarah added, sweeping farther into the room, her prim brown dress, white poke bonnet and severe hairdo giving even more emphasis to her disapproval.

"I insist you leave this house at once!" Ketti cried, too angry to think about manners. The reverend had gone too far this time.

Ketti's grandmother looked outraged, as did her mother, but it was Mari who stepped forward and spoke calmly, if coldly. "You'd better explain your statements—at once."

Sarah and her brother exchanged glances, as though bracing themselves before they began. The Reverend Mead took off his wide-brimmed black hat and handed it to Sarah, then took a thin testament from an inside pocket of his frock coat, as though to strengthen his purpose. He appeared so serious, as if he were about to begin a sermon, that Ketti would have laughed had she not been so angry.

"Ketti and John cannot marry!" he suddenly thundered. "They are sister and brother!"

For a long moment the three Foster women were stunned, speechless. Whatever they'd expected the man to say, this shocking charge came from out of the blue. Ketti's face flushed with embarrassment, and a glance at her mother told her that Mari felt as she did, except that Mari's face was completely drained of color. But before either of them could retort, Adam suddenly spoke from the doorway behind the reverend.

"What the hell is the meaning of this?" he cried, striding into the room, his sombrero hanging by its string on his back, his spurs jingling as he moved. He'd just come into the house, and was still dressed for the range in his *paniolo* riding garb. His face was set in hard lines and his eyes were scarcely more than slits as he pinned the reverend with his gaze.

"I asked you a question, man!" he said, his tone dangerous. "And you'd better come up with a goddamn good answer!"

The reverend blanched and took a step backward as Adam glared at him in a threatening manner. But Sam Mead's chin went up and his narrow face tightened with resolve. "There's no need to blaspheme!" he retorted.

Adam took a step closer. "Get on with it—before I toss you out on your ear!"

"John's mother, Jane, was once betrothed to you," he began, his tone edged with disapproval as his eyes locked with Adam's. "And when she married John's father, Stuart, in San Francisco, she was already pregnant—with your son!''

Ketti grabbed the back of a chair for support, the words lashing her with thoughts too awful to imagine. She heard her mother's sharp intake of breath. Her grandmother stood so suddenly that the papers on her lap spilled onto the floor.

"That's a damnable lie!" Adam was across the room in an instant to grab the reverend by the lapels, almost jerking the man off his feet.

Sarah flew to her brother's defense, pushing between the two men. "Take your hands off my brother!" she cried shrilly. "It's a sin to lay hands on a man of the cloth! Let him go!"

Mari and Ketti stepped forward, each taking one of Adam's arms, fearful that he was about to do bodily harm to the sanctimonious minister.

"It's a mistake, Father," Ketti said, but her voice shook. "I can't imagine why a 'man of the cloth' would say such a thing." Her eyes flashed over the two intruders, scorching them from head to foot. "But it's not true."

"Yes, it is!" Sarah retorted. "Agnes Webster's father, the Reverend Henry, who was Stuart's minister at the time, told my brother so."

Ketti wanted to slap Sarah's smug face, but she restrained herself. A glance at her mother's stricken expression told her how terribly upset she was, perhaps even more so than her father.

Before anyone could say more, Ketti's grandmother's voice rang out over the others. "This is nonsense!" she cried, every inch the haughty descendant of Polynesian kings, the outraged matriarch of the Foster family. "Reverend Mead, Sarah Mead, you're not welcome here. You will leave at once—and take your vicious lies with you!"

Sarah bristled, her face scarlet. "*We* do not lie! My brother saw the letter John's father sent to the Reverend Henry. It was with the church records."

''Then show me that letter!'' Adam demanded. ''I don't believe there was such a letter!''

''We—we don't have it!'' Reverend Mead stammered. ''The Reverend Henry burned it—he said he thought he'd burned it years earlier, right after he received it, because he didn't believe it.'' He pursed his lips, then plopped his hat back on his head. ''But the Lord works in mysterious ways. I was meant to see the letter so that I could put a stop to this—this abomination!''

''Get out, you goddamned troublemakers!'' Adam bellowed and, taking the reverend by the elbows, he propelled him out to the hall, followed by the protesting Sarah.

When the front door slammed behind the Meads, an awful silence fell over the women. Then Adam strode back, hesitating just inside the doorway.

''It's not true, Mari,'' he said, but his tone had lost its anger. His gaze was on his wife, and it was as though he'd forgotten that his daughter and mother were also in the room. ''There was never that kind of relationship between Jane and me. If there really was a letter, then Stuart lied—probably trying one last ploy to destroy our love.''

Mari nodded, but she lowered her eyes, and Ketti saw that the Reverend Mead had done more than try to destroy her own marriage to John. He'd also placed a terrible doubt between her parents.

It can't be true, she told herself. She wouldn't allow herself to believe such lies. But what about the letter? Had there really been one? The Reverend Mead had wanted to marry her. Was he capable of making up a story to prevent her from marrying John? Oh God! she thought, and a terrible agony began deep inside her. If only John weren't in Honolulu. If only she could talk to him and clarify the whole mess . . . for all of their sakes.

Later that day Adam and Mari stepped from Adam's office where they'd been having a private conversation, just as Seth and Agnes came calling with good news.

"I've secured our situation with the bank," Seth exclaimed. "I gave them the documents concerning our New England assets, to show that our ranches are solvent and that we have enough cash behind us to warrant loans."

"That is good news," Adam said, but his voice sounded flat.

"We thought we'd just ride over and tell you in person," Agnes said, smiling, "and have a visit while we're at it. Seth is still trying to catch up on what's been happening all these years he was away."

They were met with solemn smiles. Then Ketti came down the stairs, having left her grandmother napping, and overheard the conversation. "I'll have tea sent into the salon," she said, and tried to interject a light note into her voice. She was so upset inside that she felt sick, but she believed in John, and their love. The awful things that the reverend said simply couldn't be true. "It seems we've missed lunch anyway," she added.

Seth and Agnes exchanged glances, suddenly realizing that something was wrong. Ketti looked as though she'd been crying, and there was a strain between Adam and Mari.

"Perhaps we came at a bad time," Agnes said. "We weren't really going to stay long, as we want to be home before supper."

Seth nodded agreement. He couldn't figure out why they were upset, but he sensed it had nothing to do with himself and Agnes. Before he could decline the tea, Mari took Agnes's arm and led the way into the salon, while Ketti told the housekeeper to bring the tray.

Seth followed, but didn't take the offered chair. He shook his head. "I'm going to be blunt here, because I care about all of you." He hesitated. "Something's wrong and I feel that Mother and I are intruding. We can come back another time."

Ketti blinked away sudden tears, and saw that her mother's eyes were overbright as well. A sudden lump in her throat took her words, and she was unable to answer.

"You may as well hear it from us," Adam said harshly, "because the good reverend will probably spread the word." He strode to the fireplace and, leaning against the mantel, told Agnes and Seth the whole story, while his wife and daughter averted their gazes.

"But that's not true!" Agnes cried. "My father received that letter a couple of years after Stuart and Jane left Hawaii. My parents told Russell and me about its contents, but he'd already determined that Stuart was lying, just trying to get even with Mari and Adam, trying to cause trouble."

"You knew?" Mari's gaze flew to her stepmother, her hope that the Reverend Mead and his sister had lied dying within her. She'd been hanging on to that hope, knowing that the minister wanted to marry Ketti, and that his sister wanted John. She took a long shuddering breath, and forced herself not to cry. *I must trust Adam,* she told herself. Adam had never lied to her, and when he swore he'd never made love to Jane, she must believe him. But somewhere inside her, the Reverend's words didn't go away.

Agnes nodded. "We all decided to forget it, as we didn't believe it. The letter rambled and contradicted itself, and it seemed obvious to us that it was a lie." She paused, frowning. "I can't understand why my father didn't burn the letter."

"He thought he had, according to the reverend," Adam replied. "But it looks like the damn thing is doing its damage now, after all this time."

During the whole interchange Ketti hadn't said a word. She felt awful, even guilty somehow. Had it not been for her engagement, the reverend would never have revealed the contents of the old letter and caused her parents so much anguish. Yet she suddenly knew that he would have anyway. The reverend was a vindictive man.

She moved to the long windows to watch the distant ocean that lay miles below their ranch. On the horizon, clouds were piling upon each other, dark and ominous, and threatening a storm. Already an advance guard of wind fingered through the branches of the shrubs and trees in the garden. Oh God! she cried inwardly. Why this? Why these horrible doubts about the man I love? That he could be her half brother was unthinkable. Ketti turned her glance toward the serene peak of Mauna Kea in an effort to calm herself. I can't think about this now, she told herself, or remember the times John made love to me. No, she thought. First she must talk to John. She must find out the dates—when his parents left Hawaii and how soon after that he was born. His birth certificate would clarify everything.

A hand touched her shoulder, and then her father spoke, his words low and meant only for her. "Ketti, I'm so sorry about this," he said gruffly. "And I apologize for not talking to you right away, but your mother and I needed to talk—and I guess I forgot for a time the kind of pain you were suffering."

She nodded, and swallowed hard as tears welled up.

Adam turned her to him. "I want to reassure you," he said, and as their eyes met, Ketti saw his pain. "I wouldn't lie to you, Ketti, not over this." He took a ragged breath. "This is the worst situation a man could find himself in with his only beloved daughter."

"I know, Father," she managed shakily.

"John isn't my son, Ketti. There was never an intimate relationship between me and his mother—*never,* not even once."

For a moment neither spoke, and Ketti saw her mother come up behind her father. "I believe you, Father," Ketti said slowly. "You've always been a man of his word."

"I believe you too, Adam," Mari whispered. "I'm sorry if I doubted you for even a moment—I had no right—"

She broke off as Adam swooped them both into his arms. "Thank God, thank God!" was all he could manage.

A short time later, satisfied that everything had settled down, Seth and Agnes went out to their buggy, anxious to reach home before it rained.

"I'm glad we came," Agnes said before Seth signaled the two bays. "Happy that I was able to explain my father's reaction to that letter."

"We are too," Ketti replied for all of them.

Then they were off in a clatter of lava pebbles and creaking wheels. As the Fosters went back inside, Ketti made a decision. She would return to Honolulu a few days early, so she could catch John before he returned to the Big Island. Although she and her parents didn't believe the reverend, other people might. She was sure the minister wouldn't let the matter die—especially when she and John went on with their wedding plans.

The whole awful accusation must be disproved at once, she told herself. And John was the one with the proof.

"I wish you'd change your mind, Ketti," Mari said, as Ketti came down the stairs the next morning dressed in her deep green traveling suit and matching felt hat with two perky feathers. It was barely dawn; the sun was still only a blush on the distant mountains, and the lowlands were still caught in the half-light between night and morning.

"It's as I said last night, Mother," Ketti began, watching as one of the *paniolos* brought down her small trunk. "We need to stop any talk that might arise from that old letter. If John proves his birth date, that will do it."

Mari nodded, but looked worried. "You're right, dear. But on top of everything else, the weather still looks threatening."

"The storm passed during the night," Ketti replied to reassure her mother. Secretly she agreed; another storm was coming. But storms or not, she had to go. If she waited until she was originally scheduled to go, she might miss seeing John for a while. And she couldn't leave things as they were—her whole future with John was involved. Even though she believed her father without question, the thought of island gossip wasn't pleasant. She didn't want snide glances, or future problems for her own children one day.

She and John planned to spend the rest of their lives on his plantation.

Then the buggy arrived from the barn, the two bays driven by her father who was taking her down to Kawaihae. She kissed her mother, having already said goodbye to her grandmother the night before. She went outside and climbed up onto the seat. When her trunk was stowed behind them, her father cracked the reins and they were off on the journey down the long sloping road to the steamer. She waved once to her mother when they reached the rise, then settled her skirts more comfortably over her legs, content just to soak up the eternal peace of the land, a feeling that always calmed her with the knowledge that everything would be resolved in the fullness of time.

"Are you all right, Ketti?" Adam asked, his eyes suddenly on her.

"Yes, I am now," she replied with a soft smile. "Thank you for what you said yesterday, Father. It helped me put everything in perspective, although I admit I was quite upset for a while."

"We all were." His gaze returned to the road.

The quiet of the high country was all around them; even the air was still with the promise of the new day. The first rays of sunlight streamed downward from the mountains to transform the webbing of dew that covered the highlands into a fairyland of sparkling gems. Ketti gave a contented sigh, and glanced at her father, who held the reins with such a sure grip. He wore his sombrero and riding clothes, but had left his spurs at home. A real *paniolo* himself, she thought fondly. He was so lean and handsome that it was hard to imagine him old enough to have a grown son and daughter. She was proud of him, had always adored him.

A brief frown touched her brow when she remembered her thoughts yesterday. She'd even remembered comparing her father and John in the past, thinking that they had similar traits, even though they didn't resemble each other physically. But now she realized that John was the same caliber of man, that was all—which was why she'd fallen in love with him. The similarity stopped there; they had no mannerisms or characteristics that came from a blood relationship.

Thank God, she thought, and wondered how she could have had even one moment of doubt. Her mind whirled. She was glad they rode in silence, suspecting her father also enjoyed the enfolding peace of the land they all loved so much.

Her father's voice brought her back to her surroundings, and she was surprised to see they were already at Kawaihae. "The steamer is ready to leave, and it's early yet." He glanced around as he reined in the bays. "Unless they're making a run before a storm."

Ketti looked toward the horizon, which was piled with black clouds. A chill of foreboding shot through her. She didn't like the look of the sky at all. But she held up her skirts so that she could step to the ground without tripping. She was going, storm or no storm.

Her father was there to help her, before unstrapping her trunk. "I don't know if you should chance it," he said, again squinting out over the ocean.

"It'll be all right," Ketti announced with contrived confidence. "The waves aren't above normal, and they usually are before a big storm."

He studied the ocean briefly, then agreed. "But if the steamer should run into bad weather and turn back, you can always stay at our cottage here in Kawaihae," he reminded her, and she heard the worry in his voice.

"It'll be just fine." Ketti grinned at him. "The weather is no worse than usual." She hesitated, sobering. "You know I have to go, Father. I need to talk to John."

"I suppose it's fine. I reckon I'm just jumpy since the reverend paid us his visit."

They both laughed, if a bit nervously. Then Adam saw that her trunk was taken aboard. A short time later the steamer was on its way out to sea. Ketti waved from the deck, even more unsettled to see her father stand watching the ship until the distance swallowed him up.

They were only an hour out when the gale force wind hit, and she suddenly knew this was no small storm. Its unexpected severity took even the captain by surprise. Ketti knew they were in trouble.

Chapter Twenty-One

"The ship's taking on water!"

Ketti jumped up from where she'd been trying to rest and calm her nerves. Her cabin was tiny, and the rolling and rocking of the boat had made it impossible to sit anywhere but on the bunk, where she could brace herself against the walls. She should have listened to her father, she thought, and waited until the storm passed. As it was, she was the only passenger. Now she feared the steamer wouldn't make it in the heavy seas.

"Miss Foster!" A man called from beyond her door, his voice followed by loud knocking. "Miss Foster, please open the door!"

She flung it open and the captain, garbed in oilskins, immediately grabbed her arm. "Come along!" he cried, his expression urgent. "We've turned back to Kawaihae because we're taking on water. Everyone is topside, in case we have to lower the lifeboats and abandon ship."

Icy fingers of dread tightened in Ketti's stomach. As they reached the hatch, the captain handed her an oilskin cape and hat. Quickly she put them on, and then he took her hand and pulled her through the opening and onto the deck. Instantly, the wind blasted them and, had it not been for the captain's grip, she would have been thrown to the rail, and overboard into waves higher than the ship.

She'd known the storm was bad, but not this bad. But there was no time to register her horror. Ropes had been strung along the deck, and they held on to them while they struggled against the wind and rain to the pilothouse. By the time they reached the upper cabin, Ketti's hat had flown away and her hair lay plastered against her head, dripping seawater down her back.

Once the door was closed, Ketti slumped against it, but the captain and several deckhands worked furiously to keep the ship steady into the waves, fearful of being caught broadside in a trough—and swamped. Even Ketti could see how the steamer was listing to port, and knew it was because of water in the hold. The very thought was terrifying; she knew a lifeboat couldn't make it in the furious ocean. Their only chance was reaching Kawaihae before the steamer sunk.

Time seemed to blur for Ketti while the crew worked to steer the boat and keep it afloat. The wind roared around their small shelter, and the waves crashed over it so hard that Ketti wondered how the vessel managed to surface each time. Her offers of help were only waved aside; the captain made it clear that she was to stay out of the way, as they had no time to rescue her should she find herself in trouble.

Cold crept through her wet clothing to touch her skin with chills, and eventually she couldn't stop her teeth from chattering. Then a deckhand, his body twisting in the wind like a rag doll, struggled across the outside deck, hand over hand on the rope until he reached the pilothouse. The door burst in with a mighty gust of wind, propelling the man inside. Ketti quickly swung it shut behind him.

"Ain't no use!" he managed, his strength almost exhausted. "The pumps can't keep ahead of the water. It's gaining on us—only a matter of fifteen, maybe twenty minutes, and we'll have to get outta there."

The captain looked grim. "Keep at it, man!" he shouted above the noise that shook their tiny shelter. "Or it'll flood the engines and then we're done! Work your hearts out—it's our only chance to make port!''

The man just shook his head, but turned back to return to his men. Again, Ketti slammed the door shut after him. But she hadn't failed to notice that the list to port had become more severe.

We aren't going to make it! she thought desperately, and knew her fate was out of her hands. All her other problems faded into insignificance. Her mind narrowed to one thought, which she chanted over and over to keep her sanity.

I love you, John. Oh dear God, how I love you, John.

John's ship reached Kawaihae just before the storm hit, and by the look of the waves, he was relieved that he was on solid ground. His supplies would be unloaded when the wind abated. In the meantime, he decided to ride up to the Foster ranch and see Ketti. She'd been on his mind during the whole time he'd been gone, and for some reason he couldn't rid himself of the feeling that something was wrong. He chided himself as he mounted his horse and started up the road to the high country. It's only because I can't believe my good fortune in finally being able to set the date, he told himself. But still his worry persisted.

The rain beat against his oilskin coat and hat, but the wind at his back seemed to help his mount move faster. When he finally turned into the Foster driveway, he looked forward to a shot of whiskey to warm him...and to the loveliness of the woman he loved.

The Hawaiian housekeeper answered his knock, and invited him into the house. But her news shocked him. Before the storm hit, Adam and Mari had driven over to the Webster ranch on business, old Mrs. Foster was in her room, and Ketti had taken the morning steamer to Honolulu. For long seconds, John could only stare at the woman while the water ran down his oilskin to puddle on the floor. *Ketti was out on the ocean in the storm!*

"I know she thought you were still in Honolulu," the housekeeper told him. "That's why she went back early." The woman looked at him oddly, as though there were more to the story.

"Just to see me?" John asked sharply. "When she knew I'd probably be here before she was scheduled to go back?"

"She didn't want to miss seeing you—in case you were delayed."

"Why?"

The woman glanced away, wiping her hands nervously on her apron. Although she'd overheard the reverend the day before, she hadn't let on. She didn't want the family to think she was an eavesdropper. "I think Miss Ketti had something important to discuss with you," she said lamely.

"Is that all you know?" John watched her expression close, and realized she would say no more, even if she knew more.

"Would you like a hot drink?" she asked, changing the subject.

John shook his head, and moved back to the door. Something was wrong; he could feel it. God help Ketti out in that storm. His stomach lurched with sudden fear, as he remembered another time at sea when Ketti had been almost washed overboard, would have been but for him. And *I'm not there this time to save her,* he thought desperately.

He said a hasty goodbye as he ran to mount his horse. In seconds he was galloping toward the road back to Kawaihae. He'd catch the first available boat to Honolulu. The thought of going on to his plantation didn't even enter his head. He wouldn't rest until he knew Ketti was safe.

"We might make it!" the captain shouted to the other men in the pilothouse. No one acknowledged his words, and Ketti doubted anyone even heard, as the wind howled like something possessed, and the sea thundered against the hull, each wave sending a shudder through the ship. The tilt to port was so bad that Ketti expected the vessel to roll onto its side at any moment. An exceptionally high wave had hit the windows like a giant fist and knocked out the front glass, and the door hinges had sprung the last time it was opened, so that the spray drenched them each time they crested a wave. She was so cold her hands and feet were numb, and she doubted she could even talk, her teeth chattered so hard.

Still the captain hadn't ordered the lifeboats lowered, and Ketti suspected he knew their only hope was keeping the steamer afloat until they made port. She clung to a brass rail on the wall, aware that a sudden movement could propel her through the gaping door and into the ocean before she even found her voice to cry out. She could only watch, helpless, and hope for the best.

"Ahoy!" the captain shouted above the din that filled their ears. "I see port!" He took his hand from the wheel briefly, and pointed. "Thank the good lord!"

Several minutes passed before they were close enough for Ketti to see the buildings in the village. For the first time she thought they might make it after all.

As they approached land, they were somewhat sheltered from the full gale force of the wind. The captain turned over the wheel to his first mate, then, using the rope for support, he went out on deck to direct their landing.

"Run it into shallow water!" he shouted back to the first mate, and Ketti surmised that he was attempting to save the boat.

Now she could see other deckhands running to the captain's orders, all of them oblivious to the storm. She knew that the hold was filling fast now that the men had abandoned the pumps in order to secure the steamer. She held her breath as the ship closed the distance to land. Then the hull scraped bottom, and a shout went up from the men. The engines were stopped, and before Ketti had time to feel relief, she was hustled off the ship along with the crew.

"Now we can only pray that the water doesn't get to the engines before they cool!" the captain cried. "If it does, they could blow!"

His words were enough to put wings on Ketti's feet, but she could hardly walk, her feet were so numb. Two of the mates grabbed either arm and helped her down the ladder to a waiting lifeboat. Minutes later she stepped ashore. As they let go of her, she was horrified to find her legs wouldn't hold her, either. She crumpled to her knees, her green traveling suit weighing her down, cold and heavy against her body. Before the men could help her up again, a horse was reined in nearby. The rider leaped off its back and ran to help her instead. She looked up into eyes whose silvery blue color had dulled to flat gray.

"I'll take over from here," John told the captain and his men.

"John," she managed, her strength about gone. And then she swooned into his arms, her relief taking her last reserve. She didn't faint; she was simply spent.

"Thank God!" he cried, his quick glance assessing the situation. The steamer was lucky to have made land. It could have sunk . . . and Ketti would have been gone, lost forever beneath the vast Pacific Ocean. The thought jolted him to the core.

Without another word, he swooped her up closer to his body, and strode to the shelter of the first building, trying to decide what to do. He could feel the tremors shaking her body, and he immediately dismissed the thought of taking her home. She needed to get out of her wet clothes and be warmed up. He'd seen men die from a severe chill.

"John," she whispered against his chest.

"I'm here, darling," he crooned, cradling her like a precious doll, as he considered possible courses of action.

"Take—take me—to our cottage—at the end—of the village," she managed between her chattering teeth.

"Hush now," he replied softly, soothing her, as he recalled the *paniolo* cottage Ketti had once mentioned. "Someone will come for Miss Foster's trunk when things settle down," he called back to the captain.

The palms that grew in clusters around the small village twisted in a witch dance, their fronds sweeping the air like great feather dusters. The late afternoon was quickly darkening toward evening, the low charcoal clouds squeezing the light from the day. The rain pelted down, huge drops that turned the street to thick mud that sucked at John's boots as he hurried toward the cottage. When he reached it, Ketti told him where to find the key, and seconds later he'd opened the door and was putting her down on a horsehair sofa near the stone fireplace.

John tossed his hat aside, and his oilskin coat soon followed. Then he glanced around the high-beamed room, saw that a kitchen was in the back, and a door to a bedroom at the side. His expression grim, he strode into the adjoining room, quickly rummaged through a chest at the foot of the bed and found wool blankets. Then he returned to Ketti, who huddled against the back of the sofa in an attempt to warm herself.

He squatted before her, his fingers on the buttons of her sodden jacket. When he saw how white she looked, her long lashes drooping over her large eyes, he was alarmed. She didn't protest when he removed her jacket, then her ruffled, high-necked waist, followed by her shoes and skirt and underthings. When she lay naked, John quelled the desire for her swelling within him. Her flesh was icy, and he wrapped her in blankets, tucking in the corners.

She watched, allowing his touch, but her chill was so deep that even that didn't warm her. Ketti suddenly wondered if she would ever be warm again, ever stop shivering. She'd never been cold like this before, and wondered if she were suffering from shock as well as cold.

John didn't pause once he had her rolled in the blankets. He built a fire in the fireplace, feeding it with kindling until the logs were blazing, the flames leaping and crackling up the chimney. Ketti needed heat.

The kitchen had a stove, and a black iron teakettle rested on its cold top. John took it out the back door to fill at the water pump, then brought it back to place in the fireplace to heat. He found a cup and tea, and a bottle of whiskey in the cupboard. When the water boiled he made the tea, added liquor, then helped Ketti sip it.

She smiled her thanks, and he grinned back, managing to conceal his concern. She still trembled from the cold. It was as though it had gotten inside her, so that no matter how she warmed her skin, the core of her couldn't rid itself of the chill. The thought scared John. He pushed the sofa closer to the fire. When the hot tea and whiskey appeared to have no effect other than to cause a fit of coughing, he decided on a more drastic measure.

As she watched, her eyes growing large with surprise, he undressed, tossing his clothes aside. Then he uncovered her and lay down beside her, her back against the horsehair, her breasts and stomach pressed to his chest and belly. He curled her to him, one of his arms under her neck, the other around her waist, holding her cold flesh against the heat of his. He tucked the blankets around them, and willed her to come back to life.

At first Ketti was too cold to care about anything other than getting warm. She was contented to let John minister to her, although she didn't like him to look so worried. But even to express that had seemed too much effort. After her first feeling of shock that he'd climbed in with her, she soon forgot her qualms as she settled against his warmth. He didn't try to touch her in an intimate way, or make love to her, so she relaxed, and gradually the heat began to return to her limbs, and the shivers diminished and then vanished altogether.

Sensing that she was returning to normal, John allowed his fingers to begin to stroke her. Ketti felt the rich sensation of pleasure surge through her, and moaned sleepily. But when he cupped a breast, she was startled out of her reverie.

Her lashes fluttered open, and her gaze was caught by the silvery lights in his blue eyes. "No, John, we can't."

"Why not, my sweet?" he whispered huskily. "I just want to assure myself that I have my own Ketti back."

"Because—because there's something that must be settled first. Something that is so unpleasant I can't hardly say it." She hesitated. "Especially since we're together—like this."

He propped himself on his elbow, smiling down into her face. "What could be so terrible?" he asked. "Don't tell me you're worried about Sarah again, because there was—"

"No!" she cried, interrupting him. "It's not that."

"What then? What could be so bad?"

"It's the Reverend Mead," she began. "He and Sarah came to the ranch and said some awful things."

"Jesus!" he retorted. "Those two never give up. I'll have a talk with the reverend, and tell him to stay the hell out of our lives."

"He said you and I couldn't marry—" Ketti broke off, unable to meet his eyes. "He said that we are brother and sister."

Whatever reaction Ketti expected, it wasn't stunned silence. Then her words sank in. John's expression went from incredulity to rage in a matter of seconds.

"That goddamned bastard!" he thundered, and looked even more angry than Adam had after hearing the same thing. "I'll wring his damn lying neck, and then hang him out to dry."

"Please, don't be so upset, John," Ketti pleaded. "Let me finish. It's the reason why I left for Honolulu early—because I needed to tell you, and be reassured."

Then she went on to tell him the whole story, from the reverend's announcement, to her father's denial, even Agnes's part in knowing of the letter. As she talked, John's face became even more set into hard lines of anger. She suddenly knew the reverend would be made to answer for his malicious interference.

John didn't just feel anger, but black rage, not only at the minister, but at his dead father. Even though he'd changed in his last years, he'd certainly caused trouble in his earlier ones. It was like him to write a vengeful letter, John reminded himself. Hadn't it taken most of John's inheritance and every cent he had earned to pay off his father's debts and clear the family name? But it was the last straw that his father's old grudges should hurt the woman he loved. He watched her face, trying to read her thoughts.

"It's not true, Ketti. Stuart Morgan was my father, not Adam. And my parents lived in San Francisco for more than a year before I was born." He paused, again controlling his anger. "I can only apologize for my father. He was a very frightened, insecure man who tried to take what he wanted without any effort on his part, because he believed he deserved it."

John glanced away, feeling the old humiliation. "I came to pity him when I finally realized that, and the fact that he'd been neglected by his middle-aged parents, who'd kept him in private schools to grow up alone, while they traveled the world and squandered the family fortune."

"Oh, John," Ketti whispered, seeing his mental pain and embarrassment. "I'm so sorry. And I know it isn't true— because both you and my father say it isn't."

He dropped a kiss on her nose, then slipped out of the blankets. "I agree, though, that under the circumstances we should wait for a better time for lovemaking," he said dryly, anger still edging his tone. He stepped into his pants, pulled his shirt over his head and then strode off into the bedroom. Several minutes later he returned to lift Ketti from the sofa.

"I'm putting you to bed, my love. And tomorrow we'll sort out this whole mess." He took her to the bed he'd prepared by folding back the spread and blankets, and placed her between the sheets so that her head sank into the pillow. Then he tucked the covers around her.

He straightened, backlighted by the flickering flames from the fireplace, his gaze serious. "And I'll even produce a birth certificate, just to make sure your father and I are completely cleared.'' A tight smile touched his lips and was gone. "Or the gossips will chop us into little pieces.''

"John, I do believe you," she whispered, fearful that she might have hurt him, too.

He stooped and kissed her on the mouth, a long lingering kiss that sent her blood singing through her veins. When he lifted his head she saw the return of humor to his eyes.

"I know that, darling. Or I'd be kissing you like a brother...not a lover.''

And with those words he went back to the sofa, where he spent the night, except when he tiptoed to the bedroom to check on Ketti. Each time he was pleased to note that she slept soundly, her long silky lashes resting on the upper curves of her cheeks, a sweet smile on her lips that would belong to him again. She reminded him of a trusting child whose world had been made right once more.

And he would see to it that it stayed that way.

Chapter Twenty-Two

Ketti's trunk was delivered early the next morning and she was able to put on dry clothes. The first mate informed them that the steamer had been saved. The storm had abated, and while Ketti, feeling her old self, saw to her toilette, John went off to supervise the loading of his supplies onto his wagon; he knew the ship he had traveled on would lift anchor when the weather settled down. It was midmorning when he returned to the cottage to fetch Ketti.

The wind still gusted but the rain had stopped. High-flying clouds scuttled across the gray sky, and the peak of Mauna Kea was now visible, as were the northern mountains. Ketti, dressed in a navy-blue skirt and matching jacket, watched at John placed her trunk in the wagon. Then, after a glance around the cottage, she grabbed up her purse and straw hat and went out to join him.

"You're well?" he asked, his blue eyes sweeping over her, taking in her pink cheeks and dark eyes sparkling with renewed energy. Her hair lay in a simple style, falling down her back in soft shiny waves. Her lips were parted and her lashes lowered, as she considered his words. He had no way of knowing that her mind was more on him, his lean strong body and the way his brows quirked over his wonderfully brilliant eyes, than on his question.

"I feel on top of the world!" she exclaimed, her sudden exuberance surprising him. A happy giggle escaped her oh-so-kissable lips as she bounded down the steps, jumped over a water puddle and landed precariously close to a rut full of mud.

He grabbed her and held her at arm's length, the corners of his eyes crinkling a moment before his lips curved into an amused smile. The wind stilled in the palm fronds, the mighty force of the waves breaking on the shore receded, and even the sounds of the village seemed to pause, as they drank in the message they saw in each other's eyes.

Everything will be all right now. Our love is safe.

And then the world started up once more. He helped her onto the seat, and jumped up beside her. With a crack of the reins, they headed toward the uplands. Ketti couldn't hide a smile. Her trip to Honolulu had certainly been a quick one.

By the time they reached the Foster ranch the sun had broken through the clouds, sending down long, rainbow-colored rays to dry the land. Both Adam and Mari were on hand to greet them, relieved to see Ketti safe.

"The storm was a short one, but violent," Adam said, and hugged his daughter. "By the time your mother and I reached your grandfather's ranch late yesterday, we knew it was bad."

"And we were worried sick about you being out on the ocean in such violent weather," Mari added, her expression suddenly tight with remembering.

John unloaded Ketti's trunk and placed it on the veranda. As he straightened, his gaze met Adam's. "I understand the Reverend Mead has created a problem," he began. "And I think we all need to talk about it."

Adam nodded and indicated everyone should go into the salon. Once they were seated, his eyes were direct, as were his words.

"Ketti has filled you in?"

John nodded. "And before we go further, I want to add my denial to yours. Regardless of what my father wrote in that letter years ago, his accusation isn't true, and I can prove it."

"We know it's not," Mari said softly, and moved closer to her husband so that she could take his hand. "Both Ketti and I believe Adam."

John glanced at Ketti, who sat next to him on the settee, and was satisfied to see her expression confirmed her mother's statement. He again met Adam's eyes. "I have my birth certificate, which is a legal document that can't be tampered with, stating I was born in a Catholic hospital in San Francisco, fourteen or so months after my parents left Hawaii."

Adam waved a hand. "This is a terrible accusation for both of us, John. But we don't need to see any document. I *know* you're telling the truth."

"I want you and Ketti and her mother to see it anyway," he replied at once, and the strength of his character was apparent to Adam, a quality to be respected. "I don't ever want this issue to rear its ugly head again, especially since our good reverend saw that letter."

Adam started to say something, and this time John waved him to silence. "And I intend to show Mead the document as well." His tone hardened, as did the lines and planes of his face, giving him the look of a man who wouldn't tolerate malicious gossip. "I will also inform him that I will take drastic action, should he ever make the contents of that letter public."

Adam nodded agreement. He knew the reverend and his sister must be stopped at once. Ketti listened, sitting quietly in the glow of her pride for John. She could see that any final reservations her parents might have had about him were gone.

"And—I want to apologize," John said suddenly during a brief lull in the conversation. "For all the problems my father caused in the past."

"Please—" Mari began, but was silenced by John's expression, which spoke of his own humiliation in the past.

He needed to air his feelings, so that his father's memory need never be a barrier between any of them.

"My father was a bitter man," John said slowly. "And he was capable of writing that letter to cause trouble. I didn't know my mother, as she died shortly after my birth."

"She came from a good family," Mari said, trying to lessen his strain in having to discuss his own parents.

"Yes, I know. I was fortunate enough to spend some time with them, here in Hawaii when I was a boy. They gave me roots, a sense of my heritage, and I vowed then to make this island my home one day. I loved them very much," he added simply. "They, too, suffered because of my mother's headstrong ways. But they accepted some blame, too, because they'd spoiled and pampered their only child."

Straightening up on his chair, John went on. "I know it might not be necessary for you to hear all this." He gave a short laugh, although his expression was serious as he spoke directly to Adam and Mari. "But it's important to me that you do, because I'll never sail under false colors, and because you were both involved back then. I was the only heir to my grandparents' estate, and they saved the plantation here on the island that once belonged to my father. But it took almost everything to pay off the debts I inherited from my father, including the money I'd made on my own investments in California. What was left went into my plantation."

He turned to Ketti. "That was why I couldn't ask you to be my wife sooner—because with the sugar crisis, I didn't know if I'd even have a home to take you to."

"I would have married you anyway," Ketti announced brazenly, so proud of him that she could hardly contain it. Both her parents hid approving grins. They understand that kind of love.

"A few more things," John said when they thought he'd finished. "I took the maiden name of my American grandmother when I decided to live permanently in Hawaii, because I knew there would be people who'd remember my father and his dishonest involvements. You might remember, Ketti, that learning who you were gave me a start. I figured your parents might not approve of me, once they knew my real name."

"But we knew who you were," Mari said, smiling. "You can't hide anything on this island, not when people knew your grandparents, too."

He nodded slowly. "I realized that later." His eyes met Ketti's again. "My father did do one good thing. If I hadn't been paying his final gambling debt, I wouldn't have been in Chinatown that day."

Ketti acknowledged his words, her eyes shining with love, and she felt the approval of her parents as well.

John's explanation had cleared up any questions that might have arisen, and they were all relieved. Ketti felt as if she had just been secured a place in paradise with the man she would love forever. After that the talk took a general turn, and soon John stood up.

"I need to get going," he told them. "But if you don't mind, I'll ride back over tomorrow afternoon—so that Ketti and I have some time together before she returns to Honolulu."

Their agreement was unanimous, and John was invited to dinner. Ketti walked outside with him, and after his kiss goodbye, she watched him out of sight. As she went inside she was already planning what she'd wear tomorrow. She wanted to look her best, as it would be their last time together until her classes were completed and she returned for their marriage. *And she wanted him to make love to her.*

"I want you to take a look at this document," John said coldly. He'd ridden over to the Reverend Mead's cottage next to his little church, and after seeing that Sarah was present, too, he pulled his birth certificate from the inside pocket of his frock coat.

"Now see here," the reverend began. "I don't like your tone of voice."

"Too goddamned bad about that!" John retorted. "You'll examine this document, or I'll stuff it down your sanctimonious, lying throat."

"Don't be blasphemous in this house!" Sarah cried indignantly.

"Just read the paper!" John's voice brooked no refusal. "And notice the dates. Please note, too, that this is a legal certificate, duly signed and stamped by the proper authorities."

They read in silence, and then the reverend dropped the document on the table. "It would appear that the letter from your father to the Reverend Henry was a lie, just as my predecessor claimed it to be," he said, his face pinched with disapproval. He clucked his tongue. "Sinful, sinful."

Intense anger shot through John. He crossed to the other man and took hold of his lapels, jerking him up onto his tiptoes. "Yes, it's sinful! But not quite as bad as your own sin of trying to cause trouble."

Sarah pulled at his sleeve. "Let my brother go! He's a godly man!"

John released him suddenly, and the reverend stumbled backward, his eyes wide with fear, which he quickly controlled.

"And he can stay godly," John told them coldly. "But if he ever breathes another lie about me or mine—he'll wish to hell he was never born."

Snatching up his birth certificate, John turned on his heel and strode out, leaving them gaping after him. Somehow he knew that they would never mention the issue again.

He rode away from the Hamakua coast, toward the Kohala Mountains, toward the Foster ranch, and Ketti. As the miles passed, his anger died, and he finally left all the old hurt behind. It was truly over.

Joy surged up in him suddenly. He could hardly wait to see Ketti, and even the thoughts of her brought an ache to his groin. He needed her. He needed to make love to her.

"I had a talk with the Reverend Mead and his sister," John said later as he sat with the Fosters, drinking coffee in the salon. "Everything has been clarified. I'm sure they'll never mention that letter again . . . to anyone."

John's tone suggested that he had confronted the Meads with his proof, and then warned them of dire consequences if they ever spoke of the letter and its contents to anyone, Ketti thought. But she only nodded and smiled. John looked so handsome in his light blue coat and trousers, the color a dramatic contrast to his dark skin. She was pleased at how well he got along with her parents, her father in particular.

John caught her glance, and stopped talking to give her a quick smile. The flash of white teeth and the crinkling of his eyes added to his attractiveness, but the look in his blue eyes, silvered by the lamplight, took her breath away.

She lowered her lashes as a surge of tingling heat coursed through her veins. She wished they could be alone, and wondered if it were possible. She sensed that he wouldn't do anything to upset her parents now that they were to be married in a few weeks—such as make love to her in her parents' house.

Ketti suppressed a sudden grin, as an idea struck her. It was up to her—and she knew what she would do. She would miss John during those weeks she had to be in Honolulu, and she wanted at least a kiss goodbye . . . in private.

John saw her expression change, and wondered what she was thinking. Something not altogether proper, he decided. But then the Ketti he knew wasn't always proper—he knew that from past experience. Her mother and grandmother were discussing the wedding, and she nodded and made remarks at appropriate intervals, but he could tell her mind was elsewhere. Her hair, swept up into a coiffure of shiny curls and waves, was ornamented with a scarlet flower that matched the color of her low-necked gown. Her cheeks were tinged with pink, and as he watched, she caught her bottom lip between her teeth, as though she were making elaborate plans, and not for her wedding.

Finally Adam stood, followed by Mari and his mother. "I've an early day tomorrow," he said. "Time for me to retire." He indicated that John and Ketti didn't have to retire as well.

But Ketti stood, too. "It has been a long day," she agreed. She went to each one and gave them a kiss good-night, then turned to John, and in front of everyone, gave him a discreet peck on the cheek, too. As she'd anticipated, her parents and grandmother had turned away, giving the young couple a moment of privacy.

"I'll be in the loft in an hour," she whispered before she stepped back and, oblivious to his startled expression, she went upstairs with the others.

The weather had cleared and warmed up, and as Ketti sat on the window seat and stared out into the moon-haunted night, she wondered if John would really meet her at the barn, or if he'd even heard her whispered message clearly. She'd changed into a black silk nightgown and matching wrap, brushed her hair until it shone and then sat down on the velvet cushion to wait for the time to pass.

The cabinet clock in the lower hall gonged the hour, and Ketti stood. She knew she was scantily dressed, but the garments covered her entirely. She just had to make sure that no one saw her. Stepping out into the hall, she hesitated. The house was quiet, and in total darkness. Only the full moon, beaming in through long windows at the end of the hall, illuminated enough so that she could see. Quietly she crept down the back stairs to the kitchen, and then out through the back door. She stayed in the shadows as she hurried to the barn and let herself inside.

Again Ketti hesitated, sensing she was alone. Even her dog, Lapu, no longer slept in the barn. She climbed the steps to the loft, and only then did she breathe a sigh of relief. High up the walls, near the peak of the roof, the moonlight streamed inside, great swaths of silver light. The night was still, as though it waited with her, and the sweet smell of hay was heady to her senses, reminding her of the night John had first made love to her.

Time passed and she grew tired of standing, so she sat down in the hay. She had no idea if ten minutes or a half hour had gone by. But her anticipation of being with John was slipping away. Maybe he wasn't coming after all.

The soft air currents seemed to shift in the loft, and she suddenly knew she wasn't alone. Scrambling to her feet, she turned to the tall figure of a man at the top of the stairs. He stood in the shadows, and as he stepped into the moonlight, Ketti saw it was John.

Without a word he went to her and pulled her into his arms, holding her against his chest. When he spoke, his breath was a soft ripple through her hair.

"Ketti, Ketti," he murmured. "So this is what was going through your head earlier. What am I to do with you? This was a crazy thing to do."

"You can make love to me," she suggested in a whisper, lifting her head to meet his eyes. "I needed to be alone with you, because I won't be seeing you until the wedding—and because that night in Kawaihae was so strange, and I wanted everything right between us before I go."

"We have a whole lifetime ahead of us," he reminded her. "We don't want to do anything to upset your family now." John didn't know how he managed to sound normal, when his pulse beat so hard against his throat that it felt as if his voice would be pinched off.

"Are you refusing to love me?"

Her disappointment trembled on the sweet night air. John sucked in a ragged breath, wondering how he could continue to restrain himself. He reminded himself that there was a risk if someone discovered them. Even as he gave himself the reasons for caution, he knew there was little chance anyone would come to the loft.

He raked his hair, and felt the tremor of passion in his hand. "I'm not refusing. God help me, I could never refuse you even the smallest wish."

She stepped back from him then, and into the moonlight, much like an actress stepping onto a stage. With her
dark, fathomless eyes fixed on him, their lashes lowered seductively, she slowly untied her wrap, and with a whisper of
silk, it fell onto the hay. The straps of her gown were next;
first one slipped from a shoulder, then the other, until the
material rippled down over her breasts and into a heap
around her feet. She stood naked before him, a temptress
with the promise of the ages in her eyes.

With each movement she'd made, his desire for her had
grown until it tantalized every cell in his body, filling him
with his own need for her, a throbbing need in his loins that
demanded her body. She had never looked more beautiful
to him than now, offering herself in trust and love, her white
skin as perfect and smooth as a porcelain work of art.

Her gaze didn't waver as she moved forward, so graceful
that she might have been floating on the moonbeam. With
exquisite care, her fingers unfastened his shirt and drew it
from his body. Her hands feathered the hairs on his bare
chest, skimming over his skin so lightly, tickling and caressing, until he could hardly bear it. But still he didn't
touch her, allowing her to explore him and his own arousal
to climb to new heights of sensation.

She stooped to remove his shoes, dropping to her knees
to unbutton and then remove his trousers. Time seemed
suspended as Ketti stroked his nakedness, marveling that his
skin felt so soft. When she bent to kiss him, her tongue
licking a trail of fire across his belly and thighs, John could
stand no more. A groan of ecstasy tore free of his throat,
and he dropped to his knees beside her, pulling her onto the
hay. They lay together, suddenly panting, the soft folds between her legs moist, ready for him to make them one.

"My Ketti, oh my darling," he whispered, before his
mouth began the journey over her body. He tasted her
mouth, nipped at her ears, then his lips traveled downward
to the pulse hammering in her throat. Her body arched
when he took first one nipple, then the other in his mouth.

But he lingered only long enough so that she trembled and shuddered and moaned his name over and over. He wanted more; he could feel that need flowing through his entire body. Then his tongue licked over her stomach and into the hairs of her femininity, a place no other man had touched, or ever would. He tasted the rich muskiness of her, savoring the sensation of her body answering his touch.

And then John could restrain himself no longer. He took her, unable to be gentle, plunging into her. She met his passion, matched his rhythm, ever spiraling upward. Their pounding hearts became one, their sweat blended, and their love sounds bound them together as surely as their joining.

Ketti strained against him, and her hands clawed at his back, as the terrible pleasure he wrought in her became an unbearable ecstasy.

"John, John!" she cried out, as the great shudders began inside her, sensations too intense to bear, and yet she welcomed them, and wanted more.

For a brief pause in time, he looked into her eyes, bright and glazed with passion, and saw the wonder, trust and love for him reflected there.

"My love," he whispered, and knew she was the only woman for him. They were meant to be together always.

Then their bodies tore headlong toward the unfathomable abyss of their passion, each bursting their intense pleasure into the other. Ketti's last thought was one of infinite surrender, followed by a peace so profound, that at that moment she would gladly have given up her life for it.

A long time later they finally stirred from their cocoon of hay. And it was then that they said all the things that needed to be said, and their goodbyes... until their wedding day.

Chapter Twenty-Three

The wedding took place on a Sunday afternoon in the Foster salon. The large room was decorated with garlands of tropical flowers and maile boughs, and the gentle breeze that wafted in through the open garden doors added a hint of the sea to the fragrance of the lush blossoms. The dining room was prepared for the buffet, which would follow the ceremony: invitations had been sent to all the couples' relatives and friends in the Hawaiian Islands.

Ketti was alone in her bedroom, having already bathed in lavender-scented water. She was powdered, and had applied charcoal to her eyelids and lashes, and rouge to her lips and cheeks. She had only to dress her hair and step into her wedding gown and she would be ready.

But as the time drew near, she felt nervous. She stood by the open window, dressed in her white silk chemise, petticoats and stockings, and looked out at the glorious vista of mountains and valleys and ocean. This would be her last day in the bedroom that had been hers since she was born, the last time she'd awaken in her bed and know that her family was nearby. In only an hour she would become John's wife.

The guests had been arriving for the past several hours, and were being entertained with cool drinks in the garden until the ceremony began. She could hear their chatter drifting on the lazy wind currents, and the sound of buggy wheels as the vehicles were being parked down near the barn. Ketti knew that Kilia and Martin would be among the guests, as would Siu and Char.

Her thoughts lingered on Char and Siu, and the school she'd started in Honolulu for the Chinese. Siu, with Char's confidence in her abilities, was taking over Ketti's position. Ketti smiled to herself, pleased at how things had turned out for the slave girl she'd rescued that long ago day in San Francisco. How glad she was that she'd confronted the highbinders. Siu was intelligent and would go far, as Char would also.

Ketti's mind whirled with more memories, of her girlish infatuation with James, who even now was back in California for good, and of the nuns in the convent school—and of meeting John. A great sigh escaped her. It was all fate.

"Nervous, dear?"

Ketti hadn't heard her mother come into the room, and she smiled wistfully as she turned to her. "Perhaps," she replied. "I was just thinking that this is the last time I'll occupy this bedroom, the last time I'll be Katherine Foster."

Mari's blue eyes filled with tears, giving them the look of sapphire gems. Her silk skirts rustled as she moved across the carpet to her daughter and took her in her arms. "You're still our daughter, and there'll be times when you'll come to visit, and this will always be your room."

But mother and daughter both knew they were talking about another thing entirely—the closing of one book, and the beginning of another.

Mari stepped back to examine Ketti's face. "Are you all right?" Her lovely face, all powdered and lightly rouged, was suddenly concerned. "You aren't having doubts, are you?"

"Oh no, Mother!" Ketti replied at once. "It's just that I feel shaky all at once, and I don't know why, because I love John, and want to be his wife—more than anything else in the world."

Mari's expression relaxed, and she pulled Ketti back into her arms. "It's a typical case of bridal nerves," she said softly. "The deeper the feelings for your man, the more severe the nerves before the ceremony. When we love so much, we fear we might disappoint, not be everything he expects of us. It's the fear of the unknown."

"Yes, yes, maybe that's it," Ketti agreed, and felt the calming effect of her mother's wise words. "And now that you've said it aloud, I think I do feel better."

"Good," Mari said, and moved away to the dressing table. Then she turned back briefly. "And remember dear, John is probably feeling the same way right now."

Ketti darted a final glance outside to the familiar landscape. Mauna Kea loomed as the northern sentinel of the Big Island. Its mighty peak had looked down on the land long before the ancient Polynesians set foot on its shore. It was eternal, and she would still view it from the plantation, she reminded herself. Somehow that made her feel even better.

"Come on, dear," Mari prompted gently. "You can't be married in your chemise."

For a moment longer Ketti hesitated, her gaze now on her mother. She hadn't noticed before how beautiful her mother looked today; her hair, piled on her head in an elaborate coiffure, shone like spun gold. She wore diamonds and sapphires on her neck and wrist and clipped to her earlobes, and her silk gown, of the latest fashion, shimmered its blue over her slender body.

Ketti sat down before her mirror. A long arm of sunlight streamed in through the window and touched the crystal bottles with fractured light in the colors of a rainbow. Then the leaves of the trees outside shifted position as the breeze rippled through the branches, and the sunbeam vanished. An omen, she thought suddenly. She was meant to be John's wife.

Her mother brushed her hair, and Ketti smiled at her in the mirror. Mari was also touched by nostalgia—for her little girl who would soon be leaving her house forever.

With deft fingers, Mari created the simple hairdo Ketti had requested, long and loose, with white gardenias at each side of her face, like the Hawaiian girls of old. She knew the style would please her grandmother.

"Panana sent her good wishes," Mari said as she stepped back and surveyed her handiwork. "But Charles will be here, of course."

"Births and weddings," Ketti quipped, and dabbed a delicate scent of perfume on her neck, and between her breasts—*for John.* Her sister-in-law had delivered the Foster heir three nights ago, and Panana was confined to her bed, her baby son in the cradle beside her. Another good omen, she decided, and stood up. Panana and Charles had danced the fertility dance—and now had their son. She and John had danced the ancient love dance—and were getting married.

Her mother didn't notice the bemused expression that briefly touched Ketti's face. She was busy taking the ivory satin wedding dress from its hanger, pleased that the seamstress had accomplished such a work of art with only Ketti's measurements. The final fitting had taken place only two days earlier when Ketti had arrived from Honolulu, her teaching duties completed.

"Come," Mari said, her eyes soft with love, one hand caressing the delicate material. "It's time."

Mari held the gown while Ketti stepped into it. The sleeveless bodice was snug and fitted with rich lace, so that the low cut revealed only the top swell of her breasts. The lace continued over the shoulders and around to the deep neckline in the back. Her waist was cinched by a satin band covered with silver sequins, and the little sparkles had also been sewn into the bell-shaped skirt, which flared over Ketti's petticoats. She stepped into matching ivory slippers, then pulled on long, tight-fitting lace gloves. The final touch was the veil, which Mari placed on her head and fastened to the gardenias. Then she turned her daughter to the full-length mirror.

"Lovely," her grandmother said from the doorway. Behind the old woman, her father nodded agreement, his dark eyes filled with pride in the girl whose eyes, so like his own, met his in the glass. They entered the room as piano music began down in the salon. Ketti's brother Charles was right behind them.

"I wanted to wish you well, my darling Ketti," her grandmother said, and then fastened a string of pearls around her neck. "These were given to me by my dear husband." Tears glistened in her eyes. "They once belonged to his mother in Norway—I know he'd want you to have them now."

Impulsively, Ketti hugged her, and forced back her own tears, tears of happiness. "Thank you, Grandmother. I'll treasure them always."

Her brother was next. "This is a great day, little sister," he whispered as he dropped a kiss on her cheek, careful not to muss her hair or veil. "I wish you as much happiness as I have with Panana."

Adam said nothing as he held his little girl. She was so special to him, so like her mother. He loved her so much at that moment that his heart ached with it. "You have a good man, Ketti. But remember that you'll always be a part of us—your family—too."

She swallowed hard, and knew how fortunate she was, how the old gods had smiled upon her. Her grandmother nodded, as though she read her thoughts. Then Charles took the old woman downstairs to wait for the ceremony to begin. He returned for his mother.

"You're breathtaking," Mari said, and she and Adam exchanged proud glances. "John won't be able to take his eyes off you." She handed Ketti her bouquet of gardenias nestled in the tiny maile leaves that were traditional for Hawaiian weddings. She left on the arm of her son.

A few minutes later, Ketti accompanied her father to the top of the stairs where they paused. As the notes of Mendelssohn's "Wedding March" began, a hush fell over the house. They started down the steps, her arm entwined with her father's, all the way to the wide doorway of the salon where they hesitated.

The moment was suspended. It was a room of many memories: holidays and birthdays and quiet family evenings. She saw her parents and grandmother and brother, her Grandfather Webster and Agnes and Seth, Char and Siu, Kilia and Martin. Now she would add another memory: her own wedding.

She started the final walk to John, who waited with the minister by the fireplace. He was more handsome in his black formal suit than she ever remembered seeing him. The whiteness of his ruffled shirt and high-standing collar brought out the darkness of his skin. But it was his eyes, glittering like sun silvering the ocean, that drew her the most. They flamed at the sight of her, and gave her the promise of his love.

There was no sound, save the gentle whisper of the trade winds beyond the open windows, as they made their vows.

"I love you, my darling...my life," he murmured against her lips.

Her lashes fluttered. She was humbled before the power of his love. "For always and for eternity," she whispered back.

They kissed then, sealing that love, knowing it would last as long as they lived. They would never be apart again.

Epilogue

One year later Hawaii became the republic of Hawaii, duly annexed to the United States. Congress repealed the McKinley Act, and the sugar industry of Hawaii was saved. The queen went into temporary retirement, but still hoped monarchy would be restored one day so that she could again rule her people, even though Sanford Dole had been named as president.

"When the crop is ready to harvest, we have a market," John remarked as he turned from the window in their upstairs bedroom.

"And a future for our plantation," Ketti said softly, and glanced down at the sleeping baby in her arms. She sat in the big four-poster bed with pillows propped behind her back, her eyes on her husband. The evening shadows were already darkening the sugar fields beyond their lawns, and the ocean of the Hamakua coast in the distance. He stood with the approaching night behind him, the dying day in front of him, for a moment in silhouette. She was reminded of how he'd looked that long-ago day in San Francisco's Chinatown: breathtakingly handsome, fearless and slightly dangerous.

She glanced at the tiny face of their son, Jonathan. Even now, although he was only a week old, he was a duplicate of John, except that his small head was covered with a riot of black hair—Hawaiian hair. She kissed the tiny cheek gently.

How she loved this small child, the fruit of her powerful love for John.

He watched, the shadows lengthening around him, too moved to speak at that moment. Ketti was even more exquisite in motherhood: the infant in her arms, her long hair a shimmering cloud around her face and a deep abiding love shining through her eyes from the very soul of her.

He crossed to her then, holding her and his son close to his heart. His family. He would work for them, and never let them down. And his son would carry on one day, continue building for the future generations.

There was a brief knock on the door, and a moment later it opened and Ketti's Grandmother Foster stepped into the room. She paused, smiling, then crossed to the bed and took her great-grandson in her arms. "He must sleep now," she said, and placed the infant in his cradle.

Both Ketti and John grinned. Although Mari had been with Ketti since the birth, Ketti's grandmother had insisted that she wanted to help as well, had taken a special interest in the new addition to the family. John kissed his wife, a lingering kiss that held a promise for the near future, and then left Mrs. Foster to settle Ketti in for the night.

The old woman went to the window to draw the shade, but hesitated, staring out into the night that now cloaked the land. She heard Ketti's white dog, Lapu, bark briefly, and the sound of the breeze rustling through the sugarcane, like the vague whispering of the old ones, the Polynesians of the past... her ancestors. Slowly she turned back to her granddaughter, who had often been compared to the goddess Pele herself.

"The old taboos about *haoles* owning the land of ancient kings no longer applies to us," she told Ketti, her words soft but ringing with conviction, her face shining with sudden understanding. "The old ways are passing, like the monarchy. The ancients have allowed our islands to become a republic. By blood and by birthright, my family is Hawaiian now."

The moment was suspended, like a final benediction, a final healing. And in that brief flash of time, Ketti believed her grandmother. Although the world might not believe the words of a superstitious old Hawaiian woman, somehow Ketti knew they were true.

She smiled her agreement. The family had paid its dues. And as she drifted off to sleep, content within the enfolding love of her husband and child, she knew the old gods were happy, too.

* * * * *

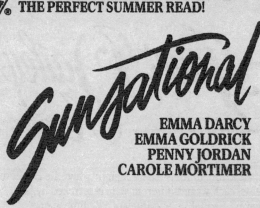

Back by Popular Demand

Janet Dailey
Americana

A romantic tour of America through fifty favorite Harlequin Presents, each set in a different state researched by Janet and her husband, Bill. A journey of a lifetime in one cherished collection.

In July, don't miss the exciting states featured in:

Title #11 — HAWAII
   Kona Winds

   #12 — IDAHO
      The Travelling Kind

Available wherever Harlequin books are sold.